CHIMERA'S GIFT

BOOK 4: INTO THE DEAD FALL SERIES

SUSAN TROMBLEY

Character Illustration by Sammi Griffin
Book cover design by Kasmit Covers

❀ Created with Vellum

CHARACTER ART

Character art of Kisk by Sammi Griffin

1

The chimera was the best scout they had, but not much in the way of companionship. Even when Tak could get the other male to talk, he never had much to say. The only one who inspired more than a few, abrupt answers from him was Asterius.

Tak and Asterius also got along quite well, considering their rocky beginnings. Though he much preferred being back in New Omni with Alice and his son, Friak, there were far worse people to travel with than his current crew as they patrolled the ruins, searching for the latest victims of the Nexus.

Someone had come through. Gray knew that much, but they didn't know anything else. That was why the chimera and Asterius were with them. They were the best scouts and hunters in the Dead Fall. Asterius could navigate the maze-like ruins blindfolded, and the chimera—well, Tak was still recovering from his initial shock when a part of the chimera had peeled away from his mane and shifted into a falcon that took to the air to scan from above.

With the bird in the air, the feathery mane the chimera usually wore had shifted to coarse hair, much like Iyaren had around his leonine head. In fact, the chimera had a leonine face similar to Iyaren's, though the chimera had two twisted, spiral horns that curled from the top of his head between his round ears.

His arms—only two of them—were covered in scales like Tak had over his entire body, and they ended in sharp-clawed hands. With feathers and fur and scales and horns, the chimera was one of the strangest of the creatures in the Dead Fall—and there were many strange creatures to be seen.

"He's not the friendliest sort, is he?" Tak asked Asterius as he jerked his chin towards the chimera, who stood atop a pile of junk, scanning the horizon with his odd, shifting eyes.

Asterius chuckled, snorting steam through his nostrils that showed just how chilly the air had grown after the last opening of the Nexus. "Prove your strength to him, and you'll have his loyalty for life, but if you can't defeat him, he won't bother with you."

Tak eyed the chimera, then lifted his gaze to the sky where the falcon circled. "I take it he's not easy to defeat."

Asterius grinned, baring sharp, gleaming teeth. "He nearly killed me before I managed to claim my victory in the gladiator pit, but at least you're immune to fire."

That much was true. Tak had an internal flame burning inside him that was part of his very soul, and he could burst into flames if threatened, without being burned himself. His entire body, inside and out, was fireproof.

Still, he was a peaceful sort. He preferred friendship to fighting. He had been a simple farmer before he'd been forced to serve in the army of his god, Ss'bek, back in his own realm. He had enjoyed his bucolic life and had not sought the adventure that had befallen him. But he wouldn't change anything now that he had his spark—his mate, Alice.

He had no plans to pick a fight with the chimera just to prove himself. There was enough fighting to do even on routine patrols, much less patrols like this one. Scavengers were always out in force after the Nexus opened, looking for new treasures —or new victims.

It was Tak's mission to reach those potential victims first, and if they were peaceful, guide them to New Omni, where they'd find a home in the ruins that were even now being renovated within the safety of the sentient forest that provided a thus-far impenetrable shield from the dangers of the Dead Fall and its inhabitants.

Since the sacrifice of life-energy by Asterius and his mate had expanded the forest, they'd been able to add six new buildings, including a sprawling marketplace that spilled out of its designated building and into the alleyways between the two buildings. They had needed every last building to house the growing settlement, because as word spread of its existence and its protection from the portal in the sky, scavengers and survivors trickled in, seeking a sanctuary where they could live out the rest of their lives in peace, and maybe even find a family.

There was no returning back home through the sky portal that had brought them to this world. Though it did work in both directions, or so Gray—the leader of New Omni—said, the artificial intelligence that controlled it would not help them find their way back to their own worlds. In fact, they were currently at war with NEX—the AI that sought to eradicate them—though they had been at a stalemate lately.

Not that Tak would ever leave the Dead Fall. This place had become his home and he had his family. His mate, his son, and his kin, Iyaren—who had become like a brother to him, even as they shared the same mate.

After a long perusal of their surroundings, the chimera motioned to Tak and Asterius and the other members of their squad that he'd spotted no sign of survivors. That didn't mean there weren't any out there. It just meant they had a long search ahead of them, until they found the creatures that had fallen through the Nexus—or far too often, the corpses.

As the chimera made his way down the pile he'd been standing on, some unseen thing thrust up from beneath the junk and twisted pallid tentacles around his ankles. Before he had a chance to react, the tentacles suddenly yanked the chimera right down into the debris, leaving behind torn flesh and blood on the jagged edges of some of the broken items that surrounded the newly-formed hole in the pile.

The falcon overhead shrieked in rage and pain, its flight faltering as it began to descend towards where the chimera had stood just seconds before.

Tak was already moving, racing towards the hole in the junk pile. He reached it just as flames burst forth, doing nothing to harm him, but sending Asterius—who'd reached the hole at the same time—staggering backwards as his fur hide caught on fire.

"Roll, Asterius," Tak shouted, not looking back at the burning minotaur, knowing the other male would figure it out.

Instead, he focused on tearing away the scorched trash around the hole in an effort to dig the chimera out as more flames burst from the opening.

A cry of agony from the falcon drew his attention as he glanced up, only to see the bird plummet from the sky.

"Yaneas!" he called to the naturally-armored insectoid that was closest to where the bird was falling. "Catch it!"

Yaneas hastened to get under the falcon before it crashed onto the jagged debris. It would still be wounded by its fall, but they had a better chance of saving it if it wasn't impaled in a hundred places.

Tak continued to tear at the opening, fearing he was almost out of time to save the chimera. The falcon had not fallen because something wounded it. It had fallen because something was killing the rest of its body. Tak still didn't understand how the chimera worked, but he could guess that the bird's condition was a good indicator of the rest of the male.

A leonine roar echoed from within the hole, growing fainter, as if the chimera were being dragged down a tunnel.

Tak finally had the hole large enough to climb through.

"I have the bird," Yaneas said, and a quick glance showed that he cradled the feathered creature in his large, three-fingered hands, where it lay lifelessly.

Asterius joined him at the hole, stinking of burnt hide and smoked meat. Tendrils of smoke still curled away from his burnt skin, but he would heal quickly.

"He still alive?" he asked, his tone revealing his concern more than his words did as he glanced at the fallen bird.

Another roar, more distant than the last, was his answer.

"I'm going in," Tak said, knowing Asterius would have to dig the hole even larger in order to follow, and they didn't have time for that.

Asterius clapped him on the shoulder. "Kill whatever did this to him and I'll buy you drinks for a month."

Tak nodded, then turned and climbed into the hole, tasting the blood of the chimera in the air along with the pheromones of some unknown creature as his tongue flicked out.

He followed the tunnel that the creature had formed, smelling it all around him—a foul, musky, slightly rotten odor, tainted with blood, both old and new. This wasn't the first time this tunnel had been used to drag a body through.

He had to proceed on hands and knees, keeping his upper hands free, one with a blade in it and the other unarmed so he could clear the way where dirt and trash had fallen in the wake of the chimera's struggling passage.

A faint roaring sound let him know the chimera still lived—and still fought—but there was pain behind the sound and Tak knew that time was running out. Fire traced along his scales as adrenaline pumped through him, stoking his internal flame.

He struggled to calm himself, deciding to proceed with stealth instead of fire as he concentrated on shifting his scales to camouflage his presence until he'd decided the best way to deal with the unknown threat.

It was pitch dark in the tunnel, so he didn't immediately spot the drop-off, until the softened earth just ahead of it suddenly gave way. Tak fell for a few breathtaking moments before he was able to snag the rock wall and gain purchase by gripping the stone with his hands—tiny scales on his finger pads allowing him a strong hold that let him proceed downwards vertically.

Climbing down the wall in darkness, he made his way towards the sounds of struggle, pausing as he heard a slithering sound, then a drawn out hiss just below him.

Keeping his sword drawn in one hand while the other three carried him down the wall, he followed that nearby sound, discovering solid ground not far below him, where a serpent coiled, hissing in distress.

As soon as he approached it, it hissed a bit louder, then slithered away from him, stopping a short distance away, then hissing again.

Tak realized it wanted him to follow it, and he wondered if it was yet another part of the chimera. It sounded like it was suffering, much as the bird had suffered.

He moved quickly, but the serpent was faster, speeding ahead despite its lack of arms or legs. It led him down a new tunnel, and drafts coming from all directions told him that it wasn't the only choice he would have had. If it hadn't been for the serpent, he could have been searching tunnels all day trying to figure out which one to take, since the scent of the creature and of death was overwhelming in all directions.

The absolute darkness of the tunnel was relieved by a faint, glowing bioluminescence from lichen on the walls as he followed in the path of the serpent. The soft, blue-green glow intensified when Tak rounded a corner, where the serpent suddenly froze and then writhed in pain, its body twisting and turning among glowing mushrooms, the whip-like movement tearing them out of their stone moorings as it flung itself this way and that.

Then it fell still, and Tak feared that meant the chimera was already dead, but when he approached the serpent, it lifted its head and its tongue darted out, showing him life still ran through it. He collected it gently and coiled its unresponsive body into the pouch slung around his waist that shifted with his armor and his scales, allowing him to remain invisible to a casual observer.

Without his guide, Tak hoped there would be no more multiple tunnels as he sped up his steps, straining to hear any sound of the chimera's roar.

When he finally did hear something, he nearly sagged in relief as he rushed towards that weak roaring, coming out into a large cavern where a massive rodent-like creature with tentacles hanging from each side of its pointed nose rather than whiskers hunched over something, jaws moving busily.

The creature was too large to have fit through the narrow tunnels, so Tak wondered how it had gotten up to the surface. As he approached on silent steps, he remained unnoticed by the massive beast, but it did lift its head, tearing away a strip of flesh and fur in its long, jagged teeth from the barely breathing beast lying on his side, blood and gore covering the tan fur that looked so much like Iyaren's that Tak had a brief moment of terror that Iyaren had somehow been captured too, before reason reasserted itself. The chimera did share some similarity to the lion-man, though the chimera had taken the form of a four-legged, powerful feline instead of a two-legged warrior.

Blood coated the chimera's massive paws and long, sharp teeth, and viscera clogged the spirals of his horns, but he had not put up enough of a fight. The rodent-creature had won, and was now feasting on the chimera while he still struggled to breathe.

Tak drew his other three swords, slow enough that they didn't ring when they broke free of their sheaths as his eyes scanned the creature in the low, bioluminescent light cast by the mushrooms and lichen. It's head and flanks looked the most vulnerable, so he moved forward with stealthy steps to stab the flank closest to him.

He buried his sword in that flank, causing the creature to rise up on its hind legs with a shriek of agony. The sudden motion jerked Tak off his feet and into the air as he kept his hold on the sword. He braced himself against the furred side of the creature and stabbed with his other three swords.

The underside of the creature writhed like a bed of worms as tentacles spilled out to encircle Tak, squeezing hard enough that even his armor buckled.

Tak unleashed his internal flame, allowing it to spread from his chest to engulf his entire body, burning away flesh and fur as the rodent squealed in agony and struggled to break free of him. The tentacles that had been squeezing him turned crisp, then disintegrated to ash, but the creature's screaming didn't stop as it raced around the cavern, scraping Tak against the stone walls with skull-bruising force.

Tak kept his swords buried it its flank to keep him attached to it while he burned it to death.

When it finally gave up the fight and collapsed in a flaming heap, barely twitching, Tak withdrew his swords, one by one, and doused his own flames, though he left the creature on fire.

He made his way to the chimera, limping slightly from where his leg had slammed against the stone in the creature's maddened attempt to shake him. In fact, his entire body ached, but the armor—gifted to him a few years ago by Gray—had undoubtedly saved his life.

The chimera's golden eyes opened as he approached. His

mane twitched as one furred ear lifted. He made an effort to move, then groaned in pain and froze in place, only his heavy, labored breaths giving away that he still lived.

Tak crouched beside him, noting the damage to his stomach, where entrails spilled out from the torn opening of his flesh. "I will get you home, my friend."

The chimera didn't respond as Tak studied the wounds, knowing he couldn't carry him out of the tunnel. There was only one other option, but Gray had told them to only use it in the direst emergency, because there was a possibility of it glitching. He had to teleport himself and the chimera back to New Omni. Only Gray had the technology to heal the chimera's grievous injuries.

He pulled the small device Gray had given him out of his pouch, where the serpent still lay coiled and silent around his survival gear. Staring at the small, silver disk, Tak took a deep, bracing breath, praying to a god who didn't hear him anymore that he and the chimera made it back to New Omni with all their parts intact and in the right place. With the way Gray's technology had been glitching lately, that was no guarantee.

"Alice, I'm coming home to you, my spark."

He reached out to lay a hand on the chimera's blood-soaked flank, then pressed the disk, activating the teleportation device to send him to Gray's main teleportation platform.

2

"That was quite the ass-chewing you gave there, Sergeant," Alice said with a grin as Lauren returned to their table in the social-gathering room after dismissing her team.

Lauren snorted as she settled into her seat and pulled the plate Alice had fixed for her closer. "That?" She waved a hand towards the team of females who'd moved to another table to take their lunch after a hard day of survival and combat training. "That was nothing more than a pep talk."

She eyed the steaming contents of her plate with appreciation. Then glanced up with slightly narrowed eyes. "Uh, you didn't make this, did you?"

Alice crossed her arms over her chest. "Hey! I'm getting better at cooking. It's not my fault we don't have decent stoves and ovens around here."

Lauren looked contrite, even if she was hesitant to pick up her fork and dig into the plate of meat and strangely colored vegetables.

"Sorry," she said, "it's just that the last time I ate your cooking, I was in the latrine for hours."

Alice held up her hands. "I swear, this time, all the meat is fully cooked! I'm also really, *really* sorry about giving you food poisoning."

Lauren grinned as she lifted the fork to her lips. "Well, you know I like to live dangerously. So, here goes nothing." She shoved the forkful of mashed vegetables into her mouth with the expression of someone facing a firing squad.

Her eyes widened a bit as she chewed, and Alice waited eagerly for a verdict. She'd been working with Iyaren to improve her cooking and better learn to use the more primitive appliances they had available, but so far, she'd had some disastrous results, and she'd gained a bit of a reputation for it. She hoped her latest attempt would help erase that reputation, but Lauren was the only woman she knew who was brave enough to keep trying her food.

"Al poisoning you again, Sarge?" Evie asked as she flopped into the chair beside Alice.

Alice shot a glare at Evie, who grinned and winked, before turning her gaze to the plate Alice had made for Lauren, her eyebrows rising with interest.

"It actually looks pretty good this time, Al. Remember the viridian root experiment?"

Lauren swallowed and spoke before Alice could respond to that reminder of another unfortunate incident. "It's really good, Al. Tastes better than A-rats."

"You've eaten actual rats?" Alice asked, not entirely surprised. Perhaps that was something army soldiers did as part of their survival training. It wasn't like eating rodents was all that unusual for them now, but it was pretty sad that Lauren would have had to eat that kind of stuff before coming to the Dead Fall.

Looking up at Alice's question, Lauren chuckled at their twin expressions of disgust, then clarified. "A-rations. The good stuff we were served in garrison."

Alice breathed a heavy sigh of relief. She'd worked hard on that plate of food, watching the fire like a hawk to ensure it didn't burn too hot or drop too low. She'd boiled the vegetables carefully, after scrubbing them vigorously, then took her time mashing them into a smooth, creamy paste before slathering on the gravy Iyaren had patiently taught her how to make.

"Taste the meat," she said, sucking in another breath to hold until Lauren finished chewing that part of her meal.

Lauren eyed the juicy, brown skin on the grilled meat with a fatalistic expression, before using the side of her fork to cut a tender piece, examining it skeptically before bringing it to her lips.

"What is it?" Evie stage-whispered to Alice.

"Barren creeper," Alice said aloud, knowing that was one of Lauren's favorites—at least when someone else other than Alice was cooking it.

Lauren's grin as she chewed gave Alice all the response she needed, but it helped when Lauren dived into the meal after finishing her first hesitant bite, scarfing the food down with evident satisfaction and a mumbled "tastes delicious," around a mouthful of meat and vegetables.

Finally!

She wanted to stand up and dance a little jig around the table in celebration that she'd finally mastered cooking in the Dead Fall. Poor Iyaren and Tak would suffer her terrible cooking mistakes no longer, though they'd always gamely and patiently choked down anything she made with carefully concealed winces and shudders. She'd still noticed.

Fortunately, Friak had only recently graduated to eating more complicated food than mashed vegetables and small chunks of fruit, or grain-based pastries and crackers. Not that she would have risked testing her food out on him until she knew she had it perfect. Iyaren did most of the cooking for their family, since he enjoyed doing so, saying it relaxed him to work at the stove.

It didn't relax Alice—it had the exact opposite effect—but she liked the challenge of it, since she'd never prepared anything more complicated or involved than a frozen dinner nuked in the microwave before she'd arrived in the Dead Fall. Her primary source of food on Earth had come from greasy fast food bags or the bakery section of the grocery store.

Cooking here was much more involved, though now that the market had been opened and traders had stocked their stalls with wares, Alice could find meat and vegetables and a variety of fruits and other—more unusual—delicacies, so she didn't have to deal with the butchering or the harvesting or the extensive preparation of the food before cooking it. That gave her more time to experiment.

"Mmm, mm, what is this seasoning you put on the meat?" Lauren asked, smacking her lips in appreciation. "It's so spicy and flavorful!"

The compliments felt so good that Alice's cheeks ached from how broadly she grinned. Coming on the heels of such a difficult time for her and her family, she needed something positive to remind her to be grateful for what blessings she had. Blessings like her best friend, Lauren—who would take a bullet for her, or just risk food poisoning—and her sister—who would also take a bullet for her, but drew the line at risking her food—and all the other ladies who surrounded her, eating their own meals and chatting away. And of course, the greatest blessings she had—her mates, Tak and Iyaren, and her precious son, Friak.

Friak, who might be her only child.

Her smile slipped as she recalled exactly what had driven her to the kitchen to distract herself with the challenges of making something truly delicious, much less edible.

Once again, she was on her period. She had hoped—prayed to whatever gods would listen—that she would be late.

Instead, she was right on schedule, just as she'd feared she would be. Just as she had been for the last six months—six months of trying not to grieve for the pregnancy that hadn't been meant to be. Gray had said that the risk of unviable pregnancies was always present, even between two humans. In a hybrid pregnancy, nonviability was an even greater risk, even with the keys that she and Tak shared that allowed them to procreate at all.

She'd already accepted that she would never be able to give Iyaren a child of his own blood, and he'd never asked her to do so, more than happy to raise Friak as his own son. Yet, she'd wanted to someday present him with a furry little son or daughter with his beautiful amber eyes and maybe someday a dark mane as impressive as his, and she wanted another child for her and Tak. She had a dream of having three children to cuddle and raise, but was beginning to fear there would be no more, despite Gray's assurances that the possibility still remained in the flux.

He'd also reluctantly confessed that there were possible futures where she had no more children. He couldn't tell her which future she was heading for.

Couldn't—or wouldn't. With Gray, it was always difficult to tell. Alice had no idea how her sister could stand it, knowing her mate kept so much information to himself.

Thus far, Gray had been unable to obtain the medical equipment he required for genetically engineering hybrids, so every pregnancy was left up to chance—and the precious keys that made it possible.

"Doshak says hatching day will probably be within the next two months," Evie said to Lauren, snapping Alice's attention back her dining companions, who'd been carrying on a conversation around her, leaving her to her own thoughts.

Alice tried not to flinch at those words, a reminder that Evie was about to have three children at once with her mate, Doshak —children who would hatch from eggs and be in a larval form for a while, but they would still be babies that shared her and Doshak's blood nonetheless. Alice would gladly deal with a squirmy larva, if she'd have the opportunity to watch that little life grow into a person who combined the best of her and one of her mates.

Evie was able to reproduce with both of her mates. She and Doshak shared gene keys that made it possible, and Gray's mutations made it possible for him to breed with Evie— creating mostly human hybrids like her delightful nephew, Sherak—her powerfully empathic and telekinetic nephew.

Lauren shook her head. "I'm happy for you, Ev. You nervous?"

Evie snorted, waving a hand dismissively. "Nah." Her eyes widened as she clutched her chest dramatically. "I'm terrified."

Alice already knew many of the reasons Evie was scared of this hatching. Her sister feared she'd be disgusted by her own children, even though Alice also knew that Evie loved them and couldn't stay away from their brooding hole, constantly scanning it with the device Gray had given her to make sure her squirmy, squiggling larvae were developing properly. Evie also feared she'd be a failure as a mother to such alien children. She was afraid she wouldn't know what to do, and Doshak had never been involved with raising the children in his nest on his own world, so he wasn't much help in that regard.

She usually took Sherak with her to meet his brothers, laughing when he'd one day told her there would only be two brothers—and one sister. After her laugh at his cuteness died down, there was a long pause. Then she'd shrieked with excitement as she'd clutched her empathic toddler to her chest. "I'm gonna have a little girl to spoil?"

That had been a difficult scene for Alice to witness, but

she'd kept it to herself how much it hurt to be constantly reminded about her own fertility problems, and her baby... no, she had to stop calling him that. He hadn't been viable, so it wasn't a baby. It was a miscarriage. Somehow, those semantics did nothing to make it hurt less.

Despite her fears about her upcoming children, Evie was happy. Blissfully happy. Alice's solemn, large-eyed nephew reassured her that his mother was happy whenever Alice felt that concern for her around him. Since she spent a lot of time with Sherak, as she babysat often so their boys could play together, she was reassured a lot. Sherak even had the awareness, despite being so young, not to comment on Alice's sadness.

Instead, her nephew would often walk up to her and place a chubby, three-fingered hand on her cheek. Then he'd tell her he loved her, and she could be his mommy too. After all, he had two daddies. Why not two mommies?

It was difficult to keep up a façade around an empathic child, and she didn't even bother pretending around Evie's mate, Gray, but she still kept a smile on around her mates and her friends. They didn't need to see her sadness—especially not the unmated females around her who were still alone and searching for the right mates to make their own families, most of which would never result in children unless something changed in the Dead Fall, or Gray could find the equipment he needed.

I'm blessed. Far more blessed than I've ever been, and I won't be greedy and ungrateful.

She told herself this every morning as she looked in the mirror, and had to remind herself throughout the day during her periods. She hated that she couldn't convince herself to be happy when she had so much to be grateful for. She hated that she allowed so much of her emotions to hinge on children that might never be—children her loving mates had never asked for or demanded from her. They felt content with the blessings they already had. Why couldn't she?

She loved her son and her two mates more than life itself. She would gladly sacrifice herself for any of them. She included her sister and her best friend in that equation, and even their mates—though she doubted any of those males would need her sacrifice to save them.

Why wasn't that enough to make her happy? What was wrong with her?

3

Iyaren warily eyed the chimera as they sat outside the unmated male housing on a stone bench, surrounded by several other males who would join him and Tak in the Fall today.

He knew the chimera's name because the creature had given Tak leave to use it, but the chimera had not extended that same courtesy to Iyaren. In fact, he barely spoke to Iyaren. He was only outside waiting with them because he wished to speak with Tak.

Ever since Tak had saved his life the previous month, Okiskeon—or Kisk, as he bade Tak to call him—had made an effort to speak to Tak. At least, more of an effort than he made with anyone else besides Asterius, who was as close a friend as the chimera had.

The creature was odd, and not just because he could split his body into many pieces that operated independently, or that his form could shift in so many ways. In fact, the strangest thing about him was how oddly he behaved. As far as anyone knew, Asterius and Tak included, the chimera pursued no friendships or relationships, and had little interest even in the unmated females and the meetings that were set up in the main building for them to find mates. He also showed no interest in any of the males.

Kisk rarely spoke to anyone, kept to his own rooms most of the time—if he wasn't out in the Fall on a mission—and often chose solitary missions. He ate alone, sat alone, fought alone, and as far as anyone knew, slept alone.

Iyaren had been alone for many years, but that had only been out of necessity, and that isolation had worn on him. Alice's arrival into his life had transformed him, making him into a better, stronger person than he had ever been before falling in love with her. He couldn't imagine ever returning to that unending loneliness. Yet, that seemed to be Kisk's preferred condition.

"Sorry I'm late," Tak said, drawing Iyaren's attention away from Kisk, who sat patiently—alone—staring at nothing.

He turned to see his kin approach, noting how weighed down Tak was by several extra packs of gear. "You appear to be overburdened."

Tak chuckled, patting a small pouch slung over one shoulder by a long strap. "Barren-flower salves, bandages, extra food, extra water, extra weapons...."

Iyaren didn't often chuckle, but he couldn't resist a huff of laughter at Tak's list. "I take it she wouldn't let you out of the house without all that?"

Tak's sharp-toothed grin softened at the reference to their shared mate. "She's worried."

More like terrified. Ever since Tak faced off a monster to save Kisk's life, returning home with several broken bones, covered in blood, and carrying the barely-breathing body of the chimera, Alice had been frantic about his safety—and Iyaren's by extension, realizing how close she could have come to losing one of them. Now, Alice never wanted them to leave the house, much less go out into the Fall, but she knew they had jobs to do, so to assuage her worry, she insisted on extra precautions.

"I do not understand," Kisk said, appearing at Tak's side, his color-shifting eyes staring without expression at the extra packs slung over Tak's shoulders. "Who is this 'she' that holds such power over you?"

He cocked his head, so similar to Iyaren's and yet literally worlds apart from him. It was odd to see such a face and mane so far from home. Even odder still to see the feathers instead of fur, and the scales that covered his arms and legs.

"Is she a mighty warrior queen?" Kisk's tone took on a mild interest. "I was told all the females in this world were weak."

Tak heaved a small sigh as he turned to Kisk. Iyaren tried to keep his expression neutral and not display his amusement at Tak's impatience with the other male. Tak was friendly, outgoing, and liked to joke with people. Kisk was the exact opposite of all those things, and lacked even basic manners, speaking bluntly and often harshly in a way that got other people's backs up. He also appeared to lack any sense of humor, which made it difficult for Tak to find common ground with him. Yet, Kisk seemed to be drawn to Tak ever since Tak had saved his life. Always waiting for a chance to speak with him when he left the family living quarters.

"We speak of my mate, Kisk. I believe I've mentioned Alice before."

There was a quelling note in Tak's tone that he rarely ever used, since it was a warning, and Tak wasn't one to seek violence as a first solution. Given how devastating his most effective attack could be, Iyaren understood his hesitation to use it. Tak didn't like hurting people, not unless he had to, and he was always aware of the possibility of collateral damage.

Iyaren's ears lifted in curiosity, wondering exactly what conversation had spawned this note of censure in Tak's voice. He shifted his attention from Tak to Kisk to study his reaction.

The chimera appeared impassive, unaffected by the obvious tension he'd caused in Tak. "How does this weak female hold such sway over a warrior of your caliber? It makes little sense. She cannot defeat you. All she can do is submit. Why would you listen to anything she has to say, much less obey her commands?"

Kisk's mane shifted from feather to fur for a single blink of an eye as wings spread from it, then melted back into his mane. "Why would you ever breed with such weakness?"

Tak was on Kisk before Iyaren—shocked by the cutting words—even had a chance to react.

"Never call my mate weak, you little snake," Tak hissed as he grabbed the chimera by his shirt—a ragged, stained thing, poorly sewn with clumsy stitches and made of more holes than fabric.

A bellowing laugh cut off any response Kisk might have made.

"I see Kisk is asking people to kill him again," Asterius said, strolling up to stand between Tak and Kisk, setting large, firm hands on both of their shoulders.

With a casual tug on each of their shoulders, he set them apart from each other. Tak took an extra step back, still glaring at Kisk, who met his eyes with ones that had shifted to gray with horizontal, elongated pupils.

Asterius glanced at Tak. "Don't let his ignorance get to you, Tak. Pity him instead. He knows nothing, and this is why he asks with such confusion."

Kisk's only response was to growl, shooting a glare at the muscle-bound minotaur, before returning his eyes to Tak.

They'd shifted to a golden color similar to the eyes Iyaren had seen so much in his early life, and they watched Tak with more curiosity than the contempt he usually showed others.

"In my world, only a queen who can defeat me is worthy of breeding. We don't allow weakness to spread through spawn."

"Bah," Asterius said, his relaxed good humor still in place as he turned with one hand still firmly on Kisk's shoulder, forcing him to turn away as well unless he wanted to visibly resist. "You don't know what strength is. Nor do the fools in your world."

He patted Kisk on the shoulder, hard enough that the chimera visibly winced, his lips peeling back in a snarl that bared teeth as sharp as Iyaren's. "Good thing you came to this one. Now you should start using your brain, before you succeed in pissing someone off enough to actually kill you."

Asterius glanced at Tak. "Did I use that right? 'Pissing off?' Lauren says it all the time when she's angry."

Tak nodded. "I'm definitely 'pissed off.'" He pointed at Kisk. "Don't come near me again, chimera, until you learn some manners—and some respect for my mate."

Iyaren again had the unusual desire to chuckle at the look of surprise that flashed across Kisk's face. The male wasn't so impassive now that his new friend wanted nothing to do with him.

For the first time, Iyaren saw uncertainty in the chimera as he glanced from Tak to Asterius, then even shot a wide-eyed look to Iyaren, almost like he was seeing him for the first time.

"What purpose would this education serve? I will never see weakness as something to respect."

Asterius shook his large, horned head. "Time to steer you out of danger, my friend." He pushed Kisk away from Tak and Iyaren, who'd risen to his feet, growing tired of the chimera's use of that word, and the implications about his mate. Insults he wouldn't stand for, whether they came from ignorance or not.

"Good luck out there," Asterius called back to them over his shoulder as he shoved Kisk so hard the other male stumbled. "Wish I was going with you... instead of *building*," he muttered the last word with resentment, never very thrilled to come up on the roster for building detail instead of fighting or patrolling the Dead Fall.

Iyaren stared after Asterius and Kisk with a thoughtful look as they disappeared into the growing crowd of unmated males coming out of their quarters to begin their busy days.

"He's an idiot," Tak growled, adjusting the straps of the extra packs Alice had insisted he bring.

"Is he young?" Iyaren pondered aloud, thinking that would be at least some explanation for Kisk's complete ignorance about life.

Tak snorted. "Ancient, from what he's said. He gave me the impression he's un-aging."

Iyaren recalled Tak's descriptions of how Kisk had looked when he was struggling to stay alive with his entrails scattered at the rodent creature's feet. "Not immortal like a god, though."

Tak pulled his lips back in a snarl that reminded Iyaren of his own angry expression, enough that it amused him to see his closest friend adopting it.

"Oh, he can bleed. And if he insults Alice again, I'll remind him of that."

4

Alice hated those days when her mates went into the Fall. Usually, it was only one or the other, so she wasn't left completely alone. She knew why Gray planned the rosters that way, and it made her ill to even think about the calculating nature of that. If she lost one mate, he reasoned, at least she'd still have the other.

Having them head into the Fall together was a double-edged sword. On the one hand, she knew they could watch each other's backs, and she trusted them to protect each other better than any of the other males that traveled with them, but on the other hand, if she lost both of them, it would completely destroy her. Even losing one of them would make it difficult to go on.

To make matters worse, she'd asked Evie if she could babysit Sherak, so at least she'd have the boys to keep her distracted, but Evie had given her an uncomfortable look, then said she'd like to take Friak for the day and let Alice have some time to relax.

When pressed, Evie had admitted that Sherak had been feeling Alice's sadness lately, and it was affecting him.

Alice had been crushed by that confession, and knew Evie didn't want to tell her and hurt her feelings, but she was a mother and had to put Sherak's needs before her sister's. She wanted Alice to talk to Gray, as many people did for counseling, since Evie's mate had a calming, stabilizing influence, but Alice was always uncomfortable around Gray and knew the peace he offered was only fleeting and false.

Ever since her miscarriage, her discontent and grief had been growing, no matter what she did or told herself to try to make it better. She'd bottled it all up inside her to protect her love ones from knowing how miserable she was, but she couldn't hide it from some of them.

Including the most vulnerable of them. She felt like a monster for putting all her despair on such a young child as poor little Sherak. She was a terrible auntie for not realizing what she'd done until it was too late and his normally happy outlook had begun to sour and turn too solemn.

Worried that her mood might even be affecting mellow Friak, maybe even enough to start him flaring again after he'd finally gotten his spontaneous combustion under control, she took Evie up on her offer to watch them both, giving Alice time to reflect.

Only, she still had no idea what to do about how she felt, and now she had no distractions from all her worries and fears and regrets—and guilt.

I shouldn't feel this way. I am blessed.

I am blessed!

Tears dampened her cheeks that she hastily swiped away before any of the other females saw them as she made her way through the unmated female wing of the family apartment building, then outside to the path that led into the ancilla forest.

She'd find more peace among the ancilla than with her enigmatic brother-in-law.

As always when she stepped from the paved pathway into the loam that surrounded the colorful trees of the ancilla forest, she felt a sense of serenity wash over her. It wasn't enough to completely soothe her troubled mind, but it helped take the edge off her sadness and grief.

The guardian trees greeted her arrival with a colorful show of lights. If she were to touch their branches, they would even speak with her telepathically. Despite the fact that they'd once belonged to a brutal, conquering race that had savaged their own galaxy until they encountered a virus they could not defeat, the ancilla possessed calm, benevolent energy now, after being forced to live bound to their forest and remain reliant on the kindness and sacrifice of others to sustain their lives. They'd grown to deeply regret their mistakes, and at the same time, feel gratitude for the outcome, because it had saved their souls.

Now, they provided absolute protection from NEX and the dangers of the Dead Fall, creating a shield from their own tree-like bodies to enclose the settlement of New Omni and their own forest that crowded against the buildings. Young saplings even grew between the buildings and on the outer edges, spreading their root-systems deep and far to increase the range of their protection.

Soon, the ancilla would be ready for another mating sacrifice, and Asterius and Lauren had already volunteered themselves, knowing that they could step into the pool at the heart of the forest, just below the towering mother tree, and survive the loss of their life-energy to fuel the production of the ancilla's mating blossoms. They'd made a vow to do this, each year or so—when the ancilla regained enough strength from the exhausting process of their reproduction—until the forest spread throughout the Dead Fall, locking NEX out of it completely and providing safety and sanctuary for all the survivors of the Nexus portal.

Alice felt a blush burn her cheeks as she made her way towards the mother tree, where the sense of peace and serenity was the strongest. The memory of the last sacrifice—the last ancilla mating—and what had happened after the trees had blossomed and shook their petals loose to fly in the breeze, was enough to briefly lift her spirits, until she truly felt blessed, instead of just having to remind herself repeatedly that she was.

When Lauren and Asterius had come together in the pool during their sacrifice, reaffirming their life and love by mating, it had changed the energy the ancilla themselves put out, so each blossom carried with it some kind of aphrodisiac that made anyone touched by it incredibly, uncontrollably horny. No one in the forest at the time had been unaffected—even Iyaren, who had begun feeling Alice up as soon as the petal had touched his fur and then sank into his skin. Despite the fact that Evie and her own mate had been standing right there at the time.

They'd made a run for it when they realized what was happening, but they hadn't made it far before Alice and Iyaren couldn't stand the raging lust inside them any longer and they fell to their knees, pulling at each other's clothes until they were stripped naked. Their hands had not stopped roaming, Alice feeling every ripple of muscle beneath the sleek fur that covered her mate, as his four hands skated over her body, touching her everywhere that he knew made her sigh in pleasure or gasp in excitement.

By the time his fingers found her entrance, she'd been soaking wet, so eager for him that her inner muscles clenched painfully on emptiness. She nearly cried with relief when his large fingers—claws carefully retracted—entered her with a wet sound that was so erotic to her heightened senses that she'd nearly come in that moment.

They were naked, outdoors in a forest of sentient trees, blossoms filling the air around them like a snowstorm, and they were touching each other as if they couldn't bear not to. They couldn't help themselves. They couldn't wait until a more appropriate time, and they couldn't find more privacy. Neither of them would have ever done this if it wasn't for the petals, but in that moment, they couldn't think of doing anything else.

His fingers pumping inside her and her hand closed around his bumpy cock had not been enough—not nearly enough—so she'd been extremely grateful when he'd jerked her roughly around until she was on her hands and knees and without any warning or preamble, rammed his thick erection into her waiting entrance.

He took her ferally, nearly wild with his need, growling in a long, drawn-out way that didn't translate to any words, claiming her as surely as his teeth had once claimed her. Only this time, the brief pain of muscles quickly stretched gave way to intense pleasure and satisfaction at the fullness of him as he thrust in and out of her.

She had no idea how long he screwed her mercilessly, his fingers digging into her ample hips, clutching her as if she would even think of trying to get away from him. He hadn't needed to, since she was pushing back into each thrust with a desperation of her own, her hands digging into the loam, crushing old, dead leaves as she held on for dear life, trying not to be completely lost to the ecstasy of their violent mating.

When he came, he roared in triumph, a lion claiming his victory, and Alice had trembled in her orgasm, her cries not enough to be heard over his as his seed warmed her insides and the barbs that were inside the bumps on his cock extended to hold him in place inside her, keeping her from escaping him to expel his seed before it had a chance to find its target.

Not that she would have. Not that she wouldn't have done anything to have that seed take root and grow into a child that shared both their blood, but she knew it wasn't meant to be.

Tak had found them lying upon the forest floor, still naked, rubbing each other into a new frenzy, their hands busy preparing them to mate yet again, even though her thighs were slick from their combined orgasm.

She'd looked up into the reptilian eyes of her other mate and had seen that he too was affected by the petals, the lust causing his ridges to swell into hard points on his head and back as obvious as the shifting at his groin, where his cock—with its knobbed head and always hard shaft—waited to be pressed against her slit.

He'd shown no distaste nor jealousy for the sight of her and Iyaren lying there naked, Iyaren's fingers delving into her slick heat as she stroked his shaft back into hardness. If anything, the sight of them like that seemed to make Tak even more excited, as his cock breeched his slit to thrust at the air when Alice spread her legs far enough for him to get a good look at Iyaren's finger penetrating her, again and again, the fur on it slick from her.

They'd never done a threesome—had never even had sex in the same room together, though Alice had broached the idea with her mates after many awkward conversations with Evie. Ultimately, they'd decided that things were already working well the way they were and it was better not to shake them up by doing something that might end up making them jealous or cause problems.

Alice had been relieved by that agreement, feeling far too intimidated by the thought of taking two of them on at once, not certain she could handle both of them, even if their own possessiveness wouldn't have made things uncomfortable.

But that day, in the ancilla forest with the petals flying, none of them had felt any inhibitions or hesitation.

When Tak dropped to his knees between her legs and grabbed her hips to pull her towards his eagerly thrusting shaft, the knobby end seeking her slit with unerring accuracy, no one made any protest.

Iyaren had trailed his wet fingers to her clit, allowing Tak access while he teased her sensitive bud with each thrust of Tak's cock. Inside her, the rounded end of it stroked over her g-spot. Outside of her, Iyaren's fingers toyed with her clit. His lips found hers, swallowing her cry of ecstasy as she came, her muscles clenching around Tak's hard length as it pumped relentlessly inside her.

A stumble over a lifted root snapped Alice out of her memories of that day. The pleasure she'd felt was still clear and sharp to her, but the details of their seemingly endless orgy had grown fuzzy over time, leaving the clearest recollections at the beginning, before the haze of lust and pleasure and exhaustion had blurred everything. She was certain that they hadn't penetrated her at the same time, as Evie had said her mates sometimes did, because Alice had been able to walk the next day—albeit shakily—her legs still weak and her insides aching from so much use.

But even if they hadn't both taken her at the same time, they'd traded her off until her body was exhausted and neither of them could continue. Only then had they all collapsed in the loam in a sweating, sated heap before her two mates situated her between them and snuggled her close, eight strong, muscled arms finding their way around her body to hold her and keep her warm.

Back in the present, she stared up at the wondrous trees around her, recalling how awkward they'd all felt after that experience, barely able to meet each other's eyes until they'd come to an unspoken agreement to never speak of it again and go back to the way they'd been mating, one at a time, gentle and intimate, always an act of love and devotion—rather than raw, uninhibited lust.

Evie and her mates had apparently had so much fun they planned to return to the forest during the next mating petal storm for a repeat, but Alice and her mates would be safe inside the walls of their apartment during the event, which Evie was now calling a "festival" and planning for as if it would be exactly that. Her crazy sister even intended to put cushions and blankets and snacks and other comforts around the trees during that time to take care of those minor irritations that barely made a dent in the haze of uninhibited sexual energy that filled the forest during ancilla mating.

Alice sighed with a mixture of contentment and exasperation at her sister—though the latter was also at herself. She wished she had Evie's courage when it came to... well, pretty much anything. Evie didn't care what other people might think about her. She never had. She did what she wanted, what felt good, and granted, that had often gotten her into trouble. Sometimes, a lot of trouble, but she'd also had a lot more fun than Alice had in her life. At least, until Alice had met her mates and experienced true passion.

Of course, Evie also seemed to be having a blast now with her two mates, making love as a threesome with complete abandon, not a single hang-up or concern to detract from the apparently delicious experience.

Alice was the worrier, the one always concerned about appearances and about "appropriate behavior."

"You need to keep an eye on your sister, Alice," her Nana would always say, shaking her head at Evie's back as the girl would race out the front door, off to school in glittery tights and homemade fairy wings, without a care for how the other kids would make fun of her. "There's too much of her father in that child," she'd mutter, just loud enough for Alice to hear.

Young Alice would always nod solemnly as she shouldered her heavy backpack over the plain tee shirt that hung down just past her ordinary jeans. "I will, Nana. You can trust me to keep her out of trouble."

Nana had nodded at that, making Alice feel momentarily proud and accepted, as if she had an important job to do and

Nana had faith in her to do it. "I know you will, Alice. You've always been the responsible one. The normal one."

Then, Nana would shoo Alice out the door, and Alice knew it was time to take her leave without bothering to wait for a kiss or a hug to see her off. That wasn't Nana's way. At least not with her granddaughters, who'd been a burden thrust upon her and her husband in their golden years, when they were supposed to be enjoying retirement.

The normal one....

It sounded boring. Boring like Evie had accused her of being on many occasions when Alice had tried to save her from her bad decisions before Evie needed an emergency bail-out.

"I don't want to be boring like you, Al," she'd always say. "I want to *live* my life!"

As if I'm not living life?

Alice looked around at the silent trees as she sank down to a kneeling position beside the small pond in the clearing where her sister had once made her home with Doshak.

"I'm living my life just fine, thank you," she said aloud, flinching at the sound of her voice, seemingly so loud in the quiet forest, where only a breeze ruffling the multicolored, teardrop-shaped leaves made a sound.

No one responded to her, not that she expected them to. The ancilla were mostly silent listeners, patient, calm, relaxing to confess all her worries and concerns to, since they never offered their own advice when she just needed somewhere to vent.

"I love my mates, and our sex is fabulous!" As she spoke, she felt a strange thrill, saying such a private, intimate thing aloud, as if she might be overheard by someone who would think her scandalous for such openness about things best left behind closed doors.

"I'm good at making them come." Her cheeks burned hot as she whispered the words, testing her newfound daring. "I make

Chimera's Gift 33

them tremble with their orgasms. I bring them to their knees, begging me to let them touch me in return." Her blush deepened until she was certain she'd be as aflame as Tak if she were a Histri'i like him. "I'm *not* boring."

Her chin lifted as if there was someone there who might deny her words.

A slight hiss was the only sound she heard, but it was enough to cause her to jump to her feet as she searched for the source of the sound. She jumped further away from the pond when she saw a snake coiling through the blades of dull, brown grass that bordered the glittering water. Its gleaming scales were brown along the top with stunning, blue stripes along its sides. As she watched it slither closer, backing away towards the nearest ancilla, its coloring shifted to a rainbow of colors, then seemed to settle on an unnatural pink that looked familiar.

Alice spared a quick glance down at her shirt, realizing the color of the snake matched her clothing. She staggered back into the ancilla tree's trunk. A thin, willowy branch swept across her cheek gently.

Safe.

The voice spoke into her mind, bringing calm with it. The ancilla guarded this forest and allowed nothing harmful to enter. If the snake was dangerous, it would already be dead, pulled down into the dirt and loam by roots to be dissolved into nutrients for the soil.

She released a shaky laugh, staring at the pink snake, which had halted its advance when she'd staggered away and now lay with tongue flicking out, head slightly lifted, beady, snake-eye seeming to be fixed on her. With the garish pink color— matching material Tak had proudly presented her after finding it in the marketplace—the snake looked like an abandoned children's toy, except for the alertness of its pose and the small tongue flicking out.

"Aren't you a pretty little thing," Alice said, leaning back against the ancilla trunk, which pulsed warmly against her palms, welcoming her touch.

She gestured to the snake, then plucked at her shirt—which she'd immediately started cutting out and sewing from the fabric when Tak had brought it to her, wanting him to know how much she appreciated his thoughtful gift. He knew she liked colorful things.

"I like your coloring."

The serpent was silent, though that was hardly surprising. Although, in the Dead Fall, any creature was possible. Even a talking snake.

She glanced up at the ancilla trees surrounding the clearing. Some of them had branches heavy with colorful, round fruit like large marbles waiting for someone to harvest for the market, where their sweet, crisp, delicious juice and pulp was used for many recipes.

A slow grin spread her lips as she returned her gaze to the snake. "Is this the part where you offer me a bite of forbidden fruit then?"

"I'm not Eve, you know. Not even Evie—but I warn you, she's probably already tasted it. Heck, she's probably eaten an entire forbidden-fruit pie, knowing my sister." If there were ever forbidden fruit to taste, Evie would be the one to damn humanity for a bite. She'd see paradise as boring anyway.

Alice's smile spread even wider as she expanded on her fanciful thoughts, voicing them aloud to the snake and the listening trees. "Me? You couldn't talk me into tasting that fruit. Better the paradise you know, right? Why take a chance on something unknown, when you have all you could ever want? Never did understand Eve's choice."

The snake lowered its head, but the eye never stopped staring in her direction.

"So, you picked the wrong girl to approach, my little friend.

I have all I need in life. I won't be tempted by the promise of something more."

Her playful smile faltered as she actually listened to her own words. Had it not been her sadness and feelings of discontent that had brought her into the forest in the first place? She had family, love, passion, a home, safety, her health, and the most precious child in any dimension. She had blessings beyond counting, yet she'd still been driven to this place—this state of mind—by a sense of grief and dissatisfaction.

5

Oskiskeon watched the odd female through the eyes of his serpent sliver, unable to speak through that part of himself, but not inclined to anyway. What would he possibly say to this worthless creature?

He was still fuming over the dismissal of the fire-warrior and his insistence that Kisk learn to respect this soft meat-pouch Tak called a mate. He had yet to see anything about the female that was worthy of his respect.

Tak had earned Kisk's respect by defeating the monster that had been eating Kisk alive. He owed the fire-warrior his life now, and that was the only reason he had bent his efforts to this seemingly impossible task, following the female from her residence into the woods, his keen falcon sliver eyes tracking her so his serpent sliver could catch up to her.

He resented her for wasting his time, though she had no idea why he was there. He wanted to resent Tak, but he'd been defeated, in a way, by the fire-warrior, so could not. Instead, he must shift his resentment onto the cause of it.

He would rather be anywhere other than this forest, with the all-too-knowing trees watching his every move, perhaps even sensing his every thought. He wasn't sure if they could or not. The Looge—now called Gray—had finally trusted him with the secret of the pool at the heart of the woods, and he'd spent some of his life energy inside it to replenish the forest, but he had not communed with the trees as others had. He did not wish to share his thoughts with them. Or anyone.

It was his preference to be alone. The presence of others meant necessary battles.

Not for the first time—not even for the millionth time—he missed the solitude of his mountain temple, so high above his own world that only the strongest, the most powerful—the worthiest—could reach it. Then, they would have to face him in combat. If they lived, they gained his respect, and his favor. The one favor they'd come for. The only thing they ever traveled so far and fought so hard to achieve.

Tak's female just talked and talked. It was inane. It was pointless. Even if her voice sounded like the bells that had once hung from the roof of his temple, and it brought back memories that stabbed him with a shaft of homesickness he refused to allow purchase in his mind, he didn't like for her to keep making noise. If he had a voice, he might've told her to shut her face-hole, or he'd ask how she managed to keep breathing when her voice droned on and on.

He had no idea what she was talking about. He hadn't even bothered to listen to her actual words. He just knew they were an annoyance that he wanted to end.

And yet....

A part of him began to tune in to the words themselves. To really listen with an ear towards understanding what she said, in a halfhearted and hopeless attempt to find a reason to respect her that didn't involve her defeating him in a bloody battle she had no chance of winning.

When meaning filtered through his veil of resentment, he surprised himself by growing interested.

She was speaking to herself, apparently, though why she would, he couldn't fathom. Was she unable to hear her own thoughts that she must speak them aloud? Kisk could not silence his thoughts, even if he wanted to. And he did want to. Many times—as the many parts of him demanded to be heard. He would never speak those thoughts aloud, giving voice to them—which gave them power to affect him.

Instead, he listened to this creature, this "Alice" speak her mind, and he was surprised to learn that she felt unhappy, when he would have imagined she'd be quite pleased with herself, capturing two acknowledged, accomplished warriors for her harem, even breeding a hybrid from the fire-warrior—though Kisk wondered how that had happened.

He knew that males from other worlds often preferred weak females, the kind they had to protect and provide for. Since he didn't pair bond like they did—since mating meant one brief interlude with every female who defeated him, rather than an extended partnership—he had no investment in females. Despite that, he found it fascinating that females from other worlds were so much weaker than the males, even when they were the ones generally tasked with caring for the youngest and most vulnerable of their kind.

It had initially shocked him when he'd learned that some males bred with females who would die easily—even from the process of breeding itself. The females in his world had to be strong enough to hunt down, defeat, and then capture their harem of males. Otherwise, they had no business breeding.

Despite having been in this world now for several of its years measured by its sun, the place and the people still baffled him. Every tale the other creatures told only raised endless questions and confusion that sent all his parts clamoring for answers. His attempt to gain those answers only seemed to anger people—like they had angered the fire-warrior, Tak.

The world itself wasn't much like his own in appearance,

but it was similar in the amount of danger that surrounded them at all times, which was why he found Alice and the existence of females like her in this world so odd. Without the ability to defend themselves, they had to rely on others, but unlike the females in his world, they lacked the strength to defeat those others in order to capture them. Clearly, Alice had used some arcane means to trap her mates, for even the warrior some called the Clawed One was renowned for being skillful and difficult to defeat, despite Kisk having never faced him in battle.

There was no way Alice could have physically wrestled them to the ground and slipped a rune-bound mating collar and leash around their neck. Nor did she seem to need those bonds to keep her mates from killing her or escaping her harem.

He studied her more closely as her bell voice continued on, pouring out words that only increased his confusion, but also let him know something deeply disturbed her. Something she didn't share with anyone else.

She was soft and round, with rolls of flesh that curved beneath her clothes that looked nothing like the hard, muscular bodies of the females he'd mated. He wondered what they felt like to her mates. If her mates enjoyed the way they moved when she did, shifting in a distracting way that made his eyes cross trying to focus on her.

He wondered what they would feel like under his hands as the flesh gave beneath his palms, easy to squeeze to clutch her to him, or perhaps jiggling and shifting in that distracting way as he took her like an animal, entering her from behind to pound relentlessly into her crucible until he spent inside her.

The thought made his shaft swell unexpectedly and he was grateful that he had taken to his own chamber in the unmated male quarters while his slivers watched Alice. He wouldn't have appreciated having others witness the sudden tent in his ragged trousers, which he impatiently pulled off and cast to the heap of other worn clothing that piled in the corner of his room.

He stood naked in the center of his room, blind to the mess around him as his focus shifted completely to his slivers and the female they watched, while one hand clamped over the tip of his erection to keep his fluid from spilling forth. One such as her wasn't worthy. He had no idea why the thought of mating her aroused him. Usually, only a good battle and his blood spilling out onto the ancient stone pavers in front of his temple stiffened his shaft.

She'd grown relaxed around his serpent, sliding down to sit against the trunk of the ancilla tree by the water, her thick legs crossed in front of her in a way that spread them so he could taste her pheromone easily with every flick of his sliver's tongue, even from the distance he kept his serpent from the female.

She tasted good—even he had to acknowledge that. He supposed that was one lure she'd used in her trap for her mates. Perhaps it was an adaptation that served as bait to draw them in along with her bell-like voice and her soft, jiggling flesh.

But how did she keep them? How did she win their loyalty, once she sprung the trap?

"I don't want them to feel like I do, you know?" Her voice rose on the end, like she asked a question, but Kisk wondered who she expected a response from.

Perhaps the trees, though her gaze had fixed on him again, but he had shifted his color to match her blindingly bright shirt in order to draw her attention to him. Her eyes were blue, like the sky of his world at dawn and dusk, when the purples and lavenders faded before night overtook the world.

She continued on without waiting for a reply he couldn't give her from his sliver, not that he had any answer to her question. He did *not* know. That was why he was listening to her so intently. He had no idea why she shielded her mates from her feelings of grief. Though he also had no idea why she would bother sharing it with them. What purpose would sharing feelings serve? If anything, it only made a warrior vulnerable, exposing their secret pain to those who might seek to take advantage.

She wanted to breed more offspring, but had failed to produce thus far, her body shedding the seed before it could grow. This was not an uncommon frustration for females even in his world, and was one reason they made the dangerous journey to his mountain.

He understood that the female would feel that desperation to breed. He just didn't understand why it involved so much emotion from her. The females he'd mated had not been sad—as if they'd lost something precious. They'd been determined.

Then he realized that, for some inexplicable reason, she mourned the seed that had not grown. She had named it, had even begun to craft tiny clothing for it, and most baffling to him, she'd done what she called "daydreaming" about its future. Now her eyes leaked as she struggled with her words, her bell tone faltering as she talked about those "daydreams" and odd concepts like a "wedding" and "graduation" and a "nursery" and counting tiny fingers and toes.

His shaft no longer swelled against his hand, and he'd completely forgotten about his arousal as he grew more and more fascinated by the tales she spun, most of which made no sense to him, yet he struggled to picture them, hanging on her every word, no matter how long it took for her to spit them out between hard breaths that shook her breasts, causing her expansive flesh to heave and jiggle in a way that almost brought that arousal back, and would have, if he wasn't so focused on understanding her words.

Was this how she held the warriors in her harem captive? Did she spin these fantasy tales each night to them, drawing word-pictures of daydreams so they would not even want to escape until they heard the end of the tale? He had to know what would happen next, after the "wedding," which appeared to involve many flowers and something called a "color-scheme." Alice did not satisfy his curiosity, her words drawing to a halt as she sniffled loudly, swiping her hands beneath her eyes with obvious impatience.

"I'm over it," she said in a firm tone, even though her chin quivered. "I'm not going to think about it anymore. I'm going to appreciate my blessings and stop dwelling." She nodded as if she was agreeing with herself. Then her face crumpled, twisting into a grimace that looked like pain before she put her hands over it.

Kisk slithered closer, so focused on her that even his body in his quarters leaned forward, as if he could move that part of him beside her as well. His falcon leapt from the balcony perch it had taken refuge on, overlooking the ancilla forest, and winged its way down to the trees themselves, despite his uneasiness around them. It perched on the ancilla branch above her head, and the sentient tree sent him a welcoming greeting in his mind, which he ignored, though—unlike most creatures—the ancilla was merely amused by his lack of social niceties.

She seemed unaware of his falcon alighting, but when she looked up, she noticed that his serpent had moved closer and she gasped, pushing herself backwards, though the ancilla trunk kept her from moving far.

Then she shook her head at her own reaction. "Sorry, little guy. I don't think I'll ever get over that primal fear of snakes, but the ancilla says you aren't any danger to me."

Kisk wondered if the ancilla was correct. He wasn't even certain himself what he thought of this creature anymore. He didn't respect her, as Tak had insisted he must before he could approach the fire-warrior again, but he also didn't think she was completely useless anymore. He supposed he wouldn't be bothered to kill her, since she was unlikely to attack him first.

She cocked her head, blinking the sheen of moisture out of her eyes as she stared at his serpent. "You're kinda cute, you know. That little snake face and adorable little tongue. I wonder if you'd make a good pet for Friak?"

Kisk jerked back, hissing in protest. There was no way he'd allow even a sliver of himself to be handled as a pet.

She stared at him—her mouth agape. "Did you... did you understand that?" A sudden panicked look crossed her face as she lifted a hand to her mouth as though she could push her words back inside. "Did you understand everything I was saying?"

Kisk decided to play dumb, suddenly unwilling to let her know he could comprehend her words, in case she chose to remain silent in the company of his serpent. He still hadn't heard the rest of her daydreams, and he wanted to hear more of her bells singing to him. He lowered his serpent's head and slithered a bit off to the side, as if there was something of interest for a reptile to explore, rather than the strangely fascinating creature before him.

"Hello?" she said in a sing-song tone, her voice soft as she stared at him. "Little snake-guy? Do you understand me?"

He continued to slither around without any apparent aim, hoping she would forget his earlier reaction and fall for his ruse.

After a couple more attempts on her part to gain his attention, she gave up, shaking her head. "Guess it was just a coincidence that it reacted when I said that."

Then she turned her head and stared off into the trees as if she'd forgotten him, but he still felt suspicious. There was something about her posture and the tension in her body that made him wary.

"Hmm," she said, tapping her chin, "I suppose it would

make a good pet for Friak, providing Gray can examine it and make certain it isn't venomous."

Kisk struggled not to react to her words, still unwilling to give himself away. He continued to amble aimlessly through the grass.

"Of course, Friak can get a little squeeze-y. I'll have to make certain he doesn't grip the poor little pinky too hard."

If Kisk didn't know better, he'd think the female was mocking him now, teasing him in an effort to gain a reaction that revealed his understanding.

"He does love to pet cute little things. Ooh, I know!"

Kisk paused, wondering what fresh nightmare the female was concocting in her fertile mind. Actually, feeling a bit concerned about it.

"He loves it when we dress up his stuffed animals. I'll bet I can sew a little hat and scarf for you, Snakey. How cute would you be with a tiny snake hat tied around your head?" She clapped her hands together in front of her as he lifted his head to stare at her in abject horror—a huge grin on her face as she looked back at him.

She winked at him, and suddenly he knew that she knew.

6

A sentient serpent that the ancilla trusted? Alice could only think of one creature that might fit that description. Or rather, the part of one creature.

She wondered if she should have let on to her suspicions so soon, even as the words she'd poured out unsuspectingly to the snake and the surrounding trees came back to her now, making her horrified that she'd revealed so much to what could potentially be Tak's acquaintance.

Would he tell Tak what she'd said?

The snake seemed as horrified as she was, though she wondered how she could read so much in the little creature's body language as it lifted its head—which really was adorable —and stared at her over its body.

Then it took off like a bat out of Hell, and Alice didn't know whether to laugh or cry as it escaped, having heard all her deepest, innermost thoughts, worries, and pain—the things she didn't even confess to her beloved mates, because she didn't want them to feel those burdens along with her. They were content—even happy. It was important to her that they stay that way. She wanted all her loved ones to be happy. She could deal with her own sadness.

She rose to her feet, brushed bits of loam off her palms and patted the ancilla tree companionably, thanking it for allowing her to use its support. It pulsed in return, along with a friendly farewell in her mind.

With a heavy sigh, she turned and headed back to the path that would lead her home, pondering the little pink serpent— and what she knew of the chimera.

Tak wasn't fond of the creature he'd rescued, though he tried to be patient whenever the other male talked to him. Apparently, Okiskeon lacked social skills—to the extreme. Tak said he was almost always insulting, blunt, and antagonistic, as if he wanted to pick a fight with everyone. In fact, Kisk often did pick fights in the unmated male quarters. It was only Gray's quelling influence that kept those fights from turning into deaths. Kisk was no joke as a warrior—absolutely lethal— capable of shape-shifting, fragmenting his body, and even breathing fire.

There weren't many who could defeat him in a fair fight. Those who could apparently earned his undying loyalty and respect—even if they had no use for either, since he was difficult to get along with, and it was much easier to ignore him when he pretended they didn't exist.

Whenever Tak talked about Kisk, Alice felt sorry for him. It was clear he had issues that kept him alone, even as the other males formed friendships and even more intimate relationships. It was also clear that Kisk had no idea how to take care of even himself, so it wasn't surprising that he couldn't nurture relationships with others. From what Alice had heard of his quarters and his appearance, he didn't really know how to clean up after himself, feed himself properly, or clothe himself in anything more than the rags discarded by other males.

He was the bachelor to end all bachelors, completely helpless and in need of someone to care about him. The poor guy needed a mother or a mate, and ever since Tak had saved him, Alice had been looking for the latter for him, more than willing to play matchmaker, because she suspected neither Tak nor Iyaren would allow her anywhere near the other male to mother him. Besides, he didn't seem very approachable anyway.

A fact which made seeking the perfect mate for him difficult. Tak had no idea if Kisk liked males or females, or if he even liked sex or was capable of it. Asterius wasn't much help in that regard either, as he'd told Alice she would be better off trying to pair up NEX itself with a mate—claiming the ruthless, murderous AI would be more sociable than the minotaur's sorta-friend.

As far as Alice was concerned, their lack of knowledge about Kisk was because they'd failed to ask him the important questions—being male, they didn't think these things mattered.

Alice had focused on the females she knew, since she wasn't permitted near unmated males—or rather, they weren't permitted to come near her, though she felt that was more six of one, half dozen of the other, since it still felt restrictive. Not that she couldn't appreciate the reasoning behind it, but as the settlement grew more civil and stable, she felt like it was time for her and the other females to be able to shop in the markets during the same time the unmated males were allowed to go there. She also felt like mixing the males and females in public would improve the chances of them meeting up and forming permanent bonds, since the mixers where select males were introduced to the females had been—thus far—only marginally successful in creating matches.

Currently, they had thirty-six unmated females in New Omni, which was a vast improvement from where they'd started, but it was still far less than the one hundred and fifty-seven unmated males, most of whom were not interested in relationships with other males.

Alice knew all thirty-six females well, since she'd interviewed every one of them, making many friends in the process. She knew their likes, dislikes, their cultures when it came to mating and bonding, and what they'd like to find in a mate. She loved talking to them, especially about love, and it drew her focus off her own problems to think about matchmaking and setting everyone up with their happily ever after.

Her sister, Evie, was the usual greeter for the females when they first came to New Omni, but once they'd been settled, Alice was the one who swept in and saw to it that they had everything they needed to feel as "at home" as she could make them. That required lots of questions in its own right, and those questions naturally evolved into discussions about family, then mating.

She'd identified a handful of females she thought might be perfect for Kisk, given what little she knew about him. She wished she could personally interview him, but knew that wasn't about to happen, although, if the serpent really was a part of him, she wondered if she might convince him to give her a few answers through it. If it couldn't talk, they might be able to play charades.

She'd felt safe enough around the serpent, though she wouldn't want to be around the rest of the chimera. According to Tak, not only could he shift into a serpent and a falcon, but also a full-sized African lion—with horns. Because lions just weren't deadly enough without them, apparently.

The only lion she wanted to meet face to face was her mate, Iyaren.

Of course, now that the serpent had heard all her bawling and carrying on about herself, he might be a greater danger to her than any physical threat he'd ever pose. If he went to Tak and said something about what Alice had talked about in the forest, it could create problems in her family that would disrupt the fragile bubble of happiness she made certain to keep around them.

Without really thinking it through, she changed direction to follow the path of the serpent, hoping to catch up to it and beg it not to reveal her secrets.

After an hour of searching fruitlessly, with no help from the ancilla, who merely sent her regrets that they couldn't assist her, she gave up on finding the pink snake, figuring it had probably changed its color to hide from her.

She had to return to her quarters, her stomach knotting in anxiety as she worried Kisk would spill all her secrets to Tak, who would immediately tell Iyaren. Then she'd be faced with both of them worrying about her, and recalling their own feelings of pain and loss. She wouldn't allow that to happen, but she had no idea how to stop it if Kisk had the chance to talk to Tak.

By the time she reached the entrance to the main apartment building in their complex where the family quarters were housed, she was nearly shaking from nerves and knew she couldn't visit Evie like that, because even if no one else suspected, Sherak would sense her distress.

Maybe it wasn't Kisk. It could have just been a random, sentient, color-shifting snake to match the color-shifting ancilla trees.

There were certainly stranger things in the Dead Fall. In fact, sentient reptiles were downright pedestrian. Alice was mated to a lizardman who had four arms and burst into flames on occasion. A smart snake was hardly outside the realm of possibility.

Yet, the coincidences made her nervous. The snake had approached her, not long after Tak saved Kisk's life. She'd never once seen a serpent in the ancilla forest before that, and the ancilla didn't allow strange creatures in—particularly sentient ones—unless they trusted them. Alice knew the chimera had been allowed into the heart—Gray having decided at some point that he could be trusted with the forest's secrets.

The fact that Gray trusted Kisk with such a secret said something about the chimera, but what that something was could be difficult to tell. Gray could see the future—or rather, many possible futures—and he wasn't averse to manipulating events to bring about the future he wanted. It was entirely possible, even likely, that Kisk had some role to play in a future Gray wanted to bring about. Whatever the truth might be, only Gray would know it unless he chose to share, and he rarely did.

Her brother-in-law was occupied with some mysterious task in the Dead Fall at the moment, and Alice suspected it had to do with unearthing his buried spaceship, since Evie had slipped and mentioned the flying saucer just yesterday.

Asterius was working on construction projects in the new parts of New Omni, claimed from the surrounding ruins by guardian ancilla saplings spreading their boundaries and root systems. Lauren was training some of the females to form a fighting unit to protect and patrol the female areas and serve as a security force. Evie was watching Friak and Sherak, and Doshak was no doubt with her, or at the brooding hole, scanning and fawning over the eggs that would someday hatch into their children.

There was no one to wonder why Alice suddenly changed direction at the entrance to her apartment, making her way instead towards the larger settlement and the unmated males' quarters.

She paused at the boundary fence, which towered ten feet above her and was painted a pale tan color, papered over with advertisements brought back from the Fall and added for color and cheeriness on the otherwise imposing structure. Despite the barrier, it was the threat of Gray's retribution rather than the fence itself that kept the unmated males from crossing that boundary into family and female territory.

Many of the males wouldn't be dissuaded by a single, wooden fence.

Gray had sensors on the fence, and security drones patrolling, in addition to a security guard walking the perimeter. As if all that wasn't enough, the female and family quarters were also secured with guards and sensors. Any attempt to breach those security measures meant death for unmated males.

Females weren't punished for crossing over to the male side, but only because none of them were stupid enough to try it, no matter how bored they got on this side of the fence. They knew they were drastically outnumbered and there were a lot of lonely males on the other side, most of whom were violent and aggressive by default.

Yet, she needed to cross the fence, find Kisk's quarters, and then beg him on hands and knees—if she must—not to tell Tak what she'd said. All she had to do was get through the secured perimeter, then make her way through an area filled with dangerous males to sneak into an apartment complex housing those males and find the one room that held one of the deadliest of them—and the surliest.

Shouldn't be a problem.

At least the timing was good. It was midafternoon, which meant most people in New Omni were working on some task or project that took them away from the boundary, and took quite a few males away from the settlement itself.

She sucked in a few bracing breaths, her gaze sweeping the perimeter, noting the current location of the drones sliding along the top of the fence, their scanners turned towards the male side.

According to the posted roster in the family quarters, Yaneas—who'd mated up with Ulgotha and four other males—was on patrol at this time of day. Fortunately for Alice, she knew his path, as she'd walked it with him on more than one occasion, chatting about his home world. Unlike many in New Omni, Yaneas didn't feel the same bite of homesickness when he talked about his life before coming to the Dead Fall, so she didn't feel guilty asking him questions, knowing he preferred his new life and his mate to what he'd had before.

She looked around for him and spotted his exoskeleton dully gleaming in the muted sunlight near one of the apartment buildings, noting his progress and calculating when he'd return this way. If she timed it right, she could be over the fence as soon as the drone passed and before Yaneas was in sight of her spot.

The trick was getting over the fence without killing herself. She wasn't exactly svelte, having turned to food for comfort lately, packing on weight that increased her already generous size and forced her to sew new clothing for herself. Tak and Iyaren never made a single complaint about her weight gain, nor did it appear to affect their desire for her, since they always signaled their need and arousal when she was with them, but the extra pounds added to her depression because she knew her coping strategy wasn't healthy.

That extra weight also made scaling a fence with a tight time limit to remain undetected a daunting task. If she wasn't so worried about Kisk revealing her secrets, she would have abandoned the prospect altogether. If she got caught, she'd get a lecture from Evie, and worse, a knowing look from Gray. Then Iyaren and Tak would find out something was wrong, which was the worst part of all.

As soon as the drone passed by, sliding along the bar at the top of the wooden, horizontally-slatted fence, she approached the fence and gripped the joints between the slats, breaking her nails in the process and digging splinters beneath them, but that did little to dissuade her. With a heave and a grunt of effort, she pulled herself up onto the fence, grateful that she'd worn a soft pair of hand-sewn hide boots that were like moccasins and allowed her toes the flexibility to grip the tightly-jointed slats of the fence.

With trembling arms and legs, she made the climb, cursing the fact that she'd let herself get so out of shape. Not that she'd intended to do this kind of activity, but she'd grown too comfortable living in the protected family quarters, sometimes even forgetting there was a homicidal artificial intelligence out there, plotting their demise.

In fact, her life had become so safe in the sheltering shield created by the forest that she barely even noticed when the Nexus opened anymore, so accustomed to the sirens that went off every few days or so that she automatically collected herself and her loved ones and made her way indoors without even glancing up at the portal in the sky as the ancilla trees began knitting their branches together above the settlement.

It had become a way of life to just ignore the most dangerous thing about their life, and the females and families would often meet in the basement for snacks and games, entertaining themselves and the fretful children until the all-clear was given by the sensors that Gray had set up to detect the changes in the Nexus.

With great, gasping breaths, her heart pounding and her lungs feeling like they were about to burst, she made it to the top of the fence, searching for the drone or Yaneas. She'd taken longer than she'd planned, because it wasn't as easy as she'd hoped it would be, but as she swung her leg over the top pole, she didn't see the drone or the guard.

All she could feel was gratitude over that, because it took a bit longer to descend low enough for her to jump off the fence without hurting herself, and when she did, she collapsed in a heap on the hard dirt, packed down from many male feet standing at the fence in the evenings as they tried to woo the females who would often walk along the other side of it, trilling and cooing for the males. Alice intended to be safely back home in her apartment before that nightly ritual began, though she often went outside to watch it, trying to match up the females with some of the males, based on what she knew about them.

Evie found Alice's desire to hook up everyone with a happily-ever-after amusing, since Alice had been so cynical about love before meeting her mates. Now that Alice had found her own happiness, she wanted everyone around her to feel that kind of love too.

Only lately, Alice hadn't felt like she could appreciate how in love she was, but she couldn't let Tak and Iyaren know that. They had to believe everything was okay. She would deal with her grief in time, but until then, she would protect her mates from it.

Pulling herself to her feet after a long moment of gasping for air, she winced at the pangs in her toes that stung from the effort of scaling the fence. She caught the sound of the drone sliding towards her and quickly made her way towards the giant mushroom that shaded the plaza that had been built between the fence and the unmated male housing.

It glowed at night and during the day, shriveled beneath a dull, leaf-like flap that curled out of its top and rolled down the sides to protect it from the light of the sun. It was a remarkable specimen, and Alice was honestly jealous they didn't have one on their side of the fence, but it was tended by a secretive male that she'd heard was some kind of a plant himself. He wasn't allowed on their side, so he couldn't tend such a delicate fungus, even if they had it.

As she hid beneath the sheltering mushroom, watching the scanner pass by, she wondered why the plant man wasn't allowed onto the female side, even for just a few hours to tend a mushroom tree like this.

He must be dangerous and violent, but she kept thinking, "He's a plant. How dangerous can he be?"

She hoped she didn't find out, and fortunately, there was no one in the plaza. There shouldn't be many males around Kisk's housing either.

She slapped a hand to her forehead, realizing that if all the males were busy, then Kisk might be too. But then again, they did get time off, and if Kisk was working, then why would he be slinking around the ancilla trees as a pink snake?

She'd come this far, so she figured it wouldn't hurt to check his quarters. Tak had told her where he lived during his stories of Kisk's antisocial attempts to socialize with Tak.

Alice knew the layout of the male side of the settlement, because the females would be led through the plaza on their way to the large market on shopping days, when the males were kept away from the area until all the females and families were safely back on their own side. She could picture Kisk's housing area in her mind and was grateful his apartment had an outside access door and was on the bottom level. It gave her the opportunity to sneak around the side of the building, her neck and back prickling from more than the sweat that had poured from her as she'd scaled the fence.

She worried about being spotted, felt like there were eyes watching her, but saw nothing other than more strange plants and clusters of fungus tucked into shaded areas beneath ancilla saplings that were already taller than the buildings they surrounded.

The presence of the ancilla made her feel a bit safer, though the saplings couldn't yet move their roots and flexible branches to stop an attacker if one presented himself—since they were still little more than younglings, despite their shielding abilities —but they didn't give any indication that a male was around and posed a threat.

She was definitely second-guessing herself at this point, sure that her impulsive decision to confront Kisk would end in disaster. Still, she was already here, and Kisk's apartment door was just ahead of her, darkened by the combined shade of the ancilla and other, non-sentient trees with blackened, twisted branches, sparse black leaves, a general aura of spookiness.

Nothing like confronting a surly male—a surly, *deadly* male —in his lair in the shade of creepy trees.

Maybe he's not home, she thought hopefully as she lifted a hand to knock on the door—a crudely-hewn wooden panel with runes scrawled in what she really hoped wasn't blood— but looked like it was—across the top half of the door.

He's probably working. She lowered her hand and took a step backwards, staring at those runes, unable to decipher them and suddenly really not wanting to know.

I'll, uh, come back later.

She made it another step, cursing herself for not thinking through her escape from the male side of the settlement. Then the door was jerked open from the inside, and she found herself face to face with a huge, snarling male—his face that of a lion, but with a mane of feathers that rippled as his snarl of irritation shifted into what might be surprise.

His eyes were very light gray, with horizontal irises that reminded her of creepy goat eyes. Spiral horns rose from his head between his leonine ears, further obscuring any comparison to her beloved Iyaren and his handsome leonine face.

She staggered backwards, shocked by his sudden appearance, her gaze taking in his ragged, stained tunic crusted with old food and grime, and his equally filthy pants, which hung baggy and ill-fitted over scaled limbs that shimmered with color as she watched before they settled on a beautiful ruby red.

He was barefoot, and she found his bird-like talons suddenly fascinating as she avoided looking into his eyes, though she'd frozen from her retreat when he'd barked a command for her to stay.

He hadn't asked. He'd commanded.

"You little fool!" he said in a low, menacing growl. "Why would you come here?"

She jerked her head up, but not far enough that she had to meet his eyes. Instead, she focused on his hand, which gripped the edge of the doorframe—scaled but human-like fingers with retractable claws like Iyaren's, only Kisk's were extended and digging into the wood of the doorframe, gouging out deep grooves as he snarled at her.

"You cannot defeat me. You would die immediately."

She gasped and took another step away from him, despite her fear of angering him by ignoring his command. "I-I didn't...."

She dared a glance at his eyes, then gulped and quickly looked away. They'd shifted to a golden color with round pupils.

He narrowed his eyes on her, his gleaming, yellowed fangs bared. "Females used to climb a great precipice to reach me, and you climbed what? A fence?" His voice, not as deep as Iyaren's, dripped with disdain. "Why do you think that would ever earn my favor?"

Her spine snapped straight as her hands shot up in a staying motion. "Whoa! Wait a minute. I think you've got the wrong idea here." She shook her hands in front of her, crossing them in a negative motion. "No way! I am *not* interested in you. Not like that!"

She managed to contain her shudder of revulsion, but just barely as she took in his crusty, filthy, tattered clothing and his bizarre appearance, from his feathered mane to his talon-clawed feet. A deep breath drew in the stench that was coming from the dark hole of an apartment behind him, and probably also from him, given the condition of his clothing—though the parts of him visible beneath it appeared to be clean—scale, fur, and feather all shining even in the little light that penetrated the shadows around his entrance.

Alice coughed at the eye-watering smell of rotting food and waste and turned her head to the side to try to cover it, reminding herself to breathe shallowly from now on.

If anything, her words only seemed to increase his tension, his claws digging deeper into the doorframe until the sound of them drilling into the wood was chillingly audible. "Then why are you here, female?" His voice sounded brittle and sharp, like broken glass.

Alice crossed her arms in front of her chest, tucking her hands under her armpits to hide their trembling as she took a deep breath through her mouth, then another. She was no stranger to being around big, intimidating males—even monstrous ones—but she also wasn't exactly fearless, like Evie and Lauren.

"I-I'm really sorry to bother you. It's just that I wondered if you might have been the little, pink snake I met earlier."

She winced inwardly at how crazy her words sounded, even to her. What if she'd only imagined the snake, and now she looked like a lunatic to this stranger? Yet, Tak had said he'd had a serpent part of him, and Tak had even been the one to carry it with him when he'd returned to New Omni with the mortally wounded chimera.

"Little?" Kisk snorted, his tone so offended at the word that it was almost comical. "My sliver is *not* little."

She felt both relief and dread at the confirmation. Relief that she wasn't going crazy and this awkward conversation wasn't a complete waste, but dread that she still hadn't gotten his agreement not to tell Tak about her monologue in the woods.

"I apologize." She held up her hands in a placating gesture, grateful to see that they weren't shaking anymore. "I didn't mean to offend."

He narrowed his eyes on her. "Then why do you look so amused, female?"

Alice's lips flattened as she realized he'd been able to detect the smile that she'd struggled to keep from revealing itself. She was still fighting a chuckle at his snort of outrage over being called "little."

She coughed and cleared her throat, covering her mouth with her fist for a moment to get the smile under control. "Anyway, I was hoping I could speak to you about what happened in the woods."

This distracted him from his suspicious glaring at her mouth, as if he waited for a smile to appear so he could crow "ah ha!" His gaze, reptilian now, with a sideways slit of a pupil and yellow eyes, shifted from her lips to her eyes.

"What happened in the woods?"

Irritation rippled through her, further stiffening her spine as she propped both hands on her hips. "You were eavesdropping on me. That's what happened. You had no right to—"

The sound of the doorframe cracking cut off her words abruptly as Alice stared at it, noticing that he'd broken it as his hand clenched, then she took a step away from him as she looked back at his face. His eyes were not looking at her face, but were fixed on her body, staring down at her hands on her hips.

His nostrils flared, broadening his already wide nose, and the strange feathery mane actually rippled like a bird fluffing its feathers. Alice stared at those feathers in awe as they shifted to coarse hair—a sandy, golden mane—then back to feathers again in a change so rapid, she might have missed it if she hadn't been looking right at it.

"I have a right to be in the woods," he said, though his tone sounded distant, distracted, and held little emotion and none of his normal attitude. His gaze still didn't lift from her hips, but she could see his eyes well enough to notice how they changed color and pupil shape, rapidly, like his mane had changed.

She took another careful step backwards, eyeing him with

alarm, wondering how fast she could get to the fence and call for help if he lunged at her.

Knowing if he lunged at her, she was already a goner.

Slowly, she uncurled her fists and lifted them away from her hips, holding them out flat in front of her, palms towards him in a placating way, as if he was a wild animal about to attack. "I wasn't suggesting you weren't supposed to be there. I just...."

She noted the shakiness of her voice and cursed herself for allowing her fear to show. Evie would have had some smartass comeback to his words and would have snapped at him for staring at her so fixedly. Alice could only try to draw his gaze upwards and away from the aggressive "fists on hips" stance that had apparently upset him.

"I wish you would have let me know you could understand me sooner than you did. I wouldn't have said the things I was saying if I knew anyone other than the ancilla was listening. Those were private thoughts." A return of her irritation at him for eavesdropping helped quell her shaking, especially since his gaze followed her hands, then lifted back to her face.

His furry brows drew together in a frown, but there was no sign of anger or aggression in it, and he didn't bare his ferocious teeth at her in a snarl. "If your thoughts were not meant to be heard, why speak them aloud?" He snorted in clear disdain, breaking the tension with the return of his condescending attitude. "Do you have something against peace and quiet? It certainly seems that way."

She could handle the attitude, and the surliness of before. It was the sudden tension in him that she wanted to avoid. She had no idea if he would actually hurt her or not, though she couldn't imagine why he would, after Tak had saved his life. She didn't think the chimera could be that much of a monster, since Gray trusted him with the secret of the ancilla forest, and so did the ancilla. They were generally the best judges of character.

Still, his moods were unpredictable, and no one seemed to really know him. She certainly didn't want to. The sooner she got this over with, the better.

"Look, the forest is large enough that you didn't have come around me and listen to all my talking. That's on you for hanging around me in the first place. All I'd like to ask is that you keep whatever you heard to yourself."

She crossed her arms again, bracing her feet as if he might try to push her away before she'd convinced him to respect her privacy.

He studied her with a golden gaze and round pupils, his expression unreadable even on a leonine face, which had become familiar to her, despite the very obvious differences between Kisk and Iyaren. Her mate had a flatter, narrower nose with more human proportions to his face, despite its unquestionable resemblance to a lion.

Kisk appeared more lion than man, with a longer face than Iyaren's, more pronounced snout and whiskers, and a furry, white chin that looked like a beard. His face looked both terrifying and adorably pet-able at the same time—very much like a deadly, man-eating big cat, which she had stopped seeing Iyaren as being a long time ago.

At the moment, she couldn't tell exactly what the mind behind that face was thinking, and not for the first time, wished she had Gray's mindreading ability.

As he stared at her in silence, she shifted her weight from one foot to the other.

"So," she finally said, when he didn't respond to her request, "will you please keep quiet about what you overheard?" She tried to sweeten her request, knowing she was asking a favor of a stranger who had no reason to concern himself with her relationship with her mates. "I'd really appreciate it if you didn't mention anything you heard to anyone."

He snorted, releasing the broken door frame as he stepped out of his doorway, his other hand pulling the door shut behind him, leaving him standing outside his apartment with its bloody rune door panel, only a few steps from Alice.

The reek of his apartment was shut out, much to her gratitude, but his clothing still stank as if it had never been washed. Yet, beneath that strong odor was a scent that was far nicer, an intriguing mixture of grassy and citrus odors, with a hint of some exotic spice. She doubted it was cologne, as it wasn't strong and cloying.

"Why does silence matter?" he asked, his tone as unreadable as his expression.

Alice was about to answer when she heard a sound that sent a chill through her blood. A brief howl from a male returning to their apartment. An apartment in this direction. She'd be spotted on the male side of the settlement, at the very least. She had no idea what the male would do when he saw her.

Kisk drew his lips back in a snarl as he turned towards the sound.

"Irritating, noisy, pathetic creature," he muttered, then grabbed Alice's upper arm roughly, his grip painfully strong, though he relaxed it when she yelped.

She wasn't certain if he was referring to her or the approaching male.

"I don't need this problem," he growled at her, dragging her deeper into the shadows, tugging hard on her arm when she dug her heels into the stone pavers that led up to his door. "Come with me, you foolish female. I know a way through the ancilla forest that will lead to your side of the fence."

He yanked harder on her arm, and Alice stumbled into him,

her face smashing into a rock-hard chest covered by gag-inducing filthy fabric.

Kisk pushed her upright, steadying her impatiently, muttering just loud enough to be heard by her, his words cursing weak, annoying creatures as he steered her into deeper shadows and thicker foliage.

7

They made it to the ancilla forest path without being spotted—at least not that Alice knew of—and she couldn't hold back a huge sigh of relief as the ground changed from paved road to packed dirt and loam. The guardian trees at the edge of the path rippled with welcoming colors. Though the ancilla had spread their saplings into the ruins that now formed the settlement, they still kept most people out of their forest. Only those trusted with the secret of the heart could come and go as they pleased, and the ancilla always seemed to be happy to see them visit.

She jerked her arm out of Kisk's grasp, and this time—unlike all the other times she'd tried to break free of him—he let her go.

Breathing heavily from being dragged through the settlement at a relentless pace, despite having to stick to the shadows, she shot him a glare of resentment. If he hadn't been so damned nosy, injecting his little, pink, snake-self into her life, she wouldn't have to deal with this problem.

"You still haven't agreed to keep your mouth shut," she snapped, before closing her eyes in dismay as she realized he held all the cards and she needed to be nice to him in order to convince him to keep her secrets.

"You still haven't answered why it matters that I do not speak of it." Rather than being angry at her tone, his voice sounded amused.

She opened her eyes to meet his curious gaze, surprised to see that same glimmer of amusement in his gray, goat eyes.

"My family life is very content and peaceful. I want it to stay that way."

He cocked his head, watching her as if she'd just sprouted two heads of her own. "You lie."

She blinked, confused by his statement. "I'm not lying. My family *is* happy."

"Are you not a part of your family?" He fell into step beside her when she tried to retreat along the path, heading back into the ancilla forest to loop around to the path leading back to the family side of the settlement.

She rolled her eyes as he matched her steps, shortening his own long-legged walk to avoid leaving her behind. It seemed she would not be rid of him that easily. She wondered if she could tread on one of his talons to convince him to give up on walking with her.

"Of *course,* I'm part of my family," *You dunce!* She bit the last words off before she made the mistake of saying them. The guy just couldn't take a hint and leave her alone.

"If you are part of your family, then you lie. Your family is not happy and content." He glanced at her with a knowing twist of his lips to bare fangs. "You told me so yourself."

"I didn't tell *you!*" she growled, clenching her hands into fists in front of her. "I was talking to myself, and your nosy self just butted in where you weren't wanted and started listening to things you weren't supposed to hear."

"I do not understand why you conceal your unhappiness

from your mates. If they already belong to you, why do you care what they think of your weakness?"

Alice drew to an abrupt halt, while Kisk overshot her, turning around in front of her as he paused when he realized she wasn't beside him anymore.

"What the—?" She took a deep, bracing breath, holding her hands out in front of her. "Wait. I need to be more patient."

He probably doesn't know any better.

Not for the first time, Alice wondered what kind of family unit the chimera had experience with. Normally, she would pose delicate questions to find out what a person's mating rituals and mores were like, because direct questions could easily offend. In Kisk's case, she was starting not to give a damn if she offended him.

"What exactly do your people do when they take mates, Kisk?" she asked, crossing her arms and regarding him with a narrow-eyed glare, trying to hide how curious she was for the answer beneath her pique at his rudeness.

He tilted his head, his mane feathers rustling in the slight breeze that filtered through the surrounding ancilla trees. "My people? I have none. I am *the* chimera."

The chimera—with emphasis on "the." He made it sound like he wasn't a member of a species formed of others like himself—he was the *only* one.

Alice wasn't sure the sudden pity that filled her was even warranted in his case. Perhaps it didn't matter to him that he had no people, no place to belong. Perhaps it was even easier for him to find a life here in the Dead Fall without having left a village or town or city of people like himself behind in his own world. Maybe it made it easier for him to be the only one of his kind here in this world, because he had never known what it was like to look into a familiar face—one similar to his own.

"You pathetic creatures that pair-bond make very little sense to me."

His words and condescending tone deflated her growing sympathy for him, reminding her that he was a jackass.

"You know what, Kisk. You stink." She waved a hand in front of her nose. "And I mean that literally too. You're an arrogant jerk, and you actually smell bad. Have your clothes ever met the wash basin?" She eyed the holes and tears in them. "Or a needle and thread?"

He glanced down at his stained, crusty shirt, plucking it away from his body with one hand. "The spirits of the temple used to clean and mend my raiment. At least these rags usually keep away irritants like you who are intent on interfering with my peace and quiet." His voice took on a defiant edge with the last words.

He released the dirty fabric, allowing it to slump back against his body, his shudder nearly undetectable. In fact, Alice would have missed it if she hadn't been staring at that gross tunic as it flopped back against him, heavy with dirt and crusted filth.

"You know, there has to be a male around the settlement willing to wash that for you in return for tokens or trade," she said, softening her tone and regretting her harsh words to him. If he'd spent his entire life alone, it was little wonder he lacked social skills.

The female side of the settlement had more than one female willing to do laundry service for tokens to spend in the market, though Alice personally didn't make use of it, content to do the laundry for her own family, as she enjoyed making and caring for their clothing.

He shrugged. "It isn't important." Again, his tone was defensive, with a quelling growl at the end of his words that told her to abandon the topic.

She wondered how well he got along with the other males, guessing from what Tak had told her that it probably wasn't very well at all. She didn't think Kisk even knew how to foster any kind of relationship, even a business one where he traded goods for services or vice versa.

Realizing she might be pushing him too far—and a defensive creature was a dangerous one—Alice dropped the subject, starting her walk along the path again without a comment. The sun lowered in the sky, and she needed to head back home to collect Friak from Evie before Iyaren and Tak returned from their foray into the ruins.

Not that her mates wouldn't take Friak for her and allow her to have all the leisure time she wanted, but they would question her in all innocence about what she'd been doing with that free time, and she didn't want to lie to them.

When Kisk fell into step beside her again, she bit back a sigh. "I can make it the rest of the way on my own, you know."

"You can barely breathe," he said, strolling along next to her without any sign of effort. "You might collapse soon. I suppose I should be there to drag your carcass back to the fire-warrior. He has earned that much from me."

She stumbled, as taken aback as if he'd slapped her across the face. That was what his casual, thoughtless remark felt like. "I'm a little out of shape, not that it's any of your damned business."

Her ire only made her heavy breathing more obvious. In that moment, she felt every single extra pound she'd put on while she'd been eating to bury her pain. Her knees ached and her heart thudded as her lungs seemed to struggle to draw in each breath. "You are so... god! You're so damned rude!"

"I have offered to drag you back to your home if you should lose all your wind, and you insult me for this boon?"

"I know you're mocking me, Kisk!"

She stopped walking and turned to him, poking her finger at him, irritated that she had to look up enough to strain her neck when she stood this close to him. Tall males would be the death of her poor neck someday, as Iyaren and Tak both towered over her. She wondered if little Friak would be as tall as his father.

Kisk looked genuinely surprised by her accusation, his furry brows lifting and his eyes widening as he glanced down at her pointing finger, tilting his head at it as if he wondered where it came from and what its purpose was. "I do not bother taunting a non-combatant. What would be the point? I merely observed your difficulty breathing and commented on it."

Alice pulled her hand back to run it through her hair, her scalp damp with sweat from the day's exertions. "You aren't... uh... making fun of my weight?"

His eyes rose from his chest that she hadn't quite dared to poke to meet her eyes. "Is it unusual for your kind? Is that why you struggle to draw breath?"

Alice felt humiliation fill her at the realization that she'd projected her own insecurity onto his words. Kisk wasn't even aware she was overweight. He had no idea what humans looked like other than her. She was so accustomed to being mocked for her weight, both slyly and overtly, more than familiar with comments that cruelly pointed out her breathlessness during physical education, or her struggle to regain her breath at the top of a staircase. Kids were assholes sometimes, not unlike Kisk. The difference was that Kisk wasn't trying to be malicious. He was just naturally a jerk, and he apparently didn't play favorites. He treated everyone the same—like they were beneath him.

There was something remarkably refreshing about that idea. She could never lift herself in his estimation, so why bother? Yet at the same time, his standards were so impossible to meet that she'd literally have to defeat him in a fight or save him from death for him to see her as anything but inferior. She couldn't do anything in her power to make him like her more, couldn't ingratiate herself to him, or be extra friendly in the hopes that he wouldn't make her the butt of his jokes.

Knowing that she had no control over what he thought of her was incredibly liberating for Alice. He didn't care about hurting her feelings, so she didn't feel obligated to protect his. She could say exactly what she wanted, and behave exactly as she felt like behaving, and not risk losing his regard—because she'd never had it.

"Did you really live in a temple?"

He was speechless for a moment, as if he struggled to understand her abrupt change of subject and the sudden change in her tone and posture.

Alice wasn't going to diminish herself for him anymore, picking her way around her questions and responses to avoid touchy subjects or the risk of offending him.

"I was the purpose of the temple," he said after a long moment where he studied her with an increasingly curious stare.

"No wonder you're so arrogant," she muttered, starting her walk again, not even bothering to protest when he once again fell into step with her.

He huffed in response, but continued to pace her. She walked on in silence, noting the peacefulness and beauty of the surrounding forest, though a part of her was well aware of the way he kept glancing her way expectantly.

After a time, her lips twitched with a grin as he began to fidget, running his claws through his little white beard, scratching them through his feather mane, then crossing his arms, dropping them to his sides, and then crossing them again.

Clearly unable to bear the extended silence, he spoke aloud. "Great warriors traveled from every corner of the world to climb the sacred mountain to my temple and face me in battle."

She smothered her grin. "That's nice. You know, it's so beautiful out here, isn't it?"

He snarled at her casual tone, glancing around them as if he was seeing the forest for the first time, before he turned his gaze back to her.

He waited.

She let him, walking along in silence that she pretended wasn't growing heavy with his expectation.

When he growled low in his throat and then opened his mouth to speak again, she couldn't resist releasing her smile.

"Do you have something against peace and quiet?" she said in a low, mocking voice. "It certainly seems that way."

He paused, staring at her with his mouth gaping open. Then he shook his head, his mane feathers puffing up, then smoothing out as he regained his composure. "I am honoring you with my speech. It's not the same as your endless blathering, female."

She took several more steps before turning on her heel to face him, laughing at his outraged expression. "Oh, you mean you *don't* like having someone throw your own words back in your face? You *do* want to tell your own story without being made to feel like someone doesn't care to listen? I never could have guessed."

He lifted his chin, his face taking on a fierce, regal look. "Did you not hear me? The *greatest* warriors battled their way up the most dangerous mountain in my world, fighting endless monsters just to challenge me and earn my favor if they succeeded in slaying me."

She nodded, about to pretend she wasn't really paying attention when the meaning of his words actually gave her pause, making her curious despite her intention to continue teasing him. "So, I'm guessing you never had to give your favor out, since you're still alive."

He squared his broad shoulders, his head lifting even further, until he looked the epitome of a snobbish aristocrat looking down their nose at the lowly creatures beneath them. "I was only slain one hundred and three times in ten thousand years."

It was Alice's turn to gape speechlessly at him for a long moment as he wore a satisfied smirk, now that he'd gotten her complete attention, as he'd so clearly wanted it.

"What the... you were *slain*? As in, 'dead' slain?"

He harrumphed as if her question was completely stupid. "Is there another definition for the word in your pitiful language?"

She crossed her arms and pursed her lips, giving him a critical once-over. "Seeing as you're standing right here and you don't look like a zombie, though your smell gives me some doubts, I'd say you're lying through your ginormous teeth."

He waved away her words with a hand, including the insults that didn't even seem to faze him. "The temple revived me afterwards."

She shook her head, again struggling to contain her shock. "Wait a minute, are you like the big boss from a video game or something? Because that's what your life sounds like." She gave a small laugh, but then realized anything was possible in the Dead Fall, so maybe it wasn't such a joke.

He blinked at her. "What's a 'video game'?" He struggled to form the words, since it was clear they didn't exist in his language, so he had to speak them in English.

She pondered how to explain the concept, not having a great deal of experience with them herself, though she'd seen enough of them to understand the basic description. When she finished explaining to the best of her knowledge, he gave her a condescending glare.

"You speak of make-believe. I am real, as was the favor I offered. I did not 'respawn' as you say. I was revived, my mortal wounds healed by the temple spirits so that I might bestow my favor, and then await the next challenger."

It still sounded like a video game big boss to Alice. She

wondered what his "favor" was. Perhaps some enchanted sword or armor for the great warrior. "So, did you have to eat and sleep in your own world?"

Or go to the bathroom? She didn't ask the last question aloud.

He frowned. "Of course I did. The spirits provided my food, and I slept in the most luxurious room in the temple." He scratched his chin hairs with retracted claws. "Not at the altar where I awarded my favor."

"Did you ever get lonely in that temple, Kisk?" The sympathy was back, though she wondered if he deserved it, or even warranted it.

Ten thousand years! The mind boggles at the very idea!

He narrowed his gaze on her, his eyes shifting through their variant appearances before settling on the goat eyes that were her least favorite. "What purpose would that have served?"

"What?"

He gestured to the forest around them. "Do the ancilla ever miss their legs? Would it do them any good to ponder such a question?"

The bubble of sympathy for this fractious male grew, despite Alice's attempts to quell it. He could have just as easily said he didn't get lonely, and didn't even know what it meant. Instead, he'd posed a question that held far more of an answer than she thought he'd intended.

"Could you ever leave the temple?" She bit her lip, wondering if perhaps she should change the subject. Perhaps this was all too touchy for Kisk, and suddenly, she cared now about hurting his feelings. She felt the chains of empathy falling back around her. So much for that feeling of liberation.

He sniffed, tossing his head as if she was an insect beneath his talon-clawed foot. "And why would I want to? There was nothing I needed to see that could possibly compare to the luxury of my temple and grounds."

"You couldn't, could you?"

He swung his head to glare at her. "What difference does it make? I'm here now. When this world blended with mine, it was this place where my temple ended up, but the seals binding me to it remained behind in my own world. I haven't found freedom to be any better than I imagined it would be."

"If that's true, why didn't you remain in the temple? Would it revive you in the Dead Fall?" Alice tried not to let too much of her sympathy show in her voice.

His fidgeting made it seem like he was uneasy at her softer tone, as if it bothered him not to be speaking in a contentious way.

He was silent for a long moment, his arms crossed over his chest, his hands tucked away beneath them. Then he shrugged, the movement so small she wasn't sure she'd seen it, but his filthy fabric had shifted with the motion and now lay differently.

"I suppose it would still revive me. I don't know. It doesn't matter. This is as a good a place as anywhere, I suppose." He bared his teeth in a cat-grin. "There are still fights to be had."

8

Alice pondered the mystery of Kisk in silence for the remainder of the walk to the familiar path that led back into the family side of the settlement. The entire time, the chimera kept in pace with her steps, shortening his own so he didn't leave her behind, not that she believed it was out of any concern for her. For whatever reason, he'd decided to hang around her, and it made her wonder if he was truly lonely and seeking companionship. She hoped he wasn't seeking a mate, because if so, he was barking up the wrong tree.

Fortunately, she didn't gain that impression from him. In fact, he barely even looked at her at all, and when he did glance her way, it was usually with his arrogant, disdainful expression, or no identifiable expression at all. She knew what desire looked like, even in an alien male, and Kisk showed no more desire for her than she had for him.

He didn't pester her with more bragging, or any words at all until she stopped at the edge of the settlement and turned to him to shoo him back to his own side of New Omni. The ancilla allowed Kisk free movement through the forest, but by Gray's orders, only family and mated males were permitted on this side of the settlement with the unmated females.

Alice covertly studied Kisk, noting that new clothes and a new attitude would make the male attractive, despite the strangeness of his appearance. He was tall and very well built, and had the strength most of the females in the Fall desired in their mates. He also had some pretty awesome abilities, from what Tak had told her, and she knew about at least one of them herself.

"Why do you separate your body into that little snake?" she asked, instead of bidding him farewell with a final plea not to tell anyone what she'd said earlier. She should have just sent him away, but she couldn't help being curious.

His eyes flickered to the reptilian ones, which regarded her without revealing any sign of his emotion. "When I realized that small parts of my body could pass beyond the seals binding me to the temple, I created my slivers to explore the world below me."

He crossed his arms over his chest and sniffed in a superior attitude, lifting his chin to further exaggerate the fact that he already looked down on her, being a head and shoulders taller than her. "I wouldn't expect a creature such as yourself, one with no abilities whatsoever, to understand the complexity of the process."

Alice sighed and rubbed her forehead as if the pressure could help the growing headache there. "Yes, Kisk. Me, weak and pathetic, you, strong and impressive. Can you go now? I have things to do, and it's getting late."

He looked surprised at her dismissal, then further surprised when he glanced up at the position of the sun. "It hasn't been that long, female. It is still midday. Is this not your day of rest?"

It *was* Alice's day of rest, one of two she got each week, and she deeply regretted wasting it on this encounter, but what was done was done. "I have to get home in time to greet my mates, and I'd like to have enough time to prepare dinner for my family." Now that she had finally mastered cooking without needing Iyaren there to guide her.

He rubbed his white chin, the coarser hairs there making a scratching sound. "I see. So instead of a leash and collar, you reinforce the bond on your mates with a greeting spell. Your words hold power. This explains much that has confused me. Now I understand why your voice is so beautiful."

The compliment took her aback, even though it wasn't spoken as a compliment, but rather a statement of fact, and she didn't think he was even directly addressing her. He seemed to be talking aloud to himself.

"You don't even like to hear me talk, Kisk! Why would you say my voice is beautiful?"

His ears pinned flat to his feathered mane. "Speak no more, sorceress!" He backed away from her, his hands lifting to cover his ears to add further protection from her "magical" voice. "I will not be drawn into your web of spells and bound to you like your mates."

Alice couldn't resist the grin that spread across her face at the slightly panicked look in Kisk's alien, reptilian eyes as he stumbled away from her, hands over his ears. "You don't need to worry, Kisk. I wouldn't want you for a mate if you were the last male in the Dead Fall."

She didn't think he'd heard her as he turned and walked quickly back into the forest, hunching his shoulders like her words might even have the physical force to attack him. Once he'd completely disappeared, Alice sniggered, then burst into full laughter.

She swept the tears from her cheeks as she walked back into the family quarters, grateful that for the first time in a long time, they'd come from her laughter, rather than her sadness. She was still chuckling to herself, deciding that Kisk likely wouldn't tell Tak anything, given his newfound terror of her magical voice, when she reached Evie's apartment to collect Friak.

She was early, since Evie had told her to take the entire day for herself to rest and relax or do whatever she wanted. Tak and Iyaren weren't likely to return home from the Fall until night time, barring any unforeseen circumstances, which she didn't want to contemplate.

She knocked on the door, eager to see her son, wishing she could tell him all about her unusual day, and the crazy chimera. Her broad grin slipped as she realized she couldn't tell anyone about her visit with the chimera, since it would reveal more than she wanted her loved ones to know. She had to protect them.

Realizing that Sherak would pick up on her anxiety, she tried to recapture her feelings of amusement, and was somewhat successful as she recalled the chimera's panicked flight into the woods as if her words alone could chase him down and collar him.

She was chuckling to herself when Evie opened the door.

Evie's hesitant expression shifted to an answering smile when she saw Alice's mood. "Hey, Al. You're a bit early."

Alice shrugged. "I was done relaxing. I thought I'd pick up Friak and have him help me prep for dinner. He likes to tend the fires in the stove."

Evie twisted her fingers together in front of her, glancing back into her apartment. "Well, they're not back yet." At Alice's raised eyebrows, Evie rushed to explain. "I sent the boys off with Doshak, because I was hoping you might show up a little early so we could talk."

Alarm shot through Alice as she stared at Evie's suddenly nervous expression. "What's going on, Ev?"

Evie gestured for Alice to follow her into the apartment, offering her something to eat or drink while Alice made her way to the sofa. Alice refused both offers as she took her seat, telling Evie to sit down and explain her strange mood.

Evie smoothed her hands over her hair, which was pulled close to her head in a ponytail that extended well down her back. Like Alice, she had long, black hair.

Her sister pulled herself up onto a massive tree stump that was partially carved with fantastic designs—Doshak's current project and future chair.

"I want to apologize, Al. About earlier today. I shouldn't have been so... I should have asked you what was wrong, instead of being so protective of Sherak."

Alice relaxed, realizing Evie didn't know anything about Kisk. She waved away Evie's words. "It's okay, Ev. I'm a mom too," she tried not to let the spear of pain she felt at the word "mom" show in her expression, "I understand completely."

Evie shook her head. "No, it's *not* okay. You're my sister, and you've always been there for me, you've always stood up for me, and you've always bailed me out of trouble. I should have been there for you. Obviously, something is upsetting you, and instead of finding out what it was, I took away your chance to spend time with the ones you love who might help cheer you up." She met Alice's eyes, hers glistening. "I'm so sorry, Alice. I want you to know that I will never do that again. I won't isolate Sherak from you just because you might be feeling something I don't want him to feel. For your sake, and his. He was very disappointed that he didn't get to spend time with Auntie Alice."

Alice struggled not to cry—and not to panic—as Evie's confession and apology threatened to come too close to the emotions Alice kept buried. She had to protect her sister. Evie had her own problems and her own concerns. She didn't need to listen to Alice whining and complaining. Gray's position as leader of New Omni was very stressful for both him and his mate, though only Evie showed the strain it put on them and their relationship. The current standoff with NEX couldn't last forever, and their enemy was no doubt using this time to plot something truly devasting to them. Plus, they would be welcoming three new children into the world soon, and Evie had her hands full preparing for that upcoming adventure, as well as her own worries about those children.

No, Evie didn't need Alice's problems adding to her burden.

"Well, I missed seeing him too, but I really do understand why you chose to do what you did, Ev, and you were right to do it. I needed a day of rest all to myself. It's getting close to that time of month, you know, and the mood swings are terrible this time, so I was definitely struggling with PMS, and poor Sherak didn't need to be exposed to that."

Evie narrowed her eyes, studying Alice in silence for a long moment. "Didn't you just have your period? I thought you just got off of it."

Alice nodded desperately. "That's what I meant. I was on my period this past week and the hormones just sent my mood on a rollercoaster."

Evie leaned forward to place a hand on Alice's knee. "Al...."

Alice didn't like the expression of concern and doubt on Evie's face. She rose to her feet, brushing her hands down the fabric of her pants to smooth the material.

"It's nothing, Ev." She stared down at her pink shirt, recalling her strange day, and the strange character she'd met. "Hey, Ev, you know how we have the Welcome Wagon?"

Evie's worried frown slipped into a confused one as she stared at Alice. "What does that have to do with—"

Alice hurried to speak her sudden thoughts aloud, to create a distraction. "We meet every female who comes here with supplies, clean clothes, a hot meal, a warm bed, and a buddy who will show them around and help them get acclimated, but does anyone do that for the unmated males who come here?"

She and Evie had implemented the Welcome Wagon after

first deciding they would bring other survivors to New Omni. When Lauren had arrived in the settlement, she'd gladly joined in on the project to help all the females feel welcomed and able to build a home here.

"You know Gray and the others handle that, Al."

Alice snorted, knowing how males, even her beloved mates, tended to view things. They would provide the basics, like food, water, and shelter, but none of it would be designed for comfort, and Alice had seen from Kisk's condition that once a male was part of the settlement, he didn't get much guidance on caring for himself. She didn't think their mates were being deliberately neglectful. It was just that they didn't think of things like adding additional comforts to the basics—making the food more palatable, the bedding softer, the clothing clean and well-made. The old settlement of Omni had been a dog-eat-dog place, where everyone had to fend for themselves and nothing was just given away for free. Gray was too busy now just trying to maintain peace, grow the settlement, and find more survivors, to concern himself with helping the unmated males, and their other mates were accustomed to a lack of luxuries and it wouldn't even occur to them to provide them to other males.

Alice pursed her lips at Evie. "You really think they do a good job of it?"

Evie shook her head, her expression saying she wasn't certain whether she should feel defensive for her mates, or acknowledge the truth. "They try."

Alice was quick to agree. "I know they do. But I—"

She almost blew it by admitting to having met a male who was an absolute mess because he had no clue how to take care of himself, since he'd been trapped within a temple his entire life with "spirits" to serve his every need—other than freedom and companionship.

"I just realized that maybe the unmated males don't have

things as nice over on that side of the fence. Maybe they could use a little more... care."

Ideas began to flow through her mind—plans for a new effort to bring the same kind of care and concern provided by the Welcome Wagon to the other side of the fence. They could put together a list of resources for the unmated males, letting them know where to go to get hot food if they couldn't cook for themselves, or where to have their laundry done, or their apartment cleaned in return for tokens. The Wagon could provide the initial basics, along with a few luxuries, like they did with the females.

And perhaps someone could teach those males who had never had to care for themselves how to do so. Her mind was on Kisk, wearing his reeking clothing, living in his miserable apartment, with no one to care about whether he had a hot meal that day or not. He'd need a more permanent solution than a Welcome Wagon. Now more than ever, she was convinced she needed to find him a mate—a female who would be willing to put up with his crap, while at the same time being willing to housetrain him.

A hand on her arm brought her attention back to Evie, who was watching her with concern again. "Where'd you go, Alice?"

Panic squeezed Alice's lungs. "Wh-what do you mean?"

"You were standing there staring off into space, and you didn't respond when I said your name."

Alice sighed in relief that she hadn't been discovered. "Oh, I just got so distracted making plans for another Welcome Wagon, or rather, an extension to the existing one. I can get the other females working on care packages. I've got a bunch of material I wasn't going to use for my family, and some new patterns I'd like to try out. I can start making some larger clothes for the wagon, and maybe even bake some treats, and we'll have to talk to Sira'shan about donating some more of her excellent soaps and lotions, and maybe—"

"Alice!"

Alice sighed and rolled her eyes. "Come on, Ev! Why aren't you excited by this idea? It would help Gray out to make the unmated males a little more comfortable, more relaxed. Maybe there would be less fights among them if they all had some creature comforts."

Evie didn't look away from Alice. "I'm not saying it's a bad idea, or that I'm against it. I'm just... I'm still worried about *you*, Al. I feel like this is just a way to distract you, or maybe me, from something else going on with you."

Alice snorted, brushing Evie's hand off her shoulder. "Give me a break! I told you *nothing* is going on with me but hormones. Don't tell me Sherak doesn't sense it when you're having your mood swings."

Evie looked away, suddenly interested in the eclectic décor that filled her apartment, which was cluttered with furniture that looked sleek and functional mixed with more primitive pieces built to be extra-large by Doshak and often carved by him. Evie's touch of décor was visible as well, in the soft, upholstered sofa, muted rugs, and framed posters of alien advertisements on her walls.

"That's all it is, Ev. Hormones. So, could we stop dwelling on that, and work on this Welcome Wagon thing?"

Evie sighed, cast Alice one last worried glance, before allowing a smile to cross her face. "I just hope this doesn't go as disastrously as your last matchmaking plan for the unmated males."

Alice chuckled. "Hey! The dating show idea entertained a lot of people."

Evie laughed. "Boy, did it ever! Unfortunately, for all the wrong reasons."

"Are you kidding? If we were reality show producers, that effort would have been considered a success. Do you know how often I get requests for another one?"

"Too bad Gray banned any and all dating shows," Evie said.

"Yes, your mate is such a spoilsport. It would've been an excellent way to pair up females with unmated males—if we could work the bugs out."

"Yeah, let's not bring up the bugs. I still have nightmares about that. Some males just don't know how to woo a girl."

9

B y the time Doshak returned to the apartment with the boys, Alice and Evie had prepared a list of items they wanted to put into care packages, not just for new male arrivals, but they hoped to get enough items together to present all the current males in the settlement with some nice things to make their lives a bit more comfortable, if not easier. They also had plans to put together a training program that would help individuals who needed extra assistance assimilating into their new life.

When Doshak entered the apartment, ducking his head to get through the door so he could stand to his full eight-feet, eleven inches tall—his head brushing the ceiling—he set Sherak down, and the young boy immediately raced to Alice, crying out her name in a happy greeting.

She caught her nephew up in a hug, marveling at how big and solid he'd already grown, despite being only around two and a half years old. His little mop of black hair fell over his face, almost concealing his ovoid, all-black eyes that spoke of his hybrid blood. Other than that, his face was human, with delightful chubby cheeks and a brilliant, baby-toothed smile for Alice.

"Hold you *me!*" Friak demanded, standing at her side where he'd ran after Doshak had lowered him from his back and set him on the floor.

Her son's scaled arms were lifted, his little fingers clutching as he reached towards her, wanting her to hold him along with Sherak. He was getting to the point where he grew jealous when she showed too much attention to his cousin.

Sherak could sense even this, and squirmed in her arms until she let him down, pausing to pat Friak on his bald, scaled head. "S'okay, Auntie Alice still love Fri Fri most."

"I love you both so much," she said reassuringly, kissing her son on his head as he laid it against her shoulder.

Sherak regarded her with dark, fathomless eyes, nodding. "We know. We love Auntie Alice s'much, too."

"Come here, you little squirt!" Evie said, snatching Sherak and swinging him up into the air as he squealed in toddler excitement, becoming a little kid again, instead of an empath who felt too much of other people's pain.

Evie tickle-attacked Sherak until he was laughing so hard he was gasping, his little baby teeth flashing in his gummy mouth as his legs kicked and squirmed. If he could still feel anyone's emotions, he wasn't showing it in that moment, and Alice was grateful that Evie had learned how to distract her remarkable son long enough to let him be a child.

"Mama." Friak patted her cheek, getting her attention.

She turned and studied her precious son, stunned as always at how perfect he was, knowing that the scientific probability of him even existing was near impossible, and yet, here he was in her arms, a sweet, little boy with a mischievous streak and the power to burst into flames and remain unharmed. And someday, he might have the power to shift his scales to conceal himself, just like his father.

I am blessed, she said to herself, for the first time in a while, feeling the truth of the words.

Friak regaled her about his exciting day with Uncle Doshak and the "squirmies," as he called his soon-to-be cousins, while she carried him back to their own apartment after saying good bye to Evie and thanking both her and Doshak for taking care of Friak.

As soon as she entered her own apartment, her son insisted he be put down so he could run into his "flaring room," which was completely empty and lined with fireproof tiles on every surface. Though he'd learned to control his flares, they often still built up inside him, and he felt better when he could just burst into flames at the end of a stimulating day.

Alice hated closing the door on her baby so he could set himself on fire, but knew it was healthy for him—at least, according to Tak, who would know best. It was easier not to see it happening, because even to this day, it terrified her to see flames engulfing her precious little boy.

Tak and Iyaren entered their apartment together while Alice sat on the chair in front of the door to the flaring room, wringing her hands as she waited for Friak's flames to die down.

Grateful for the distraction, she rose to her feet to greet them, wishing she'd had something cooking for them, but she'd gotten so distracted talking with Evie about their plans to help the unmated males that she'd forgotten to do anything about dinner.

Iyaren rubbed his cheek against her head as he pulled her close in a hug, careful not to squeeze her too tight against his armor, which was dulled by dirt from the Fall. His fur smelled of the Fall too, though he'd probably had his helmet on all day. She still welcomed his embrace, and his version of a kiss, before lifting her lips to kiss him.

"I will bathe and return to you, beloved. I've missed you."

As he passed the flaring room on his way to their bathroom, he knocked on the door. "Your papas are home, Fri Fri."

"Daddy!" An excited squeal sounded from the other side of the door. "I saw the squirmies in their egg-hole!"

Iyaren chuckled. "You can tell us all about it at dinner. Finish your flaring." At Friak's affirmative, Iyaren disappeared into the bathroom.

Tak grasped Alice to him in a hungry embrace, his lips crashing down on hers in a rough kiss that softened after a moment, even though his hands running over her body didn't. When he finally lifted his head, his eyes were glazed. "I also missed you, my spark. I think we'll need to do something about that later." He released her slowly, a promise of more to come tilting his scaled lips.

He'd removed his armor before grabbing Alice, so she'd been able to feel the heat from his furnace of a chest, which now glowed beneath his large pectoral scales.

He tilted his head towards the flaring room. "I think I'll join Friak. I have some energy to burn off. Not much happening in the Fall today."

"I'll make dinner for you guys," Alice said, noting the wince from Tak before he turned away to conceal it.

She propped her hands on her hips. "Hey! My food has gotten a lot better!"

He turned back and grabbed her into another firm embrace. "It has. It definitely has. I'm sorry, that was just habit."

He grinned, baring crocodile-sharp teeth. "Although, I admit, I have a great hunger for something else." His gaze trailed from her face to her breasts, which were plumped up against his chest scales.

She lifted a hand to his scaled cheek. "You know tonight is Iyaren's night."

He made a small sound of disappointment, then sighed

dramatically as he slowly released her. "I suppose I can wait, but it won't be easy, my spark."

Alice studied his face, wondering if there wasn't more to his teasing. Sometimes, it was difficult to balance their relationship in a way that she felt was fair to both of her partners. They'd gotten into the habit of switching out nights for lovemaking, and her mates were patient, but occasionally, they made jokes —as Tak just had—that made her wonder if they resented the arrangement. It was yet another worry she was afraid to bring up with them, because she didn't want to do anything to disrupt the harmony of their family. What if she brought up an issue that they'd already resolved, making it a problem again when it hadn't been?

Almost as if he read her mind, his smile slipped into a more serious expression and he touched her cheek with an upper hand, the tiny scales on his finger-pads tugging a bit on her skin as he brushed his thumb over it. "I only tease. You give us more than we could have ever asked for. I have never been happier, nor has Iyaren."

Alice smiled, turning her cheek to press further into his touch, before kissing the callused palm of his hand. "Your happiness is all that matters to me."

And she would do whatever it took to protect that happiness.

10

T ak sat on the tiled floor in the flaring room, Friak settled in his lap as the boy's flames engulfed them both. He enjoyed this time to snuggle his son and listen to his excited voice as he outlined his day in broken words from four different languages.

They'd tried, at first, to limit Friak's exposure to language to a single one, so learning to speak would be easier for him, but it was difficult not to slip into their own languages when talking around him, and Friak had picked up words in all of the ones he heard, not yet learning enough of any of them to communicate all of his thoughts.

Still, he was able to describe enough for Tak to follow his story, and occasionally correct his pronunciation when he used Histri'i words or the common trade language Tak and Iyaren shared from their home realm.

His son never ceased to amaze him as he watched the boy grow and mature from a flailing infant to a curious toddler. He'd never had such an active role in raising his previous children, who'd been raised by clan mothers rather than family units like his mate, Alice, was accustomed to. The Histri'i formed temporary hand-fasts to mate and breed offspring for their clan, often splitting up the children into two clans if there was a hand-fast between those clans. Though he'd taken an interest in the upbringing of his children and had maintained caring relationships with them, he hadn't been part of the day-to-day care that made raising Friak so special and awe-inspiring.

He got to see his son reach milestones, and to surpass his and Alice's expectations time and again. He had been there for Friak's first flaring, and was the one who got to guide Friak into learning to control his flame. He'd never performed such a daunting task before, and he'd had to dig back into his own memories for how the clan mothers had taught him and his siblings to control their fires. It had been a terrifying experience at first, as he feared he would let his son and his mate and his heart-brother down by failing to teach his son what Friak needed to know to be around them safely.

Yet, he'd managed to do it, he and his toddler muddling through the process with both failure and success, and more than one singed hair or patch of fur, but ultimately, no one had been irreversibly harmed by Friak's uncontrolled flaring, and Tak had been able to learn valuable lessons that might one day serve him for future children. He'd also built an incredible bond between him and his child that he'd never been blessed to have before.

He knew Alice was eager to have more children, and Tak and Iyaren both wanted that too, because having Friak was such a rewarding experience, and they'd all love to grow their family.

At the same time, it had been difficult for them all when she'd lost her pregnancy, and none of them really wanted to relive that dark time. He'd be content if Friak remained their only child, feeling like their family was complete as it was—as nice as it might be to welcome another son or daughter into it.

Besides, with the uncertainty in the Dead Fall over NEX's aggression and enmity, it probably wasn't the best time to bring more children into the world. Tak worried about protecting the one they already had.

"Sherak say Mommy sad, Daddy." Friak's voice sounded small and high-pitched as the roaring of his flame died down, returning to a single, glowing ember in his narrow chest, which was currently bare of flammable fabric.

Friak studied him with eyes that were such a startling blue that Tak was still taken aback by them. No Histri'i had ever had eyes that were such a beautiful color, but his Alice did.

"Why Mommy sad?" his son asked.

The fact that Friak didn't even question Sherak's word on this wasn't surprising. The boys were more like brothers than cousins, but even if they hadn't grown up spending most of their time together, Friak was old enough to recognize that Sherak was special and had the ability to sense a person's emotions.

What disturbed Tak was that he also didn't question Sherak's judgement on this, despite the youth of the child, who was even younger than Friak. That meant Sherak had detected a sadness in Alice that he and Iyaren had not.

Was it possible that his mate was unhappy in some way she wasn't sharing with them? And if so, how had they been so blind to miss it?

"Does mommy seem sad to *you*, Fri Fri?"

Friak stuck his thumb in his mouth as he appeared to ponder the question, with the gravity of a young mind struggling to understand not just the question, but the words themselves. Tak loved the little frown of concentration that would pinch Friak's brow into little creases in the soft scales that reminded him of Alice.

He waited for his son's answer, which came after a long moment of thought. "She no sad to Fri Fri."

Tak closed his eyes, sighing as he gathered his son against him in a hug before setting him on his feet on the tile.

As soon as Friak was on his feet, he whooped and raced for the door, no doubt eager to regale Daddy Iyaren about his exciting day watching the "squirmies" through the view screen on the scanner Gray had given Doshak to keep an eye on his developing offspring.

Tak waited until his son left the room before pushing himself to his feet, wondering if he should release his own flame as he'd originally intended, or follow his son into the dining room to visit with Alice and Iyaren while they prepared dinner, and maybe search in her demeanor for clues to how she really felt. She'd seemed as she usually was, happy and smiling, but now he wondered if her smile had stopped reaching her eyes, and he'd just been too distracted to notice.

Friak hadn't noticed anything different in his mother, but the child was just a young boy and not likely to observe tiny differences in body language that would give Alice's real feelings away. Tak wondered if he should confront Alice about what Sherak had told their son, or if that would only hurt her feelings. Alice loved Sherak like her own child, and Tak wasn't sure if it would upset her to hear that the boy thought she wasn't happy.

In the end, he decided to wait and see if Alice spoke of any sadness and disappointment on her own, rather than risk hurting her feelings, especially if Sherak had just picked up on a mood swing that Alice was having due to her hormonal changes. Reassuring himself that it had probably been just that, Tak released his flame and let it wash over him, losing the energy required to sustain it, but also feeling it burn away the tension that had gripped him during his patrol of the Fall. Friak's flame had already burned away the dirt of the Fall.

Later, during their dinner, which Alice had cooked to perfection with very little assistance from Iyaren this time, Tak watched her covertly, careful not to stare for too long at her face looking for changes in her lovely blue eyes or her full lips that might signify unhappiness. To him, she looked as beautiful and glowing as ever, teasing Iyaren in the hopes of eliciting one of his rare barks of roaring laughter, or helping Friak with his meal, or looking up to meet Tak's eyes with a bright smile whenever he made a joke.

It seemed as if their home was a perfect one, filled with love and happiness. In fact, the only one who was acting out of character was Tak himself as he struggled to fill the gaps in conversation when he was usually talking. Both Iyaren and Alice had cast him curious glances when he'd fumbled to respond to one of their questions, having not even heard them ask in his distraction.

By the time their meal was over, Alice's smile came less frequently and seemed more forced, and her eyes no longer had their normal sparkle when she hugged him before retiring to her room to spend her night with Iyaren.

She hesitated after their long embrace, then looked up into his eyes, her own uncertain.

"Are you sure this doesn't bother you?" she asked, her forehead pinched in a frown.

It took him a moment to understand what she was talking about, his mind so focused on whether she was truly happy or just pretending. When he realized what she meant, he was surprised that she was bringing up something that had been resolved years ago, when they'd first came together as mates. He wondered if she'd misread his distraction as disappointment that he wouldn't be sharing her bed that night. At least, not until much later, when he would join her and Iyaren in sleep.

He'd teased her about it earlier, well knowing it was Iyaren's night to spend with her. He hadn't meant it then, and he had no problem with it now.

Alice made love to one of them each night, and from what he'd learned from Evie and Lauren, that was quite a bit for a human relationship—many humans settling into a pattern of only mating a couple of times a week after the initial excitement of their romance faded into a deeper, less frantic love.

When he'd been handfasted to Histri'i females, they'd mate almost constantly for over a month of his realm's time after the handfasting ceremony, but once pregnancy was confirmed, usually only mated a few more times just for comfort and the release of stress during that pregnancy and the resulting birth and early rearing of young—before those young could be separated from the mother and raised by the clan.

Only those who were soulmates tended to mate more frequently when not actively trying to breed, but even they were more like humans in that respect, settling into a general pattern of a few times a week.

Mating every day would be exhausting for anyone, but Alice made the time for both of them, and now he worried that she did it only for them, and not because it was what she desired. The last thing he wanted was for her to think he was unhappy with their arrangement, when she made such an effort to satisfy them both, doing far more than they expected, and not just in their bedroom.

Her frown had deepened while he was lost in thought, and he noticed the worried look in her eyes, one that held almost an edge of panic to it that he hadn't seen in a long time.

"No, spark, this doesn't bother me and never will. I don't begrudge your time with Iyaren anymore than he does my time with you."

He would say it over and over again, a thousand times, if that was what she needed to hear to remove those shadows from her eyes. He just wished saying it alone was enough. Neither of them knew how else to convince her, but it had been so long since she'd expressed concern about this that they'd both grown complacent, assuming she was as content as they were. Perhaps that was where they'd gone wrong. It could explain Sherak's claim that Alice was sad, if she were once again doubting the stability of their relationship.

"Are you happy, Alice?" he whispered, brushing away the creases between her brow.

She nodded her head firmly. "Blissfully, my love." Then she lifted onto her toes and pressed a lingering kiss to his lips. "Good night, Tak."

Her kiss filled him with hunger for more, but he knew how to dampen his arousal until the following night, when she would welcome him with arms outstretched and her body warm and wet, beckoning for him to touch her and taste her before allowing himself the sweet torment of being inside her. The waiting and anticipation for that time made it all the sweeter when it came.

He watched her swaying hips as she made her way into her bedroom, stopping into Friak's room to tuck him in. Tak and Iyaren had already tucked the boy into his crib, each one telling a story from their own realm that was sure to fill the boy's dreams with images of adventures in deserts and jungles with mythic characters and dazzling cities and temples.

It was a nightly ritual they all shared, each one telling a tale from their world to Friak. Now that he was old enough, he had his favorites, and he would often demand the retelling of one or the other. Sometimes, they would all listen in, eager to hear the tales themselves, and they now all had their favorites from a different culture, or even from a different world.

He loved Alice's stories the most, himself, though Iyaren's made him feel bittersweet about his old realm and wistful that his people and the Sari'i were enemies instead of allies.

Once all the lights were off and all his loved ones tucked away in their rooms, Tak realized he felt too restless to retire to his own bed to wait until he could join Alice and Iyaren for sleep in hers, his concerns about Alice having never left him, even though he heard Iyaren's low roar and her soft laughter as they came together in the privacy of her bedroom.

As he left the apartment and turned his step towards the gatehouse that guarded the one opening to the unmated male side of the settlement—where the majority of the night life took place—he thought about Alice's concerns. He hadn't considered his initial jealousy of Iyaren since their first season of being together. He and Iyaren had come to an agreement then, and had slowly gotten over the difficulty of sharing, their own relationship growing and developing into something akin to brothers.

Now, the sounds of passion between Alice and Iyaren that he occasionally overheard caused a different feeling in him than jealousy. It aroused him to think of her naked body swaying as he watched Iyaren make love to her. His mind strayed far too often to their time together in the ancilla forest, when the petals had caused an unshakeable lust to push them into mating in front of each other.

It had been the most erotic experience he'd ever had, and the memories still caused his body to stir with desire, as he thought of Alice between the two of them, her mouth on him while Iyaren pounded into her from behind, filled by both of them as she cried out in pleasure. It was enough to make him shiver with lust.

He would do it again in a heartbeat, and Iyaren had once confessed that he wished to try it again as well, but they'd both decided not to bring it up to Alice, as she'd been mortified by the experience afterwards, and worried that they would be upset by it. It had taken time to convince her otherwise, so they certainly didn't want to go through that again.

At the boundary of the fence, a handful of females were sitting or standing in the packed-down area along the slats, calling out to the unmated males on the other side, of which there would undoubtedly be quite a few more. This had become a nightly ritual now that Gray had relaxed some of the restrictions on the females when it came to contact with the unmated males. Eventually, they would like to integrate the entire settlement, but that wouldn't happen until Gray felt certain—in his seemingly all-knowing way—that the violent, aggressive males wouldn't cause harm to the females in their desperate pursuit of mates.

Until then, both male and female residents—and those citizens that didn't fit into either category—took opportunities like this to get to know each other.

The females had learned to ignore Tak as an option after being warned off by Alice, and most of them were now friends of hers, so they greeted him in a friendly way as well. If some of them still cast him a calculating look, he didn't take note of it. He returned their greeting, then made his way to the gate where Lauren was pulling duty with Asterius as night guards, since that was generally the most dangerous time for attempts to cross the fence.

Lauren hung out on this side of the fence, more than capable of taking on any of the females who dared to try to make a run through the gate, especially since she'd been outfitted with a stunner and what she called a nightstick.

Tak didn't think any of the current female residents were stupid enough to try their luck against her, and as with Alice, most of them were her friends. Those who weren't knew enough to stay away from her.

Tak chatted with her briefly, grateful that her animosity towards him and Iyaren had faded over time after they'd insisted on a bloody fight in the arena against Asterius, where they'd defeated her mate. The misunderstandings that had taken place when Asterius and Lauren had first come to the settlement had been unfortunate, and though Tak and Iyaren still believed it had been necessary to clear the bad blood between them and the minotaur, he wished they'd handled it better, instead of springing it on Lauren and Asterius as they had.

As upset as she had been back then, Lauren wasn't one to hold grudges, and had quickly become friends with Alice, which meant she eventually had to forgive her mates. Since Tak and Iyaren had already become fast friends with Asterius after the battle, they'd naturally eased into a friendlier relationship with his mate.

"It's actually a quiet night on both sides of the fence," Lauren said as she unlocked the gate for Tak after their chat.

Tak chuckled. "I'm guessing that means Asterius is bored."

Lauren grinned and jerked her head towards the fence. "I'm sure he'll tell you all about his boredom himself. I'll make it up to him later."

"I'll hold you to that," the minotaur's deep voice said through the small hole in the gate, eliciting a broad smile from his mate.

"Have a good evening, Lauren," Tak said before passing through the small gatehouse.

"Be careful over there, Tak. Al would never forgive me if you scuffed those scales in a brawl or two."

Tak shook his head with a grin. "You know I'm a peace-maker, Lauren. I don't start fights."

She waved him through. "That's because we don't have an official fire department yet."

He laughed as he stepped out onto the other side of the fence, then spent some more time keeping Asterius company as they both watched the crowd of males around the fence preening and trying to woo females who couldn't see them, but could hear all their warbling and noisemaking.

"You'd think all the work they do doing the day would tire them out," Asterius said, his nostrils flaring as he snorted in disdain. "They aren't interested in fighting, though."

Tak smiled at the tone of disappointment in Asterius's voice. The minotaur loved a good brawl.

"Any of them seem like they might have a chance?" Tak asked, marveling at the number of males that clustered around the fence, all different—all alien in some way or another from the females on the other side—and yet, that hadn't stopped any of the males who had made it to the other side by finding mates.

Asterius shrugged massive shoulders. "Your guess is as good as mine. Your mate is the one with a knack for matchmaking. I just keep 'em from getting overeager. I guess I've bashed one too many over the head, because they've been on their best behavior lately."

Tak suspected that the peace was due more to the fact that allowing the males to interact with the females in some way, no matter how limited, gave them something they hadn't had before. Hope.

It might be enough, at least for a while, and Gray had mentioned in that annoyingly vague way he had of speaking that someday, he intended to bring more hope to the males, but he'd refused to expand on that remark, as he often refused to answer questions in detail.

"Where you heading tonight?" Asterius asked, his attention on a cluster of males who'd grown a little pushy at the fence.

Tak shrugged. "Nowhere in particular, although I thought I'd head to the market, see what food the stalls are serving, and maybe find a few surprises for Alice and Friak."

The males settled down, and Asterius took that moment to glance at Tak. "No plans to head to the arena?"

Since that day in the basement arena, he and Iyaren had often sparred with Asterius, though they stopped at drawing blood, mindful of how upset it made their mates. Now that a new, much larger, arena had been built in one of the reclaimed buildings, they'd moved their fights to this side of the fence, because neither of their mates wanted to witness them.

Tak rarely joined true arena battles, which Doshakeren and Asterius loved and could often be found dominating, their names rising to the top of every betting list, though they had yet to fight each other. Not surprising, after being threatened by horrible retaliation from Evie and Lauren if they hurt each other.

"I think I'll pass. I'm in no mood for a fight, and I don't like betting, unless it's a sure win, like you or Doshak."

Asterius slapped him on the shoulder in a friendly way, which was still strong enough to catch Tak off-guard, making him stumble forward. "You don't take enough risks, my friend."

Tak braced his feet in case Asterius decided to "pat" him on the shoulder again in the exuberant way he had. "My people are trained from a very young age to avoid risky behavior. It tends to result in a burning jungle. We might be fireproof, but our villages weren't."

Asterius nodded. "That's one advantage of being surrounded by stone, I suppose. Nothing ever burned in the labyrinth but the torches. Still, you don't have to fight for yourself, but tonight, Kisk is at the arena, so betting should be a sure thing."

Tak cut off an automatic groan, but not before Asterius noted it, and grinned in the unique way he had that accommodated his bullish features.

"He tends to get that reaction a lot," Asterius said with a chuckle. "That's probably why he's such a great fighter."

"He should learn how to bite his tongue," Tak said, still irritated by how often Kisk had insulted his mate before he'd finally snapped and sent the other male away from him for good.

He'd tried to be patient, but the things Kisk said pushed even Tak too far. If he hadn't sent Kisk away from them when he did, Iyaren might have been goaded far enough to actually hurt the other male.

Asterius snorted, his nostrils flaring. "I've come to the conclusion that he's incapable of it. If I didn't know some of his history, he would already be dead by my own hand."

This made Tak curious, since as far as he'd heard, no one knew Kisk's history. That wasn't so unusual, since many of the residents of New Omni kept their pasts to themselves and rarely, if ever, spoke of their own realms. Perhaps it was due to homesickness, or some cultural reserve, or simply because they had secrets to hide. In Kisk's case, Tak suspected he was just an unfriendly bastard who felt too superior to everyone else to share any information on his background.

"What gives him a pass in your estimation, Asterius?" Because Tak couldn't imagine what would make the possessive and protective behemoth of a male beside him brush off any insults to his own mate.

Asterius stared at the males at the fence with a distant expression that suggested he wasn't really seeing them, though he was undoubtedly aware of them on an instinctive level and would respond if trouble brewed.

"In some ways, his past was similar to mine. He was isolated, bound into one place for far longer than I was trapped in my labyrinth. The only people who came to him were looking for a fight, and those battles were all he'd ever known before he was cast into this realm."

With sympathy came guilt, so Tak didn't welcome it, but he also couldn't avoid it. Kisk might be insufferable, arrogant beyond any acceptable level, and completely clueless, but if what Asterius said about him was true, that wouldn't be his fault. At least, not entirely.

Perhaps Asterius's method of dealing with Kisk was the better option. Ignoring Kisk's insults to his mate, and accepting that they were just words spoken in ignorance and posed no harm to Alice herself—as long as she never heard them—was difficult for Tak, but he knew he had a better chance of changing Kisk's perception of the world and the people in it if he didn't push him away every time he said something infuriating—which usually meant every time he opened his mouth.

As far as he knew, Kisk only acknowledged a handful of males in the settlement, and had never spoken to any of the females. He'd never seen Kisk crowd around the fence with males like the ones there tonight.

Those males Kisk did acknowledge had to have shown that they were more powerful than he was himself. A difficult task, given his strength, size, and unusual abilities.

Kisk would talk to Asterius, because the minotaur had defeated him in the arena. He would acknowledge Doshak for the same reason. He had the good sense to avoid Gray altogether unless he wasn't given a choice, but around Gray, he behaved himself, perhaps knowing that if Gray did want to fight him, Kisk wouldn't have a chance of winning.

And now, he acknowledged Tak, because Tak had saved his life and earned a headache in return. A headache he now felt obligated to show more sympathy to, because Kisk couldn't be held responsible for a history he hadn't chosen.

"Think he can ever learn some manners?" Tak asked Asterius as he reconsidered his plans for the evening.

He might head to the arena after all.

Asterius shrugged. "This place changes people, but there are some things that are just a part of us that always stay the same. I'm not sure what part of Kisk you could change if you had a lot of patience, but I wouldn't get your hopes up."

11

The gladiator arena had an unforgettable smell to it that never changed, no matter how many times the stone pavers in the center were scrubbed clean of blood. It wasn't just the blood but all the heightened pheromones that scented the air, filled with excitement and aggression. It was enough to cause Tak's flame to heat his chest, the glow visible since he wasn't wearing anything more than a tunic and pants. If he had realized he would end up at the arena, he would have donned his armor before leaving the apartment, but if he'd done that, Alice would have been worried about him all night.

It wasn't a serious concern for him, as most of the fights took place within the boundaries of the arena, and the occasional brawl that broke out among the watchers was generally over bets placed and won or lost. People tended to leave Tak alone, knowing that he caused no problems, had powerful allies, and had more than enough deadly defenses to give any of the males present pause.

New Omni tokens changed hands—or whatever served as them—with loud clinks all around the arena as the battle in the pit below the stands concluded, leaving the victor standing over the bleeding body of his challenger, who was sprawled across the permanently stained stone tiles. The sound was only drowned out by the deafening cheers or cries of disappointment at the end result of the fight.

Tak had earned plenty of tokens for himself and his family since the use of the small, pressed discs had been implemented in an effort to standardize and streamline trading in the settlement, but he had no desire to spend those tokens on ventures like betting on fights. The ones currently weighing down the pouch at his waist would go to gifts for his family and food at one of the stalls in the market.

His purpose was to find Kisk and attempt to communicate with him in the hopes that he could find some reason not to want to punch the other male in the face. Since Kisk wasn't in the pit below, and Asterius had said he was fighting tonight, he was likely in the anteroom where the challengers waited for their turn or rested and recovered after their battle.

Tak had been to the anteroom more than once, and was familiar with the chaos and the even thicker odors that filled the long, narrow chamber as males paced back and forth in nervous anticipation or lay upon cots being treated by the healers that served most of the settlement.

Kisk was in the latter group, though he was sitting on his cot, glaring at nothing, while a healer—a male so delicate he might have been taken for a female, if one was inclined to die within the next few moments—treated the deep cuts and tears in his flesh that had stained his fur and scales with his blood.

The chimera's spiraled horns glistened with dark blood and his face was spattered with it so thickly that it could have been a mask, the fur clotted and stiff with blood so dark a blue it was nearly black.

The distant gaze of the chimera sharpened into alertness as Tak approached and greeted the healer. The other male, pale as a ghost and slender as a sapling, bowed his head in return, before returning all six of his eyes to the wounds his long fingers gently probed, or sewed with glimmering thread spun from his own abdomen.

Kisk's eyes narrowed on Tak as he turned his attention to the chimera and greeted him with a cool "hello."

Tak studied the wounds that slashed all over Kisk's chest and abdomen. He'd already seen those guts spilled out before. Despite his dislike of Kisk, he had no desire to see them again, so he was grateful that the abdominal wounds didn't look too deep.

"I take it you didn't win the fight?" he asked, searching for something to say that was neutral.

Kisk snorted, glancing down at his own wounds as if he barely noticed them, though he had to be feeling some pain from them. Tak already knew Kisk could feel pain. He wasn't indifferent to it, but then again, revealing that pain could be viewed as a weakness in this place.

"I held my own until the end," Kisk growled, and he didn't sound disappointed by the fact that he'd been defeated.

Tak thought he understood why. For Kisk, getting beaten in a fight was akin to making a new friend, even if the victor didn't see it that way. He wondered who had defeated the chimera and no doubt cost a lot of gamblers their tokens, but he didn't ask, nor look around the anteroom at the other males being patched up.

"What do you plan to do after this?" Tak asked, gesturing to the neat job the healer was doing on the stitches, which were already glowing in Kisk's flesh to ease the pain. They would heal faster than his body would by itself, though it wasn't instantaneous healing, which could be had from the right healers for enough tokens, but gladiators generally preferred the less expensive options so they kept the majority of their earnings for themselves.

Kisk shrugged his shoulder on the opposite side of where the healer worked, the crusted blood on his face cracking as his nose wrinkled in a wince of pain at the movement. "Eat. Then sleep... probably."

Tak hesitated on his next words, thinking there were many more things he'd rather be doing than talking to Kisk. Having his scales peeled off one by one came to mind as one of those things, but he now felt bad for being so harsh to him the last time they'd spoken.

"I'm also heading to the market. I was thinking of hitting the food stalls later for a snack. I'd be willing to join you."

Kisk cocked his head, his feathers twitching and fluffing. "Why?"

He had understandable suspicion in his voice. After all, Tak had been the one to tell the other male never to come near him again.

Tak looked away from Kisk's penetrating stare, scanning the anteroom for an excuse that didn't involve confessing to the pity he felt for Kisk, which he knew the chimera would despise from him. He spotted a cluster of males talking and laughing around their friend as the healer worked on his many wounds. Despite his pain, he was expressing his amusement in return to their attempts to cheer him up after his defeat.

Tak looked back at Kisk, who still waited for his answer as the healer moved on to stitching another deep slash in his side, the slender male's needle-like set of appendages that extended from his abdomen both feeding the silk and piercing the flesh to weave it through.

"I figured you could use the company."

Kisk's eyes flickered through their multiple appearances before settling on the gray eyes with the horizontal pupils. "I still don't respect your mate." His nose wrinkled. "Much," he muttered in a lower voice, as if he spoke more to himself than to Tak.

Tak drew in a deep breath, willing his instant tension to relax and his flame to settle in his chest. He realized he was extremely defensive of Alice, but attacking Kisk for stating the truth of his own opinion would do nothing to change it.

"It would be better if you never speak of my mate around me. There's plenty of other things we can discuss, Kisk."

Now Kisk's gaze had shifted from wary to curious. "Discuss? I figured you were here because of your mate. If not her, then what is there to talk about?"

Tak stared at Kisk, startled by his question. "What would you talk about with people from your own world?"

Kisk blinked. "I did not talk to people from my own world."

The healer made a small trilling sound as he moved to Kisk's opposite side and Tak shifted out of the way in response. Kisk's head turned as his eyes tracked Tak's movement.

"You never spoke to the people of your own world?"

As difficult as it was to believe, Tak knew it wasn't outside the realm of possibility. Asterius had also been so isolated that he rarely spoke to anyone until he'd escaped his labyrinth and ended up here in the Dead Fall.

"Only when I gave them my favor, and then only to give them direction."

This had thus far been the most words Kisk had said to him without anything antagonistic or offensive being said, and Tak was impressed the chimera had managed that much. Perhaps it was pain and exhaustion after a fight that made him too tired to pick another one.

"Do you have nothing you'd like to say? Nothing that makes you curious about this world, or that you'd like to share from your own?"

It was Kisk's turn to look away, but as his gaze took in the crowded confines of the anteroom, Tak suspected he was deliberately avoiding meeting Tak's eyes. "I have agreed not to speak of what makes me curious."

"Are you talking about my mate?" He had said Kisk shouldn't mention her to him, so perhaps that was what he meant.

Kisk's head whipped around as he stared at Tak in surprise. "How do you know this?"

Confusion at Kisk's odd reaction made Tak silent for a long moment before he answered. "I figured it was pretty obvious."

Kisk looked away again. "Her sorcery is powerful," he muttered.

Then he stiffened his back, grunting as the movement pulled on the stitches and earned a trilling censure from the healer, who had moved on to the last of the slashes. "Can you truly see her for what she is, or has she so enraptured you with her magic spells that you're blind to her control?"

Tak sighed, rubbing his forehead with an upper hand. The headache had returned, and he was already regretting his impulse to try talking to Kisk again. "Alice doesn't have magic spells, Kisk. She also doesn't control us."

Kisk snarled, pulling away from the healer as the pale creature sliced the last thread behind the knot he'd made. The chimera's reaction wasn't because of the healer, because he rose to his feet with his eyes fixed on Tak, no longer mindful of his wounds.

"She must have magic!" he growled, his tone trembling with what sounded like anger. "That is the *only* explanation!"

"We love our mate, Kisk. It's that simple. She doesn't need to cast magic spells or exert any other kind of control over us. We're with her because we want to be. She makes us happy."

The chimera ran shaking fingers through his mane, disrupting the sleek feathers that settled as he lowered his hand again. "This emotion—it makes no sense. What could possibly make you happy about it? You gain nothing from it."

Tak crossed his lower arms over his still-glowing chest,

while he massaged his temples with his upper hand. "Did you never hear of love before coming here, Kisk?"

"Mating serves only to breed more powerful offspring, but this love you speak of, it ties you to someone who is weaker. If your seed takes root, your offspring will be weaker, and like a corruption, that weakness will spread from one generation to the next. How can this serve any useful purpose for your people? For *any* people?"

"I take that as a 'no' then." Tak dug his fingers into his temples. "Physical strength isn't everything, Kisk."

"If there's no strength, then how do you fight to survive? How do you raise armies to overwhelm your foes? How do you secure your dynasty? Your legacy? What is the purpose of spawning offspring who won't be strong enough to carry your name into the legends told a thousand years from now?"

Tak thought over his response while Kisk took a moment to count out tokens from his stained waist pouch to hand over to the patiently waiting healer so the male could move on to the next client. The tokens disappeared into the healer's pouch with a quick blur of motion from his hand and then the slender male bowed to them both and moved away with a final trill of parting.

When he had Kisk's full attention again, Tak decided the best way to answer was with a question. After all, he had no idea what Kisk's world had been like, so he couldn't answer in a way that would make sense to the chimera without more information.

"What do you want for your children, Kisk? For them to be happy? Fulfilled in their lives? Or for them to forever strive for more, never knowing peace and contentment?"

Kisk snorted. "I'm *the* chimera. I cannot spawn offspring. I can only offer my favor to others."

Sudden understanding struck Tak, a clarity about Kisk that had been missing up until that point.

"What is your favor, Kisk," he said in a low voice.

Kisk narrowed his eyes, his nostrils flaring. "Do you ask it, fire-warrior? It is usually the female who must prove herself strong enough to pass on her blood to the next generation."

There was a flicker of some emotion that caused Kisk's eyes to shift briefly before returning to his eerie gray stare.

The sudden tension from the chimera made Tak very nervous, not because he feared the other male, but because he felt like he was standing on a cliff, knew the edge was close, but could not see how many steps would take him over it.

"I only ask what it is, if you will tell me. I want nothing more from you."

Kisk rose to his feet, crowding Tak, who refused to step backwards, feeling that it was important that he establish some kind of dominance over the other male.

"If you ask it from me, I will give it," the chimera said, leaning close to Tak, until they were eye to eye. "I owe you my life, and my favor has always been my repayment."

Tak decided perhaps it was time to take a step away from Kisk.

"I'm not interested," he said flatly.

Kisk's sudden bark of laughter caused all the nearby males to turn towards them, staring for a long moment before they decided nothing interesting was going to happen and they returned to their own concerns.

"Not eager to hand your female to me long enough to receive my gift, fire-warrior? Perhaps it's because of this 'love?' From what the minotaur says, it makes you foolishly possessive of a womb."

Kisk shook his head, stepping away from Tak to round the cot and lean down to collect the rest of his personal items, which consisted of nothing more than a grimy shirt, as stained and ragged as his blood-soaked pants, a leather belt to hold his token pouch, and scuffed, dirty boots scarred and worn and looking too misshapen and at least a size too small for his large, clawed feet.

Tak stared at Kisk, pondering his words, no longer so easily bothered by their insulting tone. He realized rudeness was Kisk's default tone, that mocking edge always there, intended to taunt and infuriate. Perhaps as a test in itself.

"You never said what your favor was."

Kisk sat on the cot to pull on his boots.

After wrestling on the first boot, he glanced up from a gleaming, black claw that poked through a hole in toe to meet Tak's gaze with golden eyes. "The favor of the chimera makes it possible to breed a female with anyone, no matter how different they might be from her. My favor can even allow you and your fellow male to combine your seed within your mate to spawn a new breed of child."

He tugged on his second boot with a pained grunt. "Great warrior queens...," grunt, tug, "would...," more grunts of effort, "drag their harems to my temple... umph... on their leashes... urg... and fight me for my favor to breed a new spawn to continue their dynasties."

He managed to work both boots over his claws, but Tak didn't miss his wince as he rose to his feet.

"Why don't you buy new boots that are actually made for your feet?" he asked, staring down at the worn leather straining to contain Kisk's talons.

The chimera stared down at his own feet as if he'd never seen them before. "What difference does it make what foot coverings I wear?" He looked back up at Tak, dismissing his boots. "Did you not hear me, fire-warrior? I can give you and your sorcerous mate the chance to breed successfully."

"I already have a son," Tak said, feeling a sudden surge of pity for the hopeful tone in Kisk's voice, recognizing it for what it was, even if the other male didn't understand his own motivation. "We can already do this thing you speak of." Though he wondered how Kisk was capable of it, and intended to have a word with Gray later about it.

If he thought Kisk would be defeated by the reminder of his son, Tak was mistaken.

"I don't know how you managed to breed the child, but it is only of the female and of you, is it not?" He didn't wait for an answer before carrying on. "What if you could have all three of you represented in the bloodlines of another child?"

Tak felt like he was asking questions that would lead him to the kind of problems that disrupted and even destroyed nice, peaceful, content lives. "So, you're saying your favor would make it possible for Alice to carry Iyaren's cubs to term?"

Kisk waved away the question, his ear flicking in irritation as if some biting insect pestered him. "If you want to waste my favor on just the two of them, then they will have a hybrid cub. But why have only a hybrid cub when you can cement your claim on your offspring by adding your own bloodline, so that the child is truly the spawn of all three of you."

Tak was growing interested, despite himself. "How exactly does your favor work?"

Kisk looked around the crowded anteroom, then shook his feathers and gestured for them to exit out the back way so they didn't have to walk past all the gamblers and those feeling an adrenaline rush from the fights.

He was silent until they moved far enough away from the crowds and closer to the darkest edges of the settlement, where the smallest saplings were still one-story tall, but it wasn't yet enough to complete the shield near the next buildings to be reclaimed once the saplings gained more height.

Kisk led Tak towards the marketplace, apparently unconcerned with his own raggedy, grimy appearance, and the fact that he was still covered in blood from himself and his opponent, including the coagulated blood that trickled down the spirals of his horns and ended up gumming up the feathers of his mane that surrounded his horns.

"Are you certain you wish to go to the market like that?" Tak eyed him appraisingly.

His clothing and appearance were probably the worst of any of the other males there, but by then, they all knew him and knew what to expect.

Kisk drew him to a halt in the dark, quiet alley, before they reached the marketplace. Tak flicked his tongue, testing for pheromones that shouldn't be around them. He found nothing larger than a barren creeper in the dark alley.

It was only then that Kisk explained his favor.

12

Kisk ended up following Tak to the market stalls after their discussion, intending to find some food, since he was shaking with hunger now that his focus was no longer on the pain of his cuts. The healer's silken threads glowed faintly in his wounds, somehow easing the pain of them. The slender male was a more expensive healer than some of the others, but Kisk found the pain-deadening properties of his stitches worth the extra investment, especially since he no longer had the temple to heal him and revive him.

Tak led Kisk to the cluster of food stalls in the center of the busy market. The scent of cooked meet and plant matter and a hundred different bodies from the same number of different worlds made Kisk nearly nauseous. His growling stomach probably didn't help either. He couldn't recall the last time he'd eaten. Surely, it had been before his decision to spend the night fighting in the arena, only to be defeated after his second battle, which had angered a great many people in the audience who'd bet on him.

He had felt a bit weak and lightheaded while standing in the pit, and his opponent had benefitted from that.

And from Kisk's distracted mind.

It was all the sorceress's fault. Her and her bell-tone voice speaking spell words to bind him. There could be no other explanation for why he felt a need inside him to see her again and once again hear her voice.

Though Tak had not defeated Kisk directly in battle, he'd saved his life, which Kisk acknowledged as pretty much the same thing. That meant Tak had proven himself worthy, and Kisk could speak to him as an equal. There had been a time, long ago, when he'd tried to carry on a conversation with the warriors and their harem before the battles would begin in the temple, but the spirits had punished him for that.

They had forbidden him from speaking with those who had not yet proven themselves worthy.

He wondered if the reason he had been able to talk to Alice without feeling that pinch of anxiety that he would be punished for it—the one that closed his throat and made it difficult to form words—was because she'd already somehow ensorcelled him through his serpent sliver.

He eyed Tak while he waited for some unidentifiable meat-based dish he'd purchased from the nearest vendor, not really concerned with what it was, as long as it filled the gaping void in his stomach. He couldn't remember the last time he'd eaten.

Had it been more than a day?

He'd been sleeping a lot, and sometimes, it wasn't worth the effort to go to the market to seek out fresh food, so he'd remain in his quarters and sleep to conserve his energy so he'd need less of it.

Tak was ensorcelled, though he naively called it "love," a concept that had long ago been abandoned on Kisk's world. There was only love for power and strength.

Kisk felt a strange sort of kinship with Tak, having been captured by the same spell-weaver. He knew the other male barely tolerated his presence, but Kisk rarely concerned himself with the attitudes of others. If he goaded them into a fight with his words or actions, it made no difference to him, since he had been created to fight. It was the only way he knew how to interact with others.

Well, not the *only* way.

He'd made an offer that Tak had not accepted. But the other male had also not refused outright, though it had looked for a moment as if he would immediately when Kisk explained the process. Yet, the fire-warrior had paused, his mouth opened on an automatic denial, while his gaze grew distant and thoughtful. Then he'd closed his mouth long enough for Kisk to see the frown that bent it before he opened it again to speak.

Tak's words had given Kisk a strange feeling of lightness inside him that had made the dull throb of his wounds and his pinched feet seem less annoying, and the oppressive scent of the alley less thick and smothering.

"I'll discuss this with Iyaren, and if he agrees that it's something we should take to Alice to consider, we will."

It wasn't an outright refusal. That meant there was still a possibility. Still... hope.

Alice...

Kisk wasn't sure how much, if anything, about the earlier day Alice might have told her mates. It didn't seem like Tak was inclined to discuss it, so it was possible the sorceress hadn't told him about it.

And why should she? She need only speak her spell words and her mates were bound to her. She had no confessions to make to them. Especially not if Kisk's suspicions about her power were accurate.

She wanted to keep her mates from feeling any sadness at all, if what he'd overheard using his serpent sliver could be trusted. That must mean their sadness would free them from their binding, or perhaps loosen it enough that they could escape the feeling inside them that made them want to see her again.

She guarded her emotions so carefully so her mates felt none of her despair, protecting her spell upon them.

It was the only explanation that made sense to Kisk.

Tak ordered something from a nearby food stall, carefully counting out tokens from his pouch before placing them into the eagerly extended tentacle of a creature, which wrapped around the clinking disks then slithered back to the other side of the food stall, where the vendor—who was not the owner of the tentacled appendage—began serving out the food onto a dish.

Kisk was very good at controlling his shudder, but he was also grateful the appendage had disappeared again. He would avoid that stall.

By that point, Kisk's food was done and he'd barely managed to make it to one of the rickety tables cobbled together from scavenged scrap wood and metal before he was tucking into it with his bare hands, shoveling food into his mouth with great haste in an effort to fill the yawning void that tore at his gut.

He was halfway through his heaping plate of food before Tak even had a chance to sink into a chair beside him, his lower arms folded over his stomach and his upper arms carrying the plate, which he set down on the table with a soft thud. His reptilian eyes watched Kisk, and a mild expression of disgust twisted his lips.

"You do not need to eat like an animal, simply because you can shift into one."

Kisk paused with a mouth full of meat he barely tasted, then snorted, spraying the greasy, brown sauce from his lips. "Mmphf...s'point of eating any other way?"

Tak lifted one upper hand to flick away the beads of sauce

that had spattered his tunic, using another upper hand to swipe away the ones that dotted his face.

His lower hands found his plate as his upper hands performed those tasks, and Kisk stared at the way all four arms moved without getting in the way of each other, marveling at it. He'd seen many strange people come to his temple, but never any with four arms. It seemed like it should be unwieldy, but since coming to the Dead Fall, he'd discovered that those who had more arms than him had no problem using them with great facility. Especially in combat.

He'd never actually looked at another male for this long though without initiating some sort of confrontation. Most males were confrontational with mere eye contact.

Especially with Kisk.

Tak was less likely to start a fight, and there were males in the settlement who said it was because he was a coward, but Kisk knew otherwise. It had been Tak who'd followed him down into the lair of the tentacle-mole and saved him from the agony of a death he would not be revived from.

"Some people call it manners." Tak shook his head as Kisk scooped another handful of food into his mouth. "I call it a way to avoid wearing the food your companion is eating."

Kisk lifted his head from where it hovered over his plate, grease and some spicy sauce dripping down his chin to further stain his shirt. He chewed, staring at Tak through narrowed eyes as the other male lifted some type of food neatly wrapped in a very large leaf to his mouth.

Kisk waited to swallow before asking the question that had finally occurred to him, now that he wasn't so distracted by pain and hunger. "Why are you not trying to fight me or telling me to go away?"

Tak also finished the bite of food in his mouth, none of it having gotten onto his scales, before he responded. "I am not an unfriendly person by nature, Kisk."

Kisk nodded at this, already knowing what was said about Tak. "Yes, others think it makes you weak, as did I once, but you have proven yourself worthy."

Tak shook his head, setting down his food as he sighed. "Worthy of what, Kisk?"

When he looked at Kisk, the chimera didn't like the sympathy he saw in the fire-warrior's eyes. It looked too much like pity, and Kisk would fight anyone who dared to feel pity for him.

He stiffened in his chair, forgetting about the last handful of food on his plate as he engaged in a staring match with the reptilian male. "Worthy of continuing to draw breath."

"And everyone must prove themselves worthy of being alive? By what? Not dying? I would think that's the point of surviving."

Kisk was about to respond to that, his mind churning over the words, trying to understand their meaning, when Tak asked him a question.

"What did you do to prove *yourself* worthy of surviving, Kisk?"

Kisk lifted his greasy chin. "I do not survive. I exist. Solely to test those who would be seen as strong enough to spawn a new breed of warrior."

"Ss'bek's crimped tail!" Tak said in a low voice, speaking sharply as if he were cursing. "You poor bastard."

Kisk snarled, rising to his feet as his hands slammed to the tabletop, making the plates rattle. He ignored the pain as blood rushed back into his feet, reminding him of the tightness of his boots as they throbbed in protest.

Several males from surrounding tables glanced over at the sound of the plates rattling, noticed it was Kisk, and rolled their eyes or other optical appendages before turning back to their own food. Kisk ignored them, focusing his attention on Tak.

"I am the chimera. *The* chimera! I am the embodiment of

an ideal—the perfection of a warrior. Only *I* can grant the greatest warriors the chance to spawn even more powerful ones." He gestured with one hand to the busy market. "And I can do it for any fool here, provided he brings me a female, but I offered it to you and yours, and you would call me a *poor bastard?*"

Tak stared up at him, his expression mild, unconcerned with Kisk's rising anger. "I know what you *are*, but what do you *want*, Kisk?"

Kisk didn't even have to think about it, but he kept the response behind his teeth, knowing now wasn't the time. She had ensorcelled them, but Tak didn't see it that way. He might feel threatened if Kisk answered that question with the name of his mate.

Tak shook his head at Kisk's silent fuming. "You don't even know, do you?"

Yes!

"That is why I said *poor* bastard. You are so far from under-standing that I don't know if anyone can help you find your way." He leaned forward, his upper arms settling on the table, his lower arms concealed in his lap. "I want to help you, but you have to abandon your past and your title to become some-thing more than just *the* chimera."

More? There was no more than that. The chimera was the highest anyone could achieve. The final test. The "big boss" as Alice had said, though he hadn't understood her words about "video games."

"I saved your life, Kisk. There are some here who would say it now belongs to me."

Kisk tensed, his claws extending to dig into the scarred wooden table top, adding new scratches to the surface as he glared at Tak. "It does not work that way. I owe you nothing but my favor."

Tak rose to his own feet, still staring down Kisk, neither of them breaking away first as they battled for dominance. "And if I don't take your favor?"

Since Kisk had not actually offered it to any other male in this world—as it was only the females who could make use of it —he didn't have a good answer for that. In his temple, no one had ever turned down the offer, because that was their entire purpose for being there in the first place.

Tak answered before Kisk could think of a good reply. "You owe me for your life, and until you can repay me, I must protect my investment. That means keeping you out of trouble."

He broke their stare long enough to glance down at Kisk's stained tunic, then further down at the table top. A sly smile tilted his lips.

"It also means I'll have to spend more time around you, and your smell is too much to handle on a daily basis, so the first thing you'll do is find clean clothes." He looked around in an exaggerated manner, as if only just noting their surroundings before looking back to Kisk with a wide, deadly grin. "Oh, look, we seem to be in a market. How convenient."

———

TAK MADE KISK PURCHASE boots that were custom-made to fit his talons, and though he'd been baffled by the whole "shopping" experience, having spent time in the market only for the food stalls, he would admit—though only to himself—that the new shoes felt incredible as they flexed around his feet, giving his claws room to actually move.

The other male also insisted he purchase new clothes from another stall, where an industrious male was busily sewing fabric into tunics and pants that were clean and unstained. Since Kisk scavenged everything he owned, not having the patience or the social skills to trade for anything more than food, he hadn't owned clean, tailored clothing since he'd been inside the temple with the spirits caring for all his needs.

Though Tak was making him do these things, Kisk was aware enough to recognize that the other male did it to help him, without seeming like he pitied him. It angered him to be pitied by anyone, as he was ten thousand years old and had fought every single one of those years and had died more times than anyone in this world.

They should be worshipping him, not pitying him.

Yet, he followed along with Tak, listening to him explain how to successfully trade with other males, telling him when to hold his tongue and keep rude or blunt comments about their wares, their stalls, or their persons, to himself.

He wasn't sure why he did it without complaint, but he suspected it was yet another part of the sorceress's enchantment. He wanted to see her again, so he behaved as her mate told him to behave.

No, he wanted more than to just see her again.

He wanted what Tak had.

Alice had chosen Tak to bind to her. The male had proven himself worthy by saving Kisk's life, and he wondered if he had done the same for Alice. He wondered if there would ever be a chance for him to save her life so she would continue to bind him to her, as she did her mates.

He had no idea how else he could prove his worth.

He also had no idea how any spell could be strong enough to make him want to try. Only the spirits had ever held this much power over him.

With clean clothes, a trade worked out with a launderer, new boots, and a much lighter pouch, Kisk dragged through the marketplace, ready to go home and sleep, though his home wasn't much to speak of. It was little more than a tiny chamber, paint peeling from the walls and ceilings, mold growing in the corners to darken the plaster, and rotting food and dirty clothes surrounding his sleeping mat. There were no other furnishings besides a low table and stained cushion with the stuffing coming out of it through the seams, a bucket for his waste, and another for his drinking and washing water.

He might not know how to properly clean his clothes, but he knew how to care for his fur, feathers, and scales. His falcon sliver was obsessed with clean feathers, as his wings needed to be prepared to fly, and Kisk hated having ragged, matted fur. His scales never needed more than a wipe-down, but he liked to see them sleek and gleaming.

In truth, at the moment, he needed a fully submersed bath, so when Tak finally bid him good night, even as the sky was lightening with the approaching dawn, Kisk turned his steps to the bathhouse rather than to his tiny, scummy apartment.

Steam billowed out of the opening when he tugged open the wooden paneled door, which had swollen into its frame from all the moisture on the inside of the room that had been turned into a bathing house.

He paid for a full bath at the front counter, noting he would need to dig up more of his buried tokens to refill his now-slim pouch when he got a chance.

The other males in the bathhouse barely spared him a glance. Taking note of who he was, they quickly looked away, returning to their own hygiene tasks, which for some of them, were probably quite complicated.

Kisk ignored them as well, though he made note of each of them and what threat they might pose, as any male would have. Even in New Omni, it was second nature to assess one's surroundings. The Gray One ruled with an uncompromising and ruthless response to those who broke New Omni's code of laws, but some of the males who lived in the settlement struggled to throw off old habits, and fights were always breaking out, most of which were considered barely skirting the code of laws, but close enough to the right side to avoid getting punished.

The sunken tubs that had made this building the perfect place to put a bathhouse were empty except for one, the room so filled with steam from the boilers that kept the water warm that Kisk could barely see through the cloud of it. He smelled the other male, even above the scent of soap made from fat, the scale and exoskeleton polishing oils and creams, and hot water. The male didn't stink, but he did smell of blood.

The same blood that still spattered Kisk's old clothes and still clotted in his horns.

He approached the other male, who splashed water onto his feathers in a halfhearted way. The places on his thigh where Kisk had gored him had been stitched up by the same healer who'd done Kisk's wounds, and those stitches glowed softly in the skin exposed by feathers that had been removed to clear the wounds.

Kisk well-remembered the talons on the other male's feet— which were now setting against the bottom of the pool— scratching deeply into his hide as the light-boned creature leapt up time and again during their battle.

The other male looked up as Kisk reached the edge of the pool and stripped off his new clothes.

"Chimera," the other male said by way of greeting, wariness in his tone.

"Veraza," Kisk said, returning the greeting as he took a moment to clumsily fold his clothing and set it to the side before taking off his new boots.

13

Iyaren watched his son and his nephew race around the mother ancilla tree, their excited giggles piercing the usual peaceful stillness of the grove. The ancilla didn't mind. In fact, they preferred the presence of mobile life like their tenders and the children they created. Children meant a future for the ancilla as much as it meant a future for New Omni.

Thus far, these two children were the only ones born in the Dead Fall that Gray had been able to save. There had been young ones who'd fallen into this world and had been found by the patrols before they'd been killed or died of starvation, and those alien children had been placed with a family in the growing family quarters. However, none of the other mated pairs or groups had been able to produce children from their own blood. Given the fact that all of them were from different worlds in different dimensions, that wasn't in the least bit surprising.

But Iyaren wanted a future for his child and his nephew that didn't involve waiting for someone else to fall from the portal in the sky to be a part of their family. He wanted to see New Omni grow more naturally, and he wasn't the only one.

They all did. Gray had made it one of his priorities. He said there were ways to "engineer" the seed of two different species so they could procreate, and the existence of the two children—plus the three more who would hatch soon—was proof that it was possible. Unfortunately, all of those cases had been special circumstances that had happened within the bodies of the people involved. It had not been something they could control.

Nor had Gray been able to get ahold of the necessary equipment to do whatever he needed to do to make it possible for them to create more hybrid children, though he had stripped much of his equipment from his space vessel to bring it back to New Omni. It now served as their medical ward, and because resources were so slim and the power requirements so high, it was only used in the direst emergencies, there being natural healers in the settlement with abilities to treat lesser illnesses and wounds.

The complications in obtaining the right equipment were only the start of the headaches their leader had to face, so Iyaren rarely bothered him about anything, preferring to rely instead on his mate and his heart-brother, Tak, for the rare occasion when he couldn't do something for himself. Gray was a ghost most of the time anyway, popping in and out of the settlement on some secret mission of his own so often that the only ones who ever saw him anymore were Evie, Doshak, and his son.

At one point, Iyaren had been hopeful that Gray would come up with a way for Alice to bear a cub of his bloodline and hers, blending them together as Friak was a blend of her and Tak. It would be such a miracle—an awe-inspiring wonder—gifted to one who'd been forsaken by his own goddess that he would suspect perhaps Sekhmet had not meant to forsake him at all, but instead had sent him here for just this purpose, in her wisdom.

Although, even being with his beloved mate, his life so fulfilled now with a child he loved like his own, and with Tak, whom he loved like a brother, he wondered if this hadn't been her intent all along.

Iyaren had put aside his hope for cubs as the threat of war with NEX dragged on from one year to the next, and the portal continued to open to mysteries they couldn't fathom, sending even greater threats to the Fall to ambush them.

So far, the ancilla were confident they could maintain the shield over the settlement and keep anything dangerous out. They could sense anything that approached their guardian trees, and bar it from entry unless they felt it would bring no harm to those sheltered within.

He'd seen the guardian trees move their roots to the surface to trap smaller creatures that attempted to pass the barrier, and those squirming, squealing victims had been quickly silenced by tightening roots, then dragged slowly underground to feed the soil. He suspected the same could happen to a much larger creature if it were stupid enough to try to force its way past the guardian trees to try its luck against the shield itself.

This place was as good as any to raise their children, though he always felt a pang of loss when he thought of their old home —the place where he'd first brought Alice and had first made love to her and claimed her as his mate. Someday, he would take Friak to their old home and show him where they had come from and tell the story of how they'd all met.

When he was much older, and hopefully the Fall was much safer.

Though his eyes were on the children, occasionally corralling one with his upper arms to swing them in the air, much to their delight, before setting them back down again to continue their chase, his mind was pondering Tak's words to him earlier that day.

Apparently, several days ago, Tak had spoken to Kisk, and Kisk had made him an offer that had left him distant and distracted enough that both Iyaren and Alice had noticed and commented on it.

Alice's smile when she'd asked Tak if there was anything bothering him had been brittle, and her eyes had been worried and shifted as if she struggled to meet his gaze. Iyaren worried so much about his mate lately, fearing she was close to shattering in some way, but he didn't know what to do about it, as any attempts to question her made her smile gruesomely exaggerated and her eyes frantic, panic in her voice as she insisted she was fine and that everything was perfectly lovely.

Tak had been more forthcoming about what was on his mind when Iyaren had questioned him this morning as Tak readied himself to join the construction crews for his rotation. Alice was working with her sister and the other women on a project that seemed to consume her, madly sewing garment after garment in the evenings after she'd served her daily rotation duties. On this day, she was with the other females not on rotation, putting together what she called "care packages" for the unmated males.

His mind dwelled on Alice's odd behavior because it was difficult to think about Tak's words. They sent too many emotions through him that he didn't know how to process, because a part of him was at war with himself.

Kisk could make it possible for Alice to bear a child with both his and Tak's bloodline merged with Alice's. The child would be, in every way, all of theirs.

His gaze sought Friak, who had climbed the branch the mother ancilla swept to the ground for them to jump over and was now swinging from it, his little feet barely off the loam so if he fell, he wouldn't hurt himself.

The boy was as much his son as any child of his own blood would be. He'd known that he would be, the moment Alice had told him she was carrying a child. Friak was a part of her, and that had been all that had mattered to him when Alice had told him the child wasn't his by blood. There had been no question in his mind that he would love the child.

But there had been a twinge of envy and a strong desire to see his and Alice's features in a child, just as Friak had Tak's scales and Alice's beautiful eyes and her cute little beak of a nose—though smaller and more like a button at the moment on the young child's face.

Even as he'd held his son in his upper arms, never touching the boy with his war hands—because superstitions died hard—he'd studied his features, seeing the echo of his mate and Tak in a new life and a future. One he wanted to see for himself and his mate as well.

They'd been counting on Gray, but who knew when or if Gray would come through with the answer? Now, they'd been given another possibility. One perhaps even more miraculous than a hybrid of just two of them—a hybrid of all three of them.

If Kisk's word could be trusted. The creature was an unknown element, and though Tak had pried some information out of him that made Tak feel sympathy for the other male, Iyaren had yet to be convinced Kisk could be believed, much less trusted.

He also wanted to immediately reject the offer simply because of what it would require.

That last part was what had made Tak so hesitant to even broach the subject with Iyaren, and was why it had taken several days before he'd caved and told Iyaren that he'd been considering it, despite the fact that he'd immediately wanted to reject it.

They both knew that it was their own selfish possessiveness

that had them wanting to reject Kisk's offer, because in order to give Alice his "favor," Kisk would have to mate with her before both he and Tak spent their seed inside her. Somehow, whatever it was he produced would cause their seed to blend with hers and create a new lifeform.

The idea of that particular male even coming near Alice made Iyaren snarl, much less allowing him close enough to touch her. To have him bury his staff inside her was something Iyaren didn't think he could stand for, but the reason his initial rejection of the idea had shifted to this current consideration of it was mostly because of Alice.

Iyaren believed she would want this, enough to endure whatever it took to have a child with the two of them.

That made this whole situation tricky. He and Tak now had information that could deeply affect Alice's life, and they were currently keeping it to themselves. If she knew that Kisk had made this offer, and Tak and Iyaren weren't telling her about it, she'd be furious, and hurt. She'd feel betrayed, as she'd felt betrayed when they'd first mated and Tak and Iyaren had plotted together behind her back to seduce her, unable to communicate effectively with her because of the language barrier.

The longer Tak and Iyaren kept this secret, the more likely Alice would find out about it and see it as them once again making decisions that involved her without her input. Only this time, they didn't have the language barrier as an excuse.

They only had their jealousy.

Iyaren didn't want Kisk to touch Alice, even if it would only be for a short time, and only once. It wasn't like Kisk was asking to join their family, though he wondered if that wouldn't actually make it easier for all of them to accept this offer.

If he and Tak learned to see Kisk as they saw each other—as a heart-brother—would it bother them to share Alice's bed with the other male?

According to Tak, Kisk had said they must all mate within a short span of time, and that those who usually received Kisk's favor had all mated in the same room at the same time, taking turns with the female, until they had all spent their seed inside her—sometimes as many as five different males—but only after Kisk had put what he called the "catalyst" into the female's womb, which he called a "crucible."

This favor was only given once to each female and her harem, but from what Kisk had said, all of the times he'd done it, the warrior females had gone away carrying a new breed of child in their womb, a child who would be fertile with many of the different races that had lived in the chimera's world—most of which had descended from those who'd gone to the chimera's temple and were called the "chimera-blessed."

They had one opportunity. One chance at a child who would share Iyaren's blood. Tak had told Iyaren that he would step back and allow this to be a child solely between Alice and Iyaren, since he had Friak to carry on his blood.

Iyaren had pondered that as well, and had come to a swift conclusion that this one opportunity should not be squandered. If all three of them could make a child together, then it should be done that way. The more he thought of what features such a child might have, what echoes of each parent he might see in its face, the more certain he became that he wanted all of them represented in this—if they intended to do it all.

But that last part was the sticking point. Neither he nor Tak were comfortable with the idea, or with Kisk. They also didn't know exactly how Alice would react, but Iyaren had a good idea. She'd be horrified at the process, but she'd do it anyway, without a second thought, if it meant giving him a cub. It was something she wanted so badly that even he felt her pain and heartache when time continued to pass without her being able to produce a child for him, and now, she worried about whether she could even have another child as time passed with no sign of another pregnancy since the loss of her last one.

As he rounded up the children to take them back to the settlement for their naps, he thought about the one consideration he put above all else—the happiness of his family. He would do anything to protect that, and anything to ensure it. Even if it meant allowing yet another male to be with his mate.

But Iyaren wasn't going to allow Kisk anywhere near her until he'd decided for himself whether the male was trustworthy. This could all be some trick, just to get close to a female. They had no proof that Kisk was honorable enough to tell the truth about this "favor."

It was time for Iyaren to do what he should have done when the chimera first joined the settlement of New Omni after recovering from the wounds he'd taken out in the Fall when the meteor had struck the old settlement and cratered a big portion of the ruins.

It was time for Iyaren to show Kisk exactly why he should be respectful of the Clawed One.

"Daddy, why show teeth?" Friak asked from his perch on Iyaren's right arm, tucked against his chest.

"Uncle 'Ren excited for fight," Sherak answered for Iyaren, reminding him to be more guarded in his emotions around the child he snuggled tight against him on his other side so the two boys faced each other, which made it easier for them to make a bunch of faces at each other that had them both giggling as he carried them back to their apartment.

His snarling grin fell away as he shook his head at the remarkable children in his arms. His life was already so blessed.

Were they being selfish to want even more blessings?

_____

14

Whenever Alice could find the time to get away for her walks in the forest, the little serpent joined her.

The first time he'd found her again, she'd been huffing and puffing her way along the path that wove through the trees closest to the family quarters, hating herself for how out of shape she'd gotten that even that small exertion was difficult.

The serpent had slithered up to her as she'd stood with her hands on her knees, catching her breath.

She'd stared down at it, red-faced, sweating, strands of hair loosening from her ponytail to surround her face and stick to her damp cheek.

The snake had looked sleek and glossy. The bastard had also looked smug.

"Outta my way, Kisk," Alice had said with a grunt as she'd straightened up and squared her shoulders, determined to walk at least a mile in her first effort. "I don't have time to deal with your crap today."

Kisk's serpent hadn't responded with anything other than a hiss, and Alice hadn't been able to decide what that might mean, but she'd figured if it came from the chimera, it was probably something rude, so she'd felt no guilt about stepping around it to continue on her path, her chin high in the air as she'd deliberately ignored the snake—only to trip on a dirt mound in the path and stumble, catching herself on a nearby ancilla tree before she'd fallen.

A series of hisses from the snake had definitely sounded like reptilian laughter, and Alice hadn't even been surprised anymore that such a thing could exist.

"Little snaky-bastard," she'd muttered to herself as she'd righted herself and started walking again.

She hadn't been able to hear him moving along the path behind her, but whenever she would steal a peek, he had always been there, just traveling in her footsteps.

After the second day of this, she gave up trying to completely ignore him, attempting a different tactic to get rid of him. Her efforts to insult him only met with more hissing snake laughs.

One thing she could say about Kisk. He would take as good as he gave without getting offended. Probably because he just didn't care about her opinion of him.

By the third day, she acknowledged that it wasn't so bad having the little snake following in her footsteps, since it distracted her from the exertion she was putting out to push herself a further distance each time she walked.

Instead, she answered questions she pretended he might care enough to ask.

"I'm breathing better, if you'll notice," she said, glancing over her shoulder at the snake, which was bright orange like her current tunic.

It always matched what she was wearing, and she wondered about it, but never bothered to ask.

The serpent's tongue flicked out as the only response. Not even a hiss of agreement. Stupid snake could show her a little encouragement. But this *was* Kisk, after all. The jerk probably wouldn't be impressed if she was running a marathon.

She was walking better too, feeling the effort less and less, even by only the third day of it. It felt good to get outside and be alone, away from the family she loved so much that she was afraid to be herself around them. Afraid that something she did, or said, or even felt, would hurt them if she didn't hide it away.

Out here in the ancilla forest, she didn't have to bury her feelings, and she didn't care if she upset Kisk—didn't even think it was possible, because the male didn't care about anything at all, from what she could tell. It was refreshing to be able to say whatever was on her mind, whenever she wanted, without fear that it would hurt someone else.

"I don't feel blessed, most of the time," she confessed on the fifth day. "I know I am, but I just can't feel it," she pressed against her chest, where her heart didn't pound as frantically as it had on that first walk. "In my heart, I still feel... sad. Lost. It's like, no matter what I have, it's never enough as long as the one thing I can never have is denied to me."

She shook her head bitterly. "I know it's selfish as all-hell! You don't have to be so damned judgmental, Kisk," she snapped, turning to glance at him.

He lifted his head to stare at her in what she imagined was surprise, or was it just more smugness? Hard to tell on a cute little snake face.

Turning back to face the path with a heavy sigh, she shook her head. "No, you're right. I'm ungrateful, and I don't deserve to be this lucky. I hate myself for feeling this way."

Suddenly, a long, scaly body slid over her foot, then wrapped around her ankle, forcing her to stop walking or risk treading on the snake. She might think Kisk was a jerk, but she was growing kind of fond of the little serpent and didn't want to hurt it.

She paused her steps and stared down at the creature, who was so much more fragile than the male it was a part of. It stared back up at her and hissed as loud as its little body could. There was no questioning the censure in the sound.

"Yes, I admitted I was ungrateful! You don't have to keep remind—Ow!"

She stumbled away from the snake, rubbing her ankle where it had bit her, the tiny teeth in its mouth barely digging deep enough to pierce the fabric of her pants and scrape her skin. But it had been startling for it to suddenly dart forward and grab her leg in its mouth.

She stared warily at the serpent for a long moment as she rubbed the area it had bitten after checking to make sure the skin wasn't broken. "You're not venomous, are you?"

The snake swung its little head from side to side in an exaggerated negative.

"Why'd you bite me?"

It flicked its tongue out and stared at her in silence.

"Was it because of something I said?"

This time, it moved its head up and down, the positive nod looking comical on the little creature.

She thought back over her words. "Because I said I was ungrateful?"

It nodded again.

"Why would that make you *bite* me? I mean, seriously? What kind of friend bites a person when they say something?"

The serpent tilted its head, staring at her with confusion that reminded her of the male it belonged to, cocking his big, feather-maned head.

She put her hands on her hips. "So, I'm not your friend?"

Of course not. This *was* Kisk, even if she'd started to look at the little snake as something separate, something that maybe had become like a little workout buddy for her.

She was expecting an emphatic shake of the little head, but

the serpent just flicked its tongue out a few more times, then turned and slithered down the path in front of her.

She watched it go, disappointed that she'd started to care about the little bastard and angry at herself that she'd actually miss seeing it sliding along behind her on her walks.

Then it stopped moving and lifted its head, turning to look back at her, waiting.

It didn't move again until she was almost upon it. Only then did it slide around until it was at her side. Since she'd stopped walking again, it also paused, staring up at her face, tongue flicking out.

"You wanna still walk with me?"

It bobbed its head in a nod.

"You gonna bite me again?"

The snake lowered its head like it was staring sheepishly at the dirt path. Then it slowly shook it from side to side, with a low hiss that sounded like the muttered "sorry" she might get from her son when he was forced to apologize for misbehaving.

She crossed her arms, regarding the snake and wondering if she wasn't reading too much into its body language. In truth, she had no idea what the creature was thinking, or if it even thought independently of Kisk. And if it didn't—if this really was Kisk in full control of this creature—then she had no idea what to think of his actions or his intent. It was entirely possible that the male felt as lonely as she did. The only difference being that he actually was alone, whereas she was surrounded by her family almost all the time.

"Did you get that care package I had sent over?"

She bit her lip, wondering just how the serpent would respond and what that would mean about how its connection to Kisk worked.

It looked up immediately, then slowly nodded, both reactions not really telling her anything.

"Did you like the things inside?"

Another slow nod. This one seemed almost reluctant, and she could imagine the overly-proud male acknowledging his appreciation of a gift from an "unworthy" person.

"Well, I hope they made your home a bit more comfortable. You... ah... do know *how* to use those cleaning supplies, right?"

The affirmative bobbing of the snake's head was hesitant, then defiant.

Then the little serpent hissed, tossed its little head, and slithered forward, though it didn't go far when it noticed Alice hadn't moved. It paused and cast her a glare from beady little snake eyes, refusing to move a muscle until Alice chuckled and followed in the little S-shaped tracks it had left in the path.

Alice hummed to herself as she walked, finding it helped to regulate her breathing and relaxed her, even as she increased her pace and her level of exertion, determined to work up to the physical fitness level she'd been when she'd first arrived in the Fall. If she ever found herself running from danger, she didn't want to end up falling behind because she'd grown too complacent. She might never shift the excess weight she'd put on during her depression, but she'd at least be able to move when she needed to.

Plus, walking felt surprisingly good, despite the constant chafing of her thighs, no matter how soft the fabric she wore was. With her blood pumping and her heart beating at a steadier pace every time she stepped out like this, and an odd little walking buddy to keep her company—connected in some way to an even odder creature who already knew her secrets and had not yet spilled them to her mate—she felt strangely free.

15

T ak was pulling night guard on the gate that evening, so Alice would be spending her night with Iyaren after they tucked Friak in. She was looking forward to it, her body already primed for him, eager for his touch.

Making love with her mates was the only time she felt like she could be entirely honest and open in their presence, which was why she craved that time throughout the long days of wearing a mask in front of them. At night, she'd let the mask drop, because all she felt then was anticipation and pleasure, and those were feelings she had no problem sharing.

Evie had once asked her how she maintained what they considered an exhausting schedule with her mates. Lauren and Asterius had an active love life, but even they took days off, and Evie had to set boundaries with Doshakeren, because he could mate almost constantly if she was so inclined, and Gray wasn't in the settlement that often, so she didn't have as much time with him as she wanted. Yet, both women insisted that Alice making love to one of her mates every single night was impressive.

Alice didn't feel exhausted by it at all, and had to admit,

there were nights they had to forgo sex because it was her time of month, or both her mates were too worn out from whatever rotation duty they'd been on that day, though they often still did intimate things together.

There were days where she wished she could be with them both together on one night, then take the next off, as Evie would do whenever Gray was available, but those days were rare. She was usually more than ready to have her mates all to herself in the evening, fresh energy filling her as she anticipated the night ahead.

Iyaren didn't disappoint either. After tucking Friak into bed and bidding Tak farewell for the night, they retired to her room, which was the biggest, simply because they spent most of their time there and both of her mates would sleep in the bed with her after her lovemaking with either one of them ended.

Iyaren liked to take control when it came to slowly stripping off her clothes, licking every inch of skin he revealed, which made it very interesting when he reached her panties. He steadied her with his lower hands on her calves, forcing her to stay on her feet despite the onslaught of his tongue against her sensitive clit. His upper hands kneaded her buttocks, gripping the full flesh and squeezing as if it was he who needed something to hold onto, even though his tongue was doing such wonderful things to her body.

He wouldn't release her until she was shuddering in climax and only then did he rise to his feet to sweep her up as her body collapsed in release, carrying her to the bed as if she weighed nothing to him. She'd never get over how strong both he and Tak were, and couldn't imagine a normal human man hefting her weight as if it was no real effort, the way her mates did.

They made her feel petite and fragile, and that wasn't something she was accustomed to feeling before she met them.

Once he had her on the bed, his lower hands curved

around her calves, gripping her to spread her legs apart so he could look upon her naked body with a predatory amber gaze, his eyes intent on her slick opening as his large tongue licked his lips.

He was not one to hurry this part, loving the foreplay as much as she did, if not more. He also loved the fact that he could hold her with all four of his hands, the lower ones being considered forbidden to use on females in his own culture because it was too dominating. Since Alice loved having him dominate her in the bedroom, she insisted he use all four hands, and he was eager to comply.

His tongue found her slit, delving into her damp heat with growls of pleasure rising from his deep chest as he pulled her legs over his heavily muscled shoulders. She writhed beneath the firm grip his upper hands had on her hips, as his tongue pushed deeper and deeper. Her legs tightened on his shoulders, pushing him even deeper still as his thick mane tickled her calves.

One lower hand found her clit, rubbing it in slow circles to intensify her pleasure as he thrust his tongue inside her, bringing her to another climax so he could feel her come, then lap at the nectar of it before finally releasing her.

As he sat back on his heels, his naked body glorious as perfectly proportioned, heavy muscle shifted beneath tawny fur, Alice eyed him as hungrily as he was watching her. She could stare at her mates all day, still in awe that creatures so gorgeous would want her as badly as they did, enough that they came to her every other night with eagerness in their touch. It made her feel like a goddess sometimes.

Like now, when Iyaren's powerful muscles trembled with the strain of not moving as she ran her hands over them, stroking his fur with a low moan. So much warmth flowed from his body, and he smelled incredible, the scent of soap from his bath still strong in his mane, which was damp from it. His own unique scent lay beneath that clean scent, and it was enough all on its own to make her eager for him.

Her fingers dived into his mane, tugging on the locks there, running her fingers over the small braids she wove into his hair to represent the four of them in their family. She kissed his lips, tasting herself on him as he met her tongue with his own.

Iyaren deepened their kiss, at the same time shifting their bodies so he could settle his hips between her thighs.

"I want to take you in my mouth, first," she whispered as he lifted his head.

He grunted, a small twitch of his lips the only sign of his amusement. "Not tonight, beloved. Just the taste of you has brought me to the brink. If you taste me in return, I won't last long enough to bury myself inside you."

And that was where Iyaren ultimately wanted to be. As much as he loved foreplay and oral sex, the simple act of sinking his thick, bumpy length inside her warm, wet sheath was his favorite part of making love. He'd told her he would never get enough of that moment when her body was gripping him completely, pressing against every sensitive bump that concealed his barbs until he ejaculated.

He hadn't been exaggerating when he said he was close, and it wasn't long before his gentle thrusts turned to frantic pounding as one lower hand found her clit, while another gripped her thigh, and the other two hands played with her nipples.

Alice's hands were gripping tightly to his upper arms, her fingernails digging into his fur as she cried out in passion while his fingers rubbed her nub. His thick length thrusted inside her until she arched in another powerful orgasm. His own climax followed soon after, as her muscles clenched to milk him.

She was no longer surprised by the brief sting of his barbs sinking into her highly sensitive inner flesh, though the continuing contractions of her inner muscles pulled on them enough to make it uncomfortable at times, but she'd grown accustomed to it, and now even found an odd sort of pleasure in that burn of pain. It seemed to intensify the contractions of her passage as Iyaren groaned, holding her still, his teeth at her neck in a gentle bite that reminded her to remain as still as possible until the barbs retracted.

It was in these moments when they could not immediately draw apart and Iyaren had to remain still buried inside her that they had the deepest sense of connection.

She felt like she was a part of him, and he was a part of her. Nothing made her want to simply pour out all her pain more than the comfort of his embrace in those moments.

And yet, she kept her silence, biting her lip and blinking back the tears that rose to her eyes at the thought of his sadness. He had been as grief-stricken as she and Tak had been when they'd learned that the pregnancy—in the second trimester—was ending, and that all the blood between her legs was the sign that she was going through a miscarriage.

They'd all dealt with the loss in their own way.

Tak had held Friak close to him whenever he had the chance, always reluctant to let go of his son for even a moment, as if he feared he would lose that child too. It had taken many months for Alice to convince him that Friak was safe and healthy and didn't need to be constantly held to keep him that way.

Iyaren had disappeared for hours on end, only to be found in the training yard, working through all his katas and forms until he could barely move, yet, despite swaying on his feet in exhaustion, he had to be dragged away in order to eat and sleep, his fur growing dirty and his mane ragged and lank until Alice had forced him into the tub with harsh words and threats she would never have followed through on.

As she'd bathed him for the first time in weeks, he'd broken down, confessing that he felt like he'd lost a part of his soul.

She'd never seen him suffer so much despair. Not even when they'd had to leave their home behind to come here to New Omni.

In all those months, Alice had dealt with the physical and mental effects of the miscarriage in silence. After witnessing the grief of her mates, she would have done anything not to prolong it, so she'd kept her own grief to herself, pulling her family together so they could find happiness again.

She'd even hidden away when it was time to pass the baby, feeling the contractions coming with the aching cramps in her abdomen. She'd made a quick excuse to her family, then had gone into one of the still unfinished apartments, finding the bathroom, which had been empty of all but a couple of work buckets. She'd barred the door, shutting herself away.

It was Gray who later found her, holding the tiny curled, shell-like body of the baby that would never take a breath in the palm of her hand, her blood coating her thighs and staining the floor beneath her as she sat propped against the tiled wall, staring down at hopes and dreams that would never be realized —and a love that would never be returned. The echo of a heartbeat found not so long ago and then lost had seemed to fill that bathroom, deafening her for only a moment, before the silence hurt enough that she wondered why her ears didn't bleed.

Gray had seen to it that she was cleaned up and her baby carefully wrapped away in a tiny box. He'd been the one to teleport them to the ancilla forest, where he'd helped her bury the box at the base of the ancilla mother tree, which thanked them for their sacrifice and shared her compassion and sympathy with them, even wrapping Alice in her branches while she'd sobbed.

Her brother-in-law hadn't called for anyone else to join them in that sad little ceremony. Not her mates, not her sister, nor her best friend, nor any of their mates. He had known she needed to do this alone.

He hadn't been happy about it, or about the fact that she wouldn't allow him to blunt any of her emotional pain using his telempathy, but he'd followed her wishes, being the only one to witness her pain and grief. She had to protect her mates. She had to protect her family.

She had to remain strong for them.

16

Iyaren had been so close to telling Alice about Kisk and his offer the night before, while he'd held her close in his arms after his barbs had retracted, and the warm, bonded feelings of their love-making were still upon them. But he'd held off, not having had the chance to evaluate Kisk for himself yet, since he still needed to fight him in the arena and defeat him. So far, his schedule and Kisk's were not working in his favor, as Kisk was always on a roster when Iyaren was off, and vice versa.

Iyaren had the added complication that he needed to keep his plans hidden from Alice, because she hated the gladiator pit and would be extremely upset if he told her he was planning on competing there.

He hated lying to her, but he didn't see any other way to protect her. He needed to know that Kisk could be trusted before he gave Alice false hope, and Tak's discussions with him had not been enough to convince Iyaren. They needed to have a discussion of their own.

After he'd shown Kisk that he was a more than capable opponent in battle.

The shadow of ancilla branches passed overhead, casting sudden shade over the board he had paused in the middle of cutting while he thought about contacting Kisk directly to arrange a battle.

Iyaren looked up at the ancilla saplings rapidly twining their branches, energy arcing between them.

Out of the corner of his eye, he saw the other males working construction detail on the edge of the settlement stop their work and begin stowing their tools. He straightened and carried the saw he'd been using over to the toolshed, turning it in to the supply master, who was watching the ancilla branches block out the sky above them.

"I wonder who's out on patrol" the supply master said to another male turning in tools, scratching his chins with one long, curved claw.

Iyaren didn't wait around for the answer, having already memorized this week's roster. No one he knew personally was tasked with duties that took them into the Fall, thank the goddess. Of course, Gray might still be out there, somewhere— or he might be deep underground, or within the confines of his space vessel, or even standing right behind Iyaren.

With that particular male, it was hard to know where he'd be at any moment. All the other mates should be safe within the ancilla's shield.

He wasn't too worried about Gray, since he had no doubt the male—wherever he was—would weather this incident as he did every other—without any sign that it fazed him.

The alarms on the posts throughout New Omni went off a few minutes later as the males filed back into the older part of the settlement where the ancilla were more mature and the shields stronger, heading towards the reinforced underground shelters they'd built for Nexus openings.

Despite the blaring sound of the alarm, the mood was casual, since this happened several times a week—sometimes even multiple times in one day. There had also been months that went by without a single incident.

They knew what to expect. Those in most danger were the ones on patrol, and each patrol had a route that took them close to an underground bolt-hole that was reinforced like the settlement's shelters. They should have time to get to a safe place before the Nexus opened, with Gray's early-warning alerts that were hooked into the ancilla's sensory branches and roots.

The opening of the portal, which had once been so dangerous, was now mostly a nuisance, though Iyaren was under no illusions that it would remain that way. From what he knew of NEX, he feared the strange intelligence was only biding its time.

The stoppage of work was a distraction from his thoughts, but not much of one. It did allow him an opportunity though, as he spotted Kisk standing alone in the corner of the shelter when he made his way down the stone steps. The chimera looked less unkempt than usual, and Iyaren narrowed his eyes when he noticed the tunic and trousers the other male wore.

He'd seen Alice sewing them for the "care packages" she'd then asked to be sent to the unmated males. It would seem Kisk had been the recipient of one, and the clothing—in a very finely woven fabric—looked like it fit him perfectly. Iyaren struggled with a moment of jealousy before dismissing it, realizing that Alice's charitable spirit would benefit many males on this side of the fence, and he couldn't afford to feel the desire to punch them every time he saw them wearing clothes that had been sewn by his beloved's hand.

He would never act on that desire. He was a highly disciplined warrior, trained in a restrictive code of honor. He'd just have to content himself with pummeling Kisk into the ground in the arena instead.

Honorably, of course.

Kisk pretended not to notice Iyaren approaching, but he could see the tension in the other male and the ruffling of his feathers as he entered the pocket of space around Kisk that no one else seemed to want to occupy.

With arms crossed and staring straight ahead, Kisk gave no indication he noticed Iyaren standing there, even after Iyaren paused directly in front of him and crossed his upper arms over his chest, just as Kisk's arms were crossed.

Now that he stood closer to the other male, he saw that much had changed about him. His leaner frame had filled out, as if he were eating more regular meals that softened the hollows in his cheeks, and his new clothes were spotless, which wasn't surprising, since he couldn't have had them long. There was no dirt or grime on him at all, and Iyaren wondered what Kisk did in his days off to keep his clothing so clean.

For a moment, as the other male's eyes shifted to gold from the gray they had been as he'd walked up, Iyaren recognized him.

Well, not Kisk himself, but he saw the echo of someone he used to know in Kisk's face. The shape of it reminded him of a friend from the temple, when they were both still young and barely had manes to speak of—mere little tufts of hair atop their heads. They'd been bunkmates, doing everything together, but Nerias had gone rogue before his mane even filled out, unable to endure the endless orders and worship and training of the temple—and even more unwilling to forever bind himself to a priestess.

They'd made Iyaren and the rest of his class hunt Nerias down as part of their training. For many days, they tracked him through the desert, knowing no other pride would shelter him as an uncastrated teenage male. They'd finally cornered him at an oasis, surrounding him while he slept. When he'd awakened to see them, he'd leapt up as if to fight them, all four hands holding the swords he'd stolen from the temple.

But instead of attacking them, he'd met Iyaren's eyes, sighed, and lowered his head. "They would send you, wouldn't they? It had to be you, I guess. That makes my decision easier."

"Come back peacefully, Nerias," Iyaren had pleaded, hoping to spare his friend a certain death.

Nerias had huffed, his face long and lean, and so much like Kisk's that the resemblance was uncanny. Then he'd said, "Come back to what? Castration and eternal penance to a goddess that cares nothing about us?"

And then he'd turned his swords on himself and slit his own throat before Iyaren realized what he'd intended. Nerias had died in his arms, pronouncing that he was free through a blood-choked throat, while all the members of their class looked on in silence.

Now, Kisk reminded him of that young rogue, wanting freedom more than anything else. The freedom to choose his own path, rather than have one thrust upon him by an uncaring goddess.

The sound of boot leather scraping on the dirt floor of the shelter brought Iyaren's focus out of the past and back to the male in front of him, who was perhaps not exactly like Nerias in the face, his being a bit longer, his nose more pronounced, his white chin squarer.

Yet the expression on his face—the defiance in the set of his features—that had been how Nerias had looked every single day before he'd run away from the temple.

Kisk shifted his weight from foot to foot, his gaze darting from some place over Iyaren's shoulder to Iyaren's face, then back, as if he wanted to ignore him, but couldn't avoid looking at the warrior who was taller and broader than him, though Iyaren didn't count on his physical size to be enough to win the battle against the fire-breathing chimera.

"I want to challenge you in the arena."

Kisk's gaze stopped darting back and forth and fixed on

Iyaren as he huffed with surprise. "Your female forbids you from fighting a true battle in the arena."

Iyaren was surprised at Kisk's tone when he said this. He'd expected it to be condescending and mocking. Instead, it was made as a statement of fact without any undertone, offensive or otherwise.

The reason Iyaren never fought any males in a blood match was no secret in the unmated male section of the settlement. Most males had enough hope for a female of their own that they didn't judge Iyaren for putting her wishes above any desire he might have to fight a bloody battle in the pit.

Some males simply didn't understand how a woman's word alone could hold a male back from doing whatever he wanted, and Iyaren knew those males were never likely to find a mate unless they changed.

Iyaren would have put Kisk in that second category, yet the male appeared to already be changing in some ways.

"I'm making an exception in this case. I want to challenge you to battle."

Kisk eyed him now with a more calculating look, sizing him up and debating the threat he posed. "What level?"

Iyaren raised the whiskers above his eyes. "Does it matter? Are you not *the* chimera? Are you not superior to all others?"

Kisk's lower jaw shifted as he ground his teeth in irritation. "I never said *I* was superior to all. It's my purpose to test all warriors to find those superior to me."

Iyaren leaned closer to the other male, looking down into his eyes with an aggressive stare. "Then test me, if you've the courage for it. Master level. It should be nothing for a warrior of your experience and caliber."

Kisk didn't break the stare, though his eyes shifted from golden back to gray, then briefly to reptilian, before returning to gray, which Iyaren suspected was his default color—the mask he wore the most to hide his true emotions from those around him.

"Why not Elimination Level?" he said, his growl mocking.

Iyaren chuckled at this obvious posturing. "Battle to the death is forbidden in New Omni—"

Kisk gestured to the root-bound roof of the shelter. "Then we go into the Fall to fight instead."

Iyaren narrowed his eyes in an angry glare, still not breaking eye contact. "You push too far, boy. It's not your death I seek. Nor will I ever let you hand me mine."

"I am ten thousand years old, cretin," Kisk snarled, his yellowed teeth bared with his fury as he lunged at Iyaren.

With an easy side-step and a few swift, open-handed strikes and a hold, Iyaren forced Kisk to his knees to avoid having his arm broken by Iyaren. Blood dripped from Kisk's nose as he glared up at Iyaren over his shoulder, which Iyaren was close to twisting right out of its socket.

"You *are* still a boy," Iyaren said in a low, calm tone as he met the angry glare. "It is not the years that make you an adult, but the wisdom you earn through experience."

He tightened his hold, turning it further so Kisk made a low groan in his throat, struggling to conceal the amount of pain he was in as his shoulder was extended too far even on his knees. He needed to lie on his stomach to ease the pressure, but he would not submit that far.

"I defeated you in seconds, *warrior*," Iyaren said the word with skepticism. "You throw yourself into a fight as if you're invincible, but I can see for myself that you bleed and feel pain. Who trained you?"

"I needed no training," Kisk said through gritted teeth. "I am *the* chimera. I was *born* to battle."

Iyaren shook his head and eased up the pressure on Kisk's arm, allowing him to relax just a bit. He believed he'd made his point, and it would be nothing but petty to force the respected gladiator to lie on his stomach and completely prostrate himself in front of all these watching males who had become their fascinated audience.

Crouching down while maintaining his hold, Iyaren kept his voice low, though he knew some males in the shelter would be able to hear it anyway, even if it was nothing but a mere whisper of sound. "Do you really need me to meet you in the pit, chimera? Or would you prefer to learn from a true master how to fight, instead?"

The chimera was silent for a long time, fuming as he shot a glare at every male daring to look their way, while he was forced to remain on his knees.

Finally, he turned his glare back on Iyaren. "Call me Kisk."

Iyaren nodded, keeping his expression solemn, though he felt pleased at the chimera's capitulation. He released the hold and stepped back, allowing Kisk to rise to his feet and rub the hand and wrist Iyaren had twisted so firmly. Then he moved on to his shoulder, his eyes focusing on everything but Iyaren.

Kisk growled a few times as he spotted males in the crowd staring at him with delighted expressions—at least, Iyaren assumed their faces were amused. On some, it was difficult to tell.

When the chimera sucked in a deep breath and his chest expanded as one male began to chuckle in a warbling, cackling, snorting sound, Iyaren clapped Kisk on the shoulder, distracting him from the other male, while at the same time pinning the creature with his own gaze.

"Fire should only be a last resort. If you learn from me, you will never need it again to earn the respect of others."

He released Kisk, who deflated, shooting Iyaren another toothy snarl. Then Iyaren took a step towards the warbling male, who immediately stopped making that sound and lowered his head, backing away from Iyaren.

"No harm meant," the male muttered, throwing his paws up in supplication.

"No harm taken, friend," Iyaren said with a meaningful glance at Kisk. "Our words alone must not bring us to battle. It is acceptable for a cub to lash out when he is angry, because his small body does little harm, but adults must learn that violence is only our last resort, when there is no other option left to us. This is our community, and we must protect it not just from NEX, but from ourselves." He looked out over the crowd of unmated males, now all watching him and the drama playing out before them as they waited for the sensors to tell them they could return to their work on the surface. "We must all learn this, in order to become a complete community—one where the fence doesn't separate us."

This brought mutters and growls and hisses and many other sounds that would be alarming if Iyaren wasn't already familiar with the tone of them. The males were listening, and even agreeing with what he had to say. Like the females on the other side of the fence, they were tired of the separation. Tired of trying to woo females through the slats, or through often invasive and embarrassing personal questions to set them up with chaperoned meetings under the watchful eyes of guards.

Change was coming to New Omni, or perhaps it was more accurate to say New Omni *was* change, as constantly in flux as the shadows of the future that only Gray could see.

Iyaren returned his attention to the chimera—a catalyst of change if ever there was one. "Kisk?"

He gained the focus of gray eyes as Kisk regarded him without verbal response.

"When is your next day off?"

Kisk looked blank for a moment, then his eyes shifted to gold, then back to gray. "Two days from now."

Iyaren would request a roster change for that same day. He suspected at least someone he knew would trade with him.

"Then two days from now, we train. Meet me in the training yard before the sun breaks."

Kisk's response was cut off by the sound of the bell and the rattle of the opening shelter door letting them know the Nexus had closed, all was well in New Omni, and they were free to return to the surface.

17

Kisk wandered the market stalls, not really seeing anything around him because he was more focused on his falcon, who'd taken off to seek out Alice the moment he returned to the surface.

It wasn't that he wanted to check on her to make sure she was safe. At least, that was what he told himself. He was spying, that was all. Tak had told him he had to learn respect for Alice and that was what he was trying to do. That was all.

It had nothing to do with the anxiety that plagued him every time the alarms went off and he didn't know where she was and whether she was protected enough.

He didn't relax until his falcon spotted Alice, exiting another underground bunker on the other side of the fence, carrying her son close to her chest.

The boy looked up and pointed as Kisk winged closer.

Alice also looked up, shading her eyes, and his chest tightened in an odd way when he saw the pale moon of her face, her eyes hidden in the shadow of her hand. Her smile wasn't hidden.

She lifted her hand in a wave, wincing as the full light of the sun hit her eyes.

His falcon sliver did a few aerial dips and dives that appeared to delight the child, who was clapping his little scaled hands and whooping. Then Kisk turned his wings to head out into the Fall, needing to scout for his own sake what new changes might have come with the latest Nexus opening.

He heard both Alice and her son bid him a farewell, the boy sounding disappointed as he cried out, "buh-bye, birdie!"

Once he was over the Fall, Kisk left his falcon to its own instincts, knowing he would receive its memories when the sliver rejoined his body and he could process those images when he was back in his apartment—a place he was trying to make nicer, though he acknowledged that he lacked the skill at it.

It smelled a bit better, now that he'd thrown out the old food and waste and cleaned the mold off the walls and floors with the solution Alice had sent him in a "care package."

He tried not to read too much into the large package Asterius had tossed at him as he'd pulled a heavy wagon past his apartment building, because the minotaur had gifted several other males in the complex similar packages, all of them filled with some articles of clothing, canned food, scented soaps and creams, and clearly marked cleansers for the home.

He'd once worn the finest raiment to be found in his world —cloth woven of actual gold, beaten and stretched into fine, glimmering threads that were used to embroider elaborate designs into the silken fabric of his robes. And his armor had been the stuff of legends, created by ancient masters and enchanted by sorcerers.

He'd left all those possessions behind in the temple, and if they still remained where he'd abandoned it in the Fall, it was likely those things had been scavenged by something by now.

When he'd decided to leave behind the only home he'd

ever known, he'd abandoned everything that went with it—walking out into the Dead Fall completely naked.

Of course, he'd very quickly realized his folly and had scavenged some clothes from the ruins, but he hadn't returned for anything he'd left behind. He was afraid if he went back, he'd be trapped in there again. In fact, the mere thought of returning made him tense, anxious.

There had been new clothes in the care package, and he'd smelled Alice on them, letting him know that she had been the one who'd crafted them. It had been her hands sewing the neat little stitches that were invisible from the outside of the garments. She'd been the one to cut out the material and design it to fit him.

He wasn't sure why she would do such a thing. The only reason anyone had ever given him a gift before had been a tribute to the temple rather than something meant personally for him.

He was wearing those clothes now, though he'd debated keeping them forever in their wrappings so her scent remained the strongest on them. Now, they were beginning to smell too much of him and not enough of her, but the way their scents mingled in the fabric was something else that he enjoyed, even more than the perfect fit of the garments and the luxurious softness of the fabric they were made from.

They were his "off-day" clothes, because he thought that was the day he'd be most likely to encounter Alice, though he never quite worked up the nerve to try to enter the ancilla forest from this side of the fence and make his way to her side. He wasn't sure if the ancilla would sense the change in his purpose or not, but it wasn't a concern that they'd keep him out that gave him pause.

She didn't like him—the way he looked, the way he smelled, the way he spoke—none of that pleased her. She'd used her beautiful voice to bind him, but she wasn't interested in keeping him, yet every time his serpent sliver went along on her forest walks, she bound him to her again, and he couldn't resist allowing some part of him to spend time with her.

"Kisk," a voice said from between two stalls that had fabric draping three of their sides to make shaded tents of their stands.

Very few people had been given leave to call him that, and they were all people he would pause to speak to, so he turned and noted the male who'd addressed him.

"Veraza," he said, by way of greeting the other male, noting that his feathers were ruffled over a broad chest heavy with muscles that would never work wings again.

"I would speak with you, chimera." Veraza gestured for Kisk to follow him to a more private area of the market.

Kisk's nose wrinkled when he saw where they were heading. "I don't smoke coil-leaf, and I don't like the scent of that den," he protested when Veraza stopped at a curtain to a huge, fabric-covered tent.

Veraza's hard beak clacked as his round, black eyes regarded Kisk with an angry gleam. "We must speak in private. The leaf-den is quiet at this time of day." He jerked his head towards the market. "While all the slaves are working."

Kisk's lips lifted in a low snarl, disliking Veraza's appraisal of their circumstances. All the males were paid a stipend to be on the duty roster. Additional tokens could be earned for volunteering for additional or more difficult, skilled, or dangerous tasks. That was simply the way of New Omni, and it worked very well for most males, though some—like Veraza—resented the strict rules of the settlement.

But Veraza resented a great many things.

Still, Kisk felt the other male had proven himself worthy of the chimera's respect, and therefore, he intended to hear him out, even if he found the Veraza far less interesting in his seething anger than the other males who had defeated him.

That made him think of Iyaren and how easily the Clawed One had brought him to his knees, moving so fast Kisk was down before he even registered that Iyaren had hit him. That kind of speed and skill awed him, and he'd faced many trained warriors in his lifetime—so many he'd lost count.

He'd never faced one who'd moved like Iyaren.

The offer to train Kisk was an honor the Clawed One bestowed on no one else, except perhaps his own loved ones.

It felt odd to Kisk to be included in that honor. He hadn't even known what to say when the offer had been made, so stunned by the very suggestion that the master swordsman would train him.

He, who was supposed to be a warrior-born. Did he not already know what he needed to know? Had he not survived countless, endless battles?

Not unscathed. And there had been too many he hadn't survived. That was not something he could afford in the Dead Fall, as the temple wouldn't revive him if he was beyond its boundaries, and he'd never learned to fight in a way that didn't often leave him wounded.

Deep in thought about the day's strange turn of events, he followed Veraza through the curtain without another protest, wrinkling his nose at the cloying scent of stale coil-leaf smoke, which altered the minds of some of the residents like a drug, while others simply found the experience of smoking it relaxing. Some of the patrons took advantage of the uninhibited atmosphere for more social pursuits.

That last was obvious as they passed a shrouded booth where two males were locked in an embrace, each attempting to mate in an awkward way with another unfamiliar body that still seemed to bring them both pleasure—if the grunting and soft hooting were anything to go by.

Veraza took no note of the other patrons of the den, and that made Kisk hope that he wasn't interested in the same type

of activity. Kisk felt no interest in Veraza in that way, and didn't
believe he would for another male, though he'd heard many of
them tell the tale of feeling the same way, once. Before they'd
accepted that they'd never again have a chance with a female of
their own species. Some said if the body was alien anyway,
what difference did it make?

Kisk was born for one purpose, and the only reason he
mated was to catalyze the change of other males' seed in a
female's womb. Without a crucible, there was no point in him
growing aroused.

The pleasure of mating hadn't been anything he would
pursue outside of his purpose, and his shaft rarely hardened
anymore—at least, it hadn't until lately, when even the thought
of Alice made it stiff more often than not.

He'd never experienced much satisfaction, even buried
inside a female with his catalyst pumping into her crucible—
although the non-violent physical contact with the females
he'd mated had been a guilty pleasure he'd kept to himself.

He followed Veraza to the farthest end of the tent, noting
the shrouded alcoves back there were all empty. Somewhere in
the center of the tent, someone drummed on a hide stretched
over a barrel to drown out the sounds from other patrons. He
assumed that it was to conceal whatever they were saying or
doing from others.

The birdman folded his talons beneath him on the
ragged, stained cushion that covered the floor, settling his
feathered thighs on top of the scaled skin of his lower legs.
Once seated, his feathers smoothed until his puffed-up body
once again looked sleek with glossy feathers and large, dense
muscles that had once allowed him to soar the skies like
Kisk's falcon.

Veraza cocked his head as he watched Kisk take a seat on
the cushion across from him. He lifted a feathered arm with a
scaled hand that was much like his claw-toed talons to wave

away the proprietor who brought by a tray of dried coil-leaf and a selection of pipes.

"Just stone-mold ferment for myself," he said, then gestured at Kisk with his other hand, "and whatever my friend is having."

Kisk raised his whiskers at that, not recalling any time when someone had called him a friend without it being insulting—other than Alice, but she'd been speaking to his serpent, not to him.

When the proprietor looked his way, he ordered the same drink Veraza had, having no experience whatsoever with fermented drinks. He largely stuck with water, though occasionally treated himself to the fresh juice from the ancilla fruits, which the trees awarded to those who tended their grove.

The proprietor bobbed one head in a bow while a second head turned on the shared neck to squawk over his shoulder to someone in the smoke-filled, shadowy tent.

He then bowed both heads, saying many thanks when Veraza dropped a couple of tokens onto his tray. Veraza held up his other hand in a staying motion when Kisk reached for his own pouch.

"My treat," he said, returning his dark-eyed gaze to Kisk. "After all, it isn't often that someone becomes a friend of the chimera." He trilled in amusement as Kisk narrowed his eyes. "It's a call for a celebration."

"What do you really want, Veraza?" Kisk said, folding his arms over his chest, suspicious as he eyed their surroundings, searching for potential exits.

"*The* Veraza, actually," the birdman said with the same amusement in his tone. "It's a title, as I'm sure you understand. My name? Well, that's been forgotten, because what use are such things when your title is enough on its own?"

Curiosity won out over his suspicion and Kisk decided to encourage further conversation, rather than rise to his feet and leave, as he'd been debating doing. "And what is your title enough for? Striking fear into the hearts of your enemies?"

Veraza waved his hand. "Nothing so dramatic, I'm afraid. My title identified me as the shaman of the flock—the mortal link to our gods, who flew so high they were captured in the net of stars above our world, where they whispered the secrets of the universe back to the Veraza. I used those secrets to guide my people." He fluffed his feathers. "I'm no warrior, Kisk. I did not have enemies before I came to this world."

Kisk snorted in disbelief. "Everyone has enemies." He glanced down at the talons that served as Veraza's fingers, which were curled on his knees. "And you are equipped to deal with them."

Veraza clacked his curved beak, which was shaped much like Kisk's falcon's beak. "Ah... you see everyone as a warrior or a victim. There are those who are equipped with both brains and brawn, so they might become something that is neither."

The proprietor returned with a tray heavy with two wooden mugs. Veraza picked up both of them and handed one to Kisk, who eyed it skeptically, his nostrils flaring at the sharp, rotten scent of the liquid.

"Try it, my friend. It doesn't taste as bad as it smells." Veraza stuck his beak into the mug, his tongue lapping at the liquid.

Kisk raised the mug to his mouth and took a cautious sip.

He shuddered at the bitter taste of it, but didn't want to appear as if he couldn't handle the bite of such a foul brew. Despite what Veraza might say, or what life he might have lived before, he judged—as all males judged in this world. Any sign of weakness or hesitation was noted and kept in mind.

With a grimace, Kisk tossed back the contents of the mug, swallowing as quickly as possible to avoid tasting it, though the foul brew coated his tongue. When he lowered the mug, he saw that Veraza stared at him, his own mug held in talons that had gone slack with surprise.

"You are braver than I! Small sips are all I can handle at one time." Veraza trilled, then squawked with a brief sound of what Kisk strongly suspected was his version of a full-belly laugh, his feather crest puffing out around his head with his amusement.

Kisk felt the burn of the brew in his throat and stomach, which he had failed to fill with food earlier, so now all that weighed it down was the fermented stone-mold. He knew he'd be sick later. He just wondered if he'd make it out of this place and back to his apartment before that. "Now that we've played your little social game, what did you want, birdman?"

Veraza's talons tightened around the mug for a brief moment. "A bit of a snap returns to your words, Kisk. I suppose good manners are difficult for one such as you to maintain. Those of us who don't crave battle have learned to survive by getting along with others."

Kisk was losing his patience, and he didn't particularly like the censure in Veraza's tone. He leaned forward, propping his hands on his crossed legs, feeling a bit of unsteadiness and lightheadedness at the small movement.

"Don't pretend you aren't a bird of prey, Veraza. You sit here without your wings because you picked a fight with a warrior you couldn't defeat—even you don't deny this."

Long claws dug into the wood of Veraza's mug, creating holes that leaked beads of the ferment. "That same warrior just humiliated you in front of everyone. What will you do when all those males who have lost respect for you come at you from the darkness? Do you think you can take them all down alone?"

Kisk shrugged. "Unprovoked attack ish forbidden. They'll learn to respect me again in the pitsh."

His tongue felt oddly swollen. It didn't seem to work right, and now the Veraza was peeling into two indistinct forms.

"Or, there are other options to earn back their respect." Veraza put a steadying hand on Kisk's shoulder as he slumped forward.

"Listen to me," he hissed. "The only way to earn back what was taken from you is to bring the Clawed One to his knees. Humiliate him, degrade him, and then take that which is most important to him. Only then can you have vengeance for what he's done to you."

Kisk shook his head, his own feathers fluffing as he rubbed his eyes. "Did you poison me?"

Veraza squawked with indignation. "Don't be ridiculous. I have no quarrel with you, foolish creature. You're intoxicated. The ferment is a strong one, and it looks as if you aren't accustomed to such drinks."

"Ah, I shee." Kisk rubbed his forehead hard, though his hand felt numb and tingly. It didn't seem to help clear up his vision. "How long does thish last?"

Veraza made an impatient sound halfway between a whistling trill and an angry shriek. "You'll probably have to sleep it off. But before you pass out, listen to my words. The Clawed One has invited you to train with him, but only because he thinks you are inferior. Find a way to use his own training against him, then defeat him."

Kisk struggled to focus as he stared at Veraza. He knew the story. Iyaren had defeated Veraza when the birdman had flown into his compound and challenged him for it, wanting access to the clean water. Kisk suspected there was something more to his obsession with that place, which he'd lost yet again when the meteor had struck.

Instead of killing Veraza once he'd been defeated, Iyaren had torn off his wings. They'd been broken in the battle, and probably wouldn't have healed properly anyway, but that wasn't a distinction Veraza ever made in his hatred for Iyaren.

"Why don't *you* defeat him?" he asked of the birdman, knowing the answer.

The Veraza probably wouldn't have been able to even

defeat Kisk in the pits if he wasn't so filled with rage and Kisk hadn't been distracted.

Veraza didn't bother to reply to that, at least not at first.

When he finally spoke after a long pause for a sip of his drink, his tone was thoughtful. "I would, were it in my power. I would do anything to have the strength to destroy him—as he has destroyed me."

"You want me to carry out your vengeance for you? Why would I be sho sssstupid?"

Veraza chuckled. "Is there nothing you'd like of his? Not a single thing you would take from him if you could? I think you know what... or shall I saw who... I'm talking about."

———

A POUNDING headache dragged Kisk from his straw pallet to the bucket of water that sat next to his sleeping corner. He practically drowned himself sticking his entire head in the bucket to lap up as much water as he could to ease the parched feeling of his throat and try to wash away the sickening taste on his tongue.

As soon as the water hit his stomach, it heaved with rejection, and he had to crawl to the other side of his room on hands and knees to the waste bucket, barely making it before the meager contents of his stomach were forced up into his throat and then into the bucket, which was thankfully empty at the moment.

He alternated drinking water with heaving it up several more times before he was able to keep it down, though none of that helped his aching head. When he was able to think straight, he considered the fact that he'd somehow made it back to his apartment and barred the door from any intrepid males who were stupid enough to break one of New Omni's laws for Kisk's meager possessions.

On the one shelf where he stored what little food he kept in the apartment sat a couple of odd, hard, bread-like squares wrapped in a noisy, crinkly material some males called "plastic" that he'd bought from a food stall on a whim.

They tasted sweet, if a bit stale, and he liked the crunch of them, but at the moment he was more concerned with the fact that out of the sparse collection of stored foodstuffs, they seemed the least likely to end up making him even sicker.

He selected two of the five he had remaining, knowing it wasn't likely there would be a new supply of them, though there were males in the settlement attempting to recreate many of the foods that were found by scavenging patrols. It was a pity he'd have to waste the sweet, hard-bread on a sour stomach like his, but stumbled back to his mat and sat down slowly, hoping to avoid any more insult to his aching stomach or head.

He pondered the Veraza's words as he chewed the food, washing down each dry bite with lapped-up water from the ladle he lifted out of his water bucket.

The Veraza somehow knew about Alice, but he was still ignorant about Kisk. He thought Kisk wanted Alice as a mate, but Kisk had no such inclinations.

What good would she do for him? Even if it made him happy to hear her voice and see her face, regardless of whether it wore a bright smile or an annoyed scowl, he had no use for a female like Alice.

He had no need of a mate at all, and besides, he couldn't give Alice what she wanted most. Not without the help of other males. He could never be the father she wanted for her children, nor the family she seemed to crave. He had no experience with such things. All he knew how to do was test people by fighting them.

Her current mates served her well in their roles, although he wondered why they were so blind to her misery—a sadness she only seemed to share with him. Perhaps it was because of the spell she held over them. Maybe it made them blind to her true feelings, but it didn't have the same effect on him, and he wondered if it was because she didn't care about hurting him, when she did care about hurting her mates.

She didn't have the power to hurt him anyway. There was a limit to her control over him, even if he did make it a point to find her with one of his slivers every day.

Even as he thought this, he surged to his feet, then moaned in pain, grabbing his head as it felt on the verge of splitting open. Rubbing the skin around his horns to help soothe the pain, he made his way to the door and unbarred it to look outside at the sky overhead.

It seemed he'd slept through the night and late into the morning. He had duties that day, but they wouldn't begin until the afternoon, so he still had time to rest and recover from his unfortunate choice to binge a fermented drink. He could take this time to sleep off the remaining hangover, relaxing fully.

He sighed, lowering his arms from his head, then crouched down so the little serpent that materialized as the scales on his legs drew together could crawl down to the stone that marked his threshold.

As the serpent slithered away from him—fur sprouting from his bare legs to replace the lost scales—he closed the door in its wake and returned to the mat. He wouldn't be sleeping, though he could allow his sliver to act autonomously, as he often did with his falcon.

He didn't want to though. He wanted more than just the memory of Alice's interactions with that part of him. He wanted to be there with her and watch her through the eyes of his serpent.

He wouldn't miss their daily walk, not even to rest his aching head.

18

E very day for nearly a month, Alice made it a point to take a walk in the forest during her lunch break, politely declining whenever anyone asked if she'd like them to join her. Every one of those days, the little serpent was there waiting for her, and would take on whatever color she wore for its scales, no matter how crazy the color scheme. It would even take on patterns, and she was amused by the little polka dots it spread across its body in response to the tunic she'd chosen today.

"That's a pretty cool trick you have there." She eyed the snake with curiosity, wishing it could answer her many questions about how it worked.

She supposed she could find a way to ask Kisk. Especially now, since Iyaren had decided to train the chimera, spending several of his off-days so far in the training yard on the family side of the fence, where the chimera had been allowed to travel for the first time since he'd been healed after a patrol found him barely breathing in the Fall and had brought him to New Omni after the meteor.

Alice wasn't sure why Iyaren had decided to train Kisk, but

it made her very nervous to have her mate spending so much time with the other male, given how much she'd said to his serpent. She was tense every evening, expecting either Iyaren or Tak to bring up the subject of her daily conversations with Kisk, but neither of them said a word to her about the chimera unless she asked them about him.

She had to be very careful how she asked those questions that involved him, because she didn't want them to grow suspicious, though it seemed as if they were behaving like the guilty ones, often sharing a glance she couldn't interpret whenever his name came up, before quickly finding a way to change the subject or distract her.

As usual, the snake didn't respond to her comment, sliding along beside her as she walked the paths of the forest, feeling energized by the exertion and how it had become increasingly easier for her with each day. Her clothes were fitting looser, and she'd already had to take some of the seams in, but that wasn't what made her feel so good about continuing her walks.

The truth was that she was growing so fond of her silent companion that she looked forward to the moment she would see him and get the chance to tell him about her day, feeling no guilt about confessing her worries or concerns, or talking about her problems or frustrations. She didn't feel like she was burdening him, because Kisk didn't really care about her problems, and he wasn't going to rush to try to fix them, when sometimes all she needed was to rant and vent about them to someone who wouldn't give advice or opinions.

Instead, he just listened—or appeared to—as she poured out all the stress and tension that built up over the day. It was like having a therapist, only even better, because she wasn't paying for the service, and she didn't have to see any judgment in his expression. She couldn't read snake-faces well enough to detect that sort of thing.

Sometimes, she'd spot his falcon as well, and admired the

beauty of the bird as it soared overhead, far different from the redbirds that proliferated in the Fall and the several other species of birds that had found the safety of the ancilla forest and began breeding in the branches of the sheltering trees.

She had yet to see Kisk himself again, though she'd been sorely tempted to walk out to the training yard to watch him learn from Iyaren. She loved to watch Iyaren train anyway, since he was sexy as hell when he was moving through his many fighting forms and katas, but she felt a surge of guilt whenever she thought about seeing the chimera again, because her memories had painted him as someone she might've found physically attractive if not for his repellent manners and hygiene.

She wasn't disloyal to her mates for just talking to a silent snake that she found cute like a little pet, or searching the sky for a beautiful falcon that she found awe-inspiring, like she might admire any impressive wildlife.

But seeing the male himself again might cause a different feeling inside her. One she could never forgive herself for feeling. If she began to desire Kisk, she would not be able to see any part of him again—not even the little snake she'd come to adore. The best way to avoid temptation was to quit the habit cold-turkey and cut out that part of your life.

Of course, seeing Kisk in person again might also remind her of why she hadn't found him appealing the first time, despite a body heavy with muscle and features she didn't find objectionable in the least, not to mention the intriguing way his body shifted and the changing textures of his skin and fur and scales and feathers.

She pushed the thought away, knowing it was her mind's transparent attempt to convince her to take just a peek of him and Iyaren training in the yard, and that there'd be no harm in it, but she suspected there would be. This was a concern she couldn't even share with her little, serpentine friend.

Today, she had other things she wanted to talk about anyway. Like the return of her monthly cycle. It was proof, as if she needed any, that yet again, she wasn't pregnant, despite spending every other day of the last month making love with Tak.

She'd cried when she'd checked her panties that morning and saw the blood stain, knowing what her cramps had already warned her she would see, but wanting to deny it and hold out just a little bit of hope.

"It's never going to happen, is it?" she said now, her steps slowing as she blinked back tears she didn't want to shed. What good did crying ever do for her besides convince everyone else she was weak and pathetic?

The serpent slowed its pace to match hers, its head turned to look up at her and tilted to the side in a way she figured meant it was confused by her words.

She settled her hand on her abdomen, bloated at the moment from her period. "Another baby. I'm never going to have another child."

Gray had said that was one possible future, and the more months that went by without any sign of pregnancy, the more certain Alice became that this was the future she was in. One where Friak was her only child—and a precious miracle at that —but it didn't make her disappointment and heartache any less piercing, as much as she wished it would.

"I've been thinking. I need to just stop hoping for it. It only makes it hurt more when my bleeding starts and my hopes are crushed." She stopped walking and clenched her fist over her stomach. "I just *wish* I could force myself to feel a certain way! Then I'd force myself to never feel that hope again. I hate it!"

19

Tak studied the selection of goods laid out in the storage room, noting which ones he'd picked up during their scavenging patrol and wondering if he'd made the best choices when he'd filled the limited space of his packs and cart. All of the items would be catalogued and trades would be negotiated before they were released to the market or taken back to individual homes.

Scavenging patrols were the most desirable duty for those strong enough to brave journeys into the Fall, because they got to keep the majority of their finds, putting only a small percentage of it back into the settlement to pay for the benefit of having a group of fellow males to watch their back.

He crouched down to get a closer look at an item picked up by another male when someone forcefully grabbed his upper arm and yanked him back to his feet, only to spin him around and slam him up against the wall.

Tak snarled, drawing his swords with two lower hands while his upper hands closed around the wrist of the scaled arm that pinned him to the wall by his throat.

Kisk was also snarling as he pushed his face so close to Tak's that their noses almost touched.

"Tell your mate my offer now, or I will make the offer to her myself!" Kisk growled, his golden eyes burning with fury.

Kisk growled again when the points of Tak's swords pressed against his stomach, piercing the fabric of his tunic. Despite his obvious reluctance to release Tak, he jerked his arm away, releasing Tak's throat, then took a slow step backwards.

"You haven't learned much from Iyaren after all," Tak said with an angry glare, rubbing his throat with a free upper hand while his lower hands still held his swords pointed at Kisk.

"If I wanted you dead, I would have killed you," Kisk said, clenching his fists as he stared at Tak, rather than the swords that could have gutted him.

"You might have tried." Tak grinned, but there was no amusement in it.

"Tell your mate my offer," Kisk repeated, his hands opening to reveal extended claws.

Tak sheathed his swords, reassured that even Kisk wasn't foolish enough to attack him again right under the nose of the security set to watch over the storeroom. "We're still considering it."

"You mean you're both so selfish and possessive that you will deny your mate something she wants so dearly that it's destroying her inside, and both of you are too blind to even see it!" Each word was bitten off with brittle growls of rage as Kisk stared accusingly at Tak.

Tak had never seen the chimera so enraged, and yet it wasn't his behavior that shocked Tak, but the words themselves. He felt like Kisk had successfully landed a mortal blow that nearly had him staggering.

"What are you talking about?" he whispered, his upper hands rubbing his chest as if his flame had suddenly guttered out.

"She wants another child, and fears it will never happen again." Kisk stared at Tak with a merciless glare. "Her heart is breaking because of this, and because she still grieves for the one she lost."

"How do you know this?" Tak asked, shaking his head as if he could deny Kisk's words, despite them holding a terrible ring of truth.

Kisk pointed one claw at him. "You told me to learn to respect your mate. I did my research. I studied her to understand why she deserved two powerful warriors when she was so weak."

Tak gaped at Kisk, shocked by the revelation that the other male had been watching his mate without their knowledge. Angered by it, even if it was only because Kisk had taken his words literally.

"Do you know what I discovered, fire-warrior? I learned that it was the two of *you* who did not deserve *her*." He took a step closer as Tak leaned against the wall behind him, unable to argue with such damning words—words he already knew to be true.

"You failed her when she needed you most, and you fail her again, every single day you remain blind to her true feelings. She is so much stronger than either of you that I can't believe she would waste her time loving you the way she does."

Tak remembered what had happened after she'd had the miscarriage. He'd been so heartbroken and terrified that he would lose his other child—that something would steal Friak away from him, as it had taken little Ss'terin, a child he'd never had a chance to hold. He'd withdrawn into himself, forgetting about the ones he loved in his own grief. He knew now that Iyaren had also withdrawn in his grief, and Alice had had to be the one who pulled them both out of it and helped them recover.

He couldn't remember when they'd returned the favor, and

realized to his horror and shame that they hadn't. "Why wouldn't she tell us this? Why would she suffer in silence?"

He didn't doubt it was true now. He just had to understand why he'd missed it.

"She was protecting you, because you are both too weak," Kisk growled, pacing back and forth in front of Tak. "She wanted to ensure you remained *happy*—to protect all her loved ones from grief she is ashamed to feel."

"No!" Tak cried out, holding up an upper hand as if he could ward off the blow, but the words weren't stopped by a physical barrier. "She should never be ashamed of her sadness! We never—"

"Exactly," Kisk snarled, stepping close to grab Tak by the collar of his armor. "You *never*! That's why a part of her is dying inside."

Tak didn't shove Kisk off him, even though the other male slammed him back against the wall in his fury.

It was the guard who poked an inquiring head in, and then growled a warning to Kisk to release Tak or be restrained himself that caused Kisk to release Tak and step away, though his golden eyes never left Tak's face.

"You have an opportunity to give her a gift that would help her heal, and you and Iyaren have kept this to yourselves. Why?" Kisk held his arms out to the sides. "Am I such a monster you would not have me touch her? Is the fact that you despise *me* worth punishing *her*?"

Tak and Iyaren had kept chimera's offer to themselves. They had not found the right way to broach the subject with her, both of them making the excuse that they needed to evaluate Kisk first before they dared to bring him around their vulnerable mate. Yet, they'd spent more and more time with him since then, Iyaren even training Kisk on the family side of the fence. Neither of them doubted he could be trusted not to harm Alice at this point.

But they'd kept their silence anyway.

The look in Kisk's eyes was the real reason they hadn't spoken of his offer to Alice.

"You love her," Tak said, lowering his own eyes so he didn't have to meet that glare.

"The real question is do *you*?"

Tak did flinch as if those words were a blow, because they felt like the worst one he'd ever taken.

"More than life itself," he whispered.

"Just not enough to share her," Kisk snarled bitterly.

Tak looked up, straightening his legs to push away from the wall. "We knew she would say 'yes' to the offer, even if the process would make her uncomfortable. We knew she would do anything for another child."

What they'd also feared was that she would find something in Kisk that made her want to keep him, and make this one mating a permanent one, because Alice was the kind of person who would look for the good in everyone, and somehow, she would not only find it, she'd even bring it to the surface.

"It wasn't that we didn't want to share her. It's that we didn't want to share her with someone we didn't believe was worthy of her."

"It's her right to decide who's worthy enough for her love." Kisk's expression was scathing as he looked Tak up and down. "It seems she has a lower standard than she should, given her current choices."

Tak had nothing to say to that, realizing that Kisk was correct. They'd failed Alice on many levels, including this one, because both of them had seen in Kisk the male he could be when given the chance, and both of them had come to respect him in the last month. Perhaps, that was what they'd both feared the most. What if Alice decided she loved Kisk, and then maybe even loved him more than them?

What if there was only so much room in her heart for a mate?

"We will tell her your offer tonight," he said in a low voice, looking down at the pile of salvage instead of at the other male.

Kisk snorted. "About time, but it doesn't change the fact that you kept it from her this long."

"No, it doesn't."

They would confess that too, and hope that Alice could find a way to forgive them for putting their own needs and fears above hers—again.

Kisk left the storeroom after that, apparently trusting Tak to follow through on his promise. Tak was determined to do just that as he left the room, nodding to the guard when asked if everything was okay as he passed the little umbrella-shaded guard stand.

He found Iyaren in the construction zone and motioned for him to follow him deeper into the ruins, until they stood at the edge of the ancilla boundary, out of earshot of even the most sensitive hearing.

"Kisk has demanded we tell Alice about his offer," he said without preamble. "I've agreed."

Iyaren looked off into the ruins and sighed, running his claws through his mane, touching the braids buried in the mass of hair as he lowered his hand again. "We should have done this at the beginning. She'll be hurt that we kept this from her."

Tak also stared off into the ruins, though his mind wasn't processing anything he saw within the tangle of broken buildings that would someday hopefully be absorbed into New Omni. "It's worse than that. Kisk has somehow been watching her, and apparently listening to her. Remember when Sherak said she was sad?"

At Iyaren's nod, Tak shook his head. "We should have listened then. Or perhaps noticed long before then. Alice is hurting inside, and she's hidden it away to protect *us*."

Iyaren cursed, an unusual occurrence for him because taking the goddess Sekhmet's name in vain broke about five different codes of the kanta. After he exhausted every possible epithet, he drew in a ragged breath. "We failed her."

Tak nodded. "We did."

"We have to fix this!" Iyaren began to pace back and forth, another unusual occurrence for him, since he was generally very still, capable of sitting or standing in one place without moving for hours.

"We fix it by putting our own concerns aside and trusting Alice the way we should have from the start."

Iyaren shot him a glance and Tak read the guilt in his expression. He recognized it because he shared it.

"She has enough room in her heart, my friend," Tak said as Iyaren turned away, facing the ruins fully. "That's something we should have trusted."

"We should have invited him to join our family already." Iyaren's tail whipped back and forth with his agitation.

Tak chuckled ruefully. "That has to Alice's choice as well. It isn't right for us to continue to make the decisions without getting her input too. That's the problem, isn't it? We don't trust her enough, and she doesn't trust us enough."

Iyaren turned part way to look at him in surprise. "What do you mean, she doesn't trust us enough?"

"She hid her true pain from us, because she wanted to protect us. She didn't believe we could handle it."

Iyaren looked down at the rubble beneath his feet. "Maybe at the time, she was right. I can slay a thousand enemies and survive a thousand cuts, but nothing brought me lower than losing our child."

Tak nodded, still feeling the stutter of his flame at the thought of what they'd lost. "We should have grieved together. All of us. We're too used to suffering alone. Too afraid to be vulnerable, because that might make us lose even more."

They'd already lost their entire world. They'd lost family and friends to war—and Tak had buried his own children and most of his clan. Iyaren had watched his sole purpose for living —his priestess—be torn apart by Set's minions, unable to save her, though it was all he was meant to do.

Alice had become their new purpose, a new place to build their home, and a new heart to shelter and love them. They were terrified of losing her. So terrified that they'd been selfish, hurting her even more.

"I've been trying to make Kisk a better male," Iyaren said with regret in his voice, "one I could believe was worthy of her. I should have looked closer at my own worthiness."

They'd both been doing that. Trying to mold the chimera into a mate who wouldn't steal Alice's affections and then lure her away from them. A mate who could join their family without coveting it all to himself, but Kisk hadn't been the problem. Not really. They were projecting their own selfishness onto him.

"We fix this tonight," Tak said, knowing the night ahead would be a difficult one. "I'll arrange for Friak to stay over with Sherak. I know Evie will agree to the request."

Iyaren looked up from his focus on the ground below his feet. "Do you think Evie knows how Alice feels?"

Tak slowly shook his head. "I think Alice wants to protect everyone from her pain." He released a short huff of humorless laughter. "Everyone but Kisk."

20

A lice watched Sherak and Friak tussle on the carpet, giggling and laughing as they wrestled in clumsy toddler movements that saw them toppling over onto the soft carpet more often than not.

"You're looking really good, Al," Evie said, and Alice looked up to see her sister watching her with a searching gaze.

"I lost some weight," Alice said, patting her stomach.

Evie grinned. "Good for you, but I wasn't talking about that. I meant, you look more relaxed and mellow. Less on edge. And you don't have that pinched expression around your eyes anymore."

Alice raised her eyebrows, her attention now fully redirected at Evie, confident Lauren could handle the scuffle between the boys, since she'd gotten down on her knees on the carpet and was alternating tickle attacks to give their opponent a brief advantage. The squeals of laughter from the boys grew louder, but Evie still heard Alice when she spoke.

"I do *not* have a 'pinched expression!'"

"That's what I just said. It's gone now."

Alice shook her head, touching the skin around her eyes. "Was it really pinched?"

Lauren looked up from her prone position on the carpet, where the boys had ganged up to tackle her and were now clambering all over her, trying to tickle her in revenge. "A little bit," she said, then made an "oof" sound as a toddler foot pressed against her flat stomach.

She grabbed the foot and tickled it, sending Sherak into a fresh wave of giggling. "Ev, Al's probably happy now that she gets a night all to herself with her guys. Date night." Lauren waggled her eyebrows suggestively.

Friak slid off Lauren's stomach and settled his little feet on the carpet. Then he pointed to Sherak, who was still squirming to free his foot from captivity.

"Sarge, attack!" Friak said like a little commander.

Lauren turned to look at Sherak, releasing his ankle, and he toppled to the floor in a tangle of chubby limbs, then climbed unsteadily to his feet and took off, shrieking with glee as Lauren and Friak chased him down the hall.

Alice watched Lauren herd the boys in and out of the rooms, knowing they were probably also jumping on beds and making a heck of a mess based on the volumes of their squeals. "She's really good with kids."

Evie nodded. "They are going to be completely worn-out tonight. That makes my job of watching them easier." She glanced at Alice. "Not that it's ever difficult. Friak is a good kid and they get along so well."

Alice smiled in pleased pride at Evie's comment. "Everyone gets along well with Sherak. I swear I've never met a sweeter child in my life."

Her smile faded a bit as she realized why Sherak was so much kinder than a normal toddler would be. He felt the pain of others. It was a cruel gift for such a young boy, but in time, Gray promised he'd be able to effectively shield himself.

Evie changed the subject, and Alice knew it was because she didn't want to dwell on any suffering her baby faced because of his gifts. Evie's worry would only make Sherak uncomfortable in her presence.

"So, what's the plan for you guys tonight?" She held up both hands. "I mean, not the x-rated parts."

Alice shook her head. "I'm not sure. I didn't plan this, so I have no idea what the guys have in store for me."

In fact, she hadn't even known Friak would be staying the night with Evie until Lauren had popped in to inform them of that an hour ago, saying Iyaren had stopped by the gatehouse and asked her to pass on the request when she got off work.

"Woo, a surprise, hmmm." Evie's grin was downright diabolical.

Alice snorted. "Not tonight. It's that time of month, and they both know it, so they wouldn't have made those kinds of plans."

She didn't tell Evie that they didn't do things that way, because she hadn't confirmed or denied whether they engaged in threesomes or not. She let Evie suspect they did because she didn't want her sister to keep encouraging her to try it. Evie had a way of making Alice feel boring and dull, even when she wasn't trying to.

It wasn't that Alice was against the threesome idea so much as she worried her guys would be. That one time in the ancilla forest had been incredible, but they'd also been under the influence of the petals. It would be far too awkward to do it while being fully aware of what was happening.

Her sister looked disappointed at Alice's non-answer. She had no problem sharing details of her love life, though not too much information, at least. There were some things about her brothers-in-law that Alice did not want to know.

Speaking of those family members...

"So, where's Doshak tonight?" she said, looking around the

apartment as if the nearly nine-foot-tall male would suddenly appear.

Evie's smile came with tightness around her eyes that Alice realized did look a little pinched, and she wondered if she had looked like that too.

Like she was worried.

"He's at the brooding hole. He's been given leave from the duty roster to remain at the hole until our babies hatch."

Alice knew this was a subject Evie did not want to discuss, and as the time grew closer for the larvae to hatch, Evie's trepidation was even more obvious. She'd scanned her babies a million times, and not once had she recoiled from them when she saw them squirming around in their eggs on the scanner's screen, but she still worried she wouldn't be able to hold them, or touch them, when they were out of their eggs, because she would find them gross.

For the first few months, they'd be eating rotting meat almost exclusively, so it wasn't like they needed to breastfeed, but Gray felt Evie needed to handle them as much as possible during that time, and Doshakeren—though unfamiliar with the way brooding had been done on his homeworld—did know that females from his nest had constantly tended and handled the larvae.

Evie was a good, loving mother, and she was excited about her babies, so Alice wasn't worried that she would do exactly what they needed and that she already loved them the way she should, but she'd given up trying to convince Evie that it would all be okay. She understood that Evie felt more comfortable letting Doshakeren keep watch on the brooding hole, and the giant male was more than happy to do it, as excited about the babies as Evie was.

"Where's Gray tonight," she asked, feeling a spark of irritation at him when Evie shrugged her shoulders disconsolately in response.

"He's gone again? Without a word to you about where he went? That—"

Evie held up a hand, shaking her head. "Don't, Al. I know what you're going to say. He does what he needs to do, and he's protecting us all. I'm not so selfish as to demand he dance attendance on me whenever I want attention from him."

"He could at least tell you where he is when he disappears like this."

Evie shook her head. "No, he keeps information to himself for a good reason. You have no idea the kind of burden that rests on him, Al, so please, don't judge him so harshly. Believe me, he suffers for it, even though he'll never show anyone other than me how much."

Alice lowered her gaze from Evie's steady stare, nodding her head in acknowledgement. "I'm sorry, Ev. I just hate to see you having to go through things alone all the time."

"Hey, she's not alone," Lauren said, coming out of the bedrooms where she'd apparently tucked the boys in for naps, since they were quiet now. "She's got us."

Evie grinned at Lauren's mock-offended expression. "And, you know, a pale, blood-sucking giant comes around here once in a while. He usually appears at night, when the lights are out... bonking his head on the ceiling and cursing softly in an effort not to wake me up."

Alice and Lauren chuckled at the image as Lauren plopped onto the sofa and dropped her head back on the seatback. "Whew! Those kids wore me out!"

"You don't need to stay the night with me, Sarge," Evie said, patting Lauren's arm in sympathy.

Lauren's head snapped up. "What? Are you kidding me? We've got some serious wargames planned this evening. We already built the pillow forts. They're napping in them now." She shook her head. "No way am I going to miss that!"

She dropped her head back again. "Besides, Asterius is

going out with some of the guys from the gladiator pit, so I'm on my own tonight anyway. I'd rather be here, instigating a pillow war between your kids than sitting at home with nothing to do and no television to watch."

"Oh, Asterius is going out with some friends?" Alice said, trying to sound as if she hadn't immediately become interested in this. "It-it's nice that he's made so many friends in New Omni."

Lauren shrugged. "Well, I don't know about *so* many. He's just reconnected with a lot of the guys he used to battle with in the old arena, and they aren't exactly what we'd call friends. It's more like they strut around the bar trying to one-up each other in their stories of prowess."

"Soooo, the guy version of friends, then?" Evie said with a laugh.

Lauren lifted her head enough to flash them a grin. "Something like that. Whatever you call them, he has a good time, and I wouldn't keep him from enjoying himself like that for the world." Her smile slipped. "He's been treated like an outcast for long enough. The fact that so many males now look up to him is," she blinked rapidly, turning her head away from them, but not before Alice spotted the brightness of her eyes from unshed tears. "It's good for him. I'm so proud of how he's adapted to this place, and at how so many now turn to him like he's a leader."

Asterius *was* a natural-born leader, and the charisma he possessed grew more obvious with each passing day he spent in the settlement, earning the loyalty and respect of so many of the unmated males, often with just his words alone.

Alice was always amazed at how well the minotaur had overcome a past spent alone in darkness. Somehow, he'd clung to the humanity inside him and merged it with the beast, becoming the perfect combination of both to be the future leader of New Omni, which was what Gray was grooming him for.

But it wasn't Asterius himself that had her interested in his plans for that night.

"So, who all's going with him to the bar tonight?" she asked Lauren, trying to keep her voice from sounding more than just conversational.

Lauren shrugged. "I haven't met most of them, because Asterius is still mad-possessive when it comes to introducing me to other males. I know Yaneas personally, but only because he's so over the moon about Ulgotha that Asterius isn't worried he'll try to steal me away. I guess that odd chimera will be joining them. Poor guy."

Alice stiffened, hoping neither of the other women noticed her sudden tension. "Why is he a poor guy?" she asked. "He's been training with Iyaren, and Tak has been hanging out with him too, but I've... ah... heard that he's a little tough to get along with."

Lauren sat up, her eyes blazing with righteous indignation. "Yeah, I'm sure he is. I imagine anyone would be if they'd spent ten thousand years as a captive, forced to fight anyone who came near them—to the death. People treat that guy like he's just being an asshole for the hell of it, instead of recognizing what a nightmare his past was."

Alice knew much of Lauren's anger came from the fact that she saw parallels between Kisk's past and Asterius's, but she also knew Lauren was right, and she felt ashamed of her own judgment of Kisk. He'd told her some things about his past, and it did sound like a nightmare. One she didn't think even he realized the extent of, having nothing else to compare it to.

After all, he had yet to experience anything different from the isolation and antagonism he'd lived with all his life. The unmated males treated him like they probably assumed he wanted to be treated, keeping him at a distance or allowing him to goad them into fights. The mated males kept him at a distance too, busy with their families and their own lives—too busy to make the effort to search deeper than Kisk's hard outer shell for a friend.

Tak and Iyaren had made more of an effort lately, and Alice worried that she was missing something in their sudden desire to befriend Kisk, but they'd given nothing away that he might have confided in them, so she hoped it was only because Tak felt a sense of responsibility towards Kisk after saving his life.

21

A lice sat at the table with Tak and Iyaren, playing with the food Iyaren had made and served to her, without much of an appetite. Neither of her mates appeared to have an appetite either, and that had to be due to the rising tension in the room, rather than the quality of the food, which was excellent as always, when Iyaren made it.

"So," Alice said, clearing her throat as both males looked up in unison from their plates, their intense eyes fixed on her, "Friak has a new hero in 'Sarge.' Before I left Evie's apartment, Lauren helped him capture Sherak's citadel and negotiate a treaty." She grinned. "You should have heard those boys trying to say 'citadel.'"

Tak ventured a small smile at her story, but it was strained, which made Alice very nervous. Iyaren could only manage a slight lift of his whiskered brows and a soft grunt that might have been intended to sound like amusement.

The air hung so heavy with tension that Alice felt like she was suffocating. She swallowed around the lump in her throat as she studied her mates, two of the most important people in her life. She couldn't understand how they'd come to this point, where there was so much left unsaid between them that they weren't even being themselves any more. They didn't seem any happier than she was.

Iyaren slowly set down his chopsticks—one of many eating utensils they'd learned how to use since coming to the Fall.

He then pushed his plate away from him with an upper hand, his lower hands folded in his lap. "Alice, we need to talk."

Those had to be the four worst words in any language. She jumped to her feet, her chair slamming back into the wall. "You know, I'm in the mood for dessert! Does anyone else want something? I've got cookies!"

Tak caught her wrist as she made to leave the table, tugging her towards him, trapping her. "This is important, my spark. It could mean everything to you."

She tried to jerk her hand free, feeling the terror at what they would say next close her throat. *They* meant everything to her. Were they planning to leave her? Had Kisk told them all that she'd been saying, and now they knew she wasn't happy and they thought they could fix it by leaving her? That would kill her. She couldn't bear it if they did something so terrible in an effort to "fix" things.

"He told you, didn't he?" she said, struggling to keep the tears from coming, channeling her fear into anger. "That bastard! What right does he have to tell you what I said in confidence?"

Both of her mates froze, staring at her like she'd just sprouted two heads.

"Who's 'he'?" Iyaren asked in a low growl.

"And *what* would 'he' have told us?" Tak said, his tone bleak.

Panic made Alice want to take flight from the room, but Tak's grip, though gentle, was unrelenting. She wasn't nearly strong enough to escape them—and this terrible confession that could destroy her entire life with them.

"Kisk," she whispered after she finally stopped struggling. "He told you I wasn't happy, didn't he?"

She wasn't sure what she was expecting, but it wasn't for Tak to rise to his feet and pull her into his arms, only to have Iyaren wrap his upper arms around both of them.

"I'm so sorry, my spark," Tak said, tilting his head so his cheek rubbed against the top of her hair. "I failed you."

"As did I," Iyaren's voice rumbled from above them, but she felt the vibration of his chest against her back.

"Kisk did say you were unhappy, Alice," Tak said, "but only because he was concerned about you."

She stiffened in their arms. "Nothing happened between us! Never! Mostly, I just talked to the little serpent part of him. It just kept me company on my walks. Nothing else."

Tak and Iyaren pulled away from her simultaneously, but only so Tak could touch her chin, tilting her head up to look into his eyes. "Alice, we trust you. We'd never believe you cheated on us."

He glanced up at Iyaren, who settled his upper hands on her shoulders. "Kisk never even suggested such a thing. The fact that he might be in love with you is not something you could have controlled."

She gasped and pulled away from them both, and this time, they let her go. She took several steps away from them and stared at them in shock. "What do you mean, he might be *in love* with me?"

Tak sighed and ran a hand over his crested head, pushing down on the ridges that swelled and hardened with his agitation. "This is my fault, Alice. In my anger, I told Kisk to stay away from me unless he learned to respect my mate. I believe he took this literally, thinking he needed to understand more about you before I would speak to him again."

"We realize now that Kisk craved companionship, but could not express this," Iyaren said. "In his former life, he was forbidden to speak with those who hadn't defeated him in battle or earned his respect in some other way. As far as he'd been trained, people who didn't challenge him and defeat him did not exist to him. There was no point in wanting to know them, because he would not be allowed to."

Tak wore a deep frown. "I should have noticed how lonely he was sooner. I should have been more compassionate about it. My pushing him away made him panic, I suppose—worried he would lose the opportunity to speak to one of the few people who existed for him."

"It's so easy to let ourselves be blinded by insulting words that we miss these things," Iyaren said, patting Tak on the shoulder. "I was no more pleased with him than you were."

She looked from one of them to the other, trying to comprehend what they were saying. "You mean, the only reason he came around me was because he wanted you to be his friend?"

He'd befriended her to use her so he could win back Tak's approval. A piece of her heart shattered and she grabbed her chest, startled by how much it hurt. How had someone she'd had only one real conversation with made such an impact on her?

Iyaren saw her wince and closed the distance between them, wrapping one arm around her to tuck her against his side as if he was offering support. "I think that may have been his original intent, but there's no question he cares for you now."

Tak also moved closer to her. Though he didn't put his arm around her, he ran his clawed fingers through her hair. "He made us an offer. One we were supposed to bring to you. One that would be important to you. We didn't tell you about it when we should have. We kept the secret, for our own selfish reasons." He lowered his hand. "I don't know if you can forgive me, my spark, but I'll spend the rest of my life making it up to you."

She looked from the anguish on Tak's face up into Iyaren's pained expression. "What offer?"

"A child, Alice," Tak said in a choked voice. "A very special child. One who would share all of our blood—all of our traits."

She shook her head at the impossible words. "How? Is— even Gray wouldn't have attempted that with his genetic engineering! It's too complex. There's no possible way it can be done successfully."

She knew, because it had been something she'd asked, filled with a dream of genetic engineering science waving over her and her mates like a magic wand to create a child that carried the best of all of them. Gray had quickly dissuaded that fanciful notion, explaining how difficult that would be, and how many things could go wrong.

"The chimera believes it's possible," Tak said. "He claims that this is the favor—the gift—that many warriors risked death to claim from him. It was what drove them to climb the highest mountain in his world to his temple, where they would face him in battle. If they could slay him, they would prove they were strong enough to breed a very special child."

She grabbed blindly for a chair, her hand waving in empty air for a moment before it settled on Tak's chair back, which she pulled towards her. Iyaren's arm supported her as her knees failed her, but she pulled away from his hold, shooting him a look that perhaps showed the feeling of betrayal that was growing inside her.

He lowered his amber gaze to the floor to avoid her accusing eyes.

"Why? Why would you keep this from me?" She looked from one of them to the other. "Do you know...." Her voice rose to a shriek, and she clenched her hands into fists, struggling for control.

"Do you know," she said in a calmer voice as rage built inside her, "how important this was to me? Do you have any idea how much such an offer would mean to me?"

She glared at them, feeling a hardness grow over her heart as she looked from one to the other, seeing the remorse in their stances and in their lowered gazes, but feeling no pity for them.

Only a dark anger that swelled into a void where her heart used to sit. "Does what I want mean so little to you?"

They both jerked their gazes up to meet hers.

"No!" Iyaren roared, raising all four hands as if to ward off a blow. "You mean everything to me, beloved. I would give you whatever your heart desires."

At the same time, Tak's voice was saying, "I would give you my fire itself, and gladly go into the darkness knowing it kept you warm, my spark!"

"Then why would you keep this from me!" she shouted. "This one thing! One thing that I wanted more than anything! I buried my baby and a piece of my heart with him, and you had this chance to give me another child—one from all of us—and you didn't even *tell* me about it?"

Iyaren dropped to his knees in front of her chair and took both of her clenched hands into his upper hands, trying to chafe warmth into them, but all Alice felt was cold inside at his touch.

"Please, beloved, let us make amends. We know we've hurt you. We would do anything to make it up to you."

Tak kneeled beside Iyaren, reaching to touch Alice's shoulder, flinching when she jerked away from him. "We should have trusted in your love and known that we wouldn't lose it by introducing another male into your life."

The chill spreading through her paused at those words as she looked from her fists clasped in Iyaren's hands to Tak, watching her with his crest fully swelled and hardened by his distress, making parallel ridges of spikes on his head that trailed down his back to converge into one ridge that lined his tail all the way to the tip.

"I would have had to take Kisk as a lover, is that what you mean?" she asked in a voice that sounded dead, even to her.

Inside, she wasn't sure how the thought made her feel. She couldn't even think of Kisk at the moment, because her stomach was churning and her heart aching at the feeling of being betrayed by her mates.

"It is the way his gift works," Iyaren said, staring at her intently. "He would... put it inside you, and then Tak and I would... it would have to happen quickly. We would need to be all together at the time and ready to... he said timing was important."

She pulled her hands from Iyaren's grasp and ran them over her face as the cold inside her wavered. "I—I don't know what to...."

She understood more now why they hadn't told her about this offer. It meant accepting something they hadn't been ready to accept. It meant accepting something Alice wasn't sure she was ready to accept.

"I need time to think about this," she whispered, then looked up into their faces—so dear and beloved to her—seeing their pain and regret in their expressions. She didn't doubt they were sorry for keeping this from her. "Would you have ever told me? If... he... hadn't insisted?"

She saw the truth in their eyes.

Her shoulders relaxed in relief, her body slumping back against the chair as she laughed, though she sensed the edge of hysteria to the sound. "So that's it, then? The offer is on the table, and now it just waits for us to decide to accept it?"

"Alice? Will you forgive us?" Tak asked.

She sucked in a deep breath, letting it out slowly as they waited in silence for her answer.

"I remember the last time I felt betrayed by you. I thought only of my own feelings in that situation, and didn't consider anything from your point of view." She lifted a hand to rub her aching forehead. "This time, I'm thinking of how it must have felt for both of you, to know about this, and about what it would require. I'm trying to imagine how I would feel if I were in your situation—about how I would feel if I had to watch you make love to another woman."

"We would never—"

"Not in a million lifetimes—"

Their words ran together, but Alice cut them off with a raised hand. "When I think about this, I come to the same conclusion that you did. I would make any sacrifice, even sharing your love with someone else, if it meant you would be happy." She smiled, though it was pained. "But like you, it would take me a while to grow accustomed to the idea before I'd be able to do it, and I would damn sure know the woman very well before I brought her around the two of you."

That was why they'd been spending more time with Kisk, and Alice didn't need them to say it to know. They'd already made up their minds they would tell Alice about the offer, but they wanted to know Kisk first, perhaps understanding that he would become part of their family, even if his favor only took one session to gift to them.

She had no idea if it would take more than that for his "gift" to work, but she suspected it wouldn't, if it worked at all. Either she would be impregnated by a miracle baby in that first time, or it just wouldn't take.

It didn't matter.

She couldn't remain emotionally detached from Kisk, not if she allowed him into her body and shared intimate moments between her mates with him. Whether they were prepared to grow their family in this way or not, it was the only option, if they were to accept his gift. Not because the chimera demanded it, but because Alice couldn't take it any other way.

She was afraid she might already be emotionally attached to him.

22

E vie agreed to keep Friak for the day when Alice, Iyaren, and Tak appeared at her door that morning, all of them with solemn expressions—Alice wondering whether the nerves twisting in her stomach would show on her face.

Her sister didn't ask questions, and when they entered the apartment to greet their son and break the news that he got to stay another whole day with Sherak, she saw why.

Gray was there, and Alice felt guilty for not taking the boys herself to give Evie and Gray time together. She was about to use that as an excuse to postpone the upcoming meeting when Gray shook his head at her.

This is important.

She didn't think she'd ever get used to the voice speaking in her head, but she'd learned how to respond back just fine. *So is your time with my sister. She misses you!*

Gray blinked slowly. *As I do her, which is why Doshakeren will take the children to the play area for most of the day. It is time for you to be honest with your mates, Alice. All of them.*

Alice hadn't had a response to that, and Friak's excited

greeting served as enough of a distraction that she didn't have to. By the time they'd all said their goodbyes, promising to pick up Friak at the end of the day, Gray had left the room, and possibly even the apartment.

Evie put a hand on Alice's shoulder as she turned to leave. "Listen, Al, I know this isn't easy for you—"

"How much do you know?" Alice said in a low whisper, watching Iyaren and Tak, both standing at the door, their attention focused on the boys who were playing with blocks on the carpet and talking in a gibberish mix of languages and words they'd made up on their own.

Evie shook her head. "Not enough. Gray says it's your decision how much detail to give. All I know is that you're considering...."

She glanced at Iyaren and Tak, who were working hard to ignore them, though Alice could see Iyaren's ears turn towards them.

"This isn't a whim, Evie. It-it might change everything." Alice twisted her hands together in front of her. "I think... this is important."

Evie's smile was commiserating. "That much, I already know." She squeezed Alice's shoulder, before enveloping her in a hard hug. "It'll all be okay," she whispered in Alice's ear.

"Is that Gray speaking, or Evie?" Alice whispered back, appreciating the solidness of her sister, because she felt like she was about to drown in her nervousness, anxiety, and the sense of dread that the careful life she'd been trying to build was about to crumble down around her.

"Gray doesn't tell me everything, but I don't need him to on this, Al. You'll make this work, and this guy is going to be so in love with you by the time the dust clears that he'll learn some manners, just for your sake."

She pulled back and grinned at Alice, winking as they stepped apart. "You'll have to tell me what the feathers are like."

She chuckled as Alice's cheeks blazed with heat.

————

THEY'D CHOSEN to meet Kisk in the sanctuary of the ancilla forest, where Alice always met his serpent. They figured they would see the serpent that day, as Alice had every other day and planned to ask it to bring Kisk, but he had anticipated them, and had come on his own that day, either to carry out his ultimatum to tell Alice the offer himself, or because he was certain that they would have done it.

Alice hadn't been certain what this first meeting between all of them would be like, but the schoolyard awkwardness took her by surprise as the four of them stood on the path, Alice and her mates on one side, and Kisk—wearing the clothes she'd made him and the most groomed she'd ever seen him— standing on the other side, shifting his weight from one foot to the other. His eyes were gray, with their horizontal, elongated pupils, as he avoided meeting her eyes, choosing instead to glance between her two mates as the painfully thick silence extended after their initial awkward greeting.

She realized none of the males were going to speak, so it fell to her to break the ice that seemed to crackle in the air between them. "That tunic looks good on you. The gray color I chose really brings out your eyes... well, you know... that set of them."

Kisk blinked, looked down at his shirt, even lifting a hand to pluck the fabric away from his chest. Then he lifted his head to stare at Alice with raised whiskery brows as if he'd never received a compliment before in his life.

"Does it?" He cocked his head, studying her with those same eyes. "Do you like them?"

Tak and Iyaren shifted at her side, but both of them kept all four of their arms crossed. They'd left their weapons and armor at home, determined not to imply any antagonism, and she hoped that mirrored how they felt. It was difficult to tell. They were all still dealing with this situation internally, and though they'd come to the conclusion to do this, their feelings about it had not been discussed.

"I-uh," she tried to keep her gaze from looking away from his goat eyes as she prepared to lie, "sure, I think the color is beautiful."

They shifted color, gold bleeding into gray and the pupils morphing into round ones. "Or are these easier for you to stomach?"

She clenched her fists at the mocking tone in his voice, but recognized it now as a defensive mechanism.

"When I grant my favor, I don't usually concern myself with looking into the eyes of the female," he glanced at Tak and Iyaren, "but I suspect your mates will insist I treat you as the weak creature you are and be gentle and accommodating."

She felt them tense up, and saw their arms unfolding, and knew she had to step in quickly.

That was exactly what she did. She stepped closer to Kisk. Crossing the seemingly huge gap of path that separated her and her mates from him, she approached him, noting his defensive posture shift into one of surprise, his folded arms lowering and drawing back, as if he didn't know what to do with them when she stopped in front of him, looking up into his face—similar to Iyaren's in some ways but still so different.

His mane had puffed out, the feathers ruffled and moving with a will of their own for a moment, and Alice watched in wonder as they shimmered, fading into long, golden mane hair, then shifting back to feathers in a ripple of motion. That ripple continued down his body, shifting his scales to fur, then back.

"You don't have to keep me at a distance, Kisk," she said, her voice breathless as she admired the beauty of his form, and finally allowed herself to consider what it would be like to touch him, and feel all those different textures against her.

"You are beautiful," she said, reaching out to touch his chest, feeling the fine, woven fabric beneath her fingertips as she moved them over his firm muscles, searching for a heartbeat, wondering where on such a remarkable creature would she find it.

"You wouldn't be the first female to boldly paw at me," Kisk said, but his voice sounded shaken, and he didn't make a move to step away from her, or push her hand away from him.

She found the rapid pulse of his heart, pounding against his chest, slightly off-center and on the left side, with a rhythm that suggested there was perhaps more than one, maybe even more than two hearts inside him. As she pressed her palm flat against those beating hearts, the rhythm sped up even faster. This time, he did gasp and pull away, taking several steps back as his feather mane fully fluffed up around his face.

She drew in a deep breath, filled with the scent of him, overlaid by the piney scent of some kind of soap and a familiar hint of the same oil Tak and Friak used on their scales.

"You...." He seemed to struggle to articulate, staring down at her with narrowed eyes that had turned serpentine.

Then he glanced up at her mates.

Alice glanced over her shoulder at them too, suddenly concerned they'd be jealous or upset, but instead, they both stood in a relaxed way, amusement in their expressions at Kisk's obvious discomfort.

"I don't think I've ever seen anyone unnerve the chimera so much," Iyaren said with a chuckle.

"Indeed," Tak said, tapping his chin thoughtfully with an upper hand. "Did I actually see Kisk retreat? Seems rather cowardly, doesn't it?"

"The stumbling away lacks a certain... elegance," Iyaren said, fighting the tilt of the corners of his lips that meant he was only seconds away from his rare full laughter.

Kisk squared his broad shoulders, glaring at her mates.

"You've decided to accept my favor, so there's no need for further interaction until the female is fertile."

He spun on his heel, attempting a dignified retreat, despite the fact that his feathers were still noticeably ruffled.

"No deal," Alice said firmly, crossing her arms over her chest.

Kisk froze, his back tensing, his heavy muscles shifting beneath the tunic as he turned slowly to face them again. "What did you say?"

She met his glare with her own. "I said, *no deal.*"

His nose wrinkled as his lips pulled back, baring his teeth. "You want this child."

He said it as a statement, but Alice sensed the question as well.

She sighed, smoothing a hand over her hair, where wisps escaped around her face, despite being bound in a long ponytail. "You know I want another child. Probably better than anyone." After all, he'd been the one to listen to her pour out her heart for the last month. "But no matter how much I might want that, it's not enough."

"Not enough for what?" he growled, confusion bringing his brows together.

She took a step towards him, then another when he didn't retreat. "It's not enough for me to let you touch me in such an intimate way and pretend it means nothing but reproduction. It's not enough to have you so briefly, and then watch you walk away without a backward glance. If you're going to be a part of creating this life with us, then you need to be a part of our family. You need to be a part of our child's life." She glanced over her shoulder at her mates, and they both nodded to her, giving their silent approval. "This is what we agreed to. It's all we will accept."

He cocked his head. "You would give up the chance at a child that shares all of your traits? For what?" He gestured to himself. "I won't be the child's parent. No part of me will be reflected in that child. I only provide the catalyst. What purpose would it serve to force me to be a part of your family?"

Alice looked down at the path beneath her feet, stung by his choice of words. Perhaps Iyaren and Tak had been wrong about how Kisk felt about her. She would never force anyone to belong to her, nor could she allow him to make love to her as if he were nothing but a turkey baster at a fertility clinic. "You don't want to be a part of our family?"

He growled, and Alice saw that his fists clenched before he spun on his heel and paced a few steps away, before pacing back towards her, then away again.

"I don't see the children I catalyzed until they come to me to fight for a chance to earn their own favor." At Alice's shocked look, he smirked, flashing fangs. "You see now. They are not my blood, otherwise I would never grant them my favor. Nothing of me becomes a part of them. I am *not* their father."

"You don't need to share their blood to be a father," Iyaren said, stepping forward. "My son is as much my child as any that would be born of my own blood."

Kisk ran extended claws through the soft feathers of his mane, shooting Iyaren an unreadable look through golden eyes. "You had a father of your own—family of your own—to learn from. I was created, not born. I have never been a part of a family. This isn't a battle I know how to fight."

Alice stepped close enough to capture Kisk's hand, twining her fingers with his when he didn't immediately pull away, his scales smooth and cool against her palm. "That's because this *isn't* a battle, Kisk. We're not asking you to prove yourself to us in order to win something from us. We want you to make a home with us."

He stared down at their joined hands, then looked up at Iyaren and Tak, who came up behind Alice and then spread out to flank him, each one putting a hand on his shoulder.

"You would share your home with me," he asked Tak, then turned to Iyaren.

"I saved your life. That makes me responsible for you," Tak said, clapping Kisk on the shoulder.

"And I have taken on your training," Iyaren said. "As your teacher, I also feel responsible for you."

Tak grinned toothily. "And for some reason, despite your best efforts, I still ended up liking you."

Iyaren roared with laughter, slapping Kisk on the back. "You did manage to impress me, chimera. You have potential."

Kisk stared back and forth between them with an expression that could only be called shell-shocked, then he looked at Alice and his gaze shifted to one far more predatory as his hand tightened around hers, pulling her closer.

23

K isk hadn't expected this. He'd thought only about that one chance to be with Alice, to feel what it was like to be inside her, and maybe even touch her soft body and feel its warmth for as long as it took to prime his shaft to eject his catalyst. In return, he would give her what she wanted most. What she needed to end the unhappiness that was breaking her apart.

Except that she'd refused to take his gift unless he was a part of it. He still couldn't fathom how he'd suddenly gained a family, when he'd never had anyone in his life before.

He was terrified at the very prospect of it.

They'd agreed around him—as he'd stood there still processing his shock—that they would take the time until Alice's fertility had risen to its peak to adjust to their new situation, insisting that Kisk visit Alice in the forest each day as he had been doing for her walks—only this time, in person, and that he spend his days off with all of them. They planned to coordinate the duty rosters so the four of them could spend that time together. They would be bringing their child along at some point, and that was another thing that worried Kisk.

What if the child hated him? What if he said something to the child that upset him or his parents?

He had absolutely no experience with children, and didn't know how this would ever work.

He didn't belong in a family. He wasn't made for it. He belonged in a temple, alone with nothing but the spirits of the mages that had created him.

He felt so overwhelmed that once they'd parted, the memory of Alice's hand in his still warming his palm, he'd debated making a run for it. He could be out in the Dead Fall in mere minutes, and he need never look back. He wouldn't miss his meager possessions, or his damp, dank hole of an apartment.

But he would miss his training sessions with Iyaren. He'd miss the visits from Tak, who always helped him buy the things he needed at the market and explained some of the social interactions of the other males who surrounded him. Interactions that had always baffled him and which he felt it beneath him to ask about.

Most of all, he'd miss his daily visits with Alice. He didn't think he could stand staying away from her for long, and some part of him would always end up returning to her, a sliver of himself that would always seek her out, no matter how much he told himself to stay away.

If he left, he would be denying her the child she wanted and prolonging the sadness she suffered. He might be an asshole, but he wasn't a monster. He'd made an offer, and he intended to honor it, even if it meant changing everything about his life to fit into hers.

———

THE NEXT DAY, he dressed as carefully as he had the previous day, when he'd gone to the forest to ensure that her mates had told her of his offer. He'd been nervous even then, but it was nothing compared to how he felt now. Doing the ritual with her was something he could handle. He was familiar with it, and despite that prolonged moment of intimacy he'd have with her, he felt like there wouldn't be much expectation from her.

Now, he knew she wanted more from him. The only problem was that he didn't know how to give more than that.

He had no idea how to interact with her at all, though his slivers had been visiting with her for a month.

He was grateful that Tak had helped him find, select, and purchase more clothing, and also found him a service that would launder them. The male who did this charged a very reasonable price and returned his clothes as clean and mended as any of the clothing he'd worn in the temple, even if the materials were much plainer.

Wandering along the path through the ancilla, he wondered what Alice would have thought of the golden thread embroidered silks he had worn in the temple or of the shining armor he'd fought his opponents wearing.

He felt plain and ordinary in his current clothing, as neat and clean as the tunic and pants were. At least they fit him, were newly-made, and neatly stitched.

Of course, the clothing Alice had personally given him was his favorite, and he wouldn't have traded it for all the silks and gold from his former temple.

Part of his wish for a more impressive and imposing outfit was to remind her—or perhaps more himself—that he was the chimera, and not just some common creature. He should be considered better than her, and she should be grateful for this gift.

Except that he didn't feel that way anymore, and having that confidence stripped away from him left him vulnerable to the feelings she caused in him. If she rejected him now, it would wound him far more than any sword wielded by a warrior female ever had.

Alice had proven to him that he wasn't superior, not to her, nor anyone else. He wanted to blame his feelings on the spells she'd woven with her lovely voice, but knew it was something greater than that.

She approached people with compassion and genuine interest in them. She went out of her way to make them comfortable, and if she loved them, she would bury her own pain so she could help them rid themselves of theirs. He'd never encountered someone so willing to sacrifice their own happiness to preserve someone else's. Watching the way she cared not just for her child, but also her mates, her family, and even the downtrodden unmated males through her gifts, had shown him just how shallow his life and his very purpose had been.

He had been created to test the strongest warriors in the world, so that he might grant them the gift to produce even stronger offspring. Yet his tests had only focused on physical strength and prowess. He'd never tested a candidate's wisdom, or intelligence, and he'd never even considered a candidate's compassion or kindness.

How many monsters had he spawned on his own world? Some he'd even seen for himself when they'd returned to him to challenge him for their own opportunity to spawn a new breed of warriors.

He wondered now why the mages had even created him, and it wasn't a question he'd ever bothered to ask before. Not in the ten thousand years he'd languished in that temple, with only their ghosts and the power of their unending spells to keep him company. He doubted they would ever have answered his questions. They told him only what he needed to know to carry out his purpose.

When he saw Alice waiting for him where they always met

for their walks, his major and two minor hearts thudded faster as they recognized his new purpose in life—making sure Alice found happiness again, so the hesitant smile that crossed her face when she spotted him would someday reach her eyes.

Their greeting was awkward, neither of them certain what to say now that circumstances had changed. It felt strange to be left alone with Alice, without the fear of being discovered by someone who would immediately attack him, or call down her mates upon him. It felt strange to be trusted around someone so precious and so vulnerable that it worried him to think about it.

"You look very nice today," Alice said, gesturing to his clothing.

He looked down at himself, his mind blanking on what he'd chosen to wear that morning, recognizing that it was his second-best tunic, in a ruby red color that matched the natural shade of his scales.

He plucked at it with his claws. "I just grabbed the first thing that came to hand."

Rather, he'd spent hours looking over the shelf Tak had helped him install that was stacked with clothing, in order to select the best possible choices for today's meeting with Alice.

"Oh." Her smile slipped, but she bobbed her head in an awkward nod. "Well, that's a good color for you, and it fits you nicely."

A blush darkened her pale cheeks as her gaze roved over his chest, where the fabric of the tunic clung snugly.

A rush of arousal at the heat in her gaze stiffened his shaft, forcing him to turn his back to her abruptly as he willed it back down again. "We should start walking. I don't want to be late to the food stalls for lunch. All the best options are gone once the lunch crowd has finished."

She fell into step beside him with a soft sigh. "I was hoping you might join me for lunch today, Kisk."

Spend even more time with Alice? There was nothing he wanted more. Except he didn't think he'd make it through without giving away how much he wanted the time for the ritual to arrive. He could scent that she wasn't fertile at the moment, and suspected she was in a part of her cycle where she wouldn't welcome his attention at all. Not that he was sure exactly how much of his attention she wanted, or how he should give it.

When he didn't answer right away, her sigh deepened. "I know this is... well, I know it's all pretty awkward. I felt like I could say anything to your serpent, but talking to you is... different." A soft hand settled on his upper arm, immediately drawing his steps to a halt.

Fortunately, she was looking up into his face, rather than downwards at the tent in his pants.

"Kisk—"

"Okiskeon," he said impulsively, wanting to hear her sultry, bell-tone voice as she said his full name.

She cocked her head at him. "Okiskeon? Is that your full name?"

He felt his feathers lift in pleasure at the sound of his name on her lips, the way they almost seemed to caress it. It was a name he heard so rarely, one only given to those he respected— those who'd defeated him.

"It's the name I want you to whisper in my ear when I'm inside you," he said, then realized to his embarrassment that he'd spoken the thought aloud.

Her cheeks blazed with heat, but the hand on his arm slid lower to capture his hand instead of releasing him. "I can... I can definitely do that."

She licked her lips, but not in a seductive way. It was more like she was nervous, and yet, the sight of her pink tongue sliding over her full lips felt as powerful as if she'd gripped him around his shaft and pulled him to the entrance of her crucible.

When her gaze lowered at the same time as he broke eye contact and desperately searched for something to distract them from what he'd just said, he heard a soft gasp from her and glanced down to see that she was staring at the tent in his pants.

He'd been slain many times, but never had he wished to die until this moment. He hoped the ancilla would sense his humiliation and pull him underground with their roots, never to be seen again, but they remained silent and peaceful around him, ignoring his unspoken plea.

With a quick tug he freed his hand from hers and backed away, covering the view of his erection from her eyes with his other hand.

"I should go," he stammered out, feeling the ripple of his body shifting in distress.

If he wasn't careful, he'd lose control over his form, fracturing into his slivers to run off in all directions.

"Okiskeon, wait!" she said, throwing out her hand to try to recapture his. "Please," she added when he dodged her and took several more steps backwards.

The pleading note in her voice forced him to a halt, leaving him in no doubt of her power over him. His feet couldn't move away from her even if he wanted them to, but as she approached, bringing her soft scent and lovely body closer to him, he couldn't imagine why he'd ever tried to escape.

"I'm sorry, Kisk. I shouldn't have been so rude, staring like that." She bit her lips, keeping her gaze carefully above his waist. "I have to confess to curiosity about...." Her cheeks were now as red as the burning *popta* fruit as she made a brief gesture towards his erection.

"I'm nervous," she confessed in a shaky voice. "About what's going to happen. I'm trying to act like this is a normal kind of date, but the truth is, we both know there's nothing normal about this, and all I keep thinking about is what it will be like when we do the ritual, what you look like, and whether it will hurt."

She closed her eyes and swallowed. "You're so big. I mean, I expected you'd be large because of your height and mass, but I'm afraid that maybe you're even larger than my mates, and even they could hurt me if they aren't careful."

When she opened her eyes, he saw the question in them, and he didn't know how to answer it. He'd never had to be careful or gentle with the warrior females. Their powerful, strong bodies could take the pounding as he thrust his shaft inside them to prime it until the friction was enough to release his catalyst and tighten the chains around his source so only the necessary amount was released into the female's crucible.

He'd buried himself inside the females, striking as deep as possible, his shaft long and thick to penetrate the deepest channels and still feel them tight around the beaded chains that bound it, stimulating both him and the females so their channels would pulse, dipping their wombs into the catalyst he spilled inside them.

Doubt filled Alice's eyes now, and Kisk didn't need her to say it to know that she wondered if she could go through with this, no matter how badly she wanted this baby. He had his own doubts as he swept his gaze from her toes to her head, taking note of her body along the way.

She was so soft, so fragile, her flesh giving, and any muscle underneath nowhere near enough to resist the strength of his grasp. His hands would bruise her pale skin as he impaled her, drilling into her warmth to take his own pleasure with no guarantees that she would find hers.

"Can I... see it?" she asked, gesturing to his pants, though she didn't look down at them.

Heat and tension seized his loins, chains tightening enough to make him grunt as he lifted the hem of his tunic and grasped the tie on his rope belt. He might spill his catalyst just by having her eyes settle on him, but he couldn't deny her this if it would help ease her concerns.

He also worried that it would have the exact opposite effect, having no idea what her current mates possessed for their sex organs, though he had his suspicions. Alice's words had already told him Tak and Iyaren possessed organs that penetrated her.

He had seen many matings between many different kinds of bodies, and most males in his experience possessed something to penetrate the female in order to deposit their seed. There had been a few—who like his falcon didn't have that type of organ and rubbed their seed on the female's entrance—but those had been rare enough that Kisk saw them as the anomaly.

He looked up to meet her anxious eyes, his own hearts pounding with anxiety as he slowly untied the belt and then allowed his pants to slide down his hips, lifting them away from his shaft when the fabric caught on it.

Then he stood straight, resisting the urge to cover himself as his erection pointed straight at her as if it had a mind of its own, or was reflecting his greatest desire. The chains on his source tightened further, causing a low moan from him of both pain and pleasure as her gaze lowered and she took in the sight of him, the flush on her cheeks fading to a disturbing pallor.

"Oh my god," she gasped, putting a hand to her gaping mouth as she stared at his erection.

24

Alice couldn't believe her eyes. Kisk's huge penis glowed with runes all along the length of it. It was easily around ten inches long and had a thick girth that guaranteed her fingers would not meet if she wrapped them around it. It had a similar appearance to a human cock, with the same mushroom head and a hole on the tip that leaked a single drop of clear fluid that appeared to glitter with barely visible sparkles.

The runes were definitely not human, nor was the fact that there were small chains wrapped around it, each link in the chain a rounded bump along the shaft that turned into larger chains with normal links that dangled below his massive dick and wrapped around his very large scrotum, their tightness defining three separate balls, rather than the two a human male would have.

Runes also glowed on the skin that protected those balls, though she wondered how protected they could be with freaking chains pinching them.

She didn't know what to think, or even feel, in that moment. Without thinking about it, she fell to her knees, oblivious to

Kisk's increasing tension as she knelt in front of him to get a closer look.

So close to his genitalia now, she smelled his amazing scent far more powerfully than before, and as she stared at him, the runes on his smooth, hard flesh glowed brighter, and before her very eyes, the chains—the ends of which were embedded into his flesh like they were a part of him—tightened on their own, causing his hands to clench as the chains dug into his flesh. A low growl that ended on a groan sounded from above her.

Her hands moved of their own accord to grasp the chains that defined his balls, trying to pull them free and spare him any more pain, her heart breaking and pounding at the same time at this horrible torture he must be feeling.

"No!" he said in a shaky roar, grabbing her wrists with hard hands. "You can't remove them. You will cause more pain by trying."

She closed her eyes, but tears still escaped through her lashes. "I thought you were free, Kisk, but you're still a prisoner, aren't you?"

One of his hands released her wrist and closed around his shaft, even *his* fingers not meeting around its girth. "The chains that bind me don't harm me. It is pressure I feel, not pain."

She hesitantly touched the skin of his scrotum above a chain, gently stroking over it. He shuddered in response, and moved his hand to press his palm over the tip of his dick.

"How can you say this doesn't hurt, Kisk? I know how sensitive a male's balls are. I heard the pain was unimaginable when they're injured."

He took a step away from her and her hand dropped to rest on her knee as she looked up at him.

"I'm not like the males you know, Alice. The source must be contained—bound like this so it isn't wasted."

As distracting as his genitalia was, and as delightful as it would have been to see his naked body in different circumstances, Alice was now focused completely on his face. "Kisk, what is the price of your gift?"

He looked away, breaking eye contact. "You've earned my favor. You've already paid your price."

"No, sweetheart," she said, gently, her gaze flashing back to his hand covering the tip of his shaft so firmly. "What does it cost *you* to give this gift?"

His growl was low and deep in his chest as he stared down into her eyes, his own eyes shifting from one color and pupil shape to another before settling on gray. "Nothing I'm not willing to pay to be with you, Alice."

She had no answer to that because she couldn't articulate the way his fierce words made her feel. She'd been doubting Tak and Iyaren's belief that Kisk had feelings for her, but now she suspected even they might have underestimated the strength of his feelings.

Now she understood more about why he was so defensive and kept everyone at a distance. The cost he must pay for just growing aroused was brutal. She had no idea what his catalyst cost him, and she was afraid to find out more, because it might mean forgoing the dream that had already taken root inside her and Iyaren and Tak. A child of their own that shared all of their traits would be a miracle they hadn't even dared to hope for, but if the cost to Kisk was too high, she would abandon the dream in a heartbeat. She couldn't live with herself otherwise.

She'd climbed to her feet, turning away as Kisk gained control over his erection. She heard fabric rustling behind her as he pulled his pants back up and retied his belt. The silence that fell between them was heavy after his pronouncement.

"There are other things we can do together. We don't have to mate, Kisk."

All sound of movement stopped behind her, forcing Alice to

turn around to see if he was still there. He stood frozen, staring at her, his hands still on the tie of his belt.

"You no longer want me?" he asked, his voice brittle, defensive, and as hard as it had been when they'd first spoken.

She took a quick step towards him but he backed away from her, glaring at her with golden eyes. "I just don't want to hurt you!"

"So, you reject my gift? You have a strange way of *not* hurting me," he snarled, taking another step away from her.

"Will you feel that... that pain every time we make love?" she whispered, wondering if the agony in her chest was her heart shattering at the thought that she might have to let him go, might even have to let him believe she rejected him, to save him from further suffering.

He cocked his head, his angry expression wavering with his confusion. "*Every* time? Would there be more than one time?" He looked suddenly thoughtful. "Of course, you might be able to spawn multiple children, at least until the source is depleted."

Alice held up both hands to stop him from saying more things that would only raise questions. "I think we need to talk about this, Kisk. I don't think we understand each other here. When I asked you to join our family, I was assuming you would be sharing my bed in the same way I share it with Iyaren and Tak. I thought we'd be making love often, but now I'm beginning to understand you don't do things that way."

Kisk stared at her, pondering her words, his expression still thoughtful. "Would this upset you? Would you want to make love to me often?"

"Not if it hurts you." She shook her head. "I would never want to hurt you."

He sighed and ran his claws through his feathered mane, then smoothed his palm over it. "But do you want me like that?"

She stepped up to him, putting both her hands on his chest, feeling the warmth and strength in him beneath her palms. "I just want you, Kisk. I'll take you however you come to me." She laid her head against his chest. "I don't really know you—at least not all of you, but I do know that you came to visit me every single day, without fail, when I needed someone to talk to the most. Your little serpent gave me the strength to keep going each day, and I knew that your falcon was watching over me, even though I didn't always see him. I know you've been with me this last month, giving me something I needed. An outlet. It's made me care about you, even though I never really knew your motives. I couldn't help my growing feelings for you."

His arms came around her after a long moment of silence and he held her against him hesitantly at first, as if he wasn't certain how such things were done.

"You still aren't happy, Alice," he said, lowering his face to nuzzle her hair. "If I can give you more children—"

She pulled far enough away from him to look up into his face. "That wouldn't bring back the one I lost." She shook her head, blinking away the sudden tears that made her vision blurry. "I hid my grief from everyone because I thought it would protect them, but it was also because I didn't want to appear weak. I didn't want to let people down."

He remained silent at this, listening patiently and without comment as she worked things out on her own, just as his serpent had done.

She twirled her finger in the tie that dangled from the neck of his tunic. "My sister and Lauren are so strong, all the time. They're warriors. They hate being trapped behind the walls of the settlement while their mates go off to fight in the Dead Fall. They want to join the battle, but me... I want to raise a family and make this place a home for my children. I want to watch the settlement grow and become an easier, better place to live for everyone around me. I don't want to fight endless battles just to prove myself, but I feel ashamed of that. I should be like them. They wouldn't have let this get to them."

Kisk brushed her hair off her brow, then scraped his claws gently along her scalp to the ponytail that bound her hair at the nape of her neck. "I know of these females only through reputation and your words, but I don't believe your assessment of them. Your mates are some of the strongest warriors I've ever seen, and yet their grief brought them to their knees while you kept your family whole. Perhaps these warrior women you speak of would have been able to do the same, but I doubt it. You showed me there are different ways to be strong that don't involve fighting."

He lowered his head to bump his forehead against hers, the firm ridges of his horns pressing against her skin a sharp contrast to the soft, silky feathers of his mane. "You won my respect without raising a sword against me or shedding a drop of blood."

He turned his head to rub his face against her forehead like a cat. "You won my love by showing compassion to someone who hadn't done anything to earn *your* respect."

She melted in his embrace, pressing her body fully against his, feeling the hard ridge of his erection pushing against her stomach. "You love me?" she whispered.

Her cheek turned against his hard chest so her ear heard every rapid pound of his multiple hearts.

"It was the real lesson I wanted to learn when Tak sent me away, telling me I must respect you before I could return to him. It didn't take me long to learn it—only to accept what I knew to be true."

It was on the tip of her tongue to say the same, but she held back, afraid that it was too soon to confess such a feeling to someone who was virtually a stranger to her. When had he become so important to her? How had he infiltrated her carefully planned life to throw it all into disarray, while promising so much more than she'd ever hoped she would have?

Kisk was chaos, taken form—or perhaps he was simply change—the kind that could not be undone.

25

To make love to Alice often and feel her soft arms around him, or have her touching him, as she had stroked her finger over his tormented flesh, was something Kisk couldn't stop pondering and dwelling on as the days passed in her company.

With each new day, he learned more about the life that would soon become his own.

He felt different as he walked through the unmated side of the settlement, knowing that his time there would be short. Once they performed the ritual that impregnated Alice, he would return with them to their home, which they were even now expanding so he'd have his own room. Until then, they all kept their new relationship quiet, not wishing to agitate any of the unmated males.

All around him, he saw the lonely and desperate faces, going through the motions to survive in this world, while knowing there was little in their future to make that survival worthwhile. That had been Kisk, though at least he'd never had anything in his past to look back upon with wistfulness.

He now noticed what he'd missed before, and it no longer

seemed like these other males were beneath him—even the ones who could never have taken him in a fair fight and wouldn't dream of fighting in the pit.

Many of the males seemed startled when Kisk actually spoke to them, eyeing him warily when or if they chose to respond. Some didn't, scurrying away as if he'd made a threat instead of a greeting. Others used the opportunity to pointedly ignore him, much as he'd always ignored them.

He didn't take it personal. He rarely took insults personally. Taunting was a tactic he'd always used to throw his opponents off-balance, and make them too angry to think straight. He wasn't usually affected by it himself.

His newfound friendliness didn't go unnoticed and raised enough suspicion that he overheard the whispers, but he felt such a strange feeling of lightness inside him that he ignored those whispers that seemed to follow him wherever he went. Every day, he got to see Alice, and every day it was like a blessing when her smile greeted him.

Some days, she would touch him briefly, still hesitant, as he was. Perhaps because he wouldn't return those touches, she worried that he didn't welcome them, and he couldn't find the words to tell her that he enjoyed them more than anything he could ever recall enjoying—not that there had been much in his life that had brought him pleasure outside of battle.

He just didn't know how much he could touch her without his shaft and source aching from their bindings. The more aroused he became, the harder the chains bit into him, and though he'd been mostly honest with Alice when he'd told her the chains didn't harm him, the pressure did sometimes bring pain. He didn't want her to know that the pain was sometimes a pleasure in itself.

Whenever she put her hand in his, it seemed like the entire forest glowed, though the ancilla remained unchanging. It was just the way the feeling made him see the world around him. As her shoulder bumped his arm when they walked side-by-side, he would lose his step, catching himself before he stumbled, suddenly nervous, as if he'd never been with a female before.

He hadn't. Not like this. They'd had yet to do anything more intimate than hold hands after that first day when she'd asked to see his erection, and Alice hadn't touched him with more purpose than to stroke her fingers over his fur, or lift them to touch one of his feathers briefly. Yet, those moments of contact felt more sensual than any time he'd ever buried his hard length into a female's sex to spill into her crucible.

Thoughts of Alice bent over the altar of his temple, her hands and mouth busy priming her mates while he pumped deep inside her soft body, imagining the way it jiggled with each hard thrust, made him struggle not to waste his catalyst while lying alone on his straw mat each morning.

He wanted her so badly that he ached with it almost all the time now, but he was also more nervous than he'd ever been about performing the ritual, because this time wasn't just about spending himself inside a female stranger who'd only recently slain him. This was about intimacy with a female he cared about, one who would never dream of lifting a sword against him.

The kind of woman who would never cause pain to another to benefit herself.

None of the female warriors who'd come to him in all his thousands of years—whether their harems were leashed to them or followed willingly—had ever wanted Kisk to join them. They'd never offered him a place in their harem, and he doubted they would have refused his favor if he didn't accept such an offer.

It was bizarre and unfamiliar to know he would soon have a home, filled with people he was only just coming to know.

Out of all the surprises, the child, Friak, was one of the biggest.

Despite his fears about meeting the little one, the child seemed to take to him immediately when he'd met him, and had been ecstatic when a desperate Kisk had separated his slivers and showed them to Friak in an effort to entertain him.

Now, Kisk understood that it didn't take much to entertain the child, who loved his serpent and falcon already and was even now running to greet Kisk as well whenever he was brought along on Alice's walks. It was strange to have little arms clutch his leg in a hug that had to be pried off gently by his mother, and it was even stranger to have little arms lift and a tiny voice demand to be picked up and carried in his arms.

He'd felt like he carried a glass sculpture the first time he held Friak, worried that in his inexperience, he would harm or break the child—especially when Friak would squirm in his hold, twisting this way and that as he pointed things out on their walks.

By the time he'd scented Alice's readiness for the ritual, Friak seemed to fit naturally in his arms, and the more time he spent with his new family, the more the world around him seemed to brighten, until even in the unmated male part of the settlement, he was practically blinded by the light.

When the ritual was over—when he'd spent his catalyst inside Alice—he would begin his new life with his new family. Alice had told him she had reservations about the cost he would pay to give her his gift, and he'd lied to her about it, not wanting her to reject it. If she knew the truth, he believed she would.

If she had any idea what he was planning, she wouldn't allow it.

He'd watched her blossom in those weeks they spent together as she and her mates talked about the sadness she'd been concealing, urged on by Kisk to get things out in the open so Alice's brittle smile became more genuine and less a mask to conceal the hurt inside her.

He knew that his choice would bring her grief again, but also knew that the children he would make possible for her would help her recover from it.

Once he was gone, she would still have her mates and her children to comfort her, and perhaps, some fragment or sliver of him would remain to keep her company. Until then, he would enjoy her as her other mates did, making love to her as often as possible after the ritual, even if it meant using his catalyst until nothing remained of the source, and Kisk himself faded away.

There was time yet for that. His source still held enough catalyst to keep him alive for several years. Long enough to give her more children if she should want them before it dried up.

His essence would fade during that time, and he would lose his slivers, but it would be worth it to spend as much of it making love to her as he could.

He'd lived for ten thousand years with nothing to look forward to, and now, he intended to make the most of his last few years.

26

It was time, and Alice had never been so nervous in her life. When Kisk had told her that morning that she was at her peak fertility, she'd nearly called the whole thing off, right before he'd awkwardly bowed to her—not something he'd ever done before—and then mumbled that they should meet that evening at the altar they'd prepared within the cave of the ancilla heart. He'd then rushed off as if hounds from hell dogged his heels.

She wouldn't call off their acceptance of Kisk into their family, of course, but rather the ritual itself. Kisk was now too much a part of them to ever let him go. She loved him, though she hadn't yet found the courage to tell him that. Friak loved him with the unquestioning exuberance of a child, and had no problem saying it. Tak and Iyaren loved him—finding in him a brother and companion who understood their own codes of honor and shared them, and they told him that in their own nonverbal way—which involved a lot of sparring, from what Alice understood.

Even Evie, Lauren, and their mates had embraced his inclusion into the family, not that Asterius needed any more encouragement. Evie and her mates were wrapped up in watching their eggs, waiting for the moment of hatching, yet they'd still made the time to welcome Kisk, who'd been surprised by their warm greetings, and even more surprised by the gifts they'd given him as part of a small celebration of him joining their family.

Evie wanted to do something larger after the ritual—a kind of marriage ceremony for Alice and all of her mates, since it was the first time they were in a position to do so, but the planning had been left mostly to Lauren and Alice while Evie's focus turned more and more to her own offspring.

Alice had used the mating ceremony planning to distract herself from the ritual, which would happen tonight. She'd rushed home from her walk, stopping by to visit Friak and ask Evie if she would take him overnight again, grateful that all of their duties had been shifted around and traded on the roster in order to give them these two weeks of vacation time, which she'd used to prepare the ancilla cave along with her mates, as well as to sew matching robes for her and her mates— including Kisk.

She wished she'd had time to embroider the robes or make them even flashier, but at least the task had kept her hands busy in the evenings when she'd find them shaking every time she thought about what they were about to do.

Tak and Iyaren stopped by to see Friak as she was giving him his last good night hug, holding tight as if he was her anchor, keeping her from being swept away by her nerves. They all wished him a good night, which he found baffling since it was still afternoon, but he was an easygoing child and was quickly distracted by the prospect of going with Aunt Evie and Uncle Doshak to see Gray and the squirmies.

While Doshak hoisted the giggling children up into his arms, saying a rumbling farewell before ducking his head to get out of the door and head on his way to the brooding hole, Evie remained behind long enough to speak to Alice, asking for a little privacy from Tak and Iyaren, who nodded in agreement and headed back to their own apartment.

"How are you holding up, Ev?" Alice asked as soon as the front door closed behind her mates.

Evie chuckled and shook her head. "Nice try, Al, but you're not going to distract me, or yourself, by asking about my babies."

Alice gasped, feigning outrage, annoyed that her sister could read her so easily. "That's not fair! I am very concerned about you and your babies."

Evie's smile sobered as she walked over to stand next to Alice, who was waiting for her own turn to escape out the door. "I know you do, Al. I wasn't suggesting you didn't. But I also know you're scared shitless about what's going to happen tonight, and you're looking for any way to forget about it—and any excuse to get out of it."

Alice captured the hem of her tunic and began to worry at the seam of it with shaking fingers, pinching and pressing on the thicker fold of material. She stared down at her hands toying with the fabric to avoid Evie's eyes.

"What if it doesn't work?" She swallowed hard around a lump in her throat. "What if all of this is for nothing?"

Evie put a comforting hand on her shoulder. "How do you feel about Kisk, Alice?"

Alice looked up quickly, meeting Evie's eyes. "I lo- I... care about him."

Evie gave her a knowing wink. "Are you attracted to him?"

The blush that spread across Alice's face was all the answer she needed to give.

Evie shrugged. "Then whether you get pregnant tonight or not, this isn't a waste for any of you." She studied Alice's deep blush for a long moment before shaking her head. "You know what the problem is here is that you put too much planning into this. You guys should have just had a couple of orgies beforehand—"

Alice released the hem of her tunic and held up both hands. "Stop, Ev!" Her cheeks felt like they were blazing with fire. "I'm not like that."

Evie's eyes narrowed on her. "Like *what*, exactly?" She crossed her arms over her chest. "Like *me*?"

Alice felt guilty for implying an insult, but then she felt a burst of anger for feeling guilty about hurting the feelings of someone she loved. "First of all, I didn't say there was anything wrong with how you and your mates make love, so don't try to put words into my mouth. All I'm saying is that it isn't as easy for me to accept that type of lifestyle, because I have a lot of hang ups."

Evie's tense stance relaxed, her arms dropping from her sides as she regarded Alice in a frank and assessing manner. "You know, the only look I ever see in the eyes of your mates when they glance at you is desire. If they don't find you attractive, or think any of those things you think about yourself, then they're the best damned actors I've ever seen. And by the way, I've also met Kisk, remember. I've seen the way he looks at you too, and he's so damned hot for you, he has to hold his dick to hide the fact that it's hard as a rock when you're around. I know what it means when a man sits or stands with his hand at his groin all the time. That doesn't sound like someone who will find you unattractive when you're naked. I'm just sayin', the only person here who feels that way about you, is you."

Alice shook her head at Evie's misinterpretation of her concerns. Her hang-ups weren't so much about her body anymore, though she still suffered the occasional burst of insecurity from time to time. They were more about a lifetime of trying to live "properly" and behave "appropriately," as if she could denounce the craziness in her DNA by being as normal and ordinary as possible.

"What's it like, Evie?"

Her sister blinked in confusion at the shift in conversation before a sly smile tilted her lips. "You mean having threesomes?"

"Foursome in my case," Alice said, swallowing as anxiety tightened in her chest. What was she going to do with three huge males at once? The ancilla petals had made everything easy, but this would be so different. They'd all be aware of every moment.

Evie's smile lengthened into a full-out grin. "Al, stop over-thinking this! It's not about logistics. Consider their bodies and how much you want to touch them. Think about how good they smell, and how nice their skin—er, fur and scales—feels against your skin. Get out of your own head and focus on what your body is feeling. You don't have to deny those feelings any more. No one is going to judge you, and even if they did, they can just fuck right off, because their opinion doesn't mean a damned thing."

"Nana and Papa were assholes." She held up a hand when Alice made to protest her speaking ill of the departed. "No, you need to listen. They treated us like freaks, and you keep trying to pretend you're normal like they're still watching us, but the truth was, no matter what we ever did, they were never going to think that we were like them—like we were truly 'family', because we were 'tainted' by our father's blood. You're a part of a real family now, and they love you and want to be with you, in all ways. Enjoy yourself for once and stop allowing our past to inhibit you!"

Alice shook her head, her smile rueful. "You really think it's that simple to just let go?"

"Hell yes, Al. Trust me, once you release your stranglehold on 'normal,' you're never gonna go back. They'll want this again and again, and so will you. It's that good, I promise you."

27

The altar was built of stone, but had been covered with straw, then bedding, then many soft furs and blankets. Around it sat a dozen cushions and even more blankets scattered on the thick rugs that had been brought into the cave over the last weeks by her mates and Kisk.

Torchlights illuminated the altar, but the ancilla's heart pool provided its own mellow glow to add to the ethereal atmosphere, their roots rising up through the ceiling of the cave overhead to create glowing pillars that gave the entire cave a cathedral-like appearance. The smaller ponds glimmered with the reflected light.

The ancilla were fascinated by this ritual and were more than willing to host it in their heart, offering a place that was sacred and magical in its own way to stand in for Kisk's old temple, which might still be out in the Dead Fall, but which Kisk's falcon had not been able to spot when it had been seeking it again.

Alice and her mates kneeled on the cushions before the altar, awaiting Kisk's arrival. Alice struggled not to fidget, and Tak, sitting on her right, seemed to be equally fighting the urge, as his lower hands kept tapping his knee until she captured one of them in hers and held on tight, getting an answering squeeze from him, though they didn't look at each other, staring straight ahead as if that would make it less awkward.

Iyaren seemed to take the ritual aspect of this mating far better, sitting as still as a statue, motionless and focused on the stone wall in front of him, the roots that snaked over and through it glowing softly. Yet, when she clasped one hand in Tak's, she felt Iyaren's upper hand reach for her other hand, though his lower hands remained folded in his lap.

When his callused palm pressed against hers as he squeezed her hand gently in both support and a sign of his own nervousness, she sighed and relaxed a bit, knowing she had her mates at her side, and they would all get through this new entry in their life together.

They'd been celibate since making the plans for this ritual. For one thing, Kisk said it would make their seed more potent, and Alice had heard stuff like that even on Earth with humans, so she didn't think it was some kind of ploy to keep them from making love to her.

For another thing, she, Tak, and Iyaren had a great deal to talk about each night, and since they were no longer making love every night, one at a time with her, they often spent the entire night talking, until the first rays of dawn broke through the slit in her curtains.

It had taken many nights of tear-soaked sheets, and fur and scales dampened by her weeping, to pour out all the pain she'd been holding back from them in order to protect them, and herself, from her grief. Together they talked for the first time about what they'd gone through and how it had affected each of them, and together they'd allowed each other an outlet and a safe place to pour out their sadness and their fears for the future in the darkness of Alice's room, in a bed that had sheltered the three of them, but would now need to be even bigger.

She was feeling more optimistic than she had since she'd lost her baby. She would always grieve for her child, but now she knew she could turn to her mates, and they would be strong enough to handle it. They wouldn't shatter beneath the pressure of it, or abandon her because of her weakness, and she knew they would never stop loving her, even if her body never brought forth another life.

She also knew that she couldn't guarantee anyone's happiness, not even her own, and that shouldn't have been her sole purpose in the first place. She could only protect her family from heartache for so long before she became the cause of it, and that was the confession her mates had given. The fact that Alice had hidden her pain from them had hurt them far more than if she'd been honest in the beginning and had grieved along with them.

They'd begun to fear that they were losing her, and in a way, they were. The more she withdrew into herself to conceal her pain, the less connected she was to them, so even though she always made time to take them to her bed, she was at the same time pushing them out of her head, and they'd sensed her crumbling mask of a smile, and that had made them insecure about her love—which was the last thing she'd ever wanted to do.

It was one reason they'd been so hesitant about bringing Kisk into her life, unaware that he had already found a place there.

And now, his place was about to be cemented. Assuming he ever showed up to take it.

"It's past time for his arrival," Iyaren growled, a tinge of concern in his tone. "I have trained him to be punctual. Do you think something has happened to him? Perhaps another male found out he was mated and decided to attack him."

He followed this concern up with a low growl coming from deep in his chest. Despite the fact that Kisk was significantly

older than Iyaren, Iyaren treated him like a much younger
pupil, since Kisk had very little experience at actually living
life, having spent most of it in a temple. This made Iyaren
somewhat overprotective of him, ever since he'd taken him
under his wing to train him and prepare him to become part of
their family.

Alice clenched both their hands, her palms sweating, but
neither of them pulled away, only gripping her back in reassur-
ance. "You don't think he's hurt, do you?"

She couldn't bear that thought. She'd already asked Kisk to
stay away from pit-fighting, knowing now how much time he'd
spent there, and how often he'd been wounded. The fights were
the primary source of his income, but he'd agreed to give that
up for her, since the combined income of their family was now
significantly more than he was making in the pits. She knew he
wouldn't be revived outside of his temple.

"He's as nervous as we are," Tak said, acknowledging aloud
what they were all feeling. "I think that is the reason for his
delay."

Alice made to rise to her feet, her legs shaking, but not from
the prolonged kneeling position. "I should go find him."

Her mates kept her in place, refusing to release her hands.

Iyaren took a deep breath. "No need. He's here now."

They all tensed as a large figure stalked into the cave on all
fours.

Alice gasped as a huge African lion approached them,
looking exactly like the man-eating predator from Earth, with a
massive golden and brown mane, except that on his back was
another animal—a large billy goat that had spiral horns. The
goat actually extended from his back.

Graceful, feathered wings folded at the lion creature's sides,
and as he stopped in front of them, towering over their
kneeling forms, a massive tail whipped up above the horns of

the goat, revealing that it was actually formed of a hissing serpent.

The Chimera in his true form.

Alice's jaw gaped open as she stared at the creature, who bowed his regal leonine head to the floor in front of her, bending his front legs so his maned forehead brushed the carpet beneath his massive paws. The goat on his back studied her with Kisk's gray eyes before also bowing, laying his head atop the mane of the lion.

Giant feathered wings spread out to each side of the chimera as it bowed, and the serpent tail also lowered respectfully.

She stared at him, stunned, having no idea what to say, but feeling the intense gravity of this moment. He was bowing to her, and she didn't think it was simply a whim to add flourish to this ritual. This massive, impossible creature out of myth and legend was bowing to her out of respect.

Before she could summon the words—whatever they might possibly be—to acknowledge his gesture, Kisk's body shifted before her very eyes in an awe-inspiring ripple of fur and scale and feather as the goat melted into his back and horns extended from his mane, while the feathered wings closed and then also melted into his sides. Then his golden mane shifted into feathers.

His arms and legs reformed their shape, along with his torso, and as he rose to his back feet, scales shimmered down his arms and legs. No sign of the serpent tail remained.

"You honor me," Alice whispered as he looking down at them, his body naked, and the chains wrapped around his three-balled scrotum and attached to his already-erect cock swinging with his movement. Since it was all at her eye level, the glowing runes stood out distinctly on the hard shaft and soft skin of his scrotum.

"No, Sorceress," Kisk said in a deep, growling voice, "it is you and your mates who have honored me. I came to give you my gift, but in truth, you have already given me gifts far greater than anything I could ever offer by welcoming me to your family. I am grateful for the day I fell under your spell."

Alice chuckled nervously, a little afraid and intimidated by the very formal atmosphere, despite being eye level with a beautifully adorned cock and balls—looking like some form of jeweled art sculpture with LEDs lighting it up. "You know I don't have any magic, right?"

She broke her fascinated gaze away from his groin and looked up into his eyes, which were staring down at her, the color shifting continuously.

"I disagree, Alice. You possess a power I have never encountered before. One far greater than anything I've ever faced. I will never regret falling to you, because I didn't need the temple to revive me. For the first time in ten thousand years, you actually brought me to life."

He held out his hand to her and she lifted hers, which Tak released, to put it into his.

Then he drew her to her feet, his eyes never leaving hers as she rose to stand in front of him.

"I love you, Alice. I will spend what's left of my life worshipping you, instead of those who created me." He stroked his hand down her cheek. "So soft," he whispered, his warm breath redolent of something minty that he'd used to scrub his sharp, deadly teeth until they were white instead of yellowed.

Iyaren and Tak rose to their feet at her sides, and Kisk glanced at Tak, then Iyaren, while Alice continued to stare up at his face, speechless, her mind still processing his words and the power of the emotion behind them.

She felt hands untying the belt at her waist, then felt another pair of hands catching the collar of her silken robe to slowly pull it off her shoulders, revealing her bare skin, inch by inch to all of her mates. The soft brush of fur against her collarbone told her it was Iyaren's hands disrobing her, and she felt his sleek tail stroke her ankle as it swished back and forth beside her.

A scaled hand closed around her breast as soon as it slipped free of the fabric sliding over her skin like water, and it was Tak's hand that tweaked her nipple the way she liked so much, pinching it into a hard peak beneath Kisk's watchful gaze.

With her neck bared, Iyaren's rough tongue swept along the faded scars where he'd bitten her to claim her as his. It was still one of his favorite places on her body, and she still shivered when she felt his hot tongue and hard, sharp teeth against that sensitive flesh as he licked and nipped at her neck. She was aware that he could easily rip out her throat if he wanted to, and she was also aware that he would tear out his own before he would even think of doing so.

The silken robe slid further down her body as Iyaren palmed the other globe of her breast, brushing his callused thumb over her nipple, which was already beaded from his tongue on her skin. She moaned softly and leaned back, and Iyaren caught her against his strong body, supporting her when her knees threatened to buckle. His lower hand caught around her waist, while Tak took over pulling the fabric away from her body.

Her back pressed and held against Iyaren, she could feel the hard length of his erection pushing into her spine, and was grateful that he was aroused, despite the unusual situation and the presence of Kisk, who was still watching her face as if he was fascinated by the pleasure he saw there while her other mates touched her.

When the combined light of the torches and the glowing ancilla fell upon her naked skin, she felt incredibly sensual and desirable, a feeling no doubt helped along by the fact that Tak and Iyaren slid their hands along every inch of skin that was revealed as if they couldn't get enough of touching her.

Iyaren still kissed and nibbled at her nape, his upper hand freeing her hair from the braids she'd put it in for the occasion so that it cascaded down her back, allowing him and Tak to toy with the strands while their other hands were busy finding newly revealed areas to touch and caress.

Kisk's eyes finally broke away from her face when the robe parted and fell away to leave her standing fully nude before him. As his gaze traveled down her body in the wake of that material, no doubt taking note of the possessive hands claiming her, his body tensed and the runes on his cock glowed bright enough to rival the ancilla. Alice swore she heard the links of the chains binding his groin clinking, followed by a soft moan from him.

Of pain, or pleasure, she couldn't tell, and the lust and desire clouding her mind was too much for her to think straight about it.

Kisk sucked in a deep breath, his nostrils flaring. "Usually, it is the males of the harem who prepare the female for my shaft. I don't usually touch her until it is time to put it into her crucible."

He gripped the head of his cock, his palm pressing against the tip. "But I've never felt this kind of need before. You're so beautiful, Sorceress. Your body is unlike any other I've ever seen. I want to feel its softness pressed against me, and taste every inch of you until you're trembling in my arms before I come into you to give you my gift."

"If you want to help prepare her, you have to kneel," Iyaren said in a rough growl, lifting his head from nuzzling her neck just long enough to speak before lowering it again to plant kisses along her sensitive skin, the fingers of one upper hand buried in her hair, while the other massaged her breast.

Kisk fell to his knees so fast it was like Iyaren had kicked his legs out from under him—something Alice had seen him do during training.

Tak chuckled at how quickly Kisk had moved to obey, and his lower hands trailed towards Alice's mound, showing Kisk where to focus his attention.

Iyaren tugged her upper body further back against his chest, while pressing his stiff cock against her back so her lower body pushed forward, making it easier for Tak to spread her folds with his fingers, revealing her nub, which was already throbbing with her excitement.

Tak rubbed his textured fingers over it gently a few times, his long tongue snaking out to lick the other side of her neck as if he wished it was licking her somewhere else.

"Here's where she really likes to be tasted," he said to Kisk. "But gently."

He pressed several kisses along her neck, his sharp teeth grazing her skin. "Oh, so gently, until she begs for mercy and bucks against your hold, and then you bury your tongue inside her and taste her excitement and know she's ready for all you have to give her."

His words were whispered against her ear, but the other males appeared to hear him too, since Iyaren made an agreeing grunt of a sound, his cock twitching against her back with his excitement.

Kisk moaned as he leaned closer to the pearl of hypersensitive flesh Tak revealed with his fingers holding her folds apart.

When Kisk's tongue hesitantly swept out to stroke over that nub, Alice jerked in Iyaren's restraining hold, a loud gasp rising from her lips as she writhed to escape the pleasure of it that was so intense it was almost painful. Kisk's tongue wasn't as rough as Iyaren's, but it was just as wide and wet and hot when it rasped over her a second time.

Tak caught her moan when his lips captured hers, and he proceeded to claim her mouth as Kisk grew more confident in claiming his place in her life, his tongue returning to stroke her as Tak held her open to him and Iyaren pinned her in place.

Tak caught each shriek and cry of ecstasy as Kisk's tongue brought Alice to her first orgasm, but it was Iyaren's lower hands that pulled her thighs apart as he sank back into a kneeling position to make it easier for Kisk to see her soaking slit.

After a long moment where Kisk stared at her as if he'd never seen a sight so beautiful, he lowered his head between her legs and licked his tongue inside her.

Alice grabbed a hold of his horns, pulling his head closer against her to be rewarded with his tongue delving deeper.

Iyaren's caresses grew more frantic and excited, far less calculating as she ground against Kisk's face, her wetness soaking the fur around his muzzle as he took his fill of her, his tongue thrusting inside her bringing on a second, even more powerful orgasm.

After that, Kisk lifted his head, his hands shaking as they fell upon her thighs, then roved over her stomach to clench on her rolls of soft flesh as if it turned him on, and judging by the way he moaned as he licked his chops, his intense gaze fixed on her stomach and lower body as he squeezed her gently, it did.

"So soft," he moaned, "so exquisite. The feel, the smell, the taste of you, Sorceress—"

He arched his back, crying out as if he was suddenly pained. "I can't wait much longer to be inside you, lovely Alice!"

"Tell us what to do," she gasped, worried about him even as her other mates still stroked and licked her body, never allowing her to fully come down from where she hovered at the peak of another climax.

"I need you on the altar, on your hands and knees. You must prime your mates while I am inside you. Once I spend my catalyst inside you, they must come inside you quickly. Timing is important. The catalyst won't remain active for long once it leaves my body."

If Alice had been afraid that Tak and Iyaren would be too

nervous to perform, those fears quickly evaporated as they helped her onto the altar, then divested themselves of their own robes and sat on the flat, cushioned stones in front of the altar, their naked bodies within reach of her hands and mouth.

She felt only a slight moment of hesitation and fear as Kisk positioned himself behind her, the head of his huge erection prodding her soaking entrance. As it began to slip inside her folds, she gasped and then moaned as it inched deeper, spreading her and filling her, the beaded links of the chains around the shaft rubbing against her sensitive inner walls in a surprisingly pleasing way.

As Kisk fitted his girth inside her, Alice tried to focus on Tak and Iyaren. She didn't think she had time to truly appreciate their bodies the way she normally liked to. She could stroke and pet and explore them with her mouth all day if they'd let her, since she found them both so incredibly beautiful that touching them and tasting them never got old.

She knew she would feel the same about Kisk's body, and her only disappointment was that this first time, she had not gotten the chance to truly touch him the way she wanted to before his first penetration, but afterwards, she intended to explore him to her heart's content.

Now, she focused on priming her mates to come as soon as they were buried inside her, and judging by how excited they already were, she didn't think it would take much time to prepare them, but since Kisk was clutching her thighs with a desperate grip that had grown almost painful as he sank deeper and deeper inside her, she suspected they didn't have much time before he spilled his catalyst either.

Her mouth closed over Iyaren's bumpy cock as he clutched the stone seat beneath him, rocking his hips upwards to push deeper as she sucked as much of his thick head and shaft as she could fit into her mouth.

"Not too deep," he groaned, his eyes closed as he concentrated. "I'm already close, beloved. I never thought watching you with another male would bring me so close to climax."

The sincerity in his voice and the trembling in his body as he struggled not to come in her mouth evaporated her lingering concerns that this experience would be difficult for her mates. She slowed the movements of her mouth to draw out his pleasure without bringing him to his climax.

"It was watching you come apart in our arms, your legs spread, your head thrown back as you cried out in ecstasy, clinging desperately to his horns as he made you come, that has brought me so close," Tak said, shifting his hips with a groan as Alice played her fingers along his slit, feeling the hard length of his cock moving beneath it, eager to thrust out into her warm channel.

If she wasn't careful, he might lose control of it, so she kept her touch gentle and slow as she pushed her fingers into the slit and rubbed them over the shifting, muscled length, which moved on its own when it was thrusting inside her.

"I thought about your taste, and how much I love it, and want it to be my tongue—knowing that it would be again—and I nearly lost control, my spark."

The tip of his cock poked out of his slit, and Alice lifted her head from Iyaren's erection to place a kiss on Tak's, darting her tongue out to swirl around the tip and take in the heady taste of him, thick with his spicy flavor and scented with his pheromone, which had altered to be complimentary to her own.

By this time, Kisk had sunk himself deep inside her, slowly pushing his way into her body as it stretched to eagerly accommodate his size. He felt bigger than her other mates, but not by as much as she'd feared initially, and though the head of his erection bumped her womb painfully at first, so deep that she had to adjust her position a bit to keep him from hitting it, he felt incredible inside her, the chains working like the beads on a sex toy as he began to pull back out again. They shifted around with the friction, in a way that was different from the stimulating bumps on Iyaren's shaft, which also felt incredible.

Alice knew she was going to orgasm again, and very soon, and she had to be careful not to overstimulate her mates as her own excitement grew with each thrust from Kisk. As their bodies slapped together and jerked her forward, she heard him grunting and growling, one of his hands caressing her buttocks like he was handling a priceless treasure.

"The way your body moves with mine, Sorceress," he said, his voice sounding shaken. "It's mesmerizing."

He moaned and pushed harder into her on the next thrust, where she felt the chains shifting as if they were squeezing his shaft tighter, yet it still seemed to swell thicker inside her, making her feel fuller than she ever had before.

"I've dreamed about this," Kisk said, petting her ass. "The way it ripples is even better than I imagined."

She should have been embarrassed at his words, but the excitement in them and the way her body obviously aroused him only made her feel a tremendous sense of satisfaction and even more aroused, though she hadn't thought that was possible.

Tak's cock thrust free of his slit as Kisk's increasingly harder thrusts pushed Alice's body towards them with each impact of his hips against her as he buried his length up to his chained scrotum. Alice gripped the base of Tak's thrusting shaft, trying to hold the muscular length of it still so she could close her lips around it, much to Tak's pleasure. His hiss nearly drowned out Iyaren's plea for Alice to stop tormenting him as her hand stroked up and down his length.

She alternated kissing, licking, and sucking the two of them, careful to keep them on the edge without taking them over it while Kisk chased his own release inside her, his cock thickening and the chains tightening until he was snarling in what she thought might be pleasure and pain mixed.

When he gripped her hips with both hands in a tight hold, squeezing her flesh there until it was almost painful enough for her to protest, she knew he was close, and he proved it when he began to pound frantically, thrusting into her only a handful of times before his body froze and he roared loud enough for the sound to echo for several long moments as the shuddering of her orgasm combined with his pulled her focus entirely to where they joined, as if that was the only place that existed in that moment.

He pulled out of her quickly.

"Now!" he said to Tak, who had to be the next one because Iyaren's barbs would force them to remain linked for about five to ten minutes after he came, and Kisk said that was risking the process.

Tak switched places with Kisk, and because his cock had already emerged from his slit and was moving back and forth trying to find her heat, he had to grab it and guide it into her warmth, where it thrust rapidly, and within just a handful of hard, deep thrusts that kissed her womb, spilled the hot seed that tingled against her sensitive inner flesh.

Iyaren had already pulled away from her stroking hand and teasing mouth and was standing behind her now, waiting his turn as Tak pulled out of her, struggling to catch his breath.

As Iyaren slid his thick length inside her, each bump stroking her inside until she shivered from the oversensitive feeling of her inner muscles—primed by multiple orgasms, and beaded chains, soaked by tingling seed, and now massaged by Iyaren's bumps, she climaxed again, her cervix dipping into the pool of fluid that had already been spilled inside her. It didn't take long for Iyaren to add to that pool, and Tak had barely had the chance to make his way back to the stone seats and collapse on one of them, next to Kisk, who sat in watchful silence, his gaze intent on her mates as they took their places.

Once Iyaren climaxed, Kisk's tense body relaxed and he slumped on his stone seat in front of Alice with a sigh of relief. Tak glanced down at Alice, a soft smile tilting his lips as his lower hand reached to brush her hair off her brow.

Iyaren slowly assisted Alice in lowering her body so she didn't have to remain on her knees while they were linked, allowing her to settle on her stomach while he propped the majority of his weight off of her using his arms, keeping only their lower bodies together so she didn't feel crushed beneath him.

Alice looked from Tak, whose slit was now closed tight and barely visible even from this angle, to Kisk, whose chains were slack around a flaccid penis that no longer glowed with runes, hanging down over a scrotum that looked diminished as well.

Kisk sat on the stone with his ankle propped on his other knee, resting his forearms on his leg. He seemed at ease in his nudity, despite the presence of the other males. After the intimacy they'd shared, they all seemed at ease, including Alice.

She'd been worried about how it would feel afterwards, especially considering how awkward it had been when they'd been caught in the ancilla forest after Lauren and Asterius's sacrifice that had led to the mating petals causing such sexual desire in all of them that they'd been unable to not engage in a threesome.

This time, things felt right, even in the aftermath, as if all the concerns and worries had been cleared away, and they were all in accord with how things had happened. She no longer felt any guilt about what she'd once seen as an unfairly one-sided advantage for her in the relationship. It was true that she was very lucky and had three gorgeous mates to make love to her, but she also brought a great deal to their relationship, and made sure that they all found their pleasure with her.

The fact that they were relaxed and didn't seem in the least bit resentful about how they'd had to share her body made it so much easier for Alice to relax about doing this.

Now, she understood why Evie had suggested on multiple occasions that they try this. There was something about what had just happened that seemed to only solidify and strengthen the bonds between them all, creating something deeper and more aware in their relationship. They'd opened the door to an intimacy that had been lacking up until that moment, meaning that no part of Alice's life was shut away from any of them. For once, it had all been shared openly without any type of intervention from aphrodisiacal petals.

28

Tak shifted to the floor beside the altar so he could kiss Alice, moaning as she sucked his tongue inside her mouth, deepening their kiss while they waited for Iyaren's barbs to retract. Iyaren alternated between nuzzling her neck and licking teasing paths along her vulnerable back, his hands stroking her skin as if even after his release he couldn't stop touching her.

Kisk watched them in silence for a long moment, before he rose to his feet and started to walk away.

Alice broke the kiss with Tak and turned her head to follow him. "Wait!"

When he met her eyes, she saw him distancing himself in his expression.

"Where are you going? I want you right here," she said, lifting her hand to point her finger at the cushioned seat he'd just abandoned.

He looked from her to the cushion, then to each of her mates. "I have given you my catalyst, and I won't be able to grow erect again until my source regenerates it from my essence. I can't offer you any more pleasure, so I'll leave you to your mates. At least the ritual was a success. You now carry a child that shares all of your bloodlines."

"Kisk!" Alice said, pushing herself up a bit before a pull in her vagina caused her to wince and freeze as Iyaren growled a warning.

There was so much that he'd just said that caused her mind to spin, especially his last statement—though she didn't want to get her hopes up yet. They had no idea if his "magic catalyst" would truly work as he believed in this dimension.

But what mattered to her the most now was that he was drawing away from her, as if he'd done his task and now had no more purpose. "I still need you."

He cocked his head in confusion. "For what?"

Iyaren snorted impatiently. "I suppose we should make allowances for the cub's lack of experience," he said to Tak, who chuckled in response.

Kisk's hands clenched into fists as he glared at Iyaren. "I am ten thousand y—"

Iyaren lifted an upper hand off the altar, shifting his weight to his other supporting hands, the pull in her body easing as his erection grew flaccid. "We've already been over this. Years mean nothing. Now come back here and worship your mate as you told her you did."

Tak seemed to take pity on Kisk. "Our climax is not the sole purpose of our mating with Alice, Kisk. Your presence, even after you've found your own release, is what makes her feel loved and cherished."

"Basically," Alice added with a small smile, "they're saying don't just hit it and quit it. I want to cuddle with you, Kisk. I want to run my fingers through those feathers on your head, and stroke your horns to feel the ridges. I've always wondered how soft your fur was, and the brief contact I've had with it doesn't answer that question well enough."

Her gaze dropped to his mouth, which had fallen open at

her words. "And I know, it won't be easy to kiss with a mouth like yours," she shot a knowing glance over her shoulder to Iyaren, "but I do have some experience with it, and I think you'd like it too."

Iyaren was finally able to withdraw from her body, and she worried for a moment when their combined seed and Kisk's catalyst spilled out in the wake of him pulling out, but pushed away that concern. Kisk had not warned them not to move to avoid that happening, so if he was right about his gift, the process was already in motion, and if he was wrong, then nothing they did at this point would change that.

As soon as Iyaren sat back on his haunches, allowing Alice to push herself up into a sitting position, Tak jumped to his feet and scooped her up in his arms. Before her protest fully formed on her lips, he'd carried her to the cushions where they'd been kneeling before and laid her over them, then bent and gave her a long kiss before standing again to turn and look at Kisk, who was watching them, speechless.

Tak motioned with an upper hand to Kisk as Iyaren found his robe and pulled it on over his broad, muscular shoulders, sliding all four arms into the sleeves of the robe as naturally as she would her two arms. She was always amazed at how easily her mates used their arms without any sign of awkwardness, and it had taken some trials and errors to get the patterns of their clothing just right to accommodate those extra limbs.

"Come and lay down beside our mate, Kisk," Tak said, pointing to the cushions beside Alice, who had rolled onto her side and propped herself on one elbow to watch her mates, almost distracted from their words by the beauty of their naked bodies.

"Show her how much you love her by reminding her that you find her desirable and want to touch her, even when your staff isn't hard and eager," Iyaren added, striding to Kisk to clap an upper hand on his shoulder. "There is more to mating than sex, cub. Let Alice show you what it truly means to love someone."

Alice smiled at those words—a soft smile that did nothing to stop the tingle of tears building in her eyes. This time, they were tears of joy, raised by the complete and utter conviction in the words and tones of her mates.

They felt loved. Even though she'd revealed her unhappiness, her grief, and her heartache in the past weeks, they hadn't taken it as a denial of them and what they shared with her, as she'd feared they would, which was one reason she'd hidden it for so long. They hadn't blamed her or judged her for not considering how blessed she was to have them and their son Friak. They'd accepted that she had a right to feel unhappy, and a right to grieve what she'd lost, and to fell regret for the things she might never have. They'd accepted all of this, and in doing so, had made her truly feel it when she'd repeated the words to herself, "I am blessed."

And now Kisk approached her makeshift cushion bed with hesitancy in his step, but wonder in his expression, as if he couldn't believe that he was so blessed. He kneeled down beside Alice, his gaze jumping from Tak and Iyaren to settle on Alice, his eyes now gray and odd, and eerie—and still so beautiful to her.

Tak scooped up his robe and donned it with a quick, graceful motion, swiftly tying the belt with his lower hands as his upper hands straightened the collar. He glanced at Iyaren, some unspoken meaning in their look that Alice still couldn't read—the two of them becoming more in tune with each other every day.

"We're going out for a long walk." He met Alice's eyes, a question in his, despite the fact that his words were a statement.

She nodded in response.

Tak grinned toothily, though it was filled with amusement

and not a threat. "When we return, perhaps we can try some more new things."

Iyaren's answering sound was more a purr than a growl.

"Only if Alice wishes to," he said in a choked voice.

Alice felt the wicked smile that crossed her face as she looked at Kisk, who was still kneeling beside her, watching her interact with her other mates. "Would it be safe to continue making love, now that the ritual is complete?"

Kisk blinked several times before answering. "The process began the moment your mates' seed blended with my catalyst and then found its way to your own seed. Nothing you can do now would jeopardize the life that will soon be growing inside you." He shook his head after looking at all of them in turn. "The females I've been with have occasionally brought along a harem they cared for, and they would often spend many days in my temple locked in mating, though they must have been exhausted after fighting their way to me. Their offspring were never harmed by this."

Alice placed a hand over her abdomen with relief, her excitement growing as she saw three sets of eyes follow the movement and three gazes heat with desire—even that of Kisk, who would not be able to grow aroused.

"In that case, I absolutely insist you both return after your walk." Her grin grew even wider. "We have a lot of time to make up for."

She suspected she wouldn't be walking much tomorrow, but the thought of the coming night made her so wet that she knew it would absolutely be worth it. The way Iyaren's robe tented and Tak's shifted at his groin while his chest blazed with his inner glow, told her that her mates were anticipating it too.

29

K isk felt stunned after the ritual, though his body suffered from the usual draining exhaustion that always came after releasing his catalyst. The runes were already drawing his essence from him to make more of the catalyst, so he would be drained for weeks until it regenerated.

Normally, he would fall into a deep sleep after the ritual, although, if the female and her harem remained in the temple after his part in the process was complete, he would sometimes watch the following activities with more curiosity than anything, not getting many opportunities to observe such behavior.

Mating was usually a violent affair, with a lot of growling and snarling and gnashing of teeth. In the cases where the males were leashed and bound to their harem against their will, there was great anger and resentment as they were primed to release their seed, and they often took the opportunity while they were inside the female warrior to punish her with their hard, rage-filled thrusts, which in truth, only seemed to please those females more.

Kisk had pitied all the males who were dragged to his temple, even if they came by their own will rather than by the leash. They were tools and nothing more. They served a purpose, and even when the female would play with them afterwards, it was always to her own benefit.

He could not see how Alice touching him with so much gentleness, stroking his fur and scales and feathers as if she wanted it to feel good for him, benefited her in any way, and yet, she seemed to take great pleasure in petting him, nuzzling his feathery mane and inhaling deeply as if she loved the scent of him even half as much as he loved her earthy scent—a scent that increased the more she touched him, telling him that she was growing aroused again, even though his shaft did not stand ready to serve her, and she knew it wouldn't.

Of course, her other mates would return to service her, adding more of their seed to what already spilled from her and had dampened her thighs until she'd drawn him into the ancilla pool, where the gentle current beneath the calm surface stroked around their legs, sweeping away the seed that would not take root inside her.

Kisk suspected the ancilla could make use of even the tiny amount of life energy they found in that, and wondered if there wouldn't be an advantage to making this place one of ritual mating, much as Asterius had done with his mate after his sacrifice. Perhaps the ancilla didn't need it to be a major sacrifice in order to benefit themselves, and ultimately, all of the settlers.

It was a thought that was quickly whisked away as Alice pulled his head down so she could press her lips gently against his while they were in the pool.

It was strange to touch her mouth in such a way, but he held still while her lips moved against his mouth, capturing his lower lip and sucking it between her teeth to gently nip at him.

That small bite shot a spark directly from his lip to his

groin, where to his shock, he felt the chains tighten around the two remaining lumps of his source—the third dissolving when he'd spilled the catalyst it held. It would not return until more catalyst was ready.

He had no idea why he was feeling arousal again so soon, but he pulled away from her incredible body far enough to glance down at himself, noting that the runes on his shaft had started to glow again on his stiffening length.

Only, they said something different. Something that shook him to his very core.

Normally, his runes spelled out the incantations that said *bound to create change.*

Now, they spelled out another series of words he'd never seen before. They said: *freed to create life.*

It wasn't a binding. It was an absence of one, and with the change in the runes, his energy returned to him, no longer being drained to create another catalyst.

A soft voice pulled him from his shocked stupor. "Kisk, are you okay."

Alice's warm hand stroked the feathers that framed his cheek. "Sweetheart, please say something."

Her other hand clenched around his numb fingers.

He couldn't let her know. If he told her what had happened, she wouldn't have a use for him anymore. She hadn't said she loved him—only that she wouldn't accept a gift from him if he wasn't a part of her family, but if she knew that he wouldn't be able to produce any more of the catalyst—that he wouldn't be able to give her any more children—why would she keep him around for the long term?

He had only one option to protect himself from being cut out of Alice's life. He had to be indispensable to her, and that meant he needed the spell that made his source produce the catalyst. He had to find the temple and beg the spirits to bind him again—to undo whatever it was she'd done to free him from his final captivity.

He pulled away from her, willing his erection to go back down, frustrated when just the sight of her naked body as she stared at him in stunned silence from the ancilla pool was enough to stiffen it even further.

He covered his lengthening, glowing shaft with one hand while he rushed out of the pool, turning his back to her, feeling his shift coming on.

"Kisk!" she said, apparently realizing he intended to leave as she waded out of the pool after him. "Where are you going?"

"I have to find something. I'll return as soon as I do."

That last was thrown over his shoulder just before the change came over him and he dropped to all fours, feeling his bones reform and his skin and scales ripple with his shift.

He stopped at the exit of the cave, turning to look back at her, only to notice that she'd grabbed her robe and was tugging it on with jerky, rapid movements, staring at him with wide-eyed concern.

The way her body bounced and moved made it difficult for him to focus, but he forced himself to turn away and push that image from his mind, determined to seek out his temple this very night, before Alice or her mates discovered that he wouldn't be able to give them any more than he already had and decided they no longer had a use for him.

"Stay here and wait for your mates' return," he growled, then raced out of the cave, feeling his muscles bunching as he darted into the surrounding forest.

Around him, the ancilla trees glowed, energy sparking from their branches, and he felt their dissatisfaction as roots rose from the ground in an attempt to trip him and slow his progress, catching at his paws, only for him to jerk his feet free.

He spread his wings, but the forest canopy closed above him, letting him know he wouldn't be able to escape that way.

Instead, he allowed the sliver of his falcon to peel away from his body, sending the much smaller creature up into the air to dodge through the net of the ancilla's branches, shrieking out a cry of victory as it turned its gaze to the horizon. This time, when it searched the Dead Fall, it would find his temple.

And Kisk would be right behind it, even if he had to tear through the ancilla's guardian trees to escape.

30

Alice had never wished for the convenience of a cell phone more than she did in this moment. If she could have called Tak or Iyaren, they'd be able to follow Kisk much faster than she could through the trees.

The ancilla were helping to slow down his escape, while making it much easier for her to follow in his tracks, but it wasn't enough. Kisk was simply much faster and stronger than her, and he was shaking off the ancilla with great determination and a waning concern about hurting them that they did not share when it came to harming him.

She'd seen and heard his falcon break free and then wing through the forest canopy high overhead, and this had been clear even in the night, because the ancilla were glowing until it was as bright as day, despite the high cost of this illumination to their energy levels. They weren't happy about Kisk's sudden abandonment either, and that scared Alice almost as much as Kisk's strange behavior did.

Something had happened when she'd kissed him that had sent him into a sudden and rapid retreat. A small, insecure part of her worried that it was a rejection of her, but her common sense took precedence, and she recognized that something very serious must have happened to upset him for him to leave as he did. It wasn't in his nature to retreat from anything, and he hadn't given any indication as she'd lain there petting and stroking him on the cushions that he found her touch to be anything other than pleasurable, even pressing himself into each sweep of her hands over fur or scale or feather to deepen the contact.

There was no good reason why a simple touch of her lips to his mouth would send him careening from the cave like some nightmare was chasing him. A nightmare that could threaten a massive, mythical, shape-shifting beast the size of a horse with the body of a lion and the wings of a falcon.

His behavior hadn't been spawned by nervousness, but he had seemed outright panicked for a moment before he'd pulled away from her and splashed out of the pool.

Now she was wearing nothing but a silken robe and slippers as she pursued her lover through the forest, using the ancilla's glowing trunks as guides along the path he'd taken. Around her, she could see the remnants of torn roots that had failed to contain the great beast that he'd become. As she ran, she called out for her other mates, hoping they were somewhere nearby and could help her track Kisk—and stop his inexplicable escape.

If they heard her, she saw no sign of them, and adrenaline-fueled speed of her own brought her to the edge of the ancilla forest, far faster than she'd expected—but not fast enough.

The guardian trees were healing the large hole that had been torn through their network of branches.

The hole where the chimera had escaped.

A warning glow from the trees told her to back away from the boundary of the forest, letting her know the Dead Fall beyond was too dangerous for her to proceed—letting her know they would move to stop her as they had tried to stop Kisk.

She took several steps back, and the glow of the ancilla dimmed as they bent their energy to growing back their broken limbs. The hole began to shrink, but it was still large enough that she was able to jump through it when she suddenly darted forward, catching the ancilla off-guard by her unexpected action.

The sparkle of energy from their shield tingled around her, but didn't incinerate her, as they'd recognized the need to lower its effects before she passed through it. She impacted heavily on the other side of the boundary and rolled away from the trees as roots and branches snaked towards her, the guardians flashing in distress, pleading with her to return to the safety of the forest.

She wanted nothing more than to do just that, but not until she found Kisk—before he disappeared out of her life with no explanation.

———

ALICE WAS MORE cautious in the ruins, careful not to make too much noise or barrel heedlessly in the wake of the tracks Kisk had left behind. She knew that dangers always lay in wait, and the added difficulty of a dark night didn't help matters. It would be better at this point to return to the ancilla forest and find Iyaren and Tak to help her search for Kisk, but she'd gone too far and felt like she would lose him if she didn't remain on his trail.

Already, the wind that whistled through the ruins and piles of junk erased some of his tracks. By the time she found Tak and Iyaren, the fearsome wind would have blown all evidence of his trail away.

She wound her way through the ruins, watching her steps

carefully, her slipper-clad feet nearly silent as she sought out the darker shadows in the dirt that were Kisk's tracks. The full moon cast deep shadows, and sank most of her surroundings into darkness, but there were enough points of light on the path to reveal his tracks, perhaps even better than they would have been during the day, because of the way the shadows were outlined by moonlight.

He'd taken a circuitous route through the debris piles, apparently not as concerned about his surroundings as Alice was, meaning he moved much faster than she could and had gained a large lead on her. She heard nothing but the wind as she followed him, and saw nothing but endless jagged shadows and nerve-wracking movements in darkness that turned out to be no more than tattered fabric fluttering in the breeze, or old, sagging shutters banging on their hinges—or any number of unidentifiable objects that had no lungs or heart and posed no immediate threat to her continued existence.

It had been a long time since she'd walked in the Fall, and she'd never done it alone. She began to understand how small and insignificant a person could feel among the towering ruins and broken stacks of interdimensional refuse and salvage. Viewing the Fall from her balcony where the dangers and the odors were at a safe distance was far different from walking down amongst it all. She couldn't help but admire Evie and Lauren for their courage in surviving in this place alone for any extended length of time.

She had no intention of being alone for long. She was determined to find Kisk, then get an explanation from him, and after that, have him escort her safely back to the settlement. It never even occurred to her that he might refuse to do so.

Even if, for whatever reason, he'd changed his mind about joining her family, he had too much honor to abandon her to wander the Fall on her own.

She knew that Tak and Iyaren would be very angry about

what she'd done, and hoped she could find Kisk and return to the settlement before they set off after her. She'd explain everything to them once they were all safe, and she'd promise never to leave the safety of the ancilla again without telling them first, but she also wasn't a child, and she knew how to be careful in the ruins.

She knew to keep her steps silent and her breaths shallow to avoid alerting the flesh worms to her presence. She knew to scan the ground and surroundings for traps and pitfalls and to keep her ears strained for any sound that didn't fit with the normal ones that filled the night. Her nostrils flared with each breath she drew in, seeking any scent over the ubiquitous odors of death and decay and staleness that was the natural scent of the Fall.

She had just convinced herself that everything would be okay and her impulsive decision to follow Kisk instead of going for help would pay off, when she lost his trail.

Ahead of her, a fresh tarmac pavement failed to show Kisk's footsteps, and a wave of despair struck Alice as she struggled to spot any sign of his passage. She took a few steps onto the pavement, crouching down to view it from a lower angle, noting that at least the moonlight was unobstructed from the ground in this place, which looked like a blast zone, surrounded by debris piles that had been tossed outwards from a center point where the tarmac was uncracked. Further towards the edges, she could see it breaking into chunks that crumbled back into the Fall's normal dirt ground.

This was a phase-zone, where part of another dimension had been integrated into this one, leaving behind this tarmac and what appeared to be a small aircraft standing a distance away.

In the moonlight, the aircraft was clearly defined, having the profile of a sleek stealth jet, but looking much smaller and more elongated at this distance. She wasn't so much concerned with it as she was with the dusty print she found as she walked around the area.

Judging the direction from the way the print was oriented, she spotted another one a bit further. Then another.

She'd picked up his trail again, but she was also in dangerous territory, since phased zones could contain survivors who could be as deadly—if not more so—than the normal dangers in the Fall. Though even those varied so much that it was difficult to consistently define them.

So far, the tarmac appeared to be abandoned, though there was the outline of a low-profile building that could have been a hangar or a bunker a distance beyond the aircraft. Nothing moved around Alice, but she felt exposed as she made her way swiftly over the ground, her gaze seeking more of the prints.

Kisk had come through here not that long ago, which meant if there were soldiers or some other kinds of guards, they likely would have been alerted by his passage, stirred up like a hornet's nest.

She was so convinced the place was abandoned as she followed the dust-marked tracks over the dark pavement that the voice behind her seemed almost like a dream, and she turned towards it slowly, feeling less concern than she should have in that moment.

The person facing her was the size of a child, their head coming no higher than her chest, but that made the weapon they pointed at that same chest no less dangerous. The barrel of the weapon had a small hole in it, but the weapon itself was worn like a glove on the hand of the creature, who also wore a dark uniform, boxy in shape, utilitarian in design, and apparently leaving a hole for the monkey-like tail that curled out from behind the creature.

"I repeat, remain still, giant, or I will barbecue your bare-skinned ass." The creature's simian lips pulled back in a snarl that revealed sharp canines.

Its eyes were cast in shadow by the brim of its little pilot cap.

She had no idea what language it was speaking. She only understood it because of Gray's implant that allowed her brain to translate any and all languages, using some technology known only to Gray and his people. If she tried to speak to the creature, it wouldn't understand her in return.

At least, she didn't think it would.

It looked like an adorable little monkey in a suit, but there was nothing cute about its demeanor or the arm-mounted weapon she now suspected shot some kind of flame, based on what it had said.

Even though she knew it couldn't understand her, she held up her hands slowly to show she held no weapons and posed no threat.

"I don't mean you any harm," she said, trying to keep her tone as soft and non-threatening as possible.

The little creature wasn't having any of it, and it was clear by the way it trembled that it was frightened, which meant it could be a bit too twitchy for someone pointing a weapon at her.

"I don't know what that noise you're making means, but I've already killed some of you bastards, and I'm not afraid to add you to that pile of roasted corpses."

Alice was about to try again to communicate, wondering exactly what it meant by "you bastards," when she heard the whooshing sound of wings above her head.

She closed her eyes in relief, knowing Kisk must have taken to the air with his huge falcon wings, since nothing small could have made that much of a sound. He'd probably spotted her as he took flight and had come to her rescue.

She lowered her hands, urging the little creature to lower its weapon so Kisk wouldn't attack, but the creature gasped and staggered back, raising the weapon higher, until it pointed at Alice's face.

Something struck her from behind, knocking her to her knees as a gout of plasma-hot flame shot over her head, singing her hair from the heat of it.

A heavy weight kept her pinned to the ground as someone shrieked in pain and the stench of burning flesh filled the air.

Then the monkey creature was the one shrieking as it was cast to the ground in front of her, its little hat falling off to roll away on the tarmac, and its weapon hand smashing against the ground with a loud crack.

It struggled to turn over, but its movement was quickly stilled by the pointed end of a staff that impaled it right through the chest.

Alice trailed her eyes upwards, following the line of the branchlike staff, recognizing the limb as one that had been severed at some point from an ancilla by the way the colors of it had settled into the ancilla's death gradients—gray and green— blended together and frozen in those shades.

Carrying around an ancilla branch in the settlement would be akin to adorning oneself with a severed foot or hand from some other species. It was not acceptable to the New Omnians, which let Alice know she hadn't been rescued by Kisk, and it wasn't his weight keeping her pinned to the ground.

The long curve of a wing stretched into her view, blocking out the moonlight that illuminated the corpse of the monkey creature. The wing was a hodge-podge of bones and metal, with pulleys for joints and cables and wires holding it all together beneath a tapeline of ragged flesh with gaping holes and blade-shaped, shimmering feathers at the edges of the wing.

"They aren't pretty," a rasping voice said, followed by a soft churring sound. "But they function very well. Far better than they look."

Talons dug into her back, shredding the silken fabric of her robe as they readjusted, pressing her further into the tarmac.

"The little ones have weapons with bite, I'll give them that," the voice said with a harsh, squawking chuckle. "But it's nothing my master cannot fix."

Alice struggled to turn her head to get a better look at her captor, who smelled mostly like smoldering meat, although the fire had apparently been put out. She caught another scent on him, something akin to the feathers that made up Kisk's mane most of the time, but that was it. Mostly, her nose was filled with the stench of smoke and charred flesh.

He jerked the ancilla branch staff out of the fallen body, and it made a sickening squelch, a pool of blood spreading beneath the corpse until it spilled around Alice's hand as she braced herself against the ground, pushing back against the weight keeping her pinned.

She curled her fingers into a fist, but the blood kept sluggishly flowing towards them.

"It was Kisk I was hunting tonight, never imagining I would get so lucky as to find you instead, little female."

Alice licked her lips. "Who are you? Do you work for NEX? We can help you escape it and make a home in New Omni."

A hard, bitter chuckle caused the hair to rise on the back of her neck. "New Omni?" the stranger said. "I already know about the false dreams preached in New Omni. But what about my dreams, I wonder. Will I ever have what I want the most?"

The weight of the creature shifted on her back, digging talons into her flesh as he leaned down until his voice was right by her ear, soft and menacing. "Will I ever get vengeance in New Omni? I don't think so. Instead, I have you, and the Clawed One will do anything to save you, so I need nothing more from the settlement. How many of his arms should I order him to cut off? Perhaps all but one? The one that wields the sword. Or perhaps I should make you cut them all off for him. How poetic would that justice be?"

"Veraza," Alice whispered in dawning understanding, her terror rising even higher with the knowledge of exactly who and what had her in his grasp.

"*The* Veraza," he hissed angrily.

31

A lice followed the Veraza in silence, studying his outline in the growing darkness as the moon set before the approaching dawn.

His wings were clearly a gift from NEX, as ugly and cobbled together as anything the artificial intelligence created—it having no regard for beauty or style when it put things together, choosing the most expedient paths with the least amount of waste.

Veraza's body was now burned in a long slash across one side of his chest, the feathers in that path gone completely with those around it scorched and curled from the heat. Apparently, he had shifted his body just enough to avoid a direct hit, instead getting a glancing blow from the weapon of the little monkey creature.

He carried the staff like one accustomed to using one, and not just for walking. Now that Alice understood that magic existed, she began to suspect the Veraza was from a world where such a thing as a magic staff was possible. The way the ancilla staff flickered with an inner glow as he walked made her suspect there was still some energy or life in it, but from its donor, or from the Veraza, she wasn't sure.

Whether it was magical or not, the staff was deadly enough, as she'd seen for herself. The end of it was still stained with blood that coated the gray and green gradient of the "wood" that was actually petrified ancilla flesh.

"Iyaren spared your life," she said to him after a long silence where he forced her to pick her way over a pile brimming with jagged fragments and edges, the rope that bound her wrists behind her and attached to the one around her neck tugging and tightening against her skin with each step she took.

He turned on her, his beady, dark eyes glaring with obvious hatred as his crest of head feathers rose.

"He took my wings!" His new pulley and cable wings flared out on each side of him, their blade feathers rattling against the stretched membranes that covered them. "My life would have been better to lose than that!"

He spoke in a series of trills and churrs and soft whistles, but Alice understood all of it as if he was speaking English. That didn't mean the angry shriek that came from his open beak didn't sound like a hawk to her, even though she could interpret its meaning.

"You tried to invade his home," she said, hoping to reach some reasonable part of him that would recognize that Iyaren's actions had not been done out of malice, but to protect himself from further attempts to encroach on his territory through the air.

It hadn't been personal.

The Veraza eyed her narrowly, a critical gaze sweeping her from head to foot. "The featherless, hideous little female just keeps squawking, and to what purpose, I wonder?" He clacked his hooked beak together. "Do you really believe I will just forgive your mate because you argue so passionately in his defense?"

His wings stretched and folded with creaks from the joint pulleys. "You have no idea how much I hate him, do you?"

He hopped up onto a pole pinned beneath a pile of boxy objects and gleaming, sharp metal edges, that revealed only a short length of it. He crouched down on his makeshift perch, bringing his gaze level with hers.

"If I could stomach it, I would claim you as my own and keep you until I filled your belly with my offspring and bent your spirit to my will. Then I'd return you, broken and empty, to your mate, so he would understand my pain and loss."

Alice heard the rage-filled threat, but recognized it as empty. There was no sign of lust in the Veraza's eyes, and she got the feeling that even with as much as he hated Iyaren, he wasn't the kind of male who would find rape an easy thing to do, not even for vengeance. Because of this, his threat had the opposite effect than what he was probably aiming for. Instead of making her afraid enough to silence her pleas, it made her hopeful. That he had his limits meant there was still some part of him that could be reached inside the shell of hatred that entrapped him.

"Iyaren has felt loss and pain. More than you realize. If you wanted him to suffer, then you have already had your wish."

He fluffed his feathers, eyeing her with an inscrutable expression, if that was what it could be called on a birdman. "Not enough, ugly female. Not nearly enough."

"Does it help to know that he regrets it?" Alice asked, injecting as much sorrow into her own voice as she could manage.

He shrieked a sound that translated in her mind only as a bark of laughter, and Alice knew it didn't hold any amusement. "Do you think I'm such a fool? He only regrets that he left me alive."

That was true. Iyaren had said he wished he had killed the

Veraza instead of removing his wings. He should never have left an enemy alive to hate him so virulently.

Having no answer to that without attempting a lie, she sighed heavily and shook her head. "Even with NEX backing you, you can't hope to get away with this. You'll be hunted down to the ends of the Fall, and when you're caught, you'll be dragged back to face terrible punishment."

Gray had been known to stake out the bodies of scavengers that had been turned inside-out to poles outside of New Omni to warn off the more violent survivors that saw the settlement as a potential target. That was less brutal than he used to be. In the previous Omni, he'd made the tents on the edges of the settlement from the skins of scavengers and had decorated the path leading into the settlement with a fence made from the bones of their bodies. These were the least subtle ways he had of dealing with those who broke his rules, but they weren't the most terrifying.

It was those he left alive who served the best as warnings.

If there was one thing the outwardly impassive alien hated in any universe, it was NEX, and he had no mercy for any of NEX's minions, especially those who threatened the people he loved the most in the universe.

And that was assuming the Veraza would survive long enough to face punishment. If Iyaren and Tak got ahold of him first, he would never make it to a trial before Gray.

The Veraza seemed unimpressed with her words, his feathers not even ruffled. "I have nothing left to lose and everything to gain by helping NEX. It will return me to my world, and my own flock, once I have found it a way inside the ancilla boundary."

Alice eyed his wings. "And will you return to them with your wings like this?"

The Veraza grabbed her by the throat with his free upper talon, his other claws tightening around the staff. He jerked her closer to him, the rope around her neck digging into her throat until she was gasping for air.

His sharp beak snapped together only a hair away from her nose. "Your lips look like worms, and I'm feeling like plucking them off to eat them, female. I'd stop moving them so much if I were you."

She swallowed, struggling because of the rope constricting her throat, and tried to nod her understanding.

Only with that brief, agonizing movement did he release her throat, allowing her to lean back to put slack into the rope.

"Gray could help you regrow your wings," she said in soft, pained whisper, her lips barely moving, though she suspected his threat to eat them wasn't to be taken literally.

He snapped at her impatiently. "Foolish woman. If he'd promised such a thing, I would not be here now."

"Would you forgive Iyaren if Gray helped you?" Alice asked, again keeping her lips stiff, just in case.

His gaze dropped to her arms, tied tightly behind her at the wrists. "Tell me, if I tore off your arms right now, would you be so quick to forgive me, even if your precious leader helped you grow them back."

She lifted her chin, before thinking better of it when the rope tightened around her neck. "I suppose I would, if I had brought such a punishment on myself by attacking you without provocation."

He turned away, looking off into the distant horizon, beneath the spinning clouds that surrounded the Nexus, where the sky was brightening with the coming dawn. "Beneath the Clawed One's compound lays a source of great power that could be tapped to open a portal to take me home to my flock."

She gasped in denial. "Only the Nexus—"

"And who told you that?" he snapped, turning back to her with his crest rising. "Your leader? You follow everything he says, do you? Believe every word? Even NEX does not truly understand what it does. There are other ways to open the path and return to my flock. It just requires the right timing, but I was never given that chance. First, your cursed mate blocked my way, and then NEX itself destroys that compound, forcing me to find shelter and burying the cavern beneath it forever."

"You can—you can open portals like NEX?" She shook her head in disbelief. "That's a pretty outrageous claim."

He lifted the staff in his hand and then slammed it down in front of him, where it lit up with a bright glowing light that moved across the length of it before spiraling out of the top, where the staff was twisted into a knot of small branches.

"There are lines of power to be tapped all over this world, but you are all blind to it. Your leader only understands what he calls 'science' and believes magic to be a thing of myth—something that can be measured and explained in his limited and narrow view."

She watched the lights in the staff, awed by their beauty. "If you have such power, why didn't you leave this world before now?"

He jerked the staff out of the cluster of debris that held it steady. The lightshow ended and the glow faded to darkness. "I said it must be the right time. Realities shift, and what you call dimensions are only parallel for a brief time. Only then can a doorway be opened to my own world. The Nexus anchors a parallel reality to this one so that a gateway may be opened even when it shifts away. There isn't enough power in this realm for me to do such a thing. I must wait—or find a way to access the anchor on my world."

"If all you want is to return home, I can understand why you're so driven and why you'd consider risking the wrath of New Omni, but why then waste your time and energy in a ploy for revenge?"

The Veraza regarded her for a long moment in silence before turning away to watch the Nexus. "I know my chances of breaching the barrier of the ancilla, and so does NEX. This is a game to it. Its offer is the squirm of an insect that turns out to be nothing but the waver of the air. Vengeance is all I will gain for my sacrifices." He closed his talons into fists. "And so, my vengeance will be my legacy—the only one I will leave behind."

Hopelessness. That was the undertone to the Veraza's words.

"You had a mate in your own world, didn't you?" Alice asked gently, staring at the feathers that stood up on the Veraza's bare back with the breeze, between the atrocity of crudely constructed wings that jutted from old scar tissue denuded of feathers.

"I sought a gift for my bride. The perfect one to celebrate our wedding night. A gift so magical, only the Veraza could bring it to her. Instead of the legendary artifact I'd sought, I found the anchor, and I was brought to this world. Since then, I have searched for nothing more than to return to my own. To her."

"I'm so sorry," Alice said, blinking back tears. "You must have loved her very much."

The Veraza stiffened, glancing over his shoulder at her, his wing folding down so she got a good look into his beady eye. "You aren't a bad creature, despite how ugly you are." His crest folded flat, his feathers smoothing. "It is a shame that *you* are the Clawed One's greatest vulnerability. It will bother me to hurt you."

He stretched his wings, and Alice could see the flex of muscles that bound them where the cables and wires were embedded into his scarred flesh. "I will do it anyway."

With that, he rose out of his crouch and yanked on her rope, tightening it around her neck.

32

Kisk found the temple, buried beneath the collapsed ruin of a building that must have once towered into the sky, the round top far wider than the center of the building, where it had snapped off to drop tons of building materials onto the roof of his temple.

There was still a single opening, burrowed out of the rubble, and that was how he found his way back into the structure. It wasn't what it had once been. The marble columns had collapsed, the statues were broken into pieces, and the ceiling frescos were cracked and missing.

All of the luxurious fabrics had been scavenged, along with the gold and jewelry, the weapons that had adorned the walls from all his many defeated challengers, and the armor that had filled the treasury behind the one room outside the nave that had been his chamber.

The spirits barely whispered, their magic nearly depleted just keeping the temple intact enough that the altar remained untouched, despite the ruin surrounding it.

"You have returned," they said in that multi-voiced way they had of speaking to him.

He shifted into his upright, humanoid form, revealing his groin to the pale lights that floated over the altar. "The spell is gone. I need it back."

Incomprehensible whispers filled the hushed chamber, bouncing off broken walls and fallen marble to echo back at Kisk.

"Project Chimera has been terminated," the voices finally said as one.

One of the spirits appeared before him, flickering in the way it sometimes had as it stared down at him from blank eyes in an even blanker mask. "Nano-intelligence guided retrovirus has been reprogrammed for self-destruction."

"You left us." More of the spirits flickered into view, their voices hissing in accusation.

"We could have brought great change to this world," they said as one voice in a lamenting tone. "Just think of the warriors we could have made."

A long, eerie sigh followed this statement.

"That's why I'm here," Kisk insisted, pointing to the runes on his shaft. "I'll make more warriors, but I need my catalyst!"

"You choose the unworthy," the spirits said. "We can see it in your eyes. You've given your gift to weakness."

"Never will we allow that again. It is our mission protocol to create warriors of great strength," they added.

Kisk understood now what had happened.

They'd taken the spell from him as their last punishment for abandoning his purpose. Perhaps they had left the spell active to see if he would use it as they wanted him to, but when he gifted it to Alice, they'd decided they wouldn't allow any more offspring that they considered deficient. They wanted warriors, and that was all they would accept.

"Go!"

"Leave us to fade. You have proven yourself to be unworthy, Okiskeon."

He snarled in rage, then turned to the far wall, spotting one of the weapons that had been buried so deep in the wreckage that the scavengers hadn't been able to budge it.

With a mighty roar, he heaved the battle hammer out of the broken stone and marble and turned to swing it at the altar.

"No!" the spirits said, raising their weakened voices to a single command that managed to reach the level of a shout.

Okiskeon was free of their compulsion now, and didn't hesitate to bring the hammer down on the altar.

Arcing energy like lightning crackled around the altar, making a snapping, popping sound as again and again he smashed the hammer down, until his arms and shoulders ached and nothing but gravel remained of the stone that had once stood in the center of the temple. The stone that he'd been told had held the remains of the mages that had made him.

Instead, what appeared to be inside it was wires and cables and strange devices like Gray used.

Machines.

Not magic.

The sight of such wreckage among the rubble of the altar shook him to his core. He had no idea what it all meant as he stood with his chest heaving with each lungful of air he breathed, exhausted by his actions. The air was heavy with silence, no more whispers tainting it and only his ragged breathing to break it as the dust settled around him and only the occasional snap or pop sounded from the wires.

He stared down at his shaft, noting that the chains still bound it—so much a part of him that even the destruction of the mages didn't remove them.

But the runes had stopped glowing altogether. He would never catalyze the creation of another life, but at least he'd been freed to create his own.

He left the temple in deep thought, dreading his return to

Alice, while at the same time eager for it. Now, he needn't fear the slow dwindling of his essence would result in her grief. Now, he could make love to her as her other mates did, spilling his seed inside her—his own seed.

He had no idea what a child of his would even look like, or if he could create one with Alice. After all, she'd turned to him because she'd been unable to make another child with her mates, but she'd made one. She'd made little Friak.

Perhaps there would be others. At the very least, he'd been responsible for creating the one that now grew inside her. That might be all there ever was, but for him, it would be enough.

But he feared it wouldn't be enough for her. He feared she wouldn't need him anymore if he couldn't help her create new life with her other mates.

He wasn't the chimera, anymore. He was just Kisk. Just another lonely male in a world filled with them. What did he have to offer Alice now? What could he possibly give to her that would make him worthy of staying with her and her family? He hadn't earned his place with her, like Tak and Iyaren had. His one gift to her had been to repay Tak for his life, but even then, it wasn't enough to repay her for taking him into her life permanently, giving him something he'd never had before— something he was never meant to have—a family.

He had to tell her the truth, but he didn't know how. He'd left her in the middle of the night, when they were supposed to be learning each other's bodies, as they'd discovered each other's hearts and souls over the last weeks. He should have remained there to explore her, and let her explore him. To learn about the kissing she liked to do, and make love to her again with his newfound freedom.

Instead, he'd gone on a fool's errand, and no doubt, that would have angered Alice as well, leaving him with two things to apologize for.

He retraced his steps without really paying attention to his surroundings, though a part of him was always wary of danger. It wasn't until he came across the tracks that crisscrossed his own that he snapped out of his thoughts and grew alert to the Fall itself.

Crouching down to take a better look at the double set of tracks that went over his own, he felt a frisson of fear that caused his mane to fluff out. It wasn't fear for himself.

One set of tracks showed three-toed talons—large ones, though despite their size, they were not deep, suggesting their owner was not as heavy as one would suspect with talons that size.

He had his suspicions about those tracks, but it was the other set that truly disturbed him. They were flat-soled footprints—suggesting the owner wore shoes—they were also dainty, smaller, and far too familiar.

Kisk inhaled deeply, trying to catch the scent of those who'd made the tracks, and felt relief that they'd just passed through recently. He could track them by their scent as long as he moved quickly.

When he found them, he wasn't certain what he would do. If Alice had truly been foolish enough to follow him out into the Dead Fall, was Veraza helping her find her way back—or was he a threat to her?

Kisk knew the Veraza hated Iyaren with a passion. The birdman was obsessed with vengeance. At the same time, he was one of the most peaceful males in the settlement now, which was undoubtedly the only reason Gray had allowed him to remain. He'd never directly struck out or tried to pick a fight with Iyaren, probably because he already knew he'd lose.

Because of his light bones, he was more fragile than some of the other males, but that didn't stop him from fighting in the pits, using the advantage of his lighter weight to jump and leap far above the heads of his opponents to make the best use of all four sets of his lethal talons. When he brought his hard, sharp beak into play, that made him even more dangerous.

He was a quick, fierce fighter, extremely agile, and filled with the kind of determination that refused to allow the body containing it to falter.

Kisk had never taken the Veraza to be a serious threat to Iyaren, or he'd have warned the other male after Veraza had asked him to be the instrument of his vengeance. At the time, he'd felt nothing but pity for Veraza, recognizing the futility of his impotent rage towards a male so much more powerful than he was. Although, to be fair, Kisk had underestimated Veraza in the past and ended up torn-up pretty badly because of it.

He just didn't think he'd misjudged Veraza's character so badly. He took the birdman to be the one most likely to aid another survivor in the Fall if he were able to, rather than to bring harm to them. Alice would need that sort of aid, and protection, but if Veraza knew who she was, and what she meant to Iyaren, Kisk didn't know what he'd do to her.

If he mistreated her, then he would die. Kisk knew that he himself bore most of the burden of Alice even being out in the Fall. She should have stayed safe in the cave, and she would have, if he'd only stayed there himself and made use of the fact that the spell binding him was gone. Instead, he'd panicked and had acted in haste to fix a problem that would never be fixed, and it would seem that he'd inadvertently led his mate into potential trouble.

Tak and Iyaren would not forgive him easily for this one. He only hoped he found Alice soon, or that he had not completely misjudged Veraza.

33

T he Veraza wasn't keen on taking breaks during their journey to wherever he was leading them, but Alice managed to convince him that she was far weaker than she was, stumbling often, dragging behind, even though it meant the tightening of the rope around her neck, tripping over her own heels as if it was a struggle to lift them.

She also pretended it was a struggle to breathe, heaving and huffing and puffing, which sadly, would have been the truth two months ago. Now, it was an act which not only slowed down their progress to Veraza's ultimate destination, but also convinced her that he wasn't completely lost to whatever compassion he used to possess.

He would pause, briefly as it was, to allow her to catch her breath, muttering all the while about sluggish land-walkers with unconcealed disdain. He would eye her bulk critically, making assessing comments about her weight being far too heavy for him to carry in the air, which still stung, even if she had to acknowledge their truth.

Alice had managed to get him to stop walking for the third time to give her a break, collapsing in an ungainly heap on the flattened head of a carved-stone gnome which had probably been a bench in some park.

She didn't have to pretend her legs were trembling, though it wasn't from exhaustion as the fierce eyes of the birdman stared down at her, his wings flexing and folding with his impatience and agitation.

"Have you nothing else but that robe to cover you? Your naked flesh is repulsive," he said with a shudder. "Like a diseased, molting flock mate with contagious mites."

Alice realized that in her splayed position, her robe had slid off her thighs, revealing quite a bit of her legs to him. She quickly tucked the material back around her, folding it under her thighs on the bench to keep it in place.

"I think your feathers are very pretty." She smiled when he glared at her, then ruffled said feathers, which were a glossy blue-black, like a raven's wing, except on the crest of his head. There, they were a vivid, electric blue color that startled the eye when the long, black top feathers lifted to reveal all the blue crest feathers.

He narrowed his all-black eyes. "Flattery will not help you. I don't need any convincing to like you, female. This was never about you."

She tilted her head, almost forgetting to breathe as heavily as possible to prolong the break he was giving her. If she could just delay long enough, one of her mates would find her trail. She was sure of it. She just had to keep Veraza distracted so he didn't figure that out.

"What is she like?"

He blinked at her, as if the abrupt change in subject required him to shift mental gears. "My bride?"

She nodded. "Are her feathers like yours?"

He squawked. "What a frivolous question, out of all the ones you could ask about her. She is intelligent, kind, compassionate, helpful to everyone she meets, and she has a voice that could sing the gods from the sky. What difference does it make what her feathers look like?"

Alice chuckled at his outrage, finding it far more harmless than his hate-filled desire for vengeance. "She sounds like a wonderful person."

He glowered at her. "I know what you're trying to do, and it will not work."

She stared back at him, trying to hold his eyes with hers. "Just listen to me, will you? What would your bride think about what you're doing here?"

He turned his back on her. "If I ever return to her, this will all be worth it." His tone held finality.

Then he slammed his staff into the ground at his feet. "I didn't stop us here for you to rest."

Suddenly, the ground between her and the Veraza crumbled, revealing a gaping hole that seemed to vomit flesh worms.

"We've reached our destination, female." He shook his head. "I am sorry. This isn't—"

His words were cut off by a pained shriek as a lion jumped out of the bushes that surrounded the grassy lawn area where they'd stopped for a rest. It tackled Veraza to the ground.

The birdman didn't stay down, fighting like a creature possessed, twisting to bring all four talons into play to shred the lion snapping at his neck.

Alice twisted her wrists in an effort to free them, and finally, the sweat and blood that had made the ropes slippery allowed her to slide her hands free of the ropes.

She wasted no time untying the rope around her neck next, and then jumped to her feet, scanning for some sort of weapon to use to help Kisk.

The Veraza wasn't his only challenge. Worms swarmed him, and even worse creatures crawled up from the hole in the ground.

The horrors that spilled out made the Veraza's flesh and

mechanical constructed wings look downright elegant. These creatures looked like they'd come from a malfunctioning body factory—with membranes and torn hides that could have been skinned off living victims still showing delicate veins pumping with blood, yet the bodies they covered were mostly metal, plastic, wire, or rubber.

Occasionally, there were other organic parts on the many-limbed, centipedal creatures that climbed out with the worms, but they were stuck in at odd intervals, as if there had been no plan, and they were just added because they'd been found in the Fall.

One creature, with mandibles clashing together, fell upon Kisk, it's torn membrane body spouting steam and fluid from a tube that had apparently dislodged from the rest of it, but that didn't stop the variety of limbs that made up its many legs from grasping on to Kisk to make it easier for the construct to sink its foot-long metal pincers into his tawny fur, folding and then piercing the hide beneath it as he roared in pain.

The Veraza still lived, though he was clearly broken in places by Kisk's attack, and blue blood slicked his feathers, pouring from the holes that Kisk had punctured in his neck. He rose to his feet while Kisk was rolled onto his back, his legs coming under him to kick at the construct that was coiling its flat, centipede-style body around him.

The Veraza stumbled towards his staff, clutching one talon hand to his neck to stem the flow of blood, his breath wheezing in and out of him. When he bent down to pick up the staff, bracing himself to stay on his feet, he found Alice's slipper standing on the end of it. He looked up, just as her fist connected with his eye, striking him as hard as she could above his beak.

She cursed and shook out her hand, wondering if she'd broken it and wishing she'd found something a little harder and less attached to her body to hit him with. Still, her punch seemed to have an effect on him.

"It's nothing personal," she snarled to Veraza as he staggered backwards.

She reached down to snatch up the staff and swung it at him as he regained his footing.

One of his wings listed to the side, the pulley broken and cables hanging slack beneath it, but his other wing remained functional. He brought it in front of him to block the staff, then whipped it back behind him, shoving the staff hard to the side, sending Alice stumbling with it.

Alice steadied her own footing, then backed away as the Veraza took several steps towards her, herding her closer to the hole and the worms—and the life and death battle going on between the construct and Kisk.

"You aren't a fighter, girl!" He glared at her through his one good eye. "Surrender now, and I'll ask for leniency from NEX on your behalf. You don't have to be the one to die today."

She smirked at him, swinging the staff from side to side, testing the balance and weight of it. "I wasn't planning on it."

The Veraza cried out in pain as a small falcon dropped from the sky and scratched at his good eye. He wildly flailed his arms trying to catch the bird, but it continued to dive-attack him with victorious shrieks.

Alice was almost laughing at his desperate attempts to blindly capture the falcon when the beautiful bird suddenly plunged from the sky with a very different kind of shriek, falling to the ground in a pitiful heap of feathers.

Her chuckle turned into a scream of despair as she spun around to see the construct tearing away flesh from Kisk's lion body.

"No!" she screamed, charging at the giant nightmare of a centipede construct.

It lifted its pincers from Kisk's body, which lay unnervingly still on the ground, with worms converging on it now that it was no longer moving.

The centipede monster was focused on Alice now, leaving Kisk for the flesh worms. Alice tried not to think that her beloved chimera might be dead. She swung the staff at the thing, which caught it with one of the hands that was attached to its body in lieu of a leg. The pincers clashed together with a metallic sound, stained with Kisk's blood.

The sight of it only fueled Alice's fury and adrenaline, even as the staff was yanked from her grip and cast to the side. As the flat centipede body lifted up on its many hind legs to menace her, Alice saw the system of lights and pumps through the holes of ragged membrane on one of its center segments.

It must have expected her to run from it, and no doubt it intended to herd her into the hole for a captive—perhaps to become part of some new horror of a construct. The last thing it probably expected was for her run right at it, so its response was slower than it should have been.

Though the pincers sliced through her robe and into her back, Alice struck the body of the centipede construct with the full force of her weight, anchoring herself to it as it thrashed with one hand, while her other smashed through the membrane and into the lighted box of cables and circuits and wires.

She screamed in pain as her muscles locked up from the shock when her hand made contact with the glowing lights, but her fingers managed to close around the cables and wires, and with all her might, Alice yanked them out of the box and then out of the construct, even as it folded its body down over her, sheering off a portion of her back skin with its pincers.

The construct immediately stopped moving, but the worms did not. Alice had to get Kisk away from them, and away from the hole that would pump out more constructs.

As she crawled from the wreckage of the centipede

construct, her arm was grabbed unceremoniously. A hard, talon-fingered grip jerked her free of the twisted construct and lifted her up to stare into the swollen eye of the Veraza. The other eye had been slashed clean through by Kisk's falcon and was now nothing but blood and eye slime in the torn socket.

"I underestimated you, female, and so did NEX."

The Veraza pressed something soft into her hand and then shoved her towards Kisk's unmoving body. "It won't happen again."

With those words, the Veraza leapt into the hole, where the worms were now retreating, along with the creepy, spider-like constructs that had spilled out of it to form the next wave of attacks.

Suddenly, Alice was alone with Kisk and the remains of the centipede construct, and the hole in the ground was already disappearing as she watched, either from the worms rebuilding it, or from something else. She didn't know and didn't care.

She ran to Kisk and knelt at his side, seeing that a good portion of his ribs had been exposed where the flesh had been torn off. Her gaze skittered over the wound to seek his face, praying she saw his nostrils flare with his breaths, but he seemed so still—painfully still.

Her hand clenched around the limp, soft bundle that the Veraza had given her. When she glanced down at it, she saw that it was Kisk's falcon, looking so small and fragile in comparison to how she remembered the fierce, little bird.

"Get up, damn you!" she screamed in Kisk's ear, clutching his mane with her free hand. "Don't you dare leave me!"

"Alice?" A voice cried out, followed by another, then another. They were all familiar voices, but they weren't the one she wanted to hear the most in that moment.

"Kisk, please," she begged, stroking her shaking hand over his furry cheek. "Please, don't you leave me." She sniffed. "I need you." She traced her fingertips over his closed eyes. "I love you, Okiskeon. I won't let you go."

She laid her head on his shoulder—a shoulder that was far too still.

Someone knelt beside her, but she didn't look up to see who it was.

"This is getting to be a habit, Kisk," a voice said.

The voice was one she recognized. One she loved. But not the one she needed to hear in that moment.

34

"I think it is about time you stop dying, Okiskeon."

Kisk stared mulishly at Gray, tired of the lectures. He wanted to leave this cold, sterile room now so he could find Alice and reassure himself that she was safe and well. Gray had assured him that she—and the life inside her that had barely just begun to form—were doing well, but that Kisk was not.

He'd been on the brink of death when Tak, Iyaren, Doshak, and a crew of hastily-assembled males found them and teleported them back to Gray's medical ward in the basement of the original apartment complex next to the ancilla forest.

"I do not know why you are the impatient one, Kisk," Gray said with uncharacteristic sharpness. "I am the one who must be here healing you, when I would rather be with the rest of my family, celebrating the hatching of my three younglings."

Kisk pulled his lips back in a snarl. "It wasn't my intention to be mortally wounded. That sort of thing generally happens without prior planning."

Gray blinked slowly, his expressionless face somehow still implying judgment. "In your case, I beg to disagree."

"When can I see Alice again?" Kisk crossed his arms over his chest, which was bandaged and coated in some kind of harshly scented gel that itched and burned, but apparently healed wounds rapidly. It was a pity there was so little of it left that it was only used for emergencies.

"In a mom—"

"Kisk!" Alice slammed open the door to the room, dressed in a simple gown similar to the one Kisk was forced to wear while being in the medical ward.

As soon as she saw him, she rushed towards him, running right past Gray, who stared at her with wide eyes and a gaping mouth.

"I did *not* see that coming," Gray muttered, throwing up both hands as Alice reached Kisk, then froze as if she were suddenly uncertain, her eyes fixed on his bandages.

"I suppose you would like some privacy," Gray said in a dry tone.

"If you don't mind," Alice said, not even bothering to look away from Kisk, who couldn't take his eyes off her beautiful face, wishing he had the courage to clutch her in his arms and hold her tight to him the way he wanted to.

"Of course, of course, why would I mind? This is just a sterile laboratory filled with priceless and irreplaceable equipment, so the thoughts going through both of your minds about mating on every surface of it do not concern me in the least. By all means, don't let me get in your way."

Alice didn't seem to even notice Gray's words, or note his sarcastic bow, but when he turned to leave the room, Alice looked over her shoulder at him.

"Gray... thank you. I owe you... everything."

The normally expressionless male smiled, then nodded in acknowledgement of her thanks. "You owe me nothing. You are family, Alice." The all-black eyes turned to Kisk. "As are you, now. Do not underestimate the power of that."

With those words, Gray left the medical room.

Alice turned her attention fully back to Kisk. "Is it true, what he said?"

Kisk tried to recall what Gray had said. "You mean about me being part of his family?"

She waved a hand dismissively. "Oh, I already knew that." She narrowed her gorgeous blue eyes into a glare. "And we're going to have a long discussion about you running out on me during the ritual, but that's for a later date. I was asking if it was true that you were also thinking about screwing on every surface of this room?"

Kisk grinned as he glanced around the room, filled with—as Gray had said—a bunch of arcane and no doubt irreplaceable constructs for healing and other unmentionable things Gray got up to in his laboratory. "It may have crossed my mind."

He sobered, his smile fading. "But I must explain things to you first, Sorceress. You may not want me after you hear what I have to say."

Alice grasped his feathers in both hands and pulled his face to hers, pressing her lips against his mouth in a hard kiss as her fingers speared through his ruffled feathers, then lifted to curl around his horns. She used her grip to pull him closer to her as she slanted her mouth across his. Her lips parted to let her tongue dart out. It swept across his lips, teasing over the sensitive skin there—the only part of his face not covered by fur. When he gasped at the unexpected intensity of the feeling, she took that opportunity to slip her tongue into his mouth, braving all his sharp teeth so she could tangle her tongue with his.

Before he was completely lost in the experience, she pulled away, her eyes shining brightly. "First of all, no matter what you have to say, you're mine, got that? I'm the sorceress after all, and I put an unbreakable spell on you, so you can't just up and walk away. If you try, I swear I will collar you and chain you on a leash."

She got a thoughtful look on her face, eyeing his neck, and Kisk suspected she was giving the idea serious merit.

"You know," she said in a voice that had grown husky with the arousal he scented on her, "we both might have some fun with that."

The spear of lust that shot to his groin and stiffened his shaft reminded him that as much as he'd love to break some of Gray's equipment, he had to get this all out in the open first. Things had changed for him, and he needed to know if that was going to change things for Alice.

"I can't create my catalyst anymore," he said, spitting out the truth quickly, lest he lack the courage for it.

Alice studied him in searching silence as she processed his words.

He set his hands on her shoulders, holding her in the fear that she might just turn away and leave him without another word. "It means I can't create any more children for you, Alice."

She shrugged one shoulder beneath his hold, then stroked her hand down his cheek. "Please tell me that's not why you left me on our... well, I guess we could consider it our wedding night, but I'll want a do-over."

He shook his head, gently squeezing her shoulder. "I can't give you any more children, Alice, and I know that's what you want most, so if you don't need me anymore—"

Her lips cut off his words, and her kiss was hard and almost angry before she pulled away to meet his eyes, her own as sharp as broken glass.

"If you think for one minute that all I wanted from you is a child, then you are an idiot, Kisk!" She stroked her fingers over his scaled arm as she kept her eyes locked with his. "I love you. You may have come to me when I was at my most vulnerable, but I realize now that it's exactly when I needed you in my life. Not because you gave me a child, but because you gave me a friend, a lover, and another person I could turn to whenever I need help, or whenever I get too lonely, or whenever I grow too concerned about pretending to be happy all the time, even when I'm not, so I don't bother anyone else."

She tightened her hand on his bicep, curling her fingers around it as she shifted her body closer to him. "I always said I wouldn't even consider taking another mate, because I had all I needed, and wanting anything more would be selfish, but now I understand that it isn't 'more' that you've given me, because no one could ever give me more than Tak and Iyaren do. It's just different. You're different. You've found a place in my heart that hadn't been filled to the brim already. You let me know that those places existed, and could still hold a love like you."

She smiled, and it was bittersweet and beautiful. "Love is not a finite thing. We know that as mothers, when we find the room in our heart and soul for each child we're blessed with, so I don't know why I feared that I couldn't find a place in my heart for another mate."

Kisk stared at her, wondering if it was truly that easy. Could she really love him, even though he had nothing to offer her? She had been the one to save his life, not the other way around, and yet, she still wanted him to join her family, even though he couldn't help her create any more children with her mates.

Speechless, he opened his arms, though the bandages and healing wounds pulled on his chest.

She caught his pained wince and patted his shoulder. "I guess we'll have to put off breaking Gray's equipment until you've healed up some. Until then, if you feel up to it, how about coming with me to see your new home. You never did get to, you know."

Warmth flowed through Kisk at her words. His new home. His new family.

And Alice—the sorceress who didn't believe in magic, but cast spells with her kindness and compassion. She loved him— not because he was the chimera and could make babies for her, but because he was Kisk.

35

The wedding ceremony was beautiful, as strange as it all was. Lauren and Ulgotha were her bride's maids, and Evie was her maid of honor. Asterius served as best man for Kisk, Doshak for Iyaren, and Gray for Tak, and they didn't require any groomsman with that list.

The children were ecstatic about being in the wedding party, though the "squirmies" were left on their bed of rotten meat with Yaneas serving as their nanny, perhaps not surprisingly being one of the rare people not freaked out by the giant larvae that looked unnervingly like the flesh worms, except in their heads, where mandibles chewed through their meals. On Evie's two sons, six tiny claudas surrounded their mandibles that were lacking from her daughter's currently hideous mouth.

Gray said they would be stunningly attractive once they grew out of their larval stage. As adults, they would have people falling all over themselves to get close to them. Perhaps it would make up for the fact that people tended to shy away from them in their current stage.

Except for the family, of course.

Alice looked at her wedding party, who were posing for the still images Gray's video equipment captured with a "squirmie" in Gray's, Evie's, and Doshak's arms, while Alice held Sherak and Kisk held Friak. All the smiling faces around her were so beautiful. Even though some were very alien, they were still so familiar and beloved.

They had built something in the Dead Fall that she and Evie had never found on Earth. This was their home.

Sherak patted her cheek after the last picture was taken. "Auntie Alice happy now."

She smiled, surreptitiously swiping at a tear that threatened to ruin her perfect makeup that Evie and Lauren had spent that morning getting just right for her. She nuzzled Sherak's tousled black hair with her nose. "Yes, I'm happy now. So very happy, Sherak."

He nodded with a very serious expression that reminded her of his father—the one who shared his blood, though such distinctions rarely mattered in their family. "Everyone happy today. Even squirmies." He shot her a sidelong glance from pitch-black eyes that were the most alien thing about his otherwise human face. "And Omni."

It made her feel good to think that the settlement itself was happy on this special day, a day set aside to celebrate the joining of their family as one. New Omni needed more celebrations, more holidays, and more reasons to remember all the good things about being alive.

Perhaps then, they would find something to live for besides vengeance. Her smile slipped as she thought about the Veraza and how he had been lost to NEX. She didn't think even he believed NEX would ever let him return to his bride. It was more that he didn't think he had any future in New Omni, so he'd abandoned all hope.

She and Evie were determined they wouldn't lose any more

people to despair and hopelessness. They would bring something to this settlement that it had been lacking for too long—softness, happiness, celebration, and hopefully a lot of love for the future.

"We'll make New Omni the happiest it has ever been," she promised aloud, not just to Sherak—who was propped against her shoulder—but to every survivor in the settlement.

He shook his head, squirming to be released. Since the pictures were done, Alice bent down, her wedding dress belling out around her as set him on his feet. Before she could fully rise, he put his chubby, little hand on her belly.

"Omni," he said, looking up at her with solemn, black eyes. "He is happy."

Kisk crouched down next to Sherak as he set Friak beside him, then he looked from the toddler to Alice's stomach, which had not yet begun to swell with the life inside her.

"Our child," Kisk said in a tone of awe. "He wants to be called Omni?"

She loved that he didn't even question Sherak's empathic ability. Kisk had slipped so easily into their family—with all their little quirks and foibles—that it was like he'd always been meant to be a part of it. Now that he'd freed himself from his past, he was no longer held back when it came to accepting others and interacting with them. Though he was still taciturn around new people, he had grown much easier in conversing with those who'd become his friends.

Sherak nodded sagely. "Omni his name."

Then Friak tickled him, stuck out his tongue, and raced off shrieking as Sherak giggled. He took off after Friak, as fast as his little legs could carry him.

Vincent, Alexander, and Ria squiggled desperately in the arms of their parents, already eager to follow after their sibling and cousin in the chase, though their pace at this point was somewhat slower.

Alice laughed at the struggles of Evie and Doshak to hold onto their larval offspring as they wildly wriggled until their parents relented and set them down on the floor to squirm off after Sherak and Friak.

Gray had less trouble with little Ria, but that was because he knew how to calm her. Yet, when he set her down on the floor, she still undulated as fast as her fat, segmented body could move to catch up with her siblings.

Evie rolled her eyes at her retreating babies as she stepped closer to Alice.

"Guess it's a good thing the pictures are done." She looked at Alice, who leaned back against Kisk's chest after he stood behind her and put his arms around her shoulders. "You don't think they'll get stepped on, do you?" Evie chewed her lip, clearly debating whether she should run after her youngest and round them up to put them back in their pen.

Alice pointed to Doshak and Yaneas, strolling alongside the squirming larvae, clearing the path ahead of them. "As if anyone would allow that to happen." She grinned at Evie. "I still can't believe you named your son Vincent."

Evie's answering grin was a bit sheepish. "Just don't tell Doshak about the whole 'Vincent the Vampire' thing, okay."

"What?" Alice feigned shock. "You mean you haven't told him about that? But it's hilarious!"

Evie crossed her arms and tossed her head. "It's a nice name, okay. I like it. I can't help the fact that certain odd characters just so happened to have that name."

Alice chuckled. "Oh, he was an odd character all right." She looked around at all their friends and family clustered in groups chatting in many different languages, yet still understanding each other. "I guess that guy would seem too normal in this crowd."

"Yup, and I wouldn't have it any other way," Evie said, watching Gray chatting with Tak and Asterius, a look of such

hunger and longing on her face as she watched her mate that
Alice turned her head to avoid drawing attention to the fact
that she'd noticed.

"Soooo, date night tonight?" Alice asked Evie.

Evie nodded slowly. "Not a lot of them anymore. I'll be
making the most of this one."

"You worried about him?" Alice asked in a low voice,
though if Gray wanted to, he could read everyone's mind and
didn't need to overhear their words.

"He says he's fine." Evie shrugged, her concerned frown
belying the gesture. "Not much I can do if he won't talk to me."
She turned her gaze to Alice and Kisk, a bright smile that
seemed to take a bit of effort clearing away her frown. "So, what
about the two of you? Are you all back to rotating nights?"

Alice's blush burned hot on her cheeks. She wasn't about to
go into detail on her love life. Not even with her sister.

It had been three weeks since Kisk had moved in to their
home, and during that time, he'd been healing and recovering
from his ordeal, as had Alice—the skin on her back stitched up
and itching like crazy, but the scars would fade over time, and
until then, her mates treated her like she was made of glass.

There had been some harsh words exchanged about Alice's
decision to charge headlong into the Fall after Kisk, and Tak
and Iyaren had been furious at Kisk for running like he did,
though once he'd explained things to them, they'd been
surprisingly understanding about his shock at the sudden
change, and had forgiven him.

The biggest thing both Kisk and Alice felt guilty for was the
damage done to the ancilla, but to their surprise, when they
tried to apologize to the affected trees, the ancilla brushed off
their words, and told them there was no need for them. They
did not hold any anger or ill will over the incident.

There had been many long nights of talking between the

four of them, but there hadn't yet been any mating as they all waited for Kisk and Alice to heal.

Tonight—on their wedding night—things would be different.

36

"You nervous," Tak asked as he touched the creases between Alice's brows.

She sighed, enjoying the way his touch relaxed her, smoothing out her frown lines.

He always knew how to relax her.

"I'm a little nervous. Even though we've done this before."

"This time will be a little different," Iyaren said, kneeling beside the bed, waiting in a patient position, though she could see the slightest twitch of his ear in his mane that told her he was nervous too.

"So, when do we start this?" Kisk asked, leaning against the footboard of the bed, staring at them with curiosity, and no doubt some of his own nervousness.

Alice sighed. "I guess we start now. I mean, we're all here, right? So, we should just... you know... do it."

She gestured helplessly at her three mates, who stared at her as if she was the one directing the show.

"What would you like us to do, Alice?" Kisk asked, as if he were reading her mind.

She had no idea. During the ritual, there'd been a plan.

Now, it was just a vague idea that they wanted to have a four-some, but none of them knew how to do that. Except for Kisk.

She pointed at him. "You! You've been a part of lots of orgies, right? How did they do it?"

Tak winced at her choice of words. "That word translates as a sexual free-for-all. I'd really rather not see it that way."

All eyes turned to him and he looked at them with a shrug. "What?"

"Your people have a word for such things?" Iyaren asked, staring at Tak as if he'd grown two new heads.

Tak narrowed his eyes on Iyaren. "As if the Sari'i don't?" He glanced at Alice. "And obviously, the humans do." Then he turned his gaze to Kisk. "I'm not even going to ask about your people."

It was Kisk's turn to shrug. "Good. I don't have any."

"Have you ever participated in one?" Iyaren asked, still staring at Tak.

A slight grin split Tak's scaled lips. "Not that I can recall. I won't bother asking you the same, Iyaren."

Iyaren looked away. "I've seen one, amongst the priestesses. A kanta cannot touch a female who isn't his bonded, so it was only the priestesses, while the kantas had to watch and stand guard."

"Your females were incredibly cruel," Tak said, with a sad shake of his head. "That kind of torture isn't even fair for torture."

Alice rubbed her forehead. "You guys? We're getting off-topic here! Are we going to do this or not?"

She hoped they'd take the second option. She was definitely getting cold feet. She didn't see why they needed to start doing this now, when she could just rotate nights with them as they had been doing.

Only now, with Kisk added to the schedule, it would be less time for Tak and Iyaren. If they all did this together, they'd have as much time with her as they wanted.

Kisk pushed away from his leaning position on the footboard and walked over to stand facing all three of them. Then he lifted his arms and pulled his tunic off, revealing the scars on his body where his fur was still growing in. Before anyone could comment, he lowered his hands to his pants, untying his belt and then pushing his trousers down his legs until he could kick them off.

When he stood straight again, both Tak and Iyaren flinched, Iyaren actually grabbing his crotch with a grunt of commiserating pain.

The chains were wrapped tight around Kisk's balls, which Alice could now see were missing the third bulge. The runes glowed on the sac and the shaft. Kisk said that was thanks to something Gray had done during the process of healing him—because his runes had lost their light when he was in the temple, but Gray had found a way to bring it back again.

Despite the constriction of the golden, beaded chains, or maybe even because of it, she thought the sight of his cock was surprisingly beautiful.

"Ow!" Iyaren said, massaging his own crotch. "That hurts to look at. I've known some harsh punishments, but that seems too cruel. I don't think I'll ever get used to seeing it."

Kisk grinned toothily as he lowered his hand to grasp his glowing cock. "It's actually not bad at all. Gets a little tight." He traced the dangling chains that hung beneath his cock to wrap around his scrotum. "Especially here, but it doesn't push directly on them. You'd be surprised how good it feels sometimes."

Iyaren shook his maned head, snorting through large nostrils. "I'll take your word for it." He glanced at Alice. "Is this what we do? Should we all stand and present ourselves to you?"

At Alice's uncertain expression as she sought an answer for

him, Tak stepped up next to Kisk and stripped off his own clothes, standing beside the other male in his glorious nudity, no sign of anything but the slight gap where his penis pushed against his slit in growing eagerness.

Alice looked from one gorgeous, naked body to the other, choked by the combined arousal and embarrassment over the awkward situation.

Then Iyaren rose gracefully to his feet and quickly divested himself of his clothing, going to stand on Kisk's other side naked, his bumpy cock stiffening and pushing free of the foreskin that normally concealed most of it.

Three hot males stood naked in front of Alice, staring at her in expectation, waiting for her to make the next move. She felt lightheaded and also really, really warm. She fanned herself as she looked from one nude body to the next.

"Maybe we need to make the decisions for her," Kisk said, watching her with knowing eyes.

"I agree. Perhaps we need to be the ones directing this show," Tak added, his tongue flicking out to lick his lips.

"Alice, strip your clothes off and lay back on the bed," Iyaren ordered in a low growl, his shaft stiffening into a full erection as he watched her.

She complied with jerky movements, too overwhelmed to try to strip in a sexy way, but given the hungry way her three predators were watching her, she didn't think she had to.

Once she stood naked, resisting the urge to cover her body with her hands to hide it from their intent gazes, she hesitated.

"Lay on your back before I put you on it," Iyaren said, taking a step forward, the command in his tone the same he used when training a student.

Alice rushed to comply, seeing the promise in his eyes that he would do exactly as he said, and she realized now why he was being so domineering. He was establishing dominance by giving the orders. It turned her on like crazy.

Once she was on the bed, Iyaren motioned to Tak and Kisk.

"You will sit by her head, Kisk, so she can explore your strange staff, however she decides to. And Tak, you must prepare her to take all of us. Use your tongue to make her wet and ready."

Alice shivered at the low-voiced commands and the husky tone that deepened Iyaren's already bass growl into something that caused a primal feeling of fear and excitement in her as her other mates hastened to obey him.

The mattress dipped as Kisk climbed on the bed, positioning himself so she could reach his strange, rune-covered cock, while Tak's upper hands parted her legs, revealing a slit that was already wet with her excitement. His tongue lashing her until she was writhing her hips made her even wetter as her fingers closed around Kisk's length, her thumb rubbing over the beads on the chains.

She stroked him, studying the runes in an effort to distract herself from coming too quickly, though it didn't work with Tak's tongue knowing exactly what to do to bring her to completion. When he flipped her onto her hands and knees without a word to her as her body was still convulsing, she made no protest. Not that she could have, because Iyaren was probing her lips with the head of his dick, while her hand found Kisk's again.

She alternated sucking on each of them while Tak pressed his body against hers and let his shaft pump inside her, his hands roving over her naked flesh as he moaned in pleasure with each hard, frantic thrust.

Focusing on Iyaren with her mouth, she brought him to the edge, then took him over, loving the way he roared as he pulled quickly free of her before he climaxed. It was important to time that correctly, since his barbs ejected right after climaxing, and Alice had nearly caught a mouthful of them before.

"I want to try it," she said, looking from Iyaren's exposed

barbs and the seed spilled on his stomach and thigh to Kisk's glowing cock "What we talked about."

She would have blushed at the words if she wasn't so turned on that all inhibitions were out the window. Her sister had been right about so many things, and now it was time to take it that last step.

"Are you sure," Tak whispered in her ear as he leaned over her back, his cock still thrusting inside her.

She nodded. "I'm sure."

She was nervous, but so excited that she knew she could overcome it.

Tak, Kisk, and Iyaren exchanged a glance, then Tak pulled out of her. Iyaren's hand stroking her hair distracted her from the agonizing moments she waited while Tak found the bottle of lube she'd gotten from her sister as one of her "bachelorette" gifts and coated himself with it.

Once his exposed shaft was slippery with it, he laid back on the bed, and Kisk and Iyaren helped Alice as she sat upon his length, slowly lowering herself down, facing away from Tak, as his cock pierced her second hole, pushing past the tight muscle of her rosette.

She gasped as it probed inside, and the feeling was uncomfortable and unfamiliar at first, but Kisk and Iyaren stroking her nipples and her clit as Iyaren claimed her lips helped her relax enough that Tak could slide deeper inside her, until he was fully buried in her second hole.

She laid back on his chest, staring up at Kisk and Iyaren, her lips opened in a soft gasp as Tak's cock moved inside her, slowly at first, while Iyaren continued to stroke her clit.

"Are you ready?" Kisk asked, gripping his glowing cock, his eyes fixed on Iyaren's fingers playing over her, while Tak pumped inside her second hole. "It's going to be tight."

She nodded, swallowing, her muscles clenching painfully

around Tak for a moment before the hands of her mates roving over her body relaxed her.

Kisk positioned himself, straddling her and Tak's thighs, then settled himself at her soaking entrance. Tak's cock stopped pumping long enough for Kisk to push his length inside her, stretching her until she was worried she would burst.

She felt completely stuffed, but it was incredible, and both her mates groaned as Kisk buried himself deep.

Iyaren leaned next to her ear, stroking his tongue along the shell of it, before he whispered into it. "Do you like that, beloved?"

She nodded, sucking in a breath as Kisk pulled slowly out of her again, but not all the way, the beaded chains rubbing against her internal muscles, shifting in ways that stimulated her G-spot. "Oh, yes! Very, *very* yes!"

"Then we will do this again," Iyaren said, and Alice shivered at the promise in his voice. "As many times as you want it."

With that, he claimed her lips as Kisk began to pump inside her, Tak's cock moving in a matching rhythm as they brought her and themselves to climax. She looked up into Kisk's face as he came, loving the way his lips peeled back in a snarl that bared his fierce teeth.

She smiled at him wickedly as he shuddered and stared down into her eyes. "You know, that was only the beginning."

Tak chuckled beneath her, his hot seed sliding out of her rosette as he withdrew his length. "Why did we wait so long to do this, again?"

"Damned if I know," Iyaren said with a snort. He studied Alice with a predatory gaze. "But I think we need to make up for lost time, don't you, beloved?"

She nodded wordlessly, her mouth growing dry even as her body still trembled from the aftershocks of her own orgasm.

Evie had been right again. There was no going back, but sometimes, change was a good thing.

37

A lice stood on the edge of the apartment rooftop, the wind catching her unbound hair to whip it behind her like an ebony curtain. Far down below her, the citizens of New Omni worked like ants to incorporate the new areas of the ruins where the ancilla saplings had spread since the latest breeding ritual.

This time, Alice had not been in the forest when the petals were freed from their branches to fill the air like a colorful blizzard. She'd avoided the inevitable orgy that had followed, but there had been plenty who had taken advantage of the opportunity during the outdoor festival all of the women had organized, after declaring the ancilla breeding day an official work holiday.

She and her mates had celebrated the sacrifice that Lauren and Asterius made in the safety and comfort of their own home, indoors where they wouldn't come into contact with the petals, renewing their commitment to each other as life was renewed and spread in the ancilla forest.

The fact that certain trusted, unmated males had been permitted through the fence to celebrate the festival with the females had made those with female mates more protective, and less inclined to allow them outdoors—just in case they got a little too carried away by contact with the petals.

On the other hand, several new families had been formed during the festival, with females finding their mates during the festivities, so Alice considered it a success, even if she'd had to leave the party to retreat indoors when the ancilla petals bloomed.

Lauren and Asterius would be drained for weeks, tired and worn-out. They'd sleep a lot, having given a great deal of their life energy to allow the ancilla to breed. But they felt it was worth it, and Alice couldn't help but agree as she saw the saplings sprouting within the blasted-out or burned or collapsed buildings that would someday become safe homes for survivors.

The Ancilla Breeding Festival was one of many holidays and celebrations she and the other females planned for the settlement. They now had enough safety in their life to do more than simply exist and survive. It was time that everyone who lived in New Omni had a chance to start living.

The males might be the ones responsible for building and protecting New Omni, but the females were the ones who made the settlement into a home. Alice was finally able to admit she was proud of that role, without feeling as if she was a failure, or that her contribution was less important than anyone else's.

With each new relationship that formed, with each new friendship built during social events, and with each new family member welcomed, the settlers gained something that had been lacking for far too long.

Hope for the future.

There was nothing more important than that, and nothing that would bring a lasting peace more swiftly than that simple promise. The Veraza had taught her this lesson in his despair and hopelessness. He chased a future that would never happen, a love he couldn't let go, a life that was forever lost to him—instead of looking forward to what could be.

Now, he was a puppet of NEX, and she honestly grieved for him, despite what he had done and how he'd betrayed them.

Below her, New Omni was becoming a real city, one bustling with life energy, and growing richer and more colorful by the day as a new culture emerged from the remnants of hundreds of different ones. Traditions formed along with families and friendships, and even though they could all understand each other, despite which language was spoken, the settlers began to develop a new one—a single and common trade language to show respect for their trading partners.

Alice felt awed to be a witness to the growth of a civilization, as strange as the citizens were.

"The latest breeding festival marks the dawn of a new era," a voice said behind her, startling her enough to gasp and jerk forward, her thighs bumping into the waist-high wall that kept her from toppling off the roof.

She wouldn't have fallen though. Not with the invisible force that steadied her blocking the edge of the roof.

She caught her breath, willing her racing heart to calm, and turned to face Gray, who stood staring down at the buildings below with an expressionless face.

"Ninjas make more noise than you!" she said, clasping a hand to her chest. "Damn, Gray, you almost gave me a heart attack!"

A small smile barely bent his lips. "I suspect I made more noise than you think, but you were distracted."

She let out a gust of breath in a laugh. "Probably. I was just thinking about the changes in New Omni."

"I know," he said, his eyes fixed on the settlement below them. "Your contributions have changed everything."

She stared at him in shock. "What do you mean?"

"It is always the one bright spot of color in a bleak landscape that heralds the arrival of Spring. You brought that color to New Omni. The flux is in chaos, but there are currents of calm flowing through it now that weren't there before."

She settled a hand on her growing stomach, feeling the firmness of the baby that was still very early in his development, but held such promise. "Is this change because of Omni? Is that why you said my relationship with Kisk was so important?"

"The child will be a welcome addition to our city, but it was not the creation of a new life that was important. It was the fact that you saw in Kisk a person worth loving, and in doing so, you gave hope to others."

She let out a heavy breath, stunned by his words. "I never realized something so small would have such an impact on so many people."

"People rarely do." He finally looked at her, his eyes blinking slowly. "That is why the flux is so difficult to navigate."

"Why is Evie angry at you, Gray?" It really wasn't her business to butt into someone else's relationship problems, but in this case, she was worried about her sister and her brother-in-law. Evie was growing less and less responsive when Alice asked her what was bothering her, but she knew from her observations that Evie had stopped talking to Gray.

"She believes I sometimes knowingly put innocent people in danger." His voice had no inflection, and his face didn't show any expression, so Alice couldn't really tell if he was upset or angry, or even irritated by her question. "People like her beloved sister."

Alice gasped, turning away from him to clutch the short wall with her hands, the rough concrete digging into her palms. "Did you know... what would happen?"

"I knew you could die. It was a possibility. And yes, I let it happen anyway."

Alice closed her eyes and took a deep, calming breath. When she opened her eyes, she turned to meet his unnerving gaze.

"I don't envy you, Gray. Nor do I blame you for not sharing all that you know."

He dipped his chin in a small nod. "I know. I appreciate your consideration."

"Is there anything I can do to help? I can talk to Evie—"

He lifted a hand. "There is no need. We will resolve our issues as necessary. Our love has not changed, and I believe it will prevail."

Alice nodded, knowing that if nothing else, that much was true. Evie was absolutely crazy in love with Gray, and as impassive as he seemed to be on the outside, Alice knew he felt the same way about her sister. Evie wouldn't be able to stay angry at him for long, because she would come to the realization—as Alice did—that some things had to happen in their time, in order to preserve the future.

Gray turned his gaze towards the horizon, where the Nexus hung like an ominous cloud over the Dead Fall. "The Veraza was correct about one thing," he said.

Alice shook her head in denial. "He was wrong about everything."

"I do not understand the technology the Veraza wields, and it will take me time to understand the technology that created Kisk and fueled his ability to catalyze change. I do not believe these things are magic, but since this technology remains obscured to my understanding, it might as well be."

The amount of emotion she saw in Gray's stance as he clenched a fist in front of him, his upper lip pulling upwards in a frustrated snarl, scared the hell out of her. Not because she feared him, but because she feared anything that even Gray considered a threat.

He relaxed his fist and lowered his hand. When he looked

at her, his expression was impassive again. "Enjoy this peace, Alice. I will do whatever it takes to make it last. You have my word."

With that, he disappeared from the rooftop, teleporting again, as if he no longer wanted to use his own physical energy to get around. She was afraid it wasn't because of a new, uncharacteristic laziness in him, but because he was slipping back into the old habits he'd had before he'd met Evie. Distancing himself from his physical body and his family in order to better observe the future.

Alice placed both hands on her baby bump protectively, looking down at it as she thought about Gray's words. When she looked back up at the Nexus, she curled her lips in her own version of a snarl.

"I don't care what you throw at us, NEX," she said, as if she could speak directly to the AI that controlled the Nexus. "This is our home, and Gray isn't the only one who will do whatever it takes to protect it. We'll be coming for you, you bastard. Mark my words."

EPILOGUE

The Veraza strode along the corridor, his talons clicking on the hard, tiled floor, the weapon turrets tracking his progress. The countless eyes of NEX watched his every move.

He didn't mind the constant spying, content to be NEX's servant in return for the many gifts it had given him. His wings had been significantly improved, and now, a new heart pumped in his chest, and his bones were nearly unbreakable and made of a featherlight metal.

The fact that he was nearly unrecognizable in his reflection was a small price to pay for vengeance. If he had to become more machine than alive, then so be it. He would destroy New Omni, and everyone in it, as NEX bade him to do. Then his legacy would be complete, and the Veraza would be free to return home to his bride.

A part of him screamed inside that she would never welcome him like this, and she would never forgive him for what he'd done—what he planned to do—but he silenced that voice with the hatred that filled him, and NEX never stopped whispering its own messages in his mind to drown out that voice.

NEX's voice told him to follow the corridor to a holding cell where other nodes of the AI had taken something they'd claimed from the Fall. Something special that NEX had brought forth in the last opening of the Nexus. Something NEX had been searching for, and had finally found.

The door to the cell opened to reveal a second door that wouldn't open until the first one shut behind the Veraza.

Once he stood inside the cell, he saw a strange pod. It was the size of a large person and was constructed of metal—like his new bones and wings.

A door on the front of the pod slid open as he studied it. Steam and a strange, soporific vapor spilled out of it. When his vision cleared, Veraza looked upon an odd creature that stepped free of the pod. It was clearly disoriented as it lifted arms to place long, slender fingers against its head, shaking that same head back and forth as if to clear it.

Veraza felt the presence of the creature like a physical force that extended beyond its body. When it lifted glowing eyes to meet his, he froze in place, suddenly terrified of the menace and darkness that somehow still showed through the light of those eyes. He was rendered speechless in the other being's presence, his gaze traveling over a body twisted by roots that burst from its flesh to form an armor-like covering over the naked body of the creature.

Branch-like horns formed a headdress that framed its head and face, and covered most of that same face with a wooden helmet that revealed only those glowing eyes and a slit of a mouth that split open to bare gleaming fangs.

"Where am I?" the newcomer asked in a rumbling voice. "And what manner of creature are you?"

Veraza didn't recognize the language, but the words translated as they always did. So did the disdain and condescension in the newcomer as it raked him with an assessing gaze.

The creature contained so much psychic power that it paralyzed Veraza, but NEX took control of his body, and used his beak to speak for itself.

"Your time is nearly up, but I have a proposal for you. Perhaps, even a cure."

The mouth of the creature pulled back into a snarl that showed even more jagged teeth. It lifted one hand, extending four fingers and a thumb, and roots grew from its fingers, reaching towards Veraza's frozen body.

"I can feel the life in you, creature. Answer my question, or I will drain you dry."

Veraza's terror battered against the inside of his mind like a fledgling in a cage, but NEX had control of his body and his voice, and it felt nothing akin to fear. Veraza suspected it felt nothing at all.

"You have been in stasis for eighteen thousand of your years. Your scientists could not find a cure, and your people are long gone. At least... from your dimension."

The stranger lowered its hand, the roots of its fingers retracting back into its body. It tilted its head, small leaves unfurling on the branches that made up the top of the helmet. "Speak your proposal then, inferior. Do not waste what little time I have left."

Veraza trembled in the grip of NEX, unable to move any part of his body in response to the impatient demand and threat in the newcomer.

"I offer you vengeance against the betrayer. Vengeance for your people."

"And what do you ask in return?" the newcomer said in an emotionless tone.

"Nothing," NEX answered in Veraza's voice. "Your vengeance will be payment enough."

"And what form will this vengeance take?" the newcomer said, crossing its arms over a root-twisted chest.

"You will kill Patient Zero and destroy her children. In return, I can prolong your existence as you are—and perhaps even provide a cure."

The newcomer lowered its head, fixing Veraza with a glare that had physical pressure behind it, forcing him to take several steps backwards, despite being paralyzed by NEX's control.

"So, my wife has escaped to this dimension. In that case, you need only show me the way, and I will take my revenge." His tone was filled with deadly conviction, promising hell to one he must have once called mate.

"She has grown very strong," NEX warned, steadying Veraza and strengthening his stance beneath the crushing force of the newcomer's stare. "Defeating her won't be so simple."

The newcomer brushed this warning off as if it was nothing. "I am the strongest, and have always been. This curse," he lifted a hand and extended the roots from his fingers, "will destroy me soon, but until then, it gives me the ability to drain the life of another to make me even stronger. It will be enough to destroy her and those she has corrupted to her service."

"In that case," NEX said, bowing Veraza's head, "I will loan you the use of this node to show you the way to her."

Another assessing gaze swept over Veraza. "Excellent. Soon, the *ancilla* will be avenged, by the Jagganata our queen betrayed."

AUTHOR'S NOTE

I honestly can't predict how this latest chapter in the Dead Fall series will go over. I know there are readers who didn't want Alice to take on a new mate, feeling like Iyaren and Tak were perfect for her, and more than enough for her, and I can respect that and completely understand.

However, when I sat down to write the chimera's story, I knew he would be an instrument of change, and I felt like Alice was the one still clinging to the hang-ups she'd held onto in her previous life. There was no one who needed change more than she and her mates did, despite the blessings that had come into their life. They all needed that last little bit of a push to become truly comfortable with their relationship with each other, and truly open to the possibilities of their new life.

I also felt like Kisk needed Alice and her mates, each of them bringing something into his life that he'd never had before. Something that would fulfill him. Tak was the friendly, outgoing person Kisk needed to learn from. Iyaren had the wisdom and patience Kisk lacked, and Alice could give him the unquestioning love and devotion he'd never known before. Once it was all laid out in my notes, I realized that it was almost as if it had been destined from the start. Even Kisk's character design was like a melding of Tak and Iyaren—not the least of which was because of the mythical chimera that inspired him. Though it is technology, rather than magic, that created him (and certain other mythical figures, as well as certain "shamans" who believe the "gods speak to them from the stars," just in case that wasn't made fully clear in the book ;))

I also worried about how flawed Kisk was in the beginning, knowing he was definitely going to rub some readers the wrong way. Even as I wrote each scene he was in and each line of dialogue he spoke, I cringed at the feedback I worried I would get about him (and did get from beta readers). Yet, I felt the need to continue with the story as is, instead of softening my approach to his character. Sometimes, as much as I love romance, I feel like too many romance heroes have their edges softened from the beginning to make them easier for the readers to love right off the bat, but I personally like a few jagged edges to my heroes in the beginning, especially when their heroine is the one that softens those edges by the end of the book.

One of the things that I always want to do with my stories is bring something real and visceral to the pages. That means that my characters aren't always easy to accept or get along with. They have flaws, sometimes big ones. Even Alice, Iyaren, and Tak aren't perfect characters, despite having already gone through their own story. They still have challenges to overcome in this book, and I felt like that was more akin to real life, where we are never quite perfect, no matter how far we've come in our development.

I hope that you love this book, and feel like it was the right direction for these characters to move in, and I hope you're looking forward to the next book in the series. I know that some readers would like the epilogues to focus on the main characters and reveal a future where they are all living happily ever after, and believe me, I can't wait to write some future stories for certain children (can't wait! Already started on a book, but must... resist and focus on current projects!), but in this book, I felt like it was necessary to make the epilogue focus on certain characters that were introduced and whose ends were still kind of dangling, because it drives me nuts to have characters introduced in books I'm reading that really fascinate me, but I don't know if there will be a future book to expand their stories. It's a personal preference for an epilogue, but I hope you enjoyed the sneak peek at what certain villains were up to.

For now, the residents of New Omni are safe, but NEX never stops plotting, and because of where this book falls in the series, I can't end it on a distant, rosy future yet. The overall story arc of this series will be coming to a culmination soon, and from then on, the series will focus more on single, self-contained stories without that larger arc that affects the whole world, involving residents of the Fall, and certain characters (must... resist!).

I have quite a few projects in the works (as usual, lol), but I have finished the first draft for Veraza's Choice, which is the next book in this series. I'm hoping to have it out in November of this year. The cover is so awesome! I can't wait to share it!

My current WIP is "The Fractured Mate," which will be the sixth book for my Iriduan Test Subject series, and then I'm hoping to work on a fourth book for my Shadows in Sanctuary series (it's also an alien romance series, and the aliens look like angels and demons.)

I really hope you enjoyed this book. If you did, I hope you'll share your thoughts by leaving a review. It makes a huge difference! As does sharing my book on social media and recommending it to anyone you think might enjoy it. I really appreciate all my wonderful readers do to support me! Thank you!

Also, follow me on Facebook for updates, cover reveals, etc. on The Princess's Dragon page, and follow my blog: www. susantrombleyblog.wordpress.com for updates, excerpts, and an insight into my creative process. You can also email me at susantrombley06@gmail.com. I love to hear from my wonderful readers! You guys are amazing, and you encourage me every day to keep sharing my work.

Also, be sure to subscribe to my newsletter for updates and announcements. I have added a section to my newsletter where I feature exclusive content for my subscribers, such as sneak peeks, excerpts from unpublished or pre-published works, character art and interviews, and anything else I think my fans will enjoy. I only send out newsletters when I have something to announce, so you won't be spammed. You can sign up at this link:

Susan Trombley Newsletter

Iriduan Test Subjects series
The Scorpion's Mate
The Kraken's Mate
The Serpent's Mate
The Warrior's Mate
The Hunter's Mate

Into the Dead Fall series
Into the Dead Fall
Key to the Dead Fall
Minotaur's Curse
Chimera's Gift
Veraza's Choice (Coming Soon!)

Shadows in Sanctuary series
Lilith's Fall
Balfor's Salvation

Jessabelle's Beast

Fantasy series—Breath of the Divine
The Princess Dragon
The Child of the Dragon Gods
Light of the Dragon

Standalones or Collaborations
Rampion

Made in United States
Troutdale, OR
06/08/2025